"This had better work, Doctor, for all our sakes. The entire operation depends on it."

"Hold on, Trath. Chekov's brain-wave activity indicates that he is fully conscious." The woman's voice softened, assuming a gentler tone. "You can stop pretending, Mister Chekov. I know you're awake."

"So much for playing Sleeping Beauty," he muttered. There was no point in keeping up the pretense since his captors were unlikely to let any secrets slip now that they knew he was listening. Opening his eyes, Chekov tried to sit up only to discover that he was strapped down to a biobed in what looked like a hospital room, being studied by the doctor and the Voyzr leader, Trath, with contrasting degrees of empathy visible upon their faces. The doctor appeared genuinely concerned about her unwilling patient, while Trath peered down at him more coldly, standing stiffly with his arms behind his back.

"Sleeping Beauty?" he asked, puzzled.

"A famous Russian fairy tale . . ."

THE ORIGINAL SERIES

IDENTITY THEFT

Greg Cox

Based on *Star Trek*
created by Gene Roddenberry

GALLERY BOOKS
New York   Amsterdam/Antwerp   London
Toronto   Sydney/Melbourne   New Delhi

G

Gallery Books
An Imprint of Simon & Schuster, LLC
1230 Avenue of the Americas
New York, NY 10020

For more than 100 years, Simon & Schuster has championed authors and the stories they create. By respecting the copyright of an author's intellectual property, you enable Simon & Schuster and the author to continue publishing exceptional books for years to come. We thank you for supporting the author's copyright by purchasing an authorized edition of this book.

No amount of this book may be reproduced or stored in any format, nor may it be uploaded to any website, database, language-learning model, or other repository, retrieval, or artificial intelligence system without express permission. All rights reserved. Inquiries may be directed to Simon & Schuster, 1230 Avenue of the Americas, New York, NY 10020 or permissions@simonandschuster.com.

This book is a work of fiction. Any references to historical events, real people, or real places are used fictitiously. Other names, characters, places, and events are products of the author's imagination, and any resemblance to actual events or places or persons, living or dead, is entirely coincidental.

™ and © 2025 by CBS Studios Inc. All Rights Reserved.

STAR TREK and related marks and logos are trademarks of CBS Studios Inc.

This book is published by Gallery Books, a division of Simon & Schuster, LLC under exclusive license from CBS Studios Inc.

All rights reserved, including the right to reproduce this book or portions thereof in any form whatsoever. For information, address Gallery Books Subsidiary Rights Department, 1230 Avenue of the Americas, New York, NY 10020.

First Gallery Books hardcover edition December 2025

GALLERY BOOKS and colophon are registered trademarks of Simon & Schuster, LLC

Simon & Schuster strongly believes in freedom of expression and stands against censorship in all its forms. For more information, visit BooksBelong.com.

Interior design by Kathryn A. Kenney-Peterson

Printed and bound by CPI Group (UK) Ltd, Croydon CR0 4YY

10 9 8 7 6 5 4 3 2 1

Library of Congress Control Number: 2025946654

ISBN 978-1-6680-9662-8
ISBN 978-1-6680-9664-2 (ebook)

The authorised representative in the EEA is Simon & Schuster Netherlands BV, Herculesplein 96, 3584 AA Utrecht, Netherlands. info@simonandschuster.nl

Dedicated to John Ordover,
for inviting me to join the Star Trek *crew twenty books ago*

Historian's Note

This story begins in 2269 (CE), during the *U.S.S. Enterprise*'s historic five-year mission, when Pavel Chekov is just an eager young ensign.

It continues in 2289, twenty years later, aboard the *Enterprise*-A, where Chekov is now head of security . . . and not as young as he once was.

One

Ensign Pavel Chekov, Personal Log. Stardate 5839.7: *The hostage crisis on Voyzr continues to escalate, with both sides of the ongoing civil war holding Federation relief workers captive in order to force or prevent the UFP's intervention. First the secessionists seized a party of Federation volunteers, who were providing humanitarian aid to civilian refugees and casualties, in hopes of getting the UFP to formally recognize their Alliance; then the global Republic "detained" their own hostages to discourage the UFP from acceding to the Alliance's demands. In-person negotiations with both sides have gotten nowhere fast, so Captain Kirk has embarked on a daring plan . . .*

"Anytime now, Ensign," the captain urged.

"Aye, sir." Chekov raced to make sense of the Voyzr control panel, which, on top of everything else, was inconveniently designed for beings with six fingers on each hand. Perspiration dripped from beneath his bangs and glued the back of his regulation black undershirt to his spine, but he wasn't about to let Kirk down with their entire mission at stake. A tricorder was slung on a strap over his shoulder. "Just a few moments more, sir."

"With all deliberate speed, Chekov."

"Understood, Captain."

The rescue party—consisting of Chekov, Kirk, Sulu, and Security Officer Brenda Cassidy, who had previously distinguished herself during a rescue mission in the Mogab system—was under siege in a control room overlooking the main fusion generator in a secret Alliance base hidden away in a repurposed pergium refinery. On the bright side, they had already succeeded in liberating the four hostages, who were huddled in a corner, looking more shaken than scarred by their ordeal. On the other hand, both rescuers and rescued were presently trapped inside the control room as irate Alliance soldiers tried to force their way through the protective blast door sealing off the chamber, which Kirk had welded shut with his phaser. Sidearms drawn, the captain and Cassidy had taken up defensive positions facing the barrier, while Sulu guarded the not-fully-rescued hostages. Two Voyzr soldiers—a sentry and a technician, respectively—were heaped in another corner, stunned into unconsciousness after being caught unawares by the rescue squad, their limp bodies disarmed and dragged out of the way. A thick, radiation-proof screen shielded the control room from the two-story-tall generator.

Sizzling energy blasts buffeted the sturdy duranium door, which was already growing red hot in the center. Molten metal began to trickle down the length of the door, not unlike the sweat dripping down Chekov's face. He could feel the heat radiating from the door, uncomfortably impressing on him the urgency of the situation. Flashing emergency lights and blaring sirens did not make deciphering the unfamiliar control panel any easier.

"*Attention, intruders!*" a stentorian voice bellowed from a public-address system. "*We have you cornered. If you value your lives, surrender at once!*"

One of the hostages whimpered, backing farther away from the door.

"I don't know about you, Captain," Sulu quipped, perhaps to buoy the anxious civilians' spirits, "but I'm starting to think we've worn out our welcome."

"An astute observation, Lieutenant." Kirk displayed no sign of surrendering, now or ever. "Chekov?"

The young ensign wondered if Kirk regretted leaving Mister

Spock in command of the *Enterprise*; Spock would have surely mastered the arcane controls by now. Chekov attempted to channel the Vulcan science officer's inimitable sangfroid as he used both hands to dial in what he believed to be the correct command sequence. Simply phasering the controls and/or the generator was not an option, at least not without risking a catastrophic meltdown, which would rather defeat the point of liberating the hostages.

"Aye, Captain. Here goes nothing."

Chekov held his breath as he turned the master dial to initiate a total system shutdown—in theory—and pressed down on the dial to confirm the command. It then felt as though a long Siberian winter passed before, to his relief, the background thrum of the generator slowed to a halt.

"Surrender the prisoners!" the loudspeaker blared. *"Or we cannot guarantee—"*

The P.A. system went silent abruptly, as did the alarms. The overhead lights flickered and failed, leaving only emergency glow strips to provide a cool, silvery radiance that reminded Chekov of a moonlit night back on Earth.

"Done, Captain!" Chekov grinned at Kirk. "With apologies to Doctor McCoy, it's dead, sir."

"And the shields?"

"Down, Captain!"

A deflector dome had prevented anyone from beaming in or out of the base, forcing the rescue party to infiltrate the refinery the old-fashioned way, via stealth and subterfuge, after Sulu expertly piloted a shuttlecraft beneath the Alliance's sensors. A phaser cannon had then been employed to bore their way into an obsolete underground maintenance tunnel, while taking care not to accidently breach a live plasma conduit or deuterium waste vent. The rest had been a cake walk . . . relatively speaking.

"And none too soon," Kirk said. "Good work, Ensign."

Vapor started boiling off the glowing blast door as the soldiers continued their assault, their pulse rifles unaffected by the power outage. An acrid odor assailed Chekov's nostrils. Kirk flipped open his communicator while keeping a phaser aimed at the disintegrating barrier.

"Kirk to *Enterprise*." He glanced over at Sulu and the hostages. "Five to beam up, as planned."

"*Aye, Captain,*" Mister Scott responded from the ship's transporter room, where he was standing by for just this moment. Each hostage had already been provided with emergency transponders to allow the *Enterprise* to lock onto them. "*Engaging transporter now.*"

The telltale shimmer of a transporter beam whisked Sulu and his charges up to the *Enterprise*, where Doctor McCoy and Nurse Chapel were ready to provide whatever medical care the hostages might require. Wiping the sweat from his brow, Chekov took comfort in knowing that, whatever happened next, the unlucky relief workers were safe at least and at last.

Now for the tricky part...

"And the other hostages?" Kirk asked. "Are they safe as well?"

"*Affirmative,*" Spock reported from the bridge. "*Lieutenant DeSalle's mission was a success. The former captives are securely aboard the ship, as is the rescue party.*"

The twin missions had been timed to take place simultaneously, continents apart, with DeSalle and his team tasked with liberating the Federation citizens wrongly detained by the Voyzr Republic. So far, it seemed to Chekov, the captain's plan was working smoothly enough, aside from a few anxious bumps along the way. He could only hope the rest of the operation went just as well.

"Good to hear," Kirk replied. "Spock, Scotty, you know what to do."

"*Acknowledged, Captain,*" Spock said. "*Proceeding as planned.*"

"*Aye, sir,*" Scott added. "*Company is on the way, although I can't imagine they'll be best pleased by the invitation... or the locale.*"

"Leave that to me, Scotty. Kirk out."

He nodded at Chekov, who stepped away from the controls and

drew his own phaser in anticipation. Cassidy tensed for action as well, while also keeping one eye on the embattled blast door. "Why am I suddenly feeling like a bouncer at a Venusian nightclub," she said, "struggling to keep the riffraff out while anticipating trouble from unruly VIPs?"

Kirk chuckled at the comparison. "Let's hope our incoming guests aren't that much of handful, Lieutenant."

I wouldn't bet on it, Chekov thought.

The coruscating glow of transporter beams lit up the chamber, depositing three startled Voyzr in their midst. Visibly bewildered by their new surroundings, they resembled the proverbial deer caught in headlights—in more ways than one.

Although largely humanoid, the Voyzr deviated from the norm by being descended from something akin to Terran cervids rather than primates, as evidenced by the bony antlers sprouting from the men's foreheads. Downy red fur carpeted their exposed flesh, while curly green wool, of varying shades and hues, adorned their scalps in place of hair. Both men and women sported uniforms consisting of linen jackets, vests, knee-length kilts, and boots. Gracefully contoured snouts protruded from their faces, further testifying to their cervine origins. Large green eyes widened further as they glanced about in confusion before zeroing in on the Starfleet officers, who had all three Voyzr targeted by their phasers. Energy blasts noisily assailed the blast door.

"Kirk!" trumpeted General Akton, commander of the Alliance forces. A fuzzy red pate, shorn clean of verdant wool, declared where his allegiance resided; as Chekov understood it, those loyal to the self-proclaimed Alliance of Independents—often referred to as "Indees"—sheared their heads to better display their clan markings, which were shaved into the velvety russet fur below. Moist, rubbery nostrils flared indignantly. "What is the meaning of this?"

He reached for his sidearm, but Kirk already had the drop on him. "Not so fast, General. Keep your weapon holstered . . . and your hands where I can see them."

"And that goes for all of you." Cassidy raised her voice to be heard over the furious weapons fire coming from the other side of the door. She tilted her head toward the stunned soldiers in the corner. "My phaser's already gotten a workout today."

You tell them, Chekov thought. *We already have enough hostiles beating down the door.*

"I also require answers, Kirk." Field Marshal Zavetta, the general's counterpart on the Republic side, regarded both Akton and the Starfleet team warily. Fleecy chartreuse curls crowned her antlerless head. Literal doe eyes narrowed in suspicion. "Where are we . . . and why have we been brought here against our will?"

Her bodyguard, inadvertently brought along for the ride, was armed with a rifle but, finding himself in Cassidy's sights, prudently refrained from brandishing it, at least for the present. He nonetheless positioned himself between Zavetta and Akton.

"My apologies," Kirk said to both commanders, "but you left me no choice." He indicated the door, where the volcanic red glow was spreading outward from the center, accompanied by the rising din of the pulse rifles. "For the record, General, those are your soldiers attempting to crash the party. I recommend you order them to back off, for everyone's sake."

The sooner the better, Chekov thought. He estimated the blast door was only minutes away from being breached. Granted, the rescue party could always be beamed back to the *Enterprise* in a pinch, but what about the shanghaied commanders? They'd been covertly misted with an aerosolized viridium solution of Spock's devising during Kirk's previous face-to-face negotiations with both sides, allowing Mister Scott to lock onto their coordinates from orbit. Unilaterally relocating both commanders on their own planet was provocative enough; literally beaming them off their homeworld onto a Starfleet vessel would be an interstellar incident of the first magnitude, causing the Federation's entire diplomatic corps to go supernova. That needed to be avoided at all costs.

"I'll do no such thing." Akton surveyed the dimly lit control room, comprehension dawning on his face. "If this is indeed where I suspect, you're trespassing on Alliance soil. You have no business being here."

"Tell that to the innocent relief workers held captive at this very site," Kirk said. "You can hardly claim the moral high ground, General, and neither can you, Marshal. In any event, General, I doubt you want to end up the unfortunate victim of friendly fire from your own troops. Call off your soldiers, long enough to sort this out in a civilized fashion."

The fierce assaults from outside added emphasis to Kirk's plea, as did the flowing metal rivulets and spreading fumes. The glare from the steadily disintegrating door made it hard to look at directly. Squinting, Chekov saw a red-hot spot in the center of the door turn blue, then white, before dissolving completely.

"Watch out!" he yelled. "Incoming!"

A brilliant turquoise beam punched through the formerly solid door, narrowly missing General Akton, who ducked out of the way just in time. The close call produced an immediate attitude adjustment. Keeping his head and antlers down, he snatched a blocky, handheld communicator from his belt and hastily fiddled with the settings.

"Akton to Saremis Base. This is a Command-Level transmission, Security Code Gazebo-Cumulous-Thicket. Stand down at once!"

A puzzled voice answered him. *"General?"*

"You heard me!" His finger jabbed the communicator's miniature keypad. "Transmitting confirmation numeric now. Cease fire . . . for the present."

Akton glared at Kirk, dipping his head as though he wanted to gore Kirk with his antlers. Metallic rings on the antlers denoted the general's rank and status.

"Yes, sir! Confirmation received and acknowledged, sir."

The incandescent beam blinked out of existence, leaving a coin-sized hole in the center of the door, which only slowly began to cool back to a duller hue. Chekov fanned the air with his free hand to disperse the metallic vapor.

"Stand by for further orders. Akton out." He lowered the communicator. "All right, Kirk. You've bought yourself a brief respite, but I caution you not to test my patience."

"Nor mine," Zavetta said. "What are you up to, Kirk, and how dare you interfere with the internal affairs of our sovereign world?"

"Sovereign *peoples*," Akton corrected her pointedly. "Your Republic doesn't speak for all of Voyzr."

"Only because your ruling clans want to continue running your territories like your own personal fiefdoms, just to cling to your 'traditional' power and privileges at the expense of peace and progress." She looked down her snout at her adversary. "And to lord it over those you deem below you by dint of blood and birth."

Akton snorted. "Only your sort can make 'tradition' sound like an obscenity. You have no respect for our noble history and heritage, you arrogant, overbearing—"

"Watch your mouth, Indee!" Zavetta's bodyguard dipped his own antlers, as though to butt heads with the enemy general. He was big enough to seem more moose than deer. Rubbery black nostrils flared. "Nobody speaks to the marshal like that!"

"That's enough!" Kirk said. "There'll be time to argue politics once you stop shooting and kidnapping each other. You've been fighting this war for a generation now. What can it hurt to lay down your weapons, right here, right now, and at least try to make peace for once?"

"Is that what this?" Zavetta asked. "A forced mediation, at phaser point? So much for your vaunted Prime Directive! You have no right to meddle in our affairs. The present conflict is strictly a Voyzr matter, to be decided by the Voyzr alone."

"If only that were the case." Kirk took her accusation in stride. "Unfortunately, we have good reason to believe that the Klingons have already covertly inserted themselves into your war . . . to their own benefit, not yours."

Chekov nodded, knowing where Kirk was going with this. A neutral world, Voyzr was strategically located at the junction of three major interstellar trade routes, each of which was known to be the safest and quickest way past various deep-space hazards: cosmic eddies, high-intensity gamma-ray fields, gravimetric distortions, a black hole, and such. Although the Klingon Empire had thus far refrained from attempting to conquer Voyzr, constrained by both the Organian Peace Treaty and the threat of Federation retaliation, the planet would be a key asset, in terms of supply lines, should the current cold war between the Federation and the Empire ever turn hot again.

"The Klingons?" Akton echoed warily.

"What evidence do you have of this?" Zavetta asked, her tone equally guarded.

Neither commander, Chekov noted, appeared particularly shocked or surprised by Kirk's statement. If anything, they both looked distinctly uncomfortable.

"Mister Chekov," Kirk said, "if you'll do the honors?"

"My pleasure, Captain."

A rifle, confiscated from the stunned Alliance soldier on the floor, rested against the side of the control terminal. Chekov returned his phaser to his belt, retrieved the rifle, then approached Zavetta's bodyguard, which entailed coming rather too close for comfort to the man's antlers and their sharpened points.

"Excuse me, sir. If you would kindly allow me to borrow your firearm? Strictly for demonstration purposes, I assure you."

The guard, who had presumably been in close proximity to Zavetta when she was misted with viridium, thereby accounting for his presence here, held tightly on to his rifle as he looked at his commander.

"Marshal?"

She nodded, her stony expression betraying nothing. "Go ahead, Sergeant."

Frowning, he surrendered his weapon to Chekov, who backed

away from the man's intimidating antlers as swiftly as dignity allowed. Crossing the chamber, he laid both rifles on an open work counter while Kirk and Cassidy kept their unwilling guests covered by their phasers. Chekov scanned the captured rifles with his tricorder. A rapid analysis, along parameters previously calculated by Spock, confirmed what Doctor McCoy had previously deduced based on a forensic analysis of the injuries suffered by various casualties of the war, including an Orion bystander wounded during the abduction of the hostages. The tricorder hummed vigorously.

"Well, Ensign?" Kirk asked.

"Just as anticipated, Captain. Scans confirm that these weapons, although fashioned to resemble Voyzr technology, undeniably incorporate Klingon components and materials." He switched off the tricorder. "I can explain in much more detail if you like. Why, the krogium particle injectors alone—"

"Maybe later," Kirk said, smiling. "Rest assured, General, Marshal, this evidence—and more—will be made available to you, for your own people to examine to your satisfaction, although I can guarantee you that we would not make such a claim if we weren't prepared to back it up. Isn't that right, Mister Chekov?"

Chekov grinned. "Aye, Captain. Beyond a doubt."

"Hold on," Akton said. "You said *both* rifles are of Klingon manufacture? Ours *and* theirs?"

"No." Zavetta shook her head. "That can't be true."

"I'm afraid so," Kirk said. "The Klingons have been surreptitiously providing both sides with arms and other resources, the better to prolong your war and destabilize your world. A divided Voyzr is a weaker, more vulnerable Voyzr, and one far less likely to join the Federation should you ever care to do so at some point in the future." His voice grew more somber. "Make no mistake. The Klingons didn't create your war, let alone the deep divisions that led to it; those are indeed Voyzr's problems to deal with. But they *have* taken advantage of the conflict, stoking your respective war machines to create ever more carnage, casualties, and hostility."

Chekov looked on in admiration as his captain swept a steely gaze over the abashed commanders. Kirk wasn't pulling any punches.

"So the question is, General, Marshal: How much longer are you going to let them get away with it?"

Two

Personal log, Commander Pavel Chekov, Stardate 8676.3:
When I last visited Voyzr, as a green young ensign, the planet was in the grip of a bitter civil war. Now, twenty years later, a united Voyzr is celebrating two decades of peace, and the Enterprise-A is en route back to the planet to take part in the twentieth-anniversary festivities, including the opening of the Federation's first official embassy there, at the personal invitation of former Field Marshal Zavetta, who is now the current chief executive or regnant of the planet. She is expected to personally attend the embassy opening, which I anticipate will be rather more hospitable than that besieged control room so many years ago.

A medical emergency, however, threatens to delay our arrival...

"What can you tell us about this pandemic on Tykona, Bones?"

Chekov listened intently, taking notes on a data slate, as Kirk held a meeting of senior officers in the ship's primary conference room, while Mister Scott held down the fort on the bridge. Also in attendance were Spock, McCoy, Sulu, Uhura, and a new yeoman whose name Chekov couldn't immediately recall. Was it just him or were the yeomen really getting younger every year? The former, no doubt.

"They've had a nasty outbreak of Empusan Fever on Tykona's northeast continent," McCoy explained, "which they're ill-equipped to deal with. Fortunately, the Federation has some newly developed medicines and technology that should make a difference there. We just need to deliver them, stat."

Chekov mentally reviewed what he knew of Tykona, a fiercely independent world with a somewhat prickly relationship with the Federation. Colonized generations ago by refugees from a far-off planetary disaster, the now-thriving world had since become a haven for both genuine refugees (who provided most of the planet's workforce) as well as wealthy exiles fleeing political reversals, wanted criminals, interstellar fugitives, and such. Portions of the planet were purported to have become glitzy urban playgrounds for the upper crust: luxury hotels, seaside resorts, theme parks, and so on. Tykona notably had no extradition treaty with the UFP or any other galactic powers, nor any formal relationship with the UFP.

"It's unusual for Tykona to request the Federation's assistance, isn't it?" Chekov asked.

McCoy shrugged. "A plague is a plague, I guess. And I like to think that Starfleet isn't going to let politics get the way of providing humanitarian aid during a major health crisis. Not when there's something we can do to help."

"Quite so," Kirk agreed. "I am concerned, however, about how this detour might affect our mission to Voyzr. Not that a genuine medical emergency doesn't take priority over an embassy opening, but this diplomatic breakthrough has been decades in the making and could be the first step to Voyzr ultimately joining the Federation someday. Plus, the regnant *did* invite the *Enterprise* and its crew specifically."

That was because of Kirk's historic role in bringing peace to the planet, Chekov knew. He flattered himself that he and Sulu and the others had played some small part in that long-ago turning point as well. Chekov briefly regretted that Brenda Cassidy would not be joining them for the festivities on Voyzr, but she had retired from Starfleet years ago. Last he'd heard, she was breeding pedigreed sand bats on an agricultural colony in the Manark system.

"It shouldn't take too long once we get to Tykona," McCoy said. "Just a day or two to instruct the planet's public-health officials on how to properly administer the treatment, then we can be on our way again."

"What about transit time?" Kirk asked. "To and from Tykona?"

Sulu started to open his mouth, but Spock answered first. "By my calculations, there should be sufficient time to detour to Tykona and still arrive at Voyzr in time, assuming there are no additional delays."

"Definitely," Sulu confirmed. "We're going to be calling it a little closer than before, but we have some wiggle room. Not a lot, though, so I recommend increasing speed from warp six to warp seven, at least once we leave Tykona."

Kirk nodded. "Or maybe even before then. Let me consult with Scotty on just how far we should push the engines to complete both missions in a timely fashion." He turned to Uhura. "Once we adjourn, inform Voyzr of our side trip to Tykona. Assure them that we're still on track for the celebration roughly two standard weeks from now."

"Aye, sir," she said. "I'll transmit a message via subspace relays."

"Thank you, Commander." Kirk settled back into his seat. "So, it's settled then. Tykona first, then on to Voyzr with all due speed."

Chekov leaned back in his seat as old memories resurfaced, shaking off the dust of time: a cramped control room. Sizzling energy blasts. A devilishly tricky control panel . . .

"Voyzr again," he said. "Hard to believe that it's been nearly twenty years since that mission."

A lot had changed since then. That pioneering five-year mission had passed into history. Spock had died and been reborn, and the original *Enterprise* had gone down in flames, only to be replaced by a brand-new ship. On a personal level, he'd moved onto the *Reliant* for a time, during the ill-fated Genesis mission, only to wind up back where he belonged, here on the *Enterprise*. Well, an *Enterprise*, anyway.

"And that it's taken all this time to finally get an embassy there," Sulu said. "Even after we intervened way back when."

"These things take time," Kirk said. "The Voyzr needed to get their own house in order before they could focus on interstellar relations. Generations of strife and division can't be swept aside overnight; indeed, I gather the peace process provoked at least one failed coup attempt on the part of die-hard war hawks not long after we departed Voyzr the first time around." He shook his head sadly. "When war is all you've ever known, peace can be an alarming prospect, I suppose."

"Illogical," Spock observed, "but true nonetheless."

"More's the pity," McCoy said. "You'd think we'd have learned better by now."

"Every civilization must evolve at its own pace, Doctor," Spock said. "In its own time."

Hence the Prime Directive, Chekov thought. *As frustrating as that can be sometimes.*

"As for the embassy," Kirk said, "my understanding is that the optics there were dicey for a long time. Given the way the Klingons and, yes, the *Enterprise* stuck their noses into Voyzr's affairs before, it was not politic for the new ruling coalition to embrace otherworldly alliances too eagerly. It was only a generation ago, after all, that the Voyzr fought a war over the pros and cons of a *global* government; establishing closer ties with an *interstellar* Federation was not a controversy that Voyzr was eager to ignite, not in those fragile early years of peace and reconciliation." Kirk paused to take a sip of coffee before continuing. "Meanwhile, the Federation adopted a wait-and-see attitude toward Voyzr, preferring to let matters there stabilize before moving too quickly to cement relations with the planet and its government."

"A prudent approach," Spock said. "There was no guarantee that the peace might not collapse and Voyzr fall back into conflict or disorder. As with that attempted coup you referenced before."

"Not to mention a certain hostage crisis earlier," McCoy added.

"Can't really blame the higher-ups at the UFP for wanting to maintain a discreet distance from Voyzr after that whole mess. Bound to be some lingering hard feelings there."

Chekov recalled that McCoy had been the one to treat the traumatized hostages after they were rescued. Small wonder he'd still be acutely conscious of the human consequences of that incident.

"Indeed," Kirk said. "All the more reason that the Voyzr are to be congratulated for making their hard-earned peace stick for close to two decades now. And past time to let bygones be bygones."

"Well, I'll take a gala celebration over a hostage crisis any day," Sulu said, grinning. "If nothing else, this excursion to Voyzr is bound to be less tumultuous than our last visit there."

Don't jinx us, Chekov thought, his Slavic temperament asserting itself. "One can only hope."

"Speaking of which, Mister Chekov," Kirk addressed him. "Where do we stand regarding security at the embassy opening?"

"Erring heavily toward caution, Captain. Given the planet's history."

As the ship's security chief, Chekov was determined that nothing go wrong on this vital goodwill mission. With the civil war still in living memory, it was inevitable that some festering tensions and divisions remained, so security needed to be tight, just in case. The big anniversary celebration, including the return of Captain Kirk and the *Enterprise*, had been long planned and announced, which meant that, for better or for worse, any would-be troublemakers had had plenty of time to hatch their plans.

"The authorities on Voyzr are claiming the lead on security issues, naturally, and are taking every precaution to lock down the embassy, the capital, and the planet itself during the festivities. Planetary defenses will be on high alert, watching for any unauthorized spacecraft, beam-downs, and shuttles. Traffic to and from high-value targets, most notably the new embassy, will be monitored closely. VIP guest lists and press credentials will be scrutinized with a fine-tooth comb, and armed security officers, including the regnant's personal bodyguards, will be on hand to keep watch over the proceedings, in conjunction with the embassy's own security staff."

Kirk nodded. "And on our end?"

"I am already in touch with both the Voyzr and Federation officials managing security for the event," Chekov reported, "and expect such communications to increase as we draw nearer to Voyzr, physically *and* chronologically. Rest assured, Captain, I fully intend to keep my eyes out for any potential security breaches . . . or worse." He cracked a smile. "No assassins, saboteurs, or suspicious stowaways will be tagging along on my watch."

"Good to know," Kirk said. "Keep me informed of any issues that may arise."

"Absolutely, sir. You can count on me."

Three

"So, any big plans for shore leave?"

Nurse Simone Tovar, only recently assigned to the *Enterprise*, chatted with Chekov in sickbay as she prepared to vaccinate him against Empusan Fever in preparation for the ship's imminent arrival at Tykona. Since their mission to the planet was primarily Doctor McCoy's show, the captain had offered shore leave to crew members whose services were not required by the medical stopover, including members of the bridge crew. Given all the crew had been through since their last shore leave on Arcadia Zenith more than a month ago, Kirk's offer had been widely appreciated.

"Nothing in particular." Chekov sat atop a biobed in the sterile examining room, his legs dangling over the edge. "Sulu and I are probably going to check out the sights in Yoshpur City. There are supposed to be some nice restaurants, night spots, and recreational activities by the waterfront. Not to mention some ambulatory coral reefs just offshore."

"So I hear." She approached with a hypospray, which she pressed against his jugular. Chekov tensed involuntarily; over the course of his Starfleet career, he'd had more than his fair share of unwanted trips to the sickbay. "Relax," she assured him. "This won't hurt a bit."

"I've heard that before."

Sure enough, however, only a slight tingling sensation accompanied the distinctive hiss of the hypospray. He had to admit that the devices were much improved since his early days in Starfleet, when the tingle was closer to a sting. He resisted the temptation to gingerly touch the injection site anyway. He wouldn't want the nurse to think he was too phobic about such things.

Especially when that nurse was Simone Tovar.

Truth be told, he'd been hoping Tovar would be on duty when he reported for his mandated booster shot. A statuesque brunette with lustrous black hair and striking dark eyes and lashes, roughly Chekov's own age, she had caught his attention almost as soon as she had boarded the ship a few weeks ago, although he hadn't had much of a chance to make her acquaintance until now.

"There now," she teased. "That wasn't so bad, was it?"

"Perfectly painless, as promised. Clearly I am in good hands."

"We aim to please. Now lie down while I look over your vital signs, just to see if you can expect any side effects. A routine precaution."

"Certainly."

He stretched out on the biobed, determined to be nothing less than cooperative, while she studied the diagnostic display screen mounted on the bulkhead behind the bed. A crisp white uniform, adorned with a caduceus emblem in lieu of a Starfleet delta, flattered her figure. Matching earrings displayed red crosses against a white background, which Chekov recognized as a vintage medical symbol from Earth's history. Exchanging the hypospray for a data slate, she compared the readings on the screen to whatever was displayed on the slate.

"Any wooziness? Light-headedness?" she asked. "Chills? Muscle spasms?"

"None of the above," he reported, although part of him almost regretted that some trivial symptom wouldn't require him to linger longer in sickbay, under Nurse Tovar's tender care. "Everything in order?"

"So it seems." Her gaze shifted between the slate and the display screen. "All readings conform with your baseline vitals, taken at your last physical."

"Which is a good thing, I assume?"

"Not to worry," she said, smiling. "You're fit as a fiddle as far as I can tell." She scrolled through the records on her slate. "I must say, though, you have quite the 'colorful' medical history. Just in the last decade-plus alone, you've been zapped by an alien probe, mind-controlled by a parasitic eel, and required emergency brain surgery . . . in the twentieth century no less!"

She shook her head in amazement.

"All in the line of duty." He wondered, hopefully, if he should be encouraged that she had been motivated to take a closer look at his file, or was she just being thorough? Enjoying her attention, he was grateful that, being assigned to sickbay, she was not directly under his command, thereby avoiding any impropriety should he attempt to pursue his attraction to her, provided she was interested. "Never know what you're going to run into out on the frontier."

"No doubt." She switched off the monitor and indicated that he could sit up now. "Frankly, I'm impressed that you're as fit as you are, considering your exploits."

"I owe it all to clean living," he joked, "and the medicinal benefits of fine Russian vodka, of course."

"*Da, tovarich*," she answered, a smirk lifting her lips. "But not *too* clean, I hope."

Was she flirting with him, or was that just wishful thinking on his part? It had been a while since he had tried his luck romantically. A long-distance romance with a roving holo-journalist had eventually run its course months ago, not long after he returned to Earth following the Genesis affair, while a weekend fling on Argelius had blazed brightly but all too briefly. As far as he knew, Simone Tovar was also single at present. Were his rusty sensors indeed picking up some genuine chemistry between them?

Nothing ventured, nothing gained, he thought. "I don't suppose you have plans for shore leave?"

Sulu would surely forgive him for seizing an opportunity to get to know Tovar better.

"I wish! But I'm going to be busy assisting Doctor McCoy on Tykona. No shore leave for me, I'm afraid."

"Of course. I should have realized." He hastily charted a new course. "But *after* Tykona, what is your social calendar like, if you don't mind me asking?"

"Not at all," she replied, to his vast relief. "Barring any unexpected Romulan attacks or exotic viral outbreaks, I should have some off-duty hours up for grabs." She treated him to a welcoming smile. "Doctor McCoy may play the curmudgeon sometimes, but he's no slave driver."

Chekov was glad that the diagnostic monitor couldn't betray his rush of excitement. That she had not immediately raised her shields emboldened him, suggesting that perhaps he wasn't entirely misreading her flirty bedside manner.

"In that case, can I possibly call dibs on a few of those hours, for dinner maybe or a walk in the botanical gardens?" He summoned whatever rakish charm he could muster. "Just to give me a chance to learn more about your personal history, since you're already well-acquainted with mine. Fair's fair after all."

She chuckled. "I think I'd like that."

Da! Chekov's spirits surged, as though he had just successfully made first contact with a particularly appealing new life-form. He silently thanked McCoy for requiring crew members to get freshly vaccinated before vacationing on Tykona.

Before he could fashion a suitably suave reply, the door to the examination room whooshed opened and Sulu strolled into the chamber.

"Reporting for my booster shot," he declared cheerfully. "Oh, hi, Pavel. You getting vaxxed today, too?"

"Doctor's orders," Chekov said, not too bothered by the interruption. This visit to sickbay had already gone much better than he could have anticipated. Best not to press his luck after this promising beginning. There would be time enough to discover what intriguing possibilities might lie ahead.

She stepped away from the biobed. "Looks like my next customer is here."

"I'll leave you to your work then." He hopped off the bed and started for the door.

"Thank you, Commander Chekov. Do be careful down on Tykona." She grinned impishly. "I don't want to see you back in sickbay too soon, because of another 'colorful' mishap."

He grinned back at her. "I appreciate your concern, Nurse Tovar."

"Please, call me Simone."

Sulu raised an eyebrow. He shot Chekov a look that made it clear that he expected a full briefing later.

Not that Chekov had anything conclusive to report just yet. This personal voyage into the unknown had barely left spacedock. Nevertheless, he looked forward to exploring just how far he and Tovar—*Simone*—might end up traveling together. Beaming, he exited sickbay with a bounce in his step. The artificial gravity felt lighter somehow, and any temporary light-headedness had nothing to do with a vaccine.

"Please, call me Simone."

Alone in his quarters, reviewing the layout of the new Federation embassy on Voyzr, Chekov took a moment to bask in the memory of Nurse Tovar's parting words. Something about Simone made him feel like a giddy young ensign right out of the Academy rather than a seasoned commander. The *Enterprise* had only just entered into orbit above Tykona, but he was already looking past his imminent shore leave on the planet to renewing his acquaintance with Tovar once the ship was on its way to to Voyzr.

A leisurely stroll through the botanical gardens, past the artificial waterfall, was just the ticket for their first date. Followed by drinks and dinner at the adjacent canteen? He was going to be increasingly tied up with security matters the closer they got to Voyzr, but he was sure he could squeeze in a dinner for two, with hopefully more such engagements to follow.

An electronic chime intruded on his hopeful imaginings. He answered the page via the computer terminal on his desk. "Chekov here."

Uhura's visage appeared on the screen, supplanting the architectural diagrams of the new embassy. *"Sorry to disturb you, but we just received a personal transmission from the planet, hailing you."*

"Personal?" He was puzzled. As far as he knew, he wasn't acquainted with anyone on Tykona.

"Yes, from a Grigori Ratikin."

The name caught him by surprise. He and Grigori had been boyhood friends in Moscow long ago and had stayed in touch over the years, even after Chekov had headed off to Starfleet Academy. They didn't see each other nearly as much as they used to, but he was still one of Chekov's oldest friends from his pre-Starfleet days.

"I take it you know this individual."

"Very much so."

But what was he doing on Tykona? Over the last few decades, Grigori had made a name for himself as a sought-after architect and interior designer, known for his distinctively eclectic approach, which blended disparate cultural styles in creative ways, often employing traditional, nonfabricated materials and antique furnishings. Working pre-warp Regulan glyphs into erotic Deltan mosaics, for example, complete with hardwood tiles from Tiburon and polished dragon scales from Berengaria VII. Last Chekov had heard, Grigori had been running a boutique home-design studio out of Cawdor Prime.

"Shall I put the transmission through to your quarters?"

"By all means, thank you."

"My pleasure."

Uhura's practiced efficiency meant that Grigori's familiar visage appeared on the screen at once. His ruddy complexion was as robust as ever, while his thick blond eyebrows and beard were, if anything, even bushier than before. A broad, jovial face suited his outgoing nature, and if there were a few more creases and wrinkles here and there... well, neither of them was as young as he used to be.

"Pavel!"

"Grigori! It's been too long!"

"And then some!" He spoke to Chekov in their native tongue. His thick Muscovite accent struck nostalgic chords in Chekov's soul, evoking memories of bygone days. *"It is good to see you, my friend. You haven't changed a bit."*

"Liar," Chekov said, grinning. "But time has been good to you as well, unless you've snuck a flattering enhancement filter into your transmission, that is."

He was joking, of course. If nothing else, Uhura would have flagged anything squirrelly in the signal right away.

Grigori laughed. *"Spoken like a security officer, suspicious of everything!"*

"I don't know. I still recall that prank you pulled on me when we went camping as kids, and you faked those scary footprints to convince me that there was a man-eating Siberian yeti lurking in the woods outside our tent."

"Absolutely worth it! You should have seen the look on your face." He guffawed in recollection. *"But enough about our glorious past. I wager you weren't expecting to hear from me tonight."*

"You'd win that bet." He gathered it was also evening where Grigori was calling from. "How is it you're on Tykona?"

"Work, what else? A local bigwig, with superb taste in designers, has me overseeing a full remodel of her country villa. I've been here a few months now, taking an expensively hands-on approach to the project." His head and shoulders filled the screen, offering little view of his surroundings. *"Imagine my surprise when I heard via the global news network that the* Enterprise, *of all vessels, was swinging by Tykona for a few days."*

Chekov shrugged. "It's a small galaxy, I guess."

"And getting smaller every day, it seems." He peered at Chekov from the computer terminal. *"Any chance you have time to visit an old friend who knew you when?"*

"As it happens, I do have some shore leave coming."

"Splendid! I was hoping that would be the case. We have much to catch up on, I'm sure, but that can wait until we can do so in person, over vodka and a fine meal. I don't want to use up all my credits on this call. I'm just a humble civilian after all, not a high-ranking Starfleet officer."

Chekov wondered if the villa he'd mentioned was equipped to communicate with ships in orbit, or if Grigori was using some sort of commercial communications facility.

"Humble my foot. But yes, send me your coordinates and let's set a time for me to beam down." He grinned in anticipation. "I am truly eager to see you again, my friend. Talk about a happy coincidence."

He was still anxious to see Simone Tovar after his shore leave, but in the meantime, he couldn't think of a better way to bridge the gap than by reuniting with one of his oldest comrades for the first time in ages.

"*I know*," Grigori said. "*Fortune has smiled on us, Pavel, so we would be ungrateful churls not to take advantage of her largesse.*"

Chekov couldn't agree more.

Four

"Welcome to Tykona," Grigori greeted Chekov warmly upon his arrival at the villa.

Chekov stepped down from a civilian-grade transporter pad. This being an off-duty social call, he'd traded his maroon uniform for more casual attire, consisting of a lightweight brown jacket, a white tunic, brown trousers, and boots. His communicator was clipped to his belt should the *Enterprise* need to get hold of him, while an unopened bottle of vodka, suitably pre-chilled, was cradled against his chest.

"I come bearing gifts." He held out the bottle. "Well, a gift at least."

"Your mother raised you well." Grigori came out from behind the transporter control console to accept the offering. A rumpled blue smock, with plenty of pockets, draped his stocky frame. He placed it carefully on the console before giving Chekov an enthusiastic bear hug. "I'm so glad you could make it!"

"How could I not?" Chekov said, returning the hug. "Who knows when we'll next be within light-years of each other?"

Breaking their embrace, he took a moment to survey his new surroundings. The modestly sized transporter room suffered by comparison to the *Enterprise*'s but appeared serviceable, the pad large enough to accommodate at least four average-sized humanoids at a time. Tykona was a Class-M planet, so there was no perceptible difference in the gravity. A comfortable temperature suggested that the villa's interior was suitably climate-controlled.

"A personal transporter room?" he observed. "Very ritzy."

Grigori shrugged. "My current client has deep pockets and a

pronounced taste for privacy. As you'll soon see, we're a considerable distance from the nearest neighbor, town, city, or transit system. Having one's own private transporter makes it easier to beam to and fro when desired."

"Just in case you get stir-crazy?"

"Something like that."

Chekov suspected Doctor McCoy would have something acerbic to say on the subject of household transporters. "Will your client be joining us?"

"*Nyet.* She's a busy woman, with her exquisitely manicured fingers in lots of different pies. We mostly communicate virtually, and any on-site work is on hold until we receive some crucial materials from Denobula . . . and the client signs off on my latest revised designs." Grigori reclaimed the frosted bottle and ushered Chekov out of the chamber. "In short, we have the whole place to ourselves, with no bothersome client or contractors to get in the way of our reunion."

"All the better," Chekov said. "If anything, everything is falling into place so conveniently that I find myself instinctively waiting for the other gravity boot to drop, just to balance things out."

"Same old Pavel." Grigori clucked at him. "Always the glass is half-empty with you."

"*Mea culpa.* Let us simply enjoy our good fortune."

"That's more like it!"

Grigori led him into a large, airy living area, attractively furnished. A wall-sized picture window let in plenty of sunlight while offering a panoramic view of the surrounding countryside. Rolling hills and valleys, boasting lush blue and silver foliage, were broken up by sparkling creeks and ponds. It was springtime in this part of Tykona, Chekov knew, and only a few wispy green clouds dotted a bright tangerine sky. Notably absent were any visible roads, maglev tracks, or neighboring homes or farms.

"You weren't exaggerating when you said your client liked her privacy. I've seen more populated asteroids."

"A tranquil getaway from the bustle of big urban centers and space stations," Grigori said. "For what it's worth, there's a landing pad for fliers and shuttles out back, discreetly out of sight." He gestured expansively at the spacious living room. "Make yourself at home."

Grigori retrieved a pair of glasses from a visibly well-stocked bar and they settled into a pair of plush chairs, facing each other across an ebony coffee table. He opened the vodka bottle and poured them each a glass.

"*Za vstrechu!*" he toasted Chekov.

"To our meeting!" Chekov echoed.

The high-quality vodka, which he had been saving for just such a special occasion, went down smoothly. A taste of Mother Russia, straight from their old stomping grounds, many sectors away.

"No ice?" Chekov asked after they'd emptied their glasses. "You always preferred your vodka on the rocks."

"A man can't expand his horizons?" He grinned at Chekov as he poured them another round. "Fine talk from the great space explorer."

"Point taken." Chekov raised his glass. "*Na zdorovye!*"

"To good health!"

The drink soon had the desired effect. Feeling quite relaxed, Chekov contemplated the sprawling hills and fields outside. "You don't mind being stuck here in the middle of nowhere?"

A people person, Grigori had always thrived on crowds and cities and cosmopolitan living. It was odd to find him in such a remote locale, transporter or no transporter.

"Only for the duration. Besides, it's not always just me here. There's often no shortage of local artisans underfoot."

"And yet . . ." Chekov glanced around. "Forgive me, but I expected to see more of a work in progress. Unfinished walls. Exposed girders and circuitry. Construction materials piled high on antigrav lifters. Yet the more I look around, I'm not seeing any evidence of a major remodel underway. Nor any trace of your trademark style for that matter."

"Well, we're in the early days yet. The work at present is mostly conceptual."

Chekov didn't understand. "But you said you been at it for a few months already?"

"Did I?" He gazed into his glass, almost as though avoiding Chekov's gaze. "If you must know, I'm having trouble getting the client to 'yes.' She keeps asking for changes and alternatives every time I present her with a new design." He let out a weary sigh before pouring them another round. "But enough about me. What are you up these days, my friend?"

Chekov repressed a frown. Was it just his imagination or was there something "off" about Grigori? If he didn't know better, he'd swear his friend was being evasive, which wasn't like him at all. The Gregori he'd known all his life had always been on open book, sometimes to a fault. And "Enough about me"? Since when did Grigori not want to talk about himself and his work? That was often his favorite topic.

"The usual," Chekov replied. "Still serving aboard the *Enterprise*, obviously."

The diplomatic mission to Voyzr was far from classified, having already been publicized in advance, but he didn't want to waste his short leave going over it again. Not unlike, perhaps, Gregori being reluctant to talk about work while taking a break with his old friend?

Maybe that's all there is to it, Chekov thought. *And he doesn't actually have anything to be evasive about.*

"And your family?" Grigori asked. "They are well?"

"Happily, yes, although I'm woefully overdue to visit them. And yours?"

"Very well, thank you."

Chekov smirked. "Even your daughter?"

"Daughter?" A puzzled expression came over Grigori's face. "I don't recall having a daughter, unless you know something I don't."

What the devil? Chekov was startled by his response. Grigori's "daughter" was a long-running private joke between them, dating back to their youth when Grigori's youngest sister, some fifteen years his junior, delighted in embarrassing her big brother by posing as his daughter in public, purporting to be the product of some juvenile indiscretion. Chekov had never let Grigori hear the end of it, now or then.

So how come the joke had flown over his head, as though he had no clue what Chekov was referring to?

"Your sister, I mean. You know, the one who was young enough to be your daughter . . . if you were *very* precocious."

"*Da, da*, of course. Little Katya." He laughed off the confusion. "For a moment there, I was afraid you'd mixed me up with another old comrade, which was quite a blow to my ego."

If you say so, Chekov thought, unconvinced. Perhaps, as Grigori had suggested just last night, serving as security chief, along with a lifetime spent encountering peril throughout the galaxy, *had* rendered him chronically suspicious, automatically scanning for potential threats, and yet . . . it did feel as though Grigori was awkwardly covering for his inexplicable lapse. Chekov scrutinized the very familiar figure sitting across from him, who certainly looked and sounded like the Grigori he'd known forever. Despite this, sensor alerts started chiming at the back of his mind.

Something wasn't right.

"So, talk to me. What's new with you?" Grigori pressed, changing the subject, perhaps a little too quickly. "Are you seeing anyone these days?"

"Not at present, although there might be somebody on the horizon. Too early to say."

He found himself reluctant to volunteer too much information until he figured out what was going on with Grigori, if indeed there was any actual cause for concern. *If he can be evasive, so can I.*

"Interesting!" Grigori leaned forward. "Tell me more."

"Nothing to tell. It's all purely hypothetical at this point." Chekov gestured at their surroundings, which did not look at all like it was being remodeled. "Not unlike your current project, it seems."

"Very funny, but don't think you're getting off that easily. Come on, Pavel, don't hold out on me. What's her name? What is she like? Is she also serving aboard the *Enterprise* now?"

What's with the third degree? Chekov thought as the klaxons in his head grew louder by the moment. Maybe he was just being paranoid, but Grigori seemed almost *too* inquisitive, as though he was bound and determined to pump Chekov for personal details. Chekov didn't want to suspect his oldest friend of ulterior motives, but he also knew better than to ignore his own hard-won instincts. His gut was telling him to watch out.

For Grigori?

He smiled to conceal his growing unease. "What can I say? I don't want to kiss and tell before there's been a single kiss."

"Even to your oldest, boon companion?" Grigori refilled their glasses again. "Perhaps this potent libation will loosen your tongue. Nothing like good Russian vodka to liven up a get-together."

"I don't know," Chekov said. "I recall some alleged 'Romulan ale,' of questionable provenance, that had you dancing on the table and singing at the top of your lungs at that dive in St. Petersburg back in '62." His brow furrowed. "What was that place called again?"

"No idea. That whole night is a blur. I couldn't recall the name if my life depended on it."

"But you must remember the truly prodigious hangover you had the next day?"

"Oh yes!" Grigori clutched his head with both hands. "Would that I could forget!"

"Likewise!"

Chekov forced himself to keep smiling even as his blood ran colder than the vodka. Grigori had failed the test Chekov had reluctantly thrown at him; the boisterous incident he'd cited was a total fabrication, invented on the spot. Added to the accumulating irregularities in evidence, not least his gut feelings, there was no longer any room for doubt. This Grigori was not the man Chekov once knew, if he was even Grigori at all.

Dire possibilities raced through Chekov's brain. A clone? An android duplicate? A shape-shifter or telepathic illusionist? The real Grigori under some manner of mind control? Or maybe even an alternate Grigori from a parallel universe? For better or for worse, Chekov's long career in Starfleet had taught him that almost anything was possible, no matter how fantastic. He could be certain of only one thing.

He was in trouble.

He rose from the chair, being careful not to betray his alarm. He suddenly wished he had not left his phaser back on the *Enterprise*. But who took a weapon to meet with an old friend?

"Excuse me," he said as blithely as possible, "but before we imbibe too heavily, I need to check in with the *Enterprise* regarding a few minor matters. I'll be just a minute."

He started to reach for his communicator as he stepped away from the table, but, far less casually, Grigori drew a compact disruptor from a pocket of his smock. He aimed it straight at Chekov.

"Sorry, Commander, I can't let you do that." His Russian accent evaporated as he switched to Federation Standard. "Keep your hands away from that communicator."

Not Grigori at all then, despite appearances.

"Who are you?" Chekov demanded, no longer obliged to hide his anger at the deception. "What have you done with the real Grigori?"

"Not to worry, Mister Chekov." A humanoid woman, wearing a long off-white lab coat, entered the room, accompanied by a half-dozen Voyzr bearing disruptor pistols. They converged from various entrances, spreading out to surround Chekov. "Your friend is unharmed, just temporarily indisposed."

He blinked in surprise, his mind struggling to make sense of the situation. Who was this woman, who appeared to be of East Asian descent, and what were hostile Voyzr doing on Tykona, many systems away from their homeworld? That the *Enterprise* was headed for Voyzr soon could not be a coincidence; this had to be about the embassy opening and the peace celebration, but how? Why had they gone to such lengths to lure him to the villa, using a false Grigori as bait?

"So much for this charade." An older Voyzr came forward, his bearing suggesting he was in charge. Streaks of white infiltrated his russet fur, while ruby bands adorned his antlers, signifying his status. His pate was sheared of wool, Indee-style, the better to display the clan markings shaved into his scalp. Large brown eyes turned toward the bogus Grigori. "A shame you couldn't get more out of him before he caught on."

"I did my best, sir," the imposter insisted. "Based on the intel our foreign allies supplied."

"No matter," the senior Voyzr said. "Acquiring Commander Chekov was our main objective. Any additional personal data you might extract would be just a bonus. We already have all we need to carry out the operation."

"What operation?" Chekov asked. It was clear that the imposter had indeed been attempting to pump Chekov for information, and that their supposedly private conversation had been closely monitored the whole time. "What is this all about?"

The ruby-tined leader ignored Chekov's indignant queries. "Take his communicator," he ordered the imposter.

"Yes, sir." The fake Grigori came forward, brandishing his firearm. "Thanks for the vodka, 'old friend.' Not a bad concoction . . . for humans, that is."

Chekov registered the significance of that disdainful qualifier. Was the imposter not actually as human as he appeared? He glared at his deceiver but, surrounded by armed hostiles, had no choice but to let the man pluck the communicator from his belt. That the scoundrel wore Grigori's face only made his treachery more galling.

"Cossack swine. If I weren't outnumbered . . ."

"Spare us your arrogant Starfleet attitude," the leader said. "And don't even think of trying to make a break for it." He indicated the sweeping vista beyond the picture window. "There's nowhere to run and no help to be found, for as far as the eye can see."

"You won't get away with this." Chekov refused to be cowed despite the odds against him. "Captain Kirk will be coming for me. My captain and my crew will put paid to your schemes, whatever they are."

The leader snorted. "They won't even know you're gone—until it's too late."

Despite his bravado, Chekov didn't like the sound of that. This was obviously about more than just his personal safety. The ship, or at least its vital mission to Voyzr, was surely in jeopardy.

"What do you mean?" he asked. "What do you want with me?"

"No more questions," the leader said. "We are on a tight schedule. Take him away."

"Take me where? I want to see Grigori."

"What you want is of no concern."

A trio of scowling young bucks advanced on Chekov. He noted belatedly that none of the Voyzr present wore military uniforms such as those he recalled from his long-ago visit to their planet, but they looked more than willing to use force regardless. Six-fingered fists clenched at their sides. Antlers lowered ominously.

"Please go quietly, Mister Chekov," the woman urged, a guilty expression on her face. He got the impression that she was uncomfortable with the tense confrontation and implied threats of violence. She rung her hands anxiously. "No injury need befall you if you simply cooperate."

"Listen to the doctor." A sneering buck took hold of Chekov's arms. His antlers were less impressive than his leader's, in both size and adornment, but were pointy enough to watch out for in a fight. "Don't give us any trouble."

Like hell I won't, Chekov thought.

With a sudden movement, he yanked his arm free from the buck's grasp, then pivoted to the side and drove his elbow into the other man's gut. The Voyzr doubled over, gasping, and Chekov grabbed at his disrupter pistol. If he could just get his communicator back long enough to trigger a distress signal, then maybe the *Enterprise* could beam him out of—

A blinding turquoise beam, fired by another Voyzr, lit up his world and his nervous system, a heartbeat before everything went black.

Five

"How is your patient, Doctor?"

"All indications are that the procedure was a success. He should be coming to shortly. We'll know better then."

The voices—one male, one female—penetrated Chekov's foggy consciousness as he slowly emerged from uneasy dreams. Despite the fuzziness, he instinctively recalled that he was in dire straits, so he kept his eyes shut, feigning unconsciousness, while he covertly took stock of his situation. From what he could tell, he was lying atop a bed of some sort, with electronic equipment beeping and humming in the background. Last he remembered, he had been ambushed by hostile Voyzr and stunned when he fought back. Oddly, however, he didn't seem to be experiencing any of the usual unpleasant aftereffects of a disruptor blast.

"Why should there be a problem? The transference worked perfectly with the other human and my volunteer, not to mention your earlier test subjects."

"True, but there's still a lot we don't know about this ancient, forgotten technology, even after all these years. And when you're dealing with two distinctly different humanoid species . . . well, you have even more variables to contend with. A procedure of this nature is no simple matter, Trath. It only makes sense to proceed with care."

"It had better work, Doctor, for all our sakes. The entire operation depends on it."

"Believe me, Trath, I know that all too well."

Transference? Procedure? Trying not to stir, his eyes still closed,

Chekov identified the voices as belonging to the human woman and the Voyzr leader, respectively, but what were they talking about? Ancient technology? An unspecified "operation"? He tried to make sense of it, but he was in the dark, literally and figuratively. He kept quiet, hoping to learn more.

"I would hope so, Doctor. An opportunity like this may not—"

"Hold on, Trath. Chekov's brain-wave activity indicates that he is fully conscious." Her voice softened, assuming a gentler tone. "You can stop pretending, Mister Chekov. I know you're awake."

"So much for playing Sleeping Beauty," he muttered. There was no point in keeping up the pretense since his captors were unlikely to let any secrets slip now that they knew he was listening. Opening his eyes, he tried to sit up, only to discover that he was strapped down to a biobed in what looked like a hospital room, being studied by the doctor and the Voyzr leader, Trath, with contrasting degrees of empathy visible upon their faces. The doctor appeared genuinely concerned about her unwilling patient, while Trath peered down at him more coldly, standing stiffly with his arms behind his back.

"Sleeping Beauty?" he asked, puzzled.

"A famous Russian fairy tale."

Chekov looked around. Although his arms and legs were strapped down, he could still lift his head, which felt oddly heavier than usual. Blurry vision gradually came into focus as, turning his head from side to side, he spied a generous assortment of medical equipment—some familiar, some not—arrayed against the walls, along with a few cabinets and counters. A guard, armed and antlered, was posted at the only door, standing watch. A translucent privacy screen partially concealed a portion of the room to Chekov's right; through it, he dimly glimpsed the silhouette of a patient in another biobed only a few meters away.

Grigori?

"Where am I?" he asked. His voice sounded hoarse and unrecognizable.

"Still at the villa on Tykona, not far from the room where we first met." The doctor looked him over, occasionally glancing up at the display screen over his head. Chekov flashed back to his recent visit to sickbay when he was tended to by Simone Tovar; somehow he doubted this exam was going to be as delightful. "I regret that my associates' subordinates were forced to subdue you, but you gave us little choice."

"Aside from choosing to take me captive, after luring me into a trap." He strained unsuccessfully against his bonds. "You'll forgive me for not being more cooperative."

She winced but soldiered on, still attempting a soothing bedside manner as though he was simply a patient under care and not a prisoner. "And now? How are you feeling?"

Honestly, he wasn't sure. He'd been stunned before, even subjected to a Klingon agonizer and a Triskelion collar of obedience, but this felt different. The lights, the colors, the sounds, even his own voice seemed distorted somehow, as though there was something wrong with his eyes and ears. His face felt strange, too, like it was swollen or stretched out of shape. He wasn't in discomfort, exactly, but it *was* disorienting.

"Wrong," he admitted. "Not like myself."

Trath snickered, earning a disapproving look from the doctor.

"And do you know *who* you are?" she asked.

Was she checking him for shock or brain damage? Next she'd be asking if he knew who the president of the Federation was.

"Commander Pavel Andreievich Chekov, Starfleet," he said without hesitation. They obviously knew who he was well enough to bait a trap with a simulacrum of an old friend. "Serial number 656-5827B."

A harsh laugh came from the other side of the privacy screen.

"I wouldn't be so sure of that if I were you." The reclining figure sat up and turned toward Chekov. "Which I would know."

Not Grigori's voice, although it did sound far too familiar. It took Chekov a moment to recognize his own voice. His jaw dropped, his defiant attitude slipping as a sudden dread overtook him. He shuddered beneath the straps binding him.

"What is this? What is happening?"

The figure on the other bed, who was clearly not under restraint, produced a small handheld remote, which he pointed at the screen obscuring his appearance. A click turned the screen transparent, and Chekov found himself looking at . . .

Himself?

A mirror image smirked at him from across the room. He looked so much like his reflection that even Chekov couldn't detect any telltale difference. The face, the voice, the physique . . . everything declared, impossibly, that the man on the bed, wearing Chekov's civilian attire, was none other than Pavel Chekov.

Just as the fake Grigori had been indistinguishable from the genuine article.

"Who—?" Chekov's own voice, which he still couldn't recognize, faltered. It was hard not to be unsettled by such a convincing doppelganger. "You have no right to do this, copying my face!"

"Please, Mister Chekov, try to stay calm." The doctor looked intently at the display screen, where his pulse and stress levels were surely spiking—with good reason. "Don't make me sedate you."

"Congratulations, Doctor." Trath smiled, heedless of Chekov's distress. "It seems the transference was a success after all."

"Transference?" A ghastly possibility hit Chekov like a photon torpedo. Tearing his horrified gaze away from the other "Chekov," he stared down at his shaking hands, which he raised as far as the restraints would allow.

Velvety red fur carpeted the backs of hands, which boasted six fingers each.

"*Bozhe moi!*"

He tried to reach for his face, momentarily forgetting his bonds in his panicky need to confirm his worst fears. Turning his frantic eyes downward, he belatedly glimpsed, at the lower periphery of his distorted, disorienting vision, the upper contours of . . . a snout?

"You devils! What have you done to me?"

"Please, Chekov," the doctor pleaded. "Don't upset yourself."

"WHAT HAVE YOU DONE?"

She recoiled, guilt contorting her own face.

"Don't coddle him," Trath ordered. "Show him."

She hesitated. "Please, I've done what you asked. There's no need to be cruel. He's received a dreadful shock."

"For his own peace of mind then, if that eases your conscience. Show him."

Her shoulders sagged in defeat.

"Very well." She retrieved a hand mirror from a nearby cabinet and approached Chekov with obvious reluctance. "Please brace yourself."

He didn't need the warning, already trembling in anticipation, but there was no way to truly prepare himself for the face that looked back at him from the mirror.

A Voyzr face.

Six

"*You devils! What have you done to me?*"

The naked fear and fury in her new patient's voice echoed mercilessly in Doctor Jacqueline Morval's mind as she conferred with her blackmailers in the villa's spacious living area. Adding to her guilt was the sense that she ought to be with Chekov now, helping him through his trauma instead of leaving him alone and under guard, but she hadn't been able to bear his accusing gaze any longer. She'd check on him later, she promised herself. She'd just needed to step away for a short spell to steady herself. Physician, heal thyself.

Fat chance, she thought.

An open bottle of vodka still rested on the coffee table, forgotten since Chekov's seeming reunion with Grigory Ratikin had come to an abrupt and upsetting end. Morval claimed an unfinished glass and gulped it down. No longer chilled, it had warmed to room temperature. She swallowed it anyway.

It didn't make her feel any better.

"Don't look so glum, Doctor," Trath chided her. "Your role in these proceedings is almost over. Less than two weeks to go." Following her lead, he poured himself a glass and sipped it experimentally. His cervine face twisted in disgust and he spit the mouthful back into the glass. "Vile! How do you humans tolerate it?"

Differently evolved taste buds? the scientist in her speculated reflexively. *Or just varying cultural backgrounds and traditions?*

Not that it truly mattered at the moment.

She and Trath shared the living space with two of his agents, neither of them in their original bodies, thanks to her. A dedicated Exile named Vonnu still occupied the form of Ratikin, while another young buck, Ryjo, was about to return to the *Enterprise* as Chekov.

It's all happening, just as planned, and there's nothing I can do to stop it.

Part of her had hoped that, against all odds, the life-entity transference would fail somehow, forcing the operation to be scuttled, regardless of the consequences for her, but no such luck. For better or for worse, she'd devoted much of her adult life to studying the ancient, arcane technology involved, so she knew what she was doing when it came to temporarily swapping consciousnesses between two sentient beings. Ryjo was indeed "Chekov" now, with no debilitating aftereffects that she could determine, damn it.

"How are you feeling?" she couldn't resist asking him.

"Older," he admitted. "Are all human bodies so tired and achy? I feel like I've aged thirty years."

"More like twenty-five," she said. "Chekov is actually in fine condition for a man his age, but you don't have an eighteen-year-old body anymore."

"I know." He sighed in resignation. "It just feels . . . uncomfortable . . . being so much older all of a sudden."

"I can imagine," she sympathized. Not that Ryjo probably needed to worry about getting much older in either this body or his original one. Not if he carried out his mission as planned.

"Your courage and sacrifice will not be forgotten," Trath said. "You are a credit to your clan and to your late father in particular. Are you ready to depart for the *Enterprise*?"

"Absolutely, sir."

A spike of alarm stabbed Morval. After months of anxious planning and anticipation, things were now proceeding far too fast. Was there still a chance to hit the brakes before it was too late?

"Are we certain this is a good idea?" she asked. "I'm worried about how quickly Chekov saw through Vonnu pretending to be

Ratikin." She gave the body-swapped Voyzr an apologetic look. "No offense."

He bristled anyway. "I did my best. It's not my fault our intel on Ratikin must have been incomplete."

"I'm not blaming you." In fact, they still didn't know what exactly had tipped Chekov off to the deception. "But what if the same thing happens aboard the *Enterprise*? Ryjo needs to fool Chekov's friends and crewmates all the way to Voyzr. Do we truly think he can pull that off when Chekov pegged Vonnu as an imposter in no time?"

"I can do it," Ryjo insisted. "I've spent months studying every aspect of Chekov's life: his history, his personality, his mannerisms, even his native tongue. Vonnu was working from a much thinner file since he just needed to fool Chekov long enough to lure him to this location . . . and perhaps extract a few updated details about his recent activities aboard the *Enterprise*."

"Quite true." Trath licked his own nose to keep it wet. "Our Klingon allies provided us with much more comprehensive intel on Commander Chekov than on Ratikin, who was indeed nothing more than bait." He placed a reassuring hand on Ryjo's shoulder. "Your hard work and preparation for this mission have not gone unnoticed. I have complete faith in your ability to carry out your mission."

Ryjo visibly basked in his leader's praise. "That means everything to me, sir."

"And as for you, Doctor." Trath shot a warning glance at Morval. "Kindly keep any second thoughts to yourself. I will not have you undermining the confidence of my agents. Do you understand me?"

"Yes, Trath." Her spirits sagged with her shoulders. "Too well."

How had it come to this? She had no loyalty to the Exile's cause. Indeed, less than year ago, she had never even heard of Voyzr, let alone known that Tykona hosted an entrenched community of Voyzr Exiles, still nursing a grudge over some long-ago civil war. She had certainly never set out to betray the Federation. Instead she had been tricked and trapped and turned, a step at a time, until she woke up one day to find herself hopelessly compromised, facing personal and professional ruin if she didn't do as she was told, even if that meant perverting her life's work, namely studying the incredible device discovered amidst the ruins of a dead civilization on Camus II more than two decades ago.

Ever since the Kirk/Lester incident of 2269, which remained strictly classified by Starfleet, select scientists and researchers had been quietly analyzing the long-lost technology responsible, the almost-metaphysical underpinnings of which continued to resist full explanation despite the best efforts of many of the Federation's finest minds. Morval and her predecessors and colleagues had made great strides in understanding the applications and effects of the technology, even to the extent of being to reverse-engineer similar devices, but determining precisely *why* it worked remained elusive, yielding only a flurry of contradictory theories and explanations, none of which could be conclusively proven.

That was the puzzle she'd been determined to crack, no matter what, and the ambition that ultimately led to her downfall.

It had started innocently enough, with a seemingly harmless request. She received through back channels a communication from someone who purported to be a Tellarite scientist engaged in equally classified research along similar lines, specifically instances of psychic possession and transference involving long-extinct alien civilizations such as the Arretians and Zetarians. Frustrated by the wearisome layers of security impeding open communication between their respective endeavors, he'd offered to share some of his findings with her, under the table as it were, in exchange for the same courtesy from her.

At first, his proposal had seemed reasonable enough. They were all on the same side after all, pursuing related goals, so why should an excess of bureaucratic red tape involving security clearances and restrictions get in the way of solving mysteries that had stymied determined scientists for decades? It wasn't as though they were trading dangerous military secrets; the Tellarite was simply offering a few tidbits of esoteric data that might provide fresh insights into certain problems that were defeating her.

Where was the harm?

It all seemed so innocuous in the beginning, with exchanges of obscure, rarefied test results, readings, and translations posing no possible threat to the safety of the Federation, which slowly, meticulously led to larger and more generous file swaps as she grew more at ease with their informal arrangement. That was how she'd thought of it then, as simply an "informal" exchange of ideas and information, not anything resembling espionage. And she *was* finding some provocative new data in the material she received from her obliging new Tellarite collaborator.

It was only after several such exchanges, in which she heedlessly shared ever-greater quantities of classified scientific data without authorization, that the "Tellarite" revealed himself to have been a disguised Klingon spy all along.

At that point, she was trapped. She could not come clean to her superiors without revealing that she had been covertly supplying the Klingons with top-secret intel for months. She would be facing disgrace, criminal prosecution, probably even imprisonment in a rehabilitation colony, not to mention the total demolition of her career, her reputation, her personal and professional relationships, everything. Friends, family, lovers, mentors . . . everyone would know that she had been duped into collaborating with the Klingons.

She couldn't live with that, and her Klingon handler knew it. She was a suborned Klingon asset now, whether she liked it or not.

In hindsight, she should have called it quits right away, confessed her misdeeds, and faced the music, but instead she had let the Klingon blackmail her into obtaining yet more classified scientific secrets, of a far more serious nature, which only gave him even more leverage over her. It was like being trapped aboard a runaway bullet train; it was already accelerating too fast to jump off without risking catastrophe, but the longer she delayed, the more impossible it became. All she could do was hang on for dear life, postponing the inevitable crash, until she ended up . . . here.

"Perhaps I should go check on my patient," she said, more defeated than ever. "See how he's coping."

Trath frowned.

"You worry too much about the prisoner. His welfare is not our concern." He licked his nose. "A shame we can't simply dispose of him."

Ryjo flinched at the prospect of his original Voyzr body being harmed, even though he was never expected to return to it. He kept quiet, however.

"That's not possible!" Morval snapped, despair expressing itself as impatience. "You know that."

Decades of research and experimentation had demonstrated that a Camusian life-entity transfer produced a profound connection between the two subjects, a kind of psychic entanglement that operated across even interstellar distances. Contrary to what Doctors Lester and Coleman had believed back in the day, killing one subject would not make the transference permanent; instead, it would kill both subjects simultaneously. Indeed, even keeping Chekov heavily sedated for the entire duration of Ryjo's mission risked impairing Ryjo's ability to think and function effectively over an extended period of time. Chekov needed to be kept in sound mind and body for the mission's sake.

"What about my body?" Vonnu scratched irritably at Ratikin's bushy blond beard. "Can I get it back now that I've played my part? I'd like to shed this aging human carcass sooner rather than later."

Morval shook her head. "Best to let the transference reverse itself naturally in due time, under careful observation. That's safer and less challenging than trying to undo it via another, unnecessary procedure." She turned toward Trath. "Any transplant, no matter how routine, risks complications, and this procedure is anything but routine."

For once, Trath did not question her, possibly because he preferred to keep the false Ratikin in reserve should something go wrong and Starfleet start taking a closer look at Chekov's visit to Tykona. Not that Trath would ever entertain such a possibility in front of his subordinates. The mission would succeed, period. Doubts were off-limits and bad for morale.

Luring the real Ratikin to Tykona had been easily accomplished, employing the same cover story later fed to Chekov. Ratikin had been drawn by the promise of an ambitious remodeling project, only to be waylaid when he arrived to inspect the location in person. Now he was being detained in a separate room, away from Chekov, as a precaution against the two humans conspiring together.

"Patience," Trath instructed Vonnu. "You'll be restored to your proper form soon enough."

At which point, it would be possible to eliminate the real Ratikin without harming Vonnu. Morval was under no illusions that Trath would let Ratikin go once Ryjo completed his mission; the innocent Russian would then be an incriminating loose end to be disposed of as expeditiously as possible. She didn't like to think about that, let alone her own possibly expendable status, despite her value as a Klingon asset and an expert in Camusian tech; still, she derived some small measure of comfort from the knowledge that at least one of her "patients" would survive this nightmare, even if Vonnu was a willing participant in the plot.

Chekov's prospects, on the other hand, were considerably less rosy.

She resorted to another glass of vodka and forced herself to focus on her work instead, seeking solace in the science that had always been her chief passion.

"Speaking of the reversal," she said to Vonnu, "are you experiencing any mental backwash yet?"

Past trials, conducted over the years on voluntary test subjects, had determined that the intimate psychic link between the subjects flowed both ways, with the division between the two consciousnesses becoming ever more permeable over time; the longer the link was in place, the more memories and impressions tended to filter back to their original brains, at first in the form of brief, fragmentary images and sensations lasting only a heartbeat or so. This psychic cross contamination, or "backwash," would eventually accelerate and amplify until the transposed life-entities began switching back to their original bodies, momentarily at first, but then for longer intervals and, ultimately, for good.

Vonnu hesitated before replying to her, looking uneasy.

"Speak up," Trath ordered. "Answer the doctor."

"It's probably nothing, but . . . I've been having these dreams that, well, seem to mix up my memories with people and places I don't know, but that maybe Ratikin does? Where I'm human, then Voyzr, then human again, in cities and landscapes I don't recognize, but which feel strangely familiar. If that makes any sense?"

Morval nodded, making a mental note to give Vonnu a full examination in the near future and perhaps ask him to keep a dream diary to better document his experience. "Anything else? While you're awake perhaps?"

"Maybe," he hedged. "Not anything serious. Just flashes every so often. Faces, voices, snatches of memories that don't belong to me." He shrugged unconvincingly, presenting a confident pose. "Nothing I can't handle for a little while longer."

She could tell he was more disturbed by his symptoms than he wanted to let on. Small wonder he'd been so anxious to get back into his own body. Ratikin's memories were already seeping back where they belonged.

"Don't worry," she assured him. "What you're experiencing is entirely to be expected, and absolutely temporary. Once the transference fully reverses itself, you will experience no lingering aftereffects."

She said this with confidence, based on years of meticulous research. Certainly, James T. Kirk had never reported any lasting effects from that first documented transference. The psychic entanglement had terminated once both parties were back in their original bodies. Subsequent trials had verified this outcome over and over.

"Nevertheless," Trath said, eyeing Vonnu warily, "we had best place you under guard for the present. We can't have Ratikin reclaiming his body at an inconvenient moment, not with so much at stake."

"Yes, sir. I understand."

"Good man." Trath turned his attention to Ryjo, who appeared to be following the discussion of Vonnu's unsettling symptoms more intently than the Voyzr leader might have preferred. "And Ryjo has no reason to fear any sort of reversal before his mission is complete, isn't that so, Doctor?"

She knew what he wanted to her to say, and, unfortunately, she did not need to dissemble. She was confident that she had figured out how to prolong the transference so that it would last long enough for Ryjo to carry out his assignment before it began to reverse itself, returning Chekov's consciousness to his own body. In theory.

"Yes," she said. "You will have enough time to . . . do what you intend."

She couldn't bring herself to spell it out any more than that.

"Good to know," Ryjo said, looking reassured. "Thank you, Doctor."

She felt a twinge of sympathy for the young volunteer. She didn't know much about his background, but she understood that he had grown up in the Exile community here on Tykona, no doubt raised on patriotic tales of the grievous historical injustice that had banished his clan from their native planet in the wake of a civil war and failed coup d'etat. He was clearly eager to avenge that long-ago wrong and prove himself loyal to the Exile cause, even if it meant sacrificing his own body and future.

"Go then," Trath exhorted. "Infiltrate Kirk's crew, beneath his very nose, and bring honor to your clan, your people, and the sacred memory of your mother and father. Make us proud."

Ryjo straightened Chekov's shoulders.

"I won't let you down, sir."

Seven

Here we go, Ryjo thought.

Taking a deep breath, he stepped out of the turbolift onto the bridge of *Enterprise*-A. Chekov's maroon uniform fit snugly on his stolen form; Ryjo resisted an urge to tug on the turtleneck collar. Excitement warred with apprehension as he confronted one of the first big tests before him.

I can do this. I have *to do this.*

He scanned the bridge, trying hard not to gawk. It had taken some time to adjust to seeing through human eyes, but he was getting used to it. To his relief, the bridge looked identical to the VR simulator he had logged into so many hours on, allowing for the slight discrepancies between human and Voyzr vision. Just to play it safe, he had run through the simulation one last time *after* the transference so any changes in lighting or coloration didn't throw him off.

"Welcome back, Mister Chekov. I trust you enjoyed your shore leave."

The captain's chair rotated toward him, and Ryjo found himself face-to-face with Captain James T. Kirk.

"Yes, Captain. Very much so."

Prepared for this moment, Ryjo schooled his new face to betray no trace of the powerful feelings coursing through him as he looked straight into the eyes of the infamous human who had cost his family and his people so much. In the Exile community he'd grown up in, Kirk's name was reviled. He was a devil: the arrogant Starfleet meddler responsible for the shameful "peace" that had dishonored the valor and sacrifice of all who had fought and died for the Indee cause, including Ryjo's own mother, all her siblings, and numerous other kin on both sides of his family tree. It was Kirk who'd set in motion the events that led to the Exiles seeking refuge on Tykona decades ago, their rightful fortunes and status unjustly diminished. Back on Voyzr, Ryjo's father had been a man of power and influence: a statesman and an aristocrat, presiding over a vast estate, heir to a long and distinguished line of clan leaders, generals, judges, industrialists, and scholars. On Tykona, he had been reduced to eking out a living as a barber, forever blaming Kirk and Starfleet for both the loss of his heritage and his son's truncated prospects. All Ryjo's life, for long as he could remember, he had been told of the glorious future he might have had if not for Kirk sticking his short, stubby human nose where it didn't belong. Looking at Kirk now, it was all he could do not to spit in his face.

He smiled broadly instead. "Still, it's good to be back, sir."

Not wanting to prolong the encounter, lest his true feelings slip past his amiable façade, he casually took his place at Chekov's accustomed post at the forward control console, replacing the hairless Deltan ensign keeping it warm. Settling into the seat, his back to Kirk, he was grateful that the *Enterprise* was still in orbit around Tykona, allowing him to get his bearings before he would be called upon to serve as either navigator or security chief to any significant degree. It was the latter role, of course, that had made the real Chekov the target of the operation. Being in charge of security en route to Voyzr put Ryjo in the ideal position to carry out his mission when the time came.

"So how was your reunion with your old comrade?"

Ryjo turned toward Commander Hikaru Sulu, whom he knew to be Chekov's longtime friend and crewmate, dating back to Kirk's original five-year mission. Sulu had also been involved in Kirk's unwelcome interference with the war two decades ago, but that was not what caused Ryjo to tense up inside. If anyone aboard the ship was going see through his disguise, it would be Sulu. He would have to be very careful around this man while, paradoxically, acting completely at ease with him, as though they were indeed the best of friends.

"Long overdue," he said. "But we picked up right where we left off, as though it hadn't been ages since we last saw each other in the flesh."

Sulu smiled, clearly happy for Chekov. "You'll have to tell me all about it later."

No way to avoid it, Ryjo thought, not looking forward to that conversation. If anything, he was more anxious about socializing with Chekov's peers than he was about performing his professional duties. The latter had simply required a crash course in Starfleet procedure, along with certain security codes, which he had accessed via an exacting biometric scan in the privacy of Chekov's quarters; the former would test his improvisational skills and knowledge of Chekov's interpersonal relationships. He could not afford to get overconfident; just look at how quickly Chekov had recognized "Grigori" as an imposter. He would have to do much better than Vonnu had if he hoped to succeed in his mission—and honor his father's memory.

"I want to hear all about your shore leave as well." He grinned back at Sulu. "Hope you didn't do anything I wouldn't do."

"If only!" Sulu chuckled. "Seriously—"

The turbolift doors whooshed open, heralding the arrival of an older, somewhat weathered-looking human male whom Ryjo instantly identified as Doctor Leonard McCoy, the ship's chief medical officer and another longtime associate of Chekov. According to the files provided by the Exiles' allies in Klingon Imperial Intelligence, McCoy had treated Chekov on numerous occasions over the last couple of decades, including more than a few close brushes with death.

"Home sweet home." McCoy crossed the bridge to the command well, where he leaned against a guardrail near the captain's chair. "Glad to see you haven't blown the place up in my absence."

"The day is young," Kirk quipped. "Mission accomplished, Bones?"

McCoy nodded. "We've done what we can, but I'm confident that the Tykon authorities now have the tools and training they need to bring the pandemic under control before it spreads any further . . . and quickly extinguish it altogether."

"Good work. You and your medical team are to be commended."

Ryjo was glad to hear it, too. The Empusan Fever pandemic had been just the opportunity the Exiles had needed, allowing their friends in high places to request the Federation's assistance, knowing that the *Enterprise* would be passing by the sector on the way to Voyzr. Truth be told, Ryjo privately suspected that the Klingons might have covertly engineered the outbreak for just that reason, but that was way above his rank in the movement. He didn't need to know what had caused the pandemic, and he didn't want to know. He was just relieved that the pandemic would be over soon, now that it no longer served any purpose.

"And has the rest of your staff also beamed back aboard?" Kirk asked.

"The whole team," McCoy said, "who, frankly, are entitled to some well-earned rest and recreation of their own at this point."

Sulu leaned over and whispered slyly to Ryjo, "Including a certain nurse."

Nurse? Ryjo nodded and winked at Sulu, as though he had any idea who the other man was referring to. Was Sulu involved with one of the ship's nurses or hoping to be? There had been nothing about that in Ryjo's briefings on Hikaru Sulu, so maybe it was nothing serious? Thank the stars that the bridge was not the place for idle gossip or locker-room chat. He would have to try to subtly draw the particulars out of Sulu later, assuming the topic ever came up again.

"Commander Uhura." Kirk swiveled toward a human woman, handsome by their standards, stationed at the communications station. Nyota Uhura, yet another close acquaintance of Chekov's, whose file Ryjo had studied extensively. She had served under Kirk even longer than Chekov. "Has everyone returned from shore leave?"

"Aye, Captain. All present and accounted for."

"Very good. In that case, I see no reason to delay our departure any longer." Kirk leaned back into his chair, fixing his gaze on the viewscreen. "Mister Chekov, set a course for Voyzr. Mister Sulu, take us out of orbit."

"Aye, sir," they responded, practically in unison.

Easy now, Ryjo thought, suddenly very glad that he hadn't taken Sulu's place instead. Better the navigator than the helmsman. *You can do this. You've done it a thousand times in the simulator . . .*

Despite his nerves, he felt a surge of excitement as well. Not only was his vital mission finally underway, but he was actually heading out into deep space for the first time ever, having spent pretty much his entire life on Tykona. He couldn't even remember Voyzr, which had been taken from him as an infant. Tykona, for all its hardships and humiliations, was the only home he'd ever known.

Which he would almost surely never see again.

A bittersweet pang leavened the turbulent emotions churning behind the stolen face he presented to Kirk and the others. He couldn't help thinking of Dise and how they had left things when they parted. If only he could have seen her one last time before leaving Tykona, tried again to make her understand why he *needed* to do this. Of the vow he'd made at his father's deathbed.

Forgive me, Dise. In a better universe, we could have had an amazing life together.

But that was not meant to be. History and heritage had set him on this course the moment their people were banished from their native soil a generation ago. A world that the real Chekov no doubt remembered better than Ryjo did.

All because of James T. Kirk and the crew of the *Starship Enterprise*.

"Setting course for Voyzr, sir."

Eight

"Offal," Picco swore as he failed yet another labyrinth puzzle on his data slate. Maybe he needed to lower the difficulty level?

The bored Voyzr nibbled on a bag of seasoned leaves and twigs as he glumly kept watch over the captured Starfleet officer strapped to the biobed in the locked chamber, which doubled as both a medical unit and a prison cell. Maintaining a guard over a prisoner who was already locked up and under restraint struck Picco as redundant, but Trath wasn't taking any chances. Yawning, Picco consulted a wall chronometer, which cruelly reminded him that he still had a few more hours on his shift. It was the wee hours of the morning, with dawn still distant, so everybody else in the villa—including the prisoner, Chekov—was surely asleep. Not for the first time, Picco cursed his bad luck at drawing the graveyard shift.

A hard plastiform chair seemed almost deliberately uncomfortable, perhaps to keep him from dozing off, but his eyes were drooping anyway. He was on the verge of requesting a mug of hot mushroom tea from the automated food slot when Chekov began stirring fitfully beneath his bonds and moaning piteously.

Maybe he was just having a nightmare? Picco couldn't really blame him, considering his circumstances. The Voyzr couldn't imagine waking up in somebody else's body and finding yourself a prisoner to boot. Picco grimaced at the other man's groans; that this Chekov person looked and sounded like young Ryjo only made his evident distress all the more troubling. Picco knew intellectually that this was an enemy combatant before him, party to the injustice inflicted on his forebears a generation ago, but his eyes kept telling him a fellow Exile was suffering.

"AARGH!"

Chekov let out an anguished cry and began writhing in torment. Picco lurched to his feet, his fatigue and boredom instantly vaporized by whatever was happening to the prisoner. He rushed across the darkened chamber, exiting the soft white glow around his seat.

"Lights! Full!"

Overhead illumination fired up, fully exposing the prisoner's convulsions. His eyes were wide open, pain and fear contorting his all-too-Voyzr features. Agonized moans escaped his lips. He shook like a leaf in a gale.

"What is it?" Picco asked, worried. "What's wrong?"

"Turn on the lights! I can't see. I can't see anything!"

"What the blight are you talking about?" His heart sank as a ghastly possibility occurred to him. "The lights *are* on."

"No! You must be lying. Tell me you're lying!" Chekov squirmed upon the bed. "My stomach, it hurts so much. My guts feel like they're twisting into knots!"

Picco gulped. Was this for real?

He waved six fingers before the prisoner's eyes—Ryjo's eyes—but the bulging orbs merely rolled wildly in their sockets, staring sightlessly at nothing.

"You really can't see? This isn't a trick?"

"What are you saying?" Chekov managed between groans. "That I'm blind?" Hysteria tinged his voice. "*Bozhe moi*, I'm blind!"

Picco's blood went cold. He recognized the symptoms—sudden blindness, excruciating stomach cramps—which had been all over the global news media for weeks. They were the first early warning signs of . . .

Empusan Fever!

"Oh, ordure." He backed away fearfully, a hand over his snout. Last he'd heard, the viral outbreak was still an ocean away but spreading at an alarming rate. And highly contagious.

"Help me, please!" Chekov bucked and twisted beneath his bonds. Violet Voyzr blood dribbled past his lips. "Make it stop. Somebody make it stop!"

Picco wanted desperately to flee the chamber before he could be infected, but he also knew that Ryjo's mission depended on Chekov's continued survival. He ran for a wall-mounted intercom unit instead of the door.

"Paging Doctor Morval! We have a medical emergency!"

Chekov's cries and whimpers scraped at Picco's nerves as he waited anxiously for a response, alternating between glancing worriedly at the prisoner and turning his face away from him. His eyes sought out the diagnostic display screen above the bed; he didn't see anything obviously amiss with Chekov's vitals, but what did he know? He was a foot soldier, not a medic. Seconds seemed to slow to a crawl before Morval's groggy voice issued from the speaker:

"What is it? What's the matter?"

"The Starfleet prisoner. I think he has the Fever!"

The sleepiness evaporated from her voice. He could practically hear her being jolted awake by his report.

"I'm on my way! Take care of him till I get there!"

"But—"

The intercom went dead, yielding only static, before he could request further instructions on how to treat the patient *and* avoid getting infected in the process. His brain hastily reviewed what he knew about the progress of the disease: blindness and stomach cramps at first, followed closely by nausea, vomiting, explosive hemorrhaging from every orifice, delirium, organ failure, and, ultimately, death.

Morval couldn't get here fast enough.

"Help me, whoever you are," Chekov pleaded. "I think I'm going to be sick!"

Nausea, vomiting, followed by blood from all over...

"Hold on!" Picco shouted, panicking. The last thing he wanted was contagious effluvia spraying everywhere, contaminating the sheets, the bed, everything. Overcoming his instinctive aversion, he dashed to Chekov's side and began hastily undoing the straps holding the writhing prisoner down. "Wait until I can get you to the lavatory."

"Hurry!" Chekov's jaws clenched, as though trying to hold back whatever was coming. His damp nostrils flared as he started hyperventilating. Grunts and groan seeped through gnashing teeth. "Urrrrgh!"

There was no time to rummage through the assorted drawers and cabinets for whatever protective gloves or masks might be available. Picco undid the straps and nervously helped raise Chekov to a sitting position. Newly freed, Chekov's hands clutched his abdomen, which was hidden behind a flimsy hospital gown. Gagging noises escaped his throat.

"Why is everything spinning?" Chekov mumbled, his head rolling slackly above his shoulders. Bloody drool dangled from lips. "Who turned off the gravity?"

"Keep your mouth shut. Don't you dare throw up on me!"

Chekov looked around blindly. Picco yanked him to his feet and grabbed his arm to guide him. "This way. Quickly!"

Chekov's eyes snapped into focus as he grabbed onto Picco's antlers and yanked the guard's head down toward Chekov's knee, which rose up to meet Picco's lower jaw before he even grasped what was happening. The impact staggered the guard, snapping off a tine from his right antler and leaving him defenseless against a combo of short, hard punches to his head and stomachs. One last thought flashed across Picco's mind before everything went dark for him.

At least he wasn't going to be infected.

"Never mind, *tovarich*. I feel much better now."

Chekov thanked his lucky stars that he'd paid attention to Doctor McCoy's briefing on Empusan Fever—and that his new, hopefully temporary body was apparently young and vigorous enough to be handy in a fight. He spit out a mouthful of blood, the inside of his mouth smarting where he'd bitten it, and tossed aside the broken piece of antler, which clattered onto the floor. Chekov hadn't meant to snap the other man's antler; he still didn't know his own strength.

He quickly relieved the unconscious guard of his disruptor pistol and a universal translator pendant, while casting an envious eye at the man's attire. He wished there was time to appropriate the man's tunic, kilt, and boots, but Doctor Morval—and who knew who else—were already on their way. As Spock might put it, alacrity was the order of the day, and not just for Chekov's own sake. He was only too aware that more than just his own identity and freedom were at stake. His body had been stolen for a reason, and given that Voyzr were responsible, it was safe to assume that the imposter was out to sabotage the rapidly approaching peace celebration. He needed to alert the *Enterprise* before it was too late.

And, if he could, find and rescue Grigori as well.

Rushing to the door, he found it locked. With no time to figure out a stealthier way to bypass any security codes or passwords, he set the disrupter on maximum and blasted the locking mechanism instead. Firing the weapon set off a blaring security alarm, just as it would aboard the *Enterprise*-A, making it even more imperative that he escape the cell as swiftly as possible. Exerting his new body's strength to the full, he managed to tug the door slightly open, only to smack the edges of his antlers into the sides of the narrow opening the first time he tried to dash through it. *Yebena mat'!* he cursed under his breath as he turned his head sideways to pass through unobstructed.

This was going to take some getting used to.

He found himself in a corridor in an unfamiliar portion of the villa, regretting that he hadn't prevailed upon the counterfeit "Grigori" to give him a guided tour of the residence before everything went to Hades. And yet, there *was* something about the hallway that did feel strangely familiar, like a tickle at the back of his brain or a forgotten word at the tip of his tongue. Mere déjà vu, or a flicker of someone else's memory lodged in Chekov's new brain?

It was an unnerving notion, but not one he had time to dwell on. Disruptor in hand, he looked up and down the corridor, weighing his options, even as the strident alarm continued unabated. No hostiles had converged on his former cell yet, but he knew they were only moments away. Should he try to find his way to the villa's personal transporter room and attempt to beam back to the *Enterprise*, or should he try to single-handedly rescue Grigori first, without even knowing where his friend was being held? Duty warred with concern for Grigori. It was vital that Captain Kirk and the others be alerted to the imposter in their midst, but did that mean leaving Grigori in the hands of the enemy until Chekov could return with a full security team later?

He hoped it wouldn't come to that.

First things first: putting distance between him and his cell before company arrived. He hurried down the hall, following that itchy tickle in his brain for lack of any other compass, while keeping a close eye out for oncoming hostiles. Reaching an intersection, he instinctively turned right, expertly clearing the corner, only to have Doctor Morval emerge from a stairway right in front of him. She froze at the sight of him. "Chekov!"

"Keep your voice down, Doctor." He held a finger to his lips, snout and all, and pointed the disruptor at her. "And no sudden moves, if you please."

He discreetly switched the pistol to stun before herding her back into the stairwell, relatively out of sight. He had questions that needed answers.

"Where is Grigori? The real one, I mean."

"You'll never get to him. Not on your own. Trath's people are already swarming the villa looking for you." Her tone was contrite, not defiant. She wasn't gloating. "I'm so sorry, Chekov. You have to believe me, none of this was my idea."

She sounded sincere, not that it mattered at the moment. "You forget, I have my own hostage now."

"Don't count on it." She laughed bitterly. "I'm more expendable than you are. Trath will sacrifice me in a minute to get you back under wraps. I've already done what he needed me to do."

"What *did* you do to me?" he had to ask. "How did you do it?"

"A life-entity transfer, employing ancient Camusian technology, which you doubtless recall."

"Of course." It had been decades since Janice Lester had switched bodies with Captain Kirk in a deranged attempt to take command of the *Enterprise*, but he could hardly forget Lester-as-Kirk inspiring a mutiny when she ordered the summary executions of all who challenged her authority, including Spock, McCoy, Scotty, and even Kirk in Lester's own body. That unsettling affair had certainly crossed Chekov's mind after finding himself stuck in a similar body-swap.

"I should have known."

Despite his immediate jeopardy, he seized on the fact that the transference had proved temporary in Captain Kirk's case, which meant that he still had a chance to get his own body back, provided he could manage to keep his present form intact and at liberty until the transfer reversed itself.

"Keep looking!" a harsh voice trumpeted nearby, the clamor of pounding boots and agitated chatter impressing on Chekov that his newly Voyzr fat was still in the fire. "He has to be here somewhere!"

"Go!" Morval urged him. "I'll divert them, buy you whatever time I can."

Could he trust her, or was she just playing him? Unable to perform a mind-meld like a certain Vulcan first officer, he had no recourse but to trust his gut yet again—and hope he wasn't making a dreadful mistake.

"All right." He lowered the disruptor and let her slip back into the corridor. "Don't make me regret this."

He hung back in the stairwell, taking cover, as he heard her running up to the approaching bootsteps.

"That way!" she called out. "He headed that way! He must be after Ratikin!"

So much for saving Grigori, he thought, Morval having made that choice for him. *I'll be back for you, my friend. You have my word on it.*

For now, however, he had to find the transporter room while he still could. Exiting the stairwell, he hurried in the opposite direction of the retreating Voyzr but almost immediately found himself confronted with another intersection, uncertain which way to go.

Left, he knew somehow. *Then right, then straight ahead, then right again.*

His new brain and body seemed to know the way, even if he didn't, so he didn't argue with them. Lights switched on throughout the villa as shouts and commotion awoke the formerly sleeping residence. Decades of Starfleet experience and training, now coupled to a limber young body, kept Chekov on his toes as he slipped like an antlered forest spirit through the villa, deftly ducking and evading roving teams of Voyzr until, sure enough, he arrived at the entrance to the transporter room—where an armed doe was already standing guard.

Sneaking past her into the transporter room was impossible, so Chekov opted for a frontal assault before the lone sentry could be joined by reinforcements. She spotted Chekov only a moment after he saw her, but that instant made all the difference. She only had time to shout, "Here! He's over here!" before a turquoise disruptor beam dropped her to the floor. Chekov bounded over her stunned form to charge into the transporter room, pistol first, just in case more Voyzr were waiting inside.

To his relief, the compact chamber was unoccupied. He had no idea how many agents Trath had on-site, but possibly it was just a small band of conspirators or maybe only a single discrete terrorist cell. He quickly sealed the only entrance, then welded it shut with a high-temperature beam from the stolen disruptor, much as Kirk had done in that Indee generator room nearly twenty years ago.

Talk about history repeating itself.

Chekov shook his head. He was getting heartily weary of déjà vu, even if this time the flashbacks were surfacing from his own memory and not somebody else's. That was something, he supposed.

The transporter controls had been customized to Voyzr standards. Fortunately, he had some experience with such panels, and now he even had the right number of fingers to operate it efficiently.

"Silver linings," he muttered.

He activated the built-in communications panel and keyed in the *Enterprise*'s emergency frequency, accompanied by his own priority security code.

"Chekov to *Enterprise*, can you read me? Repeat, this is Commander Pavel Chekov, hailing *Enterprise!*"

He received no answer. A display screen reported that the transmission had failed: **Hail incomplete. No response.**

Chekov froze momentarily. Had the *Enterprise* already departed Tykona, leaving him behind? If so, they were well beyond the range of the transporter or its communicator by now.

"Chekov to *Enterprise*?" he tried again, hoping against hope that the earlier failure was just a glitch. "Uhura?"

"Open up!" Trath bellowed from the other side of the door. Fists and bodies pounded against the barrier. "Surrender and you won't be harmed!"

And end up strapped to a biobed again, being fed a dispiriting diet of twigs and leaves? Not if he could help it.

"Stand away from the door if you value your life." Trath paused only a heartbeat before ordering his people, "Open fire!"

Disruptor bursts slammed into the door, triggering yet more flashbacks to that besieged generator room decades ago, but no reinforced blast shielding stood between Chekov and his pursuers this time, only an ordinary polyalloy door that was already buckling and melting under the onslaught. It wasn't going to hold back Trath and his agents for long.

"All right," Chekov said. "Time for Plan B."

He still had access to a transporter, if only for a few more moments. Abandoning his futile efforts to contact the *Enterprise*, he called up the transporter's history on the console and found preset coordinates for the nearest large urban center, a city called Jhopash.

Any port in an ion storm. Guilt stabbed at him at the prospect of leaving Grigori behind. *Forgive me, old friend, but duty requires I warn the* Enterprise *of the imposter as quickly as possible.*

He selected the displayed coordinates with the disruptors whining shrilly only a few meters away. The sealed edges of the door glowed white-hot, then sublimed into vapor. Setting the time for only five seconds, Chekov rushed onto the transporter pad, just as the door came crashing down onto the floor of the chamber. Chekov fired at the breached doorway to cover his escape.

"The console!" Trath shouted. "Blast the controls before—"

Chekov dissolved into energy.

Nine

"Welcome to Jhopash, Downtown Station. Please exit the platform promptly—and enjoy our peace and prosperity."

A recorded message greeted Chekov as he abruptly found himself on a crowded public transporter platform, minus his stolen disruptor pistol, which had apparently been confiscated by a sophisticated security filter. The platform was located within a covered pavilion at the center of a city square surrounded by broad pedestrian avenues, moving sidewalks, and towering structures of gleaming steel and crystal. Jhopash was in the same time zone as the villa, or so Chekov understood, but despite the predawn hour, the square was brightly lit and bustling with activity. Throngs of people were out and about, enjoying the warm spring weather. He joined the stream of new arrivals vacating the platform, then took a moment to survey his new surroundings.

Downtown Jhopash lived up to its reputation for lavish high living. A cosmopolitan populace, boasting a diverse assortment of sentients, humanoid and otherwise, filled the square and streets, as well as assorted elevated walkways, balconies, and terraces overlooking the scene. Founded by one of the first waves of refugees generations ago, Jhopash continued to draw displaced peoples, exiles, fugitives, and tourists from across the quadrant and beyond. This far from the Federation, familiar species like the Vulcans or Andorians were not much in evidence, and, much to Chekov's relief, only a smattering of Voyzr seemed visible at first glance.

At least for the moment, he thought.

The grandiose architecture was equally varied. Looming towers shared the skyline with massive hourglasses, helical spirals, and inverted pyramids made possible only by extravagant use of applied antigravity. Flying vehicles soared overhead along clearly defined aerial traffic patterns, while the ground level was given over to pedestrians flowing in and out of upscale restaurants, clubs, art galleries, and shops. A virtual fashion show, advertising the latest trends and styles from across the galaxy, was drawing an affluent-looking crowd, similarly decked out.

Clearly, this was a ritzy part of town.

Scandalized gasps and shocked expressions greeted Chekov from all sides as the crowd drew back from him, gaping or else averting their eyes, antennae, or other sensory organs. Heads of myriad shapes and sizes shook in dismay, abruptly reminding Chekov that he was wearing nothing but a flimsy, backless hospital gown providing little coverage to the rear. His embarrassment was only slightly mitigated by the fact it wasn't actually his own body being exposed.

"Er, my apologies, everyone." He positioned his now-empty hands over his hindquarters. "I was in such a hurry I forgot to get dressed."

Could Voyzr blush? He had no idea.

"You there!" A pair of uniformed police officers, resplendent in gleaming white pseudo-leather, shoved their way toward him, looking distinctly unhappy about the spectacle he was making. "What do you think you're up to, antlers?"

The speaker was a craggy-faced cyclops with one deep-set red eye in the center of his face, just above scowling lips and a jutting chin. A thick blue eyebrow descended sharply at its center, forming an indignant V above his solitary eye. A thatch of spiky cobalt hair sprouted from his scalp. A shock baton was affixed to his belt. His partner was some variety of flightless avian, complete with a multi-colored feathered crest and a polished black beak. Hawklike eyes looked Chekov over. Seeming younger than his partner, the avian held back, letting the senior cop take the lead. Scaly orange talons rested on the grip of his own baton.

Chekov couldn't immediately identify either species, but that was the least of his concerns. Apparently, contacting the local authorities was going to be easier than anticipated, thanks to his semi-indecent exposure.

"Officers!" he greeted them. "Am I glad to see you. Just who I'm looking for!"

"Oh yeah? I wouldn't be so sure of that." The cyclops sneered at Chekov, radiating belligerence. Meaty fingers plucked a plastic capsule from his belt and cracked it open to release a lightweight, waterproof rain slicker that he thrust at Chekov. "Cover up . . . now!"

"Yes, yes, of course." He hastily pulled on the slicker, which was mercifully opaque. He was anxious to explain his dire predicament to the officers. "Very much appreciated, but—"

"Look here." The cyclops shook a finger at Chekov. "We don't tolerate any inappropriate behavior in this district. This is a respectable neighborhood for decent people, who don't need low-rent miscreants like you putting themselves on display. Nobody wants to see that."

"That's for sure." The avian clucked at Chekov. "You got that, pal?"

"Absolutely, Officers. I quite understand." He struggled to get a word in. Given the cops' attitude, he was glad he was no longer brandishing a disruptor pistol. "I realize I'm not exactly making a good first impression here—"

"You think?" the cyclops said.

"But you must listen to me. I just escaped from armed criminals who were holding me against my will, and my friend is still their prisoner. What's more, I need to get an urgent message to Starfleet right away, on a matter of vital importance!"

"Starfleet, eh?" The cyclops eyed him dubiously. "You're a long way from the Federation, mister."

"Don't I know it! But I am quite serious, Officers. It's imperative that I contact the *U.S.S. Enterprise* immediately."

The avian chirped in amusement. "The *Enterprise* no less." He looked down his beak at Chekov. "What business could you have with Starfleet?"

Chekov hesitated, realizing just how far-fetched a true account of the body-swap would sound, yet he also needed to get these ill-disposed cops to appreciate the seriousness of the situation. Who knew what the false "Chekov" was already up to aboard the *Enterprise*?

"I swear to you, gentlemen, I am most certainly a Starfleet officer, recently ambushed and taken captive by hostile parties, and I urgently need to alert my captain and crewmates of an imminent threat."

"Come again?" the cyclops scoffed. "A Voyzr in Starfleet?"

"It's . . . complicated."

"I'll bet." The cops exchanged skeptical looks, perhaps wondering if he was an escapee from a psychiatric ward. "What are you on, antlers? Breez? Stim? Pheros?"

"I am quite unimpaired, Officers." Aside from being trapped in a someone else's body, that was. "But you have to believe me. This may well be a matter of life and death."

Frustration gnawed at him, straining his patience. This seemingly fruitless encounter was far too protracted—and public—for his liking. He glanced back at the transporter platform, where a fresh batch of civilians was preparing to depart the square, probably according to some established transit schedule. It wouldn't take Trath and his operatives long to deduce where Chekov had beamed to. He needed to be somewhere else before they came looking for him.

"We don't *have* to do anything, antlers. Let alone fall for whatever deer dung you're dishing out."

"Do you believe this guy?" the avian added. "Who does he think he's kidding?"

A shimmering glow, accompanied by the telltale whine of an active transporter, whisked the departing passengers away, replacing them with a fresh crop of new arrivals, including several stony-faced Voyzr.

Uh-oh, Chekov thought. *They've caught up with me.*

Spotting their quarry just beyond the pavilion, his pursuers started toward him, only to back off when they clocked the police officers as well. They dispersed into the crowd, joining a growing circle of curious bystanders observing Chekov's run-in with the cops. Feeling even more exposed than before, he knew better than to expect his Voyzr foes to retreat entirely. They would be sticking close to him, waiting for an opportunity to recapture him. He could practically feel their predatory eyes upon him.

"We're getting nowhere," he protested to the cops. "I insist you escort me to your superiors at once. I need to speak to someone in authority."

"Oh, you insist, do you? Now you're telling us how to do our job?" The cyclops unhooked his shock baton, gripping it ominously. "Get lost, antlers. Take your fuzzy red butt back to your own turf and don't let me see you on my beat again."

"You heard him," the avian said. "Beat it."

Not a good idea, Chekov knew. Not with his former captors lurking nearby.

And me without a disruptor.

"Respectfully, I would prefer not to."

"You deaf, antlers?" The cyclops's face flushed angrily. "Don't make me run you in."

"Yes, please, run me in. That's what I'm saying!"

Looking about, he spied the gullible Voyzr guard he'd kayoed back at the villa, who glared murderously at Chekov from the ring of spectators taking in the show. A bandaged antler testified to the damage he'd sustained from Chekov earlier; the Voyzr massaged his sore jaw while subtly pointing his remaining tines at Chekov, as though he couldn't wait to lock horns with him. Literally.

"I don't know what game you're playing," the cyclops growled, "but I've had enough. Get a move on." He didn't switch on his baton but prodded Chekov with its business end. "The slicker is on me. You're welcome."

Chekov glanced down at the concealing rain gear. A desperate ploy occurred to him.

"I'm sorry, Officers, but you forced my hand."

He stripped off the slicker—and the hospital gown as well.

"Hello? I need to talk to somebody!"

In Chekov's experience, interrogation rooms were the same all over, regardless of which Class-M world you found yourself on. He paced back and forth across the stark, boxlike compartment, where a bluntly utilitarian metal table and chairs sat unused, waiting for someone to join him. The walls were similarly gray and unadorned, aside from a glossy black viewscreen that doubtless served as a one-way monitor. He assumed he was under surveillance, unless somebody had forgotten he was there. With no chronometer in sight, he had no way of knowing exactly how long he'd been left to stew, but he figured the sun must have risen by now. (How long was Tykona's daily rotation again?) Fatigue lurked at the fringes of his endurance, kept at bay by adrenaline and sheer frustration. Every minute that passed was another minute the imposter was free to commit who knew what heinous acts in Chekov's body.

I need to let the captain know that's not me on the bridge!

At least his jailers had provided him with some rudimentary attire, if only for propriety's sake. A plain white tunic, black trousers, and slippers provided a degree of dignity the hospital gown had lacked. The clothes were basic enough but struck him as resembling simple civilian garb, not obviously prison togs. He chose to take that as a good sign.

"Hello! Is anybody listening? I know you can hear me!"

"No need to shout, citizen."

The sealed doorway slid open, admitting an older, reptilian woman in crisp professional attire, accompanied by a uniformed officer who looked as though he had some Klingon in his family tree. He silently posted himself by the door, which automatically closed behind him, and crossed his beefy arms across his chest. A surly expression warned Chekov not to provoke him.

Not if I can help it, he thought.

"Please sit down." The woman gestured at the table, a data slate tucked beneath her other arm. Coppery, iridescent scales gleamed beneath the harsh white light of the cell. Slitted yellow eyes scrutinized Chekov, her serpentine features betraying nothing. A forked tongue flicked briefly between her thin lips. "Let's get down to business, shall we?"

"Yes, ma'am."

Chekov took a seat at the table. Perhaps this was somebody he could finally get to listen to him? He resolved to keep his cool and avoid sounding like a lunatic. As a security head himself, he had occasionally been on the opposite side of such interviews. He liked to think he knew how to appear calm, cooperative, and, with any luck, credible.

"I am Station Chief Cesss." She sat down across from him. "And I understand you claim to be . . . ?"

"Commander Pavel Chekov, Starfleet, of the *U.S.S. Enterprise*."

He braced himself for the inevitable skepticism. Unfortunately, he saw no way to explain the emergency to the local authorities, and convince them to take immediate action, without addressing the matter of his stolen identity.

Here's hoping this Cesss person has an open mind.

"So you keep saying, but you know who I see?"

She tapped her slate and an image appeared on the viewscreen to Chekov's right: a mug shot of a smirking young Voyzr, alongside blocks of text in Tykonese. His personal translator had been confiscated, but the station itself was clearly equipped with a passive translation system. He recognized a police file when he saw one.

"Ryjo mur Zimble," she read off the slate. "Age: nineteen solar years. Born on Voyzr, emigrated to Tykona as an infant, after a failed coup on your homeworld, which your clan was inconveniently on the losing side of. Occupation: assorted menial jobs, mostly in the service and tourism industries. Prior arrests for various minor offenses, including loitering, shoplifting, vandalism, disturbing the peace, public intoxication, and now, it appears, indecent exposure." She fixed cool, appraising eyes on him. "Starfleet seems to have lowered its standards considerably."

He gazed at the screen, finally putting a name to his new face. *Ryjo.*

He struggled to reconcile the portrait painted by Ryjo's police record with the Voyzr's hijacking of Chekov's body. How did he go from petty crimes and misdemeanors to taking part in an ambitious conspiracy to infiltrate the *Enterprise*, via classified alien technology no less? Had he perhaps been radicalized by embittered Voyzr exiles? Chekov knew from his prep work for the peace celebration that not every Voyzr had put the civil war behind them, both at home and abroad. Old grudges lingered, even after twenty years.

"I know what it looks like," he said. "Nonetheless, I *am* Pavel Chekov, as I have tried to explain. If you can just contact the *Enterprise* to verify—"

"Let me stop you right there. You may be interested to know that, according to our very meticulous records, the *U.S.S. Enterprise* departed Tykona last evening with all hands aboard, including one Commander Pavel Chekov."

He grimaced. "I was afraid of that. All the more reason to alert Captain Kirk at once."

Chekov was sure he could expose the imposter if given half a chance. If nothing else, Spock could always determine the truth via a mind-meld, as he had when Kirk's body was stolen by Janice Lester.

"This is a municipal police station," Cesss said. "We are not in the business of sending subspace messages across the cosmos to foreign vessels far beyond our jurisdiction, and certainly not on the basis of a tall tale from a known delinquent."

"But what if I am telling the truth?"

"About a—let me see if I have this right—'life-entity transference' that allegedly switched your body with Ryjo's?"

"Precisely! Well, more like it swapped our minds, but close enough." He tried to head off any objections in advance. "This is not unheard-of, I assure you, and entirely possible. I speak from personal experience."

"Oh, really? Do tell."

He faltered. "Er, that's classified."

"Of course it is. Listen here, Ryjo—"

"Chekov."

"*Ryjo*," she persisted. "The way I see it, you're pulling my leg, for some juvenile reason I can't begin to fathom, or you're mentally ill and belong in a psych ward. You tell me: Which way is this going to go?"

He swallowed hard, rapidly reassessing his options. It was becoming all too clear that there was little hope of convincing Cesss, let alone persuading her to bump his plea up the ladder to some higher authority who was actually in a position to communicate with the *Enterprise* or Starfleet, assuming they were even motivated to do so. Tykona was not part of the Federation after all; the security of the *Enterprise* and its mission was hardly their concern. There wasn't even a Federation embassy on the planet to appeal to.

I'm on my own, he realized, that hard truth sinking in. *I need to find my own way off Tykona and back to the ship, by any means possible.*

And he couldn't do that if he was locked up in a padded cell.

Time to change tactics.

"You got me." He smiled sheepishly, throwing up his disturbingly six-fingered hands. "It was . . . a prank."

"A prank?" She leaned back from the table, looking both vindicated and thoroughly unamused. "You wasted my time, and that of my officers, for a laugh?"

"Ha-ha?" he said weakly. "I'm sorry. I didn't mean for it to get so out of hand. Things just sort of . . . escalated."

"That's all you have to say for yourself?" She consulted her slate again. "A sobriety scan found lingering traces of a mild sedative in your system, but not enough to account for such egregious behavior, so don't even try to claim you were under the influence."

"I wouldn't dream of it."

At this point, his best shot was to plead for mercy in hopes of avoiding further confinement.

"It was stupid, I see that now. For what it's worth, I've been going through some rough times lately and what happened last night . . . well, I wasn't myself."

To put it mildly.

"I would hope not." She continued to peruse his file. "I see that your father, Kletz mur Zimble, passed away some weeks ago."

A foreign memory flashed behind his eyes:

A geriatric Voyzr on his deathbed, gazing forlornly at his wayward son.

Chekov's throat tightened, caught off guard by a sudden, intense stab of guilt. Ryjo's *guilt*? His eyes watered, hot tears stinging them.

"Yes." Choking up for real, he seized on the tragic biographical detail, as well as the powerful emotional echoes it provoked, to help his case. He dabbed at his wet eyes with the back of a fuzzy red hand. "I'm still not over it."

Exploiting Ryjo's grief to win Cesss's sympathy troubled Chekov's conscience, making him feel badly in need of a sonic shower. Then again, Ryjo *had* stolen Chekov's body and was even now up to no good on the *Enterprise*. He needed to stay focused on the bigger picture and his duty to the ship. This was no time for an excess of scruples.

"My condolences." Cesss's tone softened somewhat. "In fact, it looks as though you made a genuine effort to clean up your act after your father's unfortunate demise. You've stayed out of trouble, and off our sensors, ever since his passing . . . until last night."

"What can I say? I have been trying to be a better person, to honor my father's memory, but I . . . slipped."

"Explain it to me."

He racked his sleep-deprived brain to come up with something plausible but not too incriminating, that wouldn't torpedo whatever possible leniency Cesss might be contemplating.

"This is your chance," she prodded him. "Make me understand."

He looked abjectly at the floor.

"It was a dare, that's all. An idiotic dare: to beam downtown wearing nothing but that skimpy hospital gown." He shrugged. "To be honest, I didn't expect it to be quite so busy at that hour."

"And the business with Commander Chekov and the 'life-entity transference'?"

Chekov thought fast. "I saw a news report about the *Enterprise* visiting Tykona, to provide medical relief, and glanced at a profile of the ship and its senior officers." He studied Cesss's face to see if she was buying this. "As you saw from my work history, I often deal with tourists from other worlds. It pays to keep up with interplanetary news. Makes for bigger tips sometimes."

"Why Chekov?"

"The name just stuck in my head, I guess. Has a nicely exotic ring to it, don't you think?"

"If you say so," she said, unimpressed. He tried not to take it personally. "And the mind-swapping nonsense?"

"Popped into my brain when those officers confronted me in the square. It seemed funny at the time."

"And now?"

"Not so much." He attempted to act as contrite as possible, without laying it on too thick. "I'm very sorry, ma'am."

"You should be. You think your father would be proud of your antics last night?"

"No, ma'am. Not at all."

Whether Ryjo's late father would approve of his son impersonating a Starfleet officer was another question. Chekov didn't know enough about the father's politics, or Ryjo's family issues, to hazard a guess.

"So what possessed you, after doing your best to turn over a new leaf?"

It seemed peer pressure alone was not enough of an explanation for Cesss. He groped for a deeper motive that might satisfy her. What, hypothetically, might drive a grieving youth to do something so ridiculously irresponsible?

"If you must know, I was trying to impress a girl."

She nodded. "This girl?"

A tap on her slate, and a new police file appeared on the viewscreen. Ryjo's mug shot was replaced by an image of an attractive young Voyzr woman with striking, forest-green doe eyes, velvety russet fur, and an impudent expression. Standing woolen pigtails, sprinkled with glitter, mimicked antlers. She smirked at Chekov from the screen, shamelessly unrepentant despite whatever offense had gotten her in hot water with the law.

Chekov started, his new heart beating faster. He *knew* this face, even though he'd never seen it before. The mug shot triggered a powerful surge of emotions: love, loss, regret. Whoever this woman was, she was obviously very important to Ryjo, so much so that his feelings for her were still imprinted on his brain and body, even if his actual mind and personality were elsewhere. Her name suddenly landed on his tongue.

"Dise."

"Listed here as a known associate," Cesss confirmed. "She the doe you were trying to impress?"

Why not? Chekov thought, going with it. He remained oddly captivated by the portrait on the screen. "Yes. Things have been rocky between us since, you know, my father died. She complained that I had changed, that I wasn't fun or daring anymore. I was afraid of losing her, so . . . I behaved foolishly."

Cesss rolled her serpentine eyes, hissing beneath her breath. "Mammals."

"Can I say again how truly sorry I am?"

He put himself in her place, using his own experience in security to calculate what tack to take next. Perhaps if he offered her a chance to avoid any additional hassles and paperwork?

"You're a busy person, obviously, who surely has better, more important things to deal with than my temporary bout of brainlessness. I don't want to take up any more of your valuable time."

"That's the first sensible thing you've said." She sighed and put down the slate. "Very well. I'll let you off with a warning this time. Do yourself a favor, though, and stay out of this district for the time being. I don't want to see you back at my station anytime soon."

"Understood, ma'am. Loud and clear. Thank you for being so very understanding. I sincerely appreciate it." He refrained from grinning in order to maintain a properly chastened and repentant appearance. "Er, just one more thing?"

She regarded him warily. "Yes?"

"Can I keep these clothes?"

"Please do."

Ten

"Hit the road."

"That is my intention, Officer."

Chekov exited the police station, having been briskly escorted off the premises, into a warm, sunny afternoon. Despite his newly acquired clothing, courtesy of the Jhopash city police, and the return of his confiscated universal translator, he felt naked without a phaser, communicator, or even a tricorder. A full Starfleet landing party, complete with a complement of security officers, would have also been nice.

If wishes were horses...

He glanced around warily, concerned that Trath's agents might be lying in wait, having trailed him to the station, but didn't spy any ominously lurking antlers. Perhaps luck was with him for once and they had lost track of him and didn't know when or where he might be released? With no idea where to go next, he paused on the pavement to look around, finding himself in what appeared to be more of an administrative sector than the posh commercial district he had first beamed into. Scrolling signage, in a generous variety of major languages, including Federation Standard, identified a town hall, courthouse, and office buildings housing an assortment of governmental departments and services, along with miscellaneous small shops and eateries to accommodate both municipal employees and citizens with business before them. The buildings, which were far less extravagant in design than those overlooking that downtown transporter pad, surrounded a small urban park radiating out from an obelisk-shaped monument to something or another. Park benches seated random Tykons enjoying an outdoor snack beneath a clear tangerine sky. Other locals milled about on the sidewalks and in the plaza, seeming in no particular hurry.

Lunch hour, perhaps?

A shadow fell over Chekov. Peering upward, he saw a levitating public transport picking up passengers from a balcony-like "dock" or "bus stop" several stories overhead, accessible from an upper floor of a looming skyscraper, as well as by a convenient outdoor lift. Another double-decker transport cruised by on the opposite side of the park, its top deck open to the pleasant spring weather. Perhaps he should try to catch the next one—but to where?

The nearest available spaceport? In hopes of catching up with the *Enterprise* somehow? Or at least coming within subspace communications range, should the opportunity and resources arise? The ship already had a sizable head start on him, which was growing larger by the moment. The *Enterprise* was traveling at warp speed, while he was stranded on in a strange city on a foreign planet in an alien body. It was a wonder he hadn't lost his mind as well.

The *Kobayashi Maru* scenario seemed a piece of cake by comparison.

He took a deep breath. The odds were against him, but he refused to lose heart. He was still a Starfleet officer, even cut off from his ship, his crew, and his own identity. He had to forge ahead, undaunted, and find a way to prevail, as Captain Kirk always did.

I can do this, he resolved. *Now that I'm no longer being held against my will.*

Then he saw the antlers among the crowd.

A Voyzr glowered at Chekov from across the plaza, mingling among the myriad pedestrians populating the park and sidewalks. The buck wasn't alone either; suddenly alert to the danger, Chekov clocked at least five Voyzr converging on him from different directions, silently making their way through unsuspecting cops and civilians. Unfriendly expressions betrayed their hostile intentions, at least if you were their target; Chekov was pretty sure he recognized some of them from both the villa and the city square where he'd eluded them before. Their persistence was commendable, if also personally inconvenient.

So much for him catching a lucky break. Had they been staking out the police station since his arrest or had someone tipped them off that he was being released? Did they perhaps have a mole on the police force, or had they been automatically pinged when Ryjo's file was accessed at the station? Had Cesss deliberately released him so that these Voyzr could recapture him? Just how highly placed were the conspirators anyway?

Something to worry about later. Right now, job one was not getting taken prisoner again.

On the bright side, he was in public, in front of a police station, surrounded by witnesses, and in broad daylight no less. Indeed, he was far from the only person being discharged from police custody at present; random locals emerged from the station to be met by friends, relations, or accomplices, receiving a wide range of receptions, from tearful embraces to angry recriminations. A disappointed elder picked up a sullen younger relation, while, only a few meters away, an abashed buck apologized profusely to an unhappy doe. Uniformed officers maintained a visible presence, keeping any tense reunions from getting out of hand. Chekov suspected that the entire plaza was under remote surveillance as well, given the concentration of government offices and facilities. His former captors were going to have to be discreet in pursuing him if they wanted to avoid undue attention. They couldn't just roughly snatch him off the street in full view of everyone.

Too bad he had to keep a low profile, too. Appealing to the police for assistance would just put him back where he was before, trying to unsuccessfully explain why the other Voyzr were after him—with predictable results. Ending up in custody again, and possibly a psychiatric ward, was not going to alert the *Enterprise* to the imposter in their midst.

So, evasive maneuvers then.

He started down the sidewalk, away from the nearest Voyzr, only to see another stony-faced buck heading toward him from the opposite direction. Chekov veered off into the park, picking up his pace while scanning for an escape route that didn't lead straight back into the enemy's clutches. Sticking to busy, public spaces hindered his pursuers, but he couldn't rely on that indefinitely. They were bound to corner him soon enough. And what if he took a wrong turn and ended up in a less-populated setting? He was a stranger to Jhopash. His hunters surely knew the city's nooks and crannies better than he did. He was out of his element as well as his body.

And Trath's agents were already closing in on him.

Seeking refuge, he spotted locals coming and going from what looked to be a neighborhood watering hole, located on the ground floor of a looming cylindrical tower on the other side of the plaza. Zigzagging through the crowd to keep one step ahead of his foes, he darted into the tavern, if only to buy time to come up with a viable plan for shaking the Voyzr tailing him.

They can't nab me inside a busy tavern, can they?

Befitting the cylindrical shape of the tower, the interior of the tavern was laid out like a wheel, with a circular bar counter at the center and booths lining the outer circumference of the room. A bartender occupied the rotating hub of the wheel; at first glance, Chekov couldn't immediately tell if the waxy-skinned humanoid was literally a cyborg or was simply piloting an elaborate exoskeleton sporting several gleaming chrome tentacles with various prosthetic attachments at their ends. Federation policies regarding extreme humanoid augmentation did not apply to Tykona, so either possibility was possible. Mounted viewscreens hyped the planet's myriad tourist attractions—beaches, powdered lava slopes, vibrant night lives—on a continuous loop. Glancing around, Chekov was glad to see plenty of locals patronizing the tavern this afternoon, just as he'd hoped.

Thank goodness!

He rushed to claim an empty stool at the bar, between two other customers, right before two Voyzr followed him into the tavern. Seeing him flanked by two unwitting patrons, they took a booth across from Chekov, who recognized one of them as the guard he had tricked back at the villa. The one with the bandaged antler. A baleful expression made it clear he was not inclined to let bygones be bygones.

The bartender rotated toward him. "What are you having?" Clear goggles protected two entirely organic-looking gray eyes.

Chekov doubted he could keep his seat without ordering anything. *Just as well*, he thought. Frankly, he could use a stiff drink after all he'd been through, strictly to settle his nerves, of course. Doctor McCoy would no doubt agree.

"I don't suppose you carry . . . vodka?"

"Let me see." The bartender's goggles lit up as a heads-up menu scrolled across the lenses before his eyes. "Some manner of tuber-based brew, I gather." He shrugged. "Don't get much call for that, but I'm sure I can synthesize it for you."

"If you don't mind." Chekov kept one eye on the two Voyzr keeping tabs on him. They appeared to be ordering their own drinks from a self-serve menu panel at their booth. Drinks appeared from a tabletop food slot. "Thank you."

The bartender cleared his throat. "Payment in advance."

"Oh, yes. Of course." Chekov tried to remember the particulars of Tykona's economic system. As was customary for shore leaves outside Federation space, he had been provided with a modest quantity of the local currency, but he had lost that along with his body. How exactly did one pay for drinks in Jhopash again?

"Your palm," the bartender prompted, extending a tentacle with a glowing scanner at its tip. He looked at Chekov expectantly.

"Right." Chekov recalled that most of Tykona utilized a credit system employing a subdermal chip implanted in a hand or equivalent appendage. He extended his right palm, hoping Ryjo had some ready credits to his name. "Sorry. I have a lot on my mind."

To put it mildly.

"Your *other* palm."

"Yes. Sorry again." He switched hands. "Guess I really need that drink." Forcing a smile, he watched nervously as the bartender scanned his palm. "Er, are there sufficient funds on hand? No pun intended."

"You can manage it." Numerical figures flashed briefly across the bartender's goggles. "But I'd think twice about buying too many refills."

"Glad to hear it. Please proceed with the transaction, thanks. I appreciate your patience."

The bartender fished a glass from a shelf beneath the counter. "Just doing my job, buddy."

Chekov took a moment to consider how Ryjo's finances (or lack of same) might impact his own ability to reach the *Enterprise*, one way or another. He supposed he should consider himself fortunate that Ryjo hadn't completely emptied his account before hijacking Chekov's body; just the same, how far was he going to get on Tykona with only Ryjo's meager credits? He didn't have time to raise enough funds to book a flight off the planet, let alone across the sector.

"Here you go."

A different steel tentacle, equipped with a tap at the end, filled Chekov's glass, which was small enough that he didn't have to worry about drinking too much while in dire straits. The clear liquid looked like vodka at least. Condensation on the glass even suggested that it had been properly chilled. A promising sign.

"*Na zdorovye,*" he toasted the bartender before tossing the shot down the hatch.

It came right back up again, his new body violently rejecting the drink, which tasted worse than the most rancid Tholian egg cider. Spitting it out, he managed to get *most* of the drink back into the glass.

"No refunds." A tentacle vacuumed up the spillage.

Seriously? Chekov thought. *I'm allergic to vodka now?*

Mocking laughter came from the broken-antlered Voyzr in the booth. Chekov shot him a dirty look before wiping the now-revolting taste from his lips. And the worst part was, he feared that the bartender had synthesized the drink correctly. It was his new body that was the problem.

"Friends of yours?" the bartender asked.

"Not exactly."

The bartender frowned. "I don't want any trouble."

"You and me both."

Another customer flagged the bartender, who rotated away from Chekov, leaving him to mull over his next move. That his pursuers were evidently constrained by the public setting implied that their mysterious "operation" was not officially sanctioned by the Tykon authorities, which was encouraging; nevertheless, he couldn't camp out at the bar forever, and the other Voyzr were almost certainly watching any front and back entrances, just waiting for a chance to get him alone. Feeling badly outnumbered, Chekov wished he had somebody, anybody, he could turn to on Tykona.

Dise?

The young doe's face, both familiar and not, flashed without warning across his mind's eyes, accompanied by a rush of warm feelings. He shook his head to dispel them. This Dise person was close to Ryjo, not him. She was no one he could trust, even if he'd had the slightest idea how to find her.

The patron on his left, a rangy blond simian of uncertain gender, polished off their drink. They got up and left, opening up the stool next to Chekov.

Uh-oh, he thought.

Broken-Antler wasted no time claiming the seat, leaving his companion to keep watch from the booth. He brought his own glass with him. Chekov tensed up, ready for fight or flight, depending.

"Not blind anymore?" the buck said in a low tone. "Quite the amazing recovery."

"False alarm, I guess." Chekov kept his voice down as well. The last thing he wanted was for the wary bartender to eject them both back out into the street. "No hard feelings?"

Broken-Antler snorted. "You wish." He leaned toward Chekov, as though confiding in him, and Chekov felt something sharp and pointy press against his ribs. Glancing down, he saw that the snapped-off fragment of antler had been repurposed as a shiv.

To get past any security filters, he assumed. *Clever.*

"Get up," the buck ordered. "Time to go."

"I don't think so," Chekov said, calling his bluff, albeit uncertainly. Would Broken-Antler risk stabbing him in public, in full view of whatever security monitors the tavern was equipped with? Moreover, was he truly willing to do mortal injury to Ryjo's body? Chekov wasn't entirely sure what killing him would do to the imposter aboard the *Enterprise*, before or after the transference reversed itself, but Trath and his people *had* taken care to keep Chekov alive and in one piece back at the villa. They hadn't just disposed of him once Ryjo took possession of his body.

"You want this body alive."

I hope.

"Only for now." Frustration colored the buck's voice. He quietly withdrew the sharpened tine. "Don't think you're getting away from us again. I'll sit here until closing if necessary. And then . . ."

He left the rest to Chekov's far too vivid imagination.

The bartender rotated back to them, his eyes narrowing behind the goggles. "Everything okay here?"

"Couldn't be better." Chekov gestured at Broken-Antler's glass. "Two more of what he's having." He met the buck's eyes, one of which was notably swollen and bloodshot. "On him."

The bartender looked to the bandaged Voyzr for confirmation.

"Fine," he muttered. "Why not?"

Chekov savored this small victory. If nothing else, the other man surely knew what Voyzr actually liked to drink. None of which, alas, got him any closer to escaping the snare tightening around him.

"I don't suppose playing sick is going to work again?"

"Don't count on it, Starfleet."

A tentacle-tap refilled their glasses with a thick, nutty-smelling liqueur, but before Chekov could sample the libation, an electronic chime announced the arrival of a new customer, who rushed up to the bar. Chartreuse freckles complemented scarlet skin and a fringe of hot-pink cilia framing her face. She seemed in high spirits and a little breathless, as though she was in a hurry. Professional attire suggested that possibly she had come straight from an office.

"Excuse me, I'm looking for the Zulongesh party?"

"Rooftop lounge." A tentacle indicated a lift entrance a few meters away, between two booths. "You're running late. They've already started."

"I know, I know!" She hurried toward the lift. "Thanks!"

Chekov saw his chance. "Hang on, did you say Zulongesh?" Grabbing his drink, he hopped off the stool and joined the newcomer before Broken-Antler knew what was happening. "I was wondering where everybody else was!"

She eyed him quizzically. "You know Oxny, too?"

"Do I know Oxny?" He attached himself to the freckle-faced stranger as though nothing could be more natural. Caught off guard, the two Voyzr scrambled to their feet, visibly unsure how to react. "Do I know Oxny!"

The lift door slid open, sensing their presence. Chekov graciously ushered his new companion into the compartment, then darted in after her before his dumbfounded pursuers could catch up with him.

"Rooftop lounge, express!"

The door slid shut in the other Voyzr's faces.

"Oops!" the woman said. "Should we have held the lift for them?"

"And keep Oxny waiting? Perish the thought!"

The lift swiftly brought them to the roof of the tower, where an open-air lounge spun slowly high above the city streets. Somewhat swankier than the ground-floor tavern, the lounge boasted attractive flesh-and-blood waitstaff and live music provided by a diverse trio of life-forms employing exotic alien instruments. A dapper Vulcanoid host greeted Chekov and Freckles as they emerged from the lift.

"Reservations?"

Chekov strode forward confidently. "The Zulongesh party. We are expected."

"There they are!" Freckles exuberantly waved at a large party seated around a table beyond the host's station. "That's our group over there."

The host stepped aside as the celebrants beckoned the latecomers over. Approaching the table, Chekov observed that one guest occupied a position of honor atop a dais at the center of the table. A sparkling metallic cape and matching fez also singled out the individual in question: a silver-haired woman whose extravagantly lobed ears betrayed Tiburonian roots.

Oxny Zulongesh, I presume.

"Happy retirement!" Freckles squealed. "Sorry we're late!"

"Not to worry," Oxny called out. "The party's just getting started. How good of you to come!"

"Wouldn't miss it for worlds." Chekov attempted to blend in, despite being the only Voyzr present, all the while scoping out the terrain tactically. A low rail circled the lounge, which was located atop a leisurely rotating platform, treating guests to a panoramic sky-high view from at least a dozen stories up. Edging toward the rail as casually as possible, he attempted to orient himself with regard to the plaza and sidewalks below. He raised his glass to her. "Happy retirement. Well deserved!"

"I couldn't agree more." Oxny squinted at him. "Excuse me, you are . . . ?"

He cringed inwardly. He had hoped he could just pass as a friend of a friend.

"You are joking of course." He clasped a hand to his heart, feigning dismay. "Surely you have not forgotten . . . Ryjo? Say it is not so."

Confusion creased Oxny's brow. He couldn't tell if she was embarrassed or suspicious. Maybe a little of both?

"Refresh my memory?"

Across the rooftop, Broken-Antler and his associate arrived via the lift and started toward Chekov. The host intercepted them.

"Reservations?"

Scowling, Broken-Antler pointed at Chekov. "We're with him!"

"Just a minute." Oxny frowned, now looking more concerned than confused. "I mean it, who are you exactly?" She turned toward Freckles. "Is he with you?"

"Just met him downstairs. He said he knew you."

So much for blending in, Chekov realized. "About that—"

The two Voyzr shoved their way past the Vulcanoid host, eliciting shouts and gasps all across the lounge. Had the frustrated bucks run out of patience, or were they just aiming to get the three of them shown the door so they and their confederates could snatch Chekov off the street at last?

He didn't want to stick around to find out.

"Sorry to crash and run," he apologized to Oxny. "Enjoy your golden years."

Abandoning the party and his drink, he bolted for the edge of the roof and climbed up onto the rail, balancing more precariously than would ordinarily be prudent. Peering down, he confirmed that he was indeed overlooking the plaza, several floors below. From his elevated vantage point, the people going about their business in the park and on the sidewalks looked as though they had been miniaturized by some sort of insidious matter-compression beam. Vertigo beckoned, but his Starfleet training kept it a bay. If he could endure a slingshot maneuver through time, he could stay cool teetering on the brink of a precipice.

"Stay back!" he warned. "Don't come any closer!"

Shrieks erupted from alarmed diners. The two Voyzr froze, confirming that they definitely didn't want Ryjo's body splattered all over the pavement below. *Good to know,* Chekov thought.

"Don't jump!" Oxny pleaded. "Whoever you are!"

Not my intention, he thought. He had something else in mind, depending on how punctual Jhopash's public-transit system was. *But if they want to think I'm about take a nose-dive to oblivion . . .*

"Take it easy, Starfleet." Broken-Antler inched slowly toward Chekov. "Let's not do anything crazy."

"Back!" Chekov stalled for time. "Not another step—or you'll answer to Trath!"

The bucks exchanged confused looks. Chekov peered up and down the plaza, searching anxiously for . . .

Yes! Right on schedule!

Another levitating double-decker, its upper dock open beneath the sunny orange sky, cruised toward the tower, passing just a few stories beneath the top of the tower. An old Russian saying came immediately to Chekov's lips:

"Geronimo!"

He threw himself off the rail. Class-M gravity seized him, more forcefully than he would have preferred, and he braced for a crash landing, hoping that Ryjo's fit, young frame was just as resilient as it seemed. The top deck of the transport seemed to rocket toward him as he plunged through empty air, but the craft also proceeded horizontally faster than he had hastily estimated. Instead of landing squarely in the middle of the upper deck, in the aisle dividing rows of seated passengers, it looked as though he was going to miss the transport altogether.

Which meant a straight drop to the sidewalk—at terminal velocity!

The rear of the double-decker moved on, leaving him behind, just as his downward trajectory brought him level with it. Twisting frantically in the air, he reached out for the railing at the back of the departing vehicle. Six desperate fingers grabbed onto the sturdy steel rail, halting his descent so abruptly that his right arm was nearly yanked from its socket. He grunted in pain but hung on for dear life. Dangling many stories above the plaza, he swung around and seized the rail with his other hand as well. Gravity stubbornly tugged on him even as he was dragged along in the transport's wake. Startled passengers turned around in their seats, boggled by his unorthodox arrival.

"A little assistance here," he asked, "if you don't mind?"

Eleven

Bowling was trickier than Ryjo expected.

The *Enterprise*'s bowling alley was located on G deck, just off the main rec deck. Six synthetic wooden lanes attracted off-duty crew members out to enjoy the traditional human pastime, which seemed to bear some resemblance to Cebboon rock-hurling contests. He had noted this particular recreational facility while memorizing the ship's layout back on Tykona and had briefly reviewed the particulars of the sport in case he was ever called upon to participate in a match. More recently, as in less than an hour ago, he had hastily delved deeper into the topic after Sulu casually reminded him of what was apparently their standing Wednesday night bowling competition. Despite the short notice, Ryjo had not anticipated much difficulty in getting through the game with his cover intact. How hard could rolling a heavy sphere toward an array of unmoving targets be?

That was *before* his ball kept swerving into the gutter as though caught by a tractor beam.

"Damn it," he vented, human-style, as his ball bounced twice down the lane before veering once more into the gutter, bypassing the pins entirely as it barreled out of sight. Perspiration soaked through his regulation black undershirt as he grew increasingly anxious (and embarrassed) by his dismal showing. Phantom antlers, which he sometimes still seemed to feel despite his rackless new human cranium, itched uncomfortably. How was he ever going to explain this away?

"Ouch." Sulu winced in sympathy. "If there's such a thing as beginner's luck, you've definitely got the opposite going on tonight. Expert's slump, maybe?"

The two men occupied the seating area at the approach to the lane, facing a distressingly full complement of upright pins, none of which were even wobbling. Their voices added to the general hubbub of the busy alley, where cheers and chatter competed with the clatter of falling pins in the other lanes. A display panel rubbed the brutally lopsided score in Ryjo's face; after a full ten frames, he had managed to topple only a few pins, mostly by accident, while Sulu had pulled off two strikes, three spares, and bowled over at least a few pins on every frame, with one more turn to go. He hadn't lost his ball to the gutter once.

"I don't know what's the matter," Ryjo said. "Perhaps I've been working too hard?"

"Or maybe you enjoyed your shore leave a little too much?" Sulu teased him good-naturedly, even though they'd left Tykona behind days ago. "Unless . . . ?"

A worried look came over Sulu's face, causing Ryjo's stomach to churn. *Keep calm*, he told himself as his ball returned to the rack via a hidden conduit beneath the lane. There was no way Sulu could've have guessed the truth, not from a few (okay, several) gutter balls.

"Unless?" Ryjo echoed.

Sulu eyed him suspiciously. "You haven't been replaced by your double from a mirror universe, have you?"

Ryjo froze, feeling like a glider skink caught in a snare, until a broad grin replaced Sulu's "troubled" expression. The helmsman chuckled at his own joke. "Seriously, Pavel, if I didn't know better, I'd swear you've never touched a bowling ball before."

"Ha-ha." Ryjo reclaimed his ball and stuck his sweaty fingers into it, wondering again why there were only three holes and not five. "Very funny."

"Guess you're just off your game tonight." Sulu shrugged. "Happens to us all."

Keep thinking that, Ryjo thought. Although Sulu was clearly just ribbing his old friend, all in good fun, Ryjo worried that he was already endangering his cover by failing so conspicuously at bowling. He had only one more roll left. He needed to turn this around before anyone started getting suspicious for real.

If he could.

He had hoped that his new body's muscle memory, and maybe even some lingering impressions on Chekov's brain, would get him through this challenge, or at least compensate for his newness at both bowling and being a human, but those hopes had gone sadly unrealized so far. Perhaps he was trying too hard? Maybe he needed to step aside, mentally, and let Chekov's brain and body do what came naturally to him?

Worth a try, he thought. *I couldn't possibly do any worse.*

Hefting the ball, which had been automatically cleansed of any stray dust or grit on its return to the rack, he took a deep breath and tried to clear his mind completely. Easier said than done under the circumstances, but letting the pressure get to him was not helping any. His displaced mind had to get out of this body's way.

Relax. It's just a game. "We've" done this dozens of times before . . .

Approaching the lane, being careful not to step over the foul line in his mandatory bowling shoes, he released his ball one last time. For once, it didn't bounce before rolling down the center of the lane. He watched anxiously, waiting for the ball to succumb to the seemingly insatiable pull of the gutter, but, to his amazement, it stayed on track for the pins, hooking only slightly to the left.

That's it, he urged the inanimate sphere, furiously willing it to remain on course as though he actually possessed telekinetic abilities. He swerved his body in an instinctive, irrational attempt to influence the ball. *Keep going . . .*

Strike!

Falling pins knocked over others, triggering a chain reaction that left no pin standing. The resulting clatter was music to Ryjo's ears. He punched the air in triumph as the thrill of victory swept away his growing anxiety.

Thank you, Mister Chekov! You trained this body well!

"That's more like it!" Sulu leapt to his feet, openly happy for his friend. He gave Ryjo a hearty slap on the back. "You're on a roll now, literally."

A rush of warmth and camaraderie lifted Ryjo's spirits—before he caught himself.

Sulu was not his friend. Nobody on the *Enterprise* was.

He mustn't forget that.

"Congratulations," a new voice chimed in. "I'd applaud if I didn't have my hands full."

He turned to discover a dark-haired woman, attractive by human standards, approaching from the adjacent snack bar, bearing a bag of the exploded grain kernels humans seemed to find so snackable. A crisp white uniform and telltale medical insignia (bizarrely mixing wings and serpents) revealed she was assigned to sickbay, but he didn't recognize her from his careful study of the *Enterprise*'s crew roster back at the villa. A recent addition to the crew? He had been afraid that the intel provided by Imperial Intelligence might not be entirely up to date. He kicked himself for not scouring the ship's current roster for any such additions at the first opportunity, but it wasn't as though he hadn't been occupied impersonating Chekov on and off duty.

"Er, thank you . . . Nurse?"

"'Nurse'?" She looked slightly nonplussed. "A tad formal when off duty, don't you think? Pretty sure I asked you to call me Simone."

Anxiety came creeping back, gnawing at whatever transitory relief his lucky strike had brought him. The woman—Simone—eyed him expectantly, while Sulu looked on with what struck Ryjo as rather too much interest. He felt he was missing some crucial subtext here. Was this the unnamed nurse Sulu had alluded to on the bridge a few days ago, when Ryjo had first taken Chekov's place at the nav controls? The one he'd assumed Sulu was interested in? For better or for worse, she hadn't come up since, and Ryjo had been reluctant to press further for fear of betraying that he'd had no idea whom Sulu had been referring to.

"Sorry," he improvised. "Force of habit, I suppose."

She regarded him quizzically. "Habit?"

"Addressing people by their ranks and titles, I mean, after serving on the bridge all day. You can take the officer off the bridge, it seems, but not the bridge out of the officer." He congratulated himself on the deft use of a human expression while attempting to smooth over his apparent faux pas. "Nothing personal, Simone. How are you this fine night?"

And who are you to Chekov?

"My social calendar is still fairly open." She held out the popcorn, offering to share. "Speaking of which, I haven't seen you around sickbay since I got back from Tykona. Not exactly sure what to make of that, to be honest."

What did she mean by that? He helped himself to a handful of popcorn as he assumed Chekov would. The exploded kernels were surprisingly tasty as human refreshments went, not all that different from the salted nuts and seeds Voyzr enjoyed snacking on. He munched on the treat while he formulated a hopefully innocuous reply.

"Just lucky, I guess."

"Lucky for who?" She stepped back, withdrawing the popcorn. Her sunny smile dimmed a few degrees. "You or me?"

Out of the corner of his eye, he saw Sulu cringe. *I'm messing up,* Ryjo gathered, but he wasn't precisely certain why. He peered into Simone's dark, enigmatically human eyes, searching for a clue. Doctor Morval had warned Ryjo that there might be some psychic seepage between his memory and Chekov's; he could really use a stray flashback regarding this nurse right now. Who was this woman? What did she expect from Chekov? What was he doing wrong? The merest flicker of a memory crossed his mind, like a fragment of a half-forgotten dream:

Simone leans toward him in sickbay. "This won't hurt a bit."

He was once her patient?

"Me, of course," he hastened to explain. "Lucky in that I've been fortunate enough not to require your expert care . . . as exceptional as it is, to be sure."

"I see," she said coolly, any previous warmth turning wintry. "Well, in that case, I'll leave you to your game. Do try not to strain anything, *Commander*. Heavens forbid you should have to swing by sickbay again."

She strode away briskly, tossing a piece of popcorn into her mouth before vacating the bowling alley altogether. Ryjo experienced a peculiar pang as he watched her depart, which made no sense. He ought to be relieved that their perilous encounter had ended sooner rather than later, before he could seriously endanger his cover, yet he felt a sudden, distinct sense of regret about whatever had just transpired between him and this "Simone" person, as though he'd let something precious slip through his fingers. A missed opportunity?

For Chekov, he reminded himself. *Not for me.*

"Wow." Sulu shook his head in dismay. "You really are off your game tonight, and I'm not talking about bowling. What *was* that even?"

That's what I need to know. Ryjo wanted to ask Sulu what the other man thought had just happened and what exactly he was reacting to, but how to do so without raising suspicion? He couldn't afford to seem too oblivious about matters that ought to be familiar to him.

"You think I said the wrong thing?"

"You tell me," Sulu said. "I thought you were keen on getting to know Nurse Tovar better the first chance you got, and that you and she had definite potential, but you barely tried to connect with her just now, let alone chat her up. Did I miss a major course correction somewhere?"

Offal, Ryjo cursed silently. Seemed he'd misread Sulu's earlier remark on the bridge; it was Chekov who was interested in "Nurse Tovar," not Sulu. He replayed his brief encounter with her to see how badly he'd flubbed it. He hadn't actually snubbed her or brushed her off, that he recalled, but he probably should have appeared more enthusiastic when she approached him, given his previous interest in her, however far that might have gone. Calling her "Nurse" had clearly been a misstep, but how was he supposed to have known that? She wasn't in his briefings. If only Vonnu had extracted this vital bit of gossip out of the real Chekov like he was supposed to!

"Well," Sulu persisted, "have you even reached out to her since we left Tykona? I'm just asking as a friend."

Ryjo felt another snare tightening around him. How was he to handle this? A romantic entanglement, under false pretenses no less, could only complicate his mission and, honestly, struck him as distasteful to boot. On the other hand, his unaccountable coolness toward Simone Tovar was already raising eyebrows. How was he to finesse this dilemma?

"You're up." Ryjo nodded at the bowling lane, where the pins had been automatically reset in anticipation of Sulu's final turn. "You still have to finish this frame."

"Uh-uh. You're not changing the subject that easily." Sulu hoisted his ball and pulled off another strike with aplomb. He didn't wait for the echoes of the falling pins to die down before picking up where he left off. "No more evasive maneuvers, my friend. You getting cold feet where Tovar is concerned?"

"Not exactly," Ryjo hedged. "I don't think."

An incoming party of bowling enthusiasts, waiting patiently for their lane, bought Ryjo a little more time as he and Sulu surrendered their spot and, at Sulu's insistence, relocated to the snack bar, where they found a relatively quiet corner to continue their conversation. Sulu acquired a cup of tea and a plate of synthetic sushi from one of several available refreshment slots, and Ryjo ordered the same; he would have liked something stronger to steady his nerves, but he needed to keep his wits sharp to avoid any more mistakes. He nibbled on the sushi; it lacked the satisfying crunch of his favorite stems and nuts, but his newly human palate found it agreeable. Sulu's persistence was much less so.

"Talk to me, Pavel. What's up? Last I knew, you and Tovar were hitting it off pretty well. So what, if anything, has changed?"

Mind your own business, he wanted to reply. Unfortunately, everything he knew about Chekov's close friendship with Sulu ran counter to that impulse. Regardless of what it felt like to him, this wasn't Sulu mercilessly grilling a suspect; this was simply two old friends taking an interest in each other's personal lives, no different from the way he and his cohorts used to talk about does back on Tykona, before he fully committed himself to the Exile cause. Chekov would not take offense at Sulu helpfully inquiring about his love life, so neither could he.

"I'm not sure," he said, deliberately vague. "Maybe now is not the right time? With the mission to Voyzr and all?"

"It's just an embassy opening," Sulu countered, "not a covert mission deep into the heart of the Romulan Empire. Nothing that precludes a date or two along the way."

Just an embassy opening? Ryjo seethed inwardly at the human's blasé attitude toward the despicable state of affairs of Voyzr. Easy for Sulu to make light of the Federation sinking its hooks deeper into Voyzr, cementing its ties to the corrupt regime that had cost the Exiles everything; he hadn't lost his family and future to the very "peace" the *Enterprise* was on its way to celebrate.

Not that this would bother Chekov . . .

"Maybe." He swallowed his resentment, as though he indeed had nothing more important on his mind than a pretty human nurse. "But perhaps I should take things slow? How well do I truly know her?"

Feel free to volunteer any details, please. How well do *I know her?*

"That's the whole point of asking her out," Sulu said, less than helpfully. "Learning more about her, getting to really know her, is the fun part. Well, one of the fun parts, that is. You'll never know if you slow to impulse now. Faint heart ne'er won fair maid, et cetera." He gave Ryjo an encouraging smile. "Where's the brash, hot-blooded Russian I've known all these years? The one who somehow managed to romance that Troyian envoy years ago, even while we were being held hostage by a renegade artificial intelligence?"

Ryjo balked, recalling the trap Vonnu seemed to fall for back at the villa while pretending to be Ratikin. He couldn't be sure, but it probably wasn't a coincidence that Chekov had tried to make a rapid exit right after Vonnu pretended to remember some scandalous episode from their past. From what Ryjo had seen, observing the "reunion" via hidden cameras, he suspected that Chekov had tricked Vonnu into exposing himself by inventing a fictitious anecdote out of whole cloth.

Was this a similar test? He recalled studying the exploit in question, rogue computer program and all, but there had been nothing about any alleged romance in the official Starfleet records, although that was perhaps simply a matter of discretion and privacy. Was Sulu testing him? Should he "remember" this dalliance or not? Or just try to duck the issue entirely?

"Maybe not so brash anymore." He affected a self-deprecating air. "I'm not getting any younger, you know."

"Don't give me that." Sulu wasn't having it. "You're younger than I am, kid, and I like to think that neither of us is ready to swear off affairs of the heart just yet." He took a sip of tea. "Just think about what I'm saying, okay?"

Ryjo pretended to take Sulu's unwelcome meddling in the spirit in which it was intended, smiling amiably. "When have I not?"

"You want a list?"

"I'll take your word for it."

"Sulu, Chekov!" Lieutenant Godwin from engineering dropped in on them, along with a few other crew members, whose faces Ryjo mercifully recognized. "Sorry to interrupt, but we need a few more players for a round of shufflelight. You interested?"

"Count me in." Sulu looked at Ryjo. "Up for trying your hand at another game?"

Not remotely. Ryjo saw a chance to make a smooth escape. "Think I'll call it a night if you don't mind." He politely fended off efforts to change his mind. "Probably better off reviewing the latest security reports."

And studying Nurse Tovar's file.

"All right," Sulu assented. "See you tomorrow."

He and the others wandered off, quickly finding volunteers to fill out their shufflelight teams. Ryjo lingered in the snack bar, finishing his tea and sushi before judging it safe to head out himself.

The nearest turbolift was located at the forward end of the *Enterprise*'s spacious, split-level rec deck, one of the largest public spaces on the ship. It was roomy enough to accommodate a wide assortment of recreational amenities and diversions, including an immense wall-sized viewscreen, currently displaying vintage twenty-second-century fractal-art videos; reading lounges; gaming tables; sunken conversation pits; and a large arcade platform offering various interactive entertainments, including a tournament-length shufflelight board, where Sulu and company were already getting started. Players used ionized paddles to try to speed or deflect a luminous puck to or from the goal pockets at each end of the board; the trick being to keep track of which phosphorescent disk was the real puck and which were just holographic decoys. Ryjo gave them a friendly wave as he leisurely made his way toward the portside turbolift, not wanting to appear too eager to get away from his fellow crew members.

Nice and easy, he told himself. *We're almost clear.*

Then he spotted Simone Tovar dead ahead.

She was exiting a recessed conversation pit between the arcade and the viewscreen. He paused, unsure if she had noticed him yet or if she was simply ignoring him. Perhaps he could slip past her and postpone any further interactions until after he'd thoroughly reviewed her file and devised a suitable strategy for dealing with her? Or would conspicuously giving her the cold shoulder now just compound his earlier missteps?

He peeked over his shoulder, hoping Sulu was too immersed in his shufflelight match to be watching, but once again fortune was not with him. Sulu nodded at him from across the crowded deck, egging him on. Ryjo could practically feel Sulu giving him an encouraging nudge with his elbow. He sighed in resignation. It appeared there was no way out.

Maybe just as well. The sooner I remedy this, the better.

He strolled toward Tovar, resolved to make the best of the situation now that it had been forced upon him. This was his chance to lay to rest any questions about his recent incongruous behavior.

"Hello again."

She turned toward him, making eye contact. "Commander."

"Touché. I had that coming, I suppose. My apologies for being so . . . impersonal . . . before. My head was elsewhere."

"How flattering." Her expression resisted ready interpretation. Wary but not entirely on red alert, with perhaps a hint of amusement as well. She looked him over, arms across her chest, as though trying to diagnose a particularly elusive medical mystery. "For a minute there, I half expected you to pretend not to see me and walk on by."

"Never," he lied. "I was just taking a moment to . . . collect my thoughts."

"About what, precisely?"

Careful, he thought. He needed to walk a fine line between acting interested but not getting too involved with Tovar. He couldn't risk anyone getting too close to "Chekov" before he completed his mission. That would be courting disaster.

"About how to get back into your good graces." He assumed what he hoped was a disarmingly sheepish air. "Can we perhaps start over again, Simone?"

She rewarded him with a smirk. "All right. Let me ask you again: How come you haven't come by to see me since Tykona?"

Was he expected to? He was fumbling in the dark, with no idea how Chekov had left things with Tovar before beaming down to the villa. *Curse you, Vonnu. You had one rutting job . . .*

"Waiting for the right moment? An inspired excuse?"

"What made you think you needed an excuse?" She stepped closer, seeming to lower her shields by a few percentages. "So, about that stroll you promised me?"

Stroll? Aboard the ship? He glanced up at the mezzanine overlooking the rec deck, where miscellaneous crew members were stretching their legs while enjoying an unobstructed view of the *Enterprise*'s secondary hull and warp nacelles through the tops of several large viewports stretching the entire height of the deck. Was that what she meant?

"In the gardens," she prompted, frowning. "Remember?"

His momentary confusion had not escaped her, it seemed. He castigated himself for failing to think of the *Enterprise*'s lush botanical gardens, which he had yet to visit. He felt himself losing whatever ground he'd regained with Tovar.

"Naturally!" He smacked his forehead. "How could I forget?"

"That's what I'm wondering."

"A stroll in the gardens sounds delightful," he said, feigning enthusiasm. *But potentially far too romantic.* He could easily imagine things going too far and too fast during a cozy amble through so much lovely, concealing foliage. Like that time he and Dise had ended up making out in that thicket in Arbor Park.

"It was *your* idea," she said pointedly. Her eyes narrowed. "Unless you're having second thoughts?"

"Not in the least." He groped for a way to delay the outing before he found himself dealing with a much more complicated situation. "Let me consult my schedule and get back to you promptly."

"Come again?" An aggrieved tone signaled that he had landed smack-dab in the manure again. "Might I remind you, Mister Chekov, that *you* asked *me* to keep my calendar clear for you . . . and then activated your cloaking device until I put you on the spot just now."

"I'm sorry." He faltered, at a loss as to how to salvage the situation. "That is, I mean, I—"

She held up her hand to silence him.

"Let me save you the trouble, Commander, of trying to squeeze me into your oh-so-busy schedule. You don't need to bother."

Turning sharply on her heels, she marched toward the very turbolift he had hoped to employ in the first place. For the second time in less than an hour, a rueful pang stabbed his heart as he watched her depart, her back to him.

"This won't hurt a bit."

Could that have gone any worse? Looking back over his shoulder at Sulu, he saw the other man facepalming, obviously embarrassed for Ryjo. *Sorry*, he thought, knowing he had let his friend down.

No, not my friend. Chekov's *friend.*

Trath had warned him about this. One had to be careful, when working undercover among the enemy, not to get too caught up in the role and start bonding with the very foes you were infiltrating. And all the more so in this case, when he was literally stepping into the life and identity of another person.

But only as a mean to an end.

He must never forget that. Never forget who he truly was and why he was here. Never forget that it was Captain Kirk and his crew who were responsible for his family being driven into Exile decades ago.

I'm not Chekov. I am not Starfleet. I am Voyzr.

And he would assassinate the regnant, no matter what.

Twelve

Chekov exited the cruising public transport at the very next stop, both to shake his pursuers, who could too easily look up the transport's scheduled route, and to escape his anxious and overly solicitous fellow passengers, who were understandably agitated by the way he had dropped in on them from above, nearly falling to his death in the process. Not an everyday occurrence, apparently.

"No, no, I'm fine, thank you very much..."

Deflecting a barrage of well-intentioned queries, along with a few less charitable reactions, he scurried off the transport onto another elevated dock several blocks from where he'd leapt from the roof. Thankfully, no transit security officers had arrived to question him yet.

A convenient lift carried him down to a busy open-air market, which he hastily crossed to catch another transport heading in the opposite direction, all the while scanning for any prowling antlers, broken or otherwise. Thankfully, a day pass on Jhopash's public-transportation system proved be within his palm's budget, so he proceeded to transfer randomly from one transport to another to throw his once and would-be captors off his trail. The way he saw it, if he didn't know where he was going, neither would they.

Just staying out of Trath's clutches was not enough, however, not when Ryjo was still taking his place on the *Enterprise* for undoubtedly nefarious reasons. As Chekov played hopscotch from transit line to transit line, keeping a wary eye out for Broken-Antler and his cohorts, he searched for a strategy beyond simply eluding capture. Exposing the imposter took priority over his own predicament, but how to accomplish that while stranded, homeless and nearly broke, on a planet light-years away from the *Enterprise*'s present destination, let alone the nearest Federation starbase or embassy? He liked to think he was resourceful enough to find shelter and gainful employment in the short term, but the clock was clicking. He didn't have time to earn his way off Tykona and back to the *Enterprise*. Ryjo needed to be stopped, and Trath's insidious plans foiled, as soon as possible.

If he wasn't already too late.

"End of the line," an artificial voice announced as the latest transport pulled up to a dock. Not wanting to stand out, Chekov joined the remaining passengers in exiting the vehicle. On reflection, it was probably past time he left the transit system altogether, just in case his enemies were fanning out across every route in pursuit of him. Plus, cruising around the city endlessly wasn't getting him any closer to protecting the *Enterprise* from whatever Ryjo was up to.

I need to stop running and start finding a way to fix this.

Descending to street level, he found himself in an outlying part of Jhopash that appeared considerably less luxe than both the high-end commercial district he'd first beamed into or even the administrative sector he'd just escaped from. Not a slum, exactly, but definitely more low-rent, verging on seedy. Basic, boxlike buildings settled for function over form; no fancy, gravity-defying architecture here, just simple, somewhat rundown structures, many of which looked as though they hadn't been refurbished in years, receiving at best only minimal maintenance. Litter besmirched the streets and sidewalks, which were pitted with potholes. Azure weeds sprouted from cracked pavement. Weather-beaten facades, fading in color, conveyed a general sense of neglect on the part of the powers that be. Not a fashionable neighborhood, in short, and well off the tourist routes.

Perhaps not a bad place to lie low while he came up with a plan?

A quick survey of the surrounding streets didn't detect much of a police presence, which was, sadly, just as well. That the local authorities were more likely to hinder than help him spoke volumes about the fix he was in. Still fuzzy on what his next move was, he explored the neighborhood, which began to feel ominously familiar even though he'd never set foot in it before. Or rather *Pavel Chekov* had never walked these streets and alleys before, but possibly Ryjo had? A distressing possibility struck him: He had thought he was navigating randomly, the better to shake his pursuers, but what if his new brain had been unconsciously guiding him back to Ryjo's old haunts all along?

That could be a problem.

He nervously searched the faces around him, feeling more than a little paranoid. If Ryjo *had* frequented this neighborhood, would Trath's people anticipate him winding up here? Or was this the last place they'd expect to find him? A case could be made for either scenario.

A sinking sun threw elongated shadows onto the uneven pavement before him. He flinched at the sight of "his" own shadow, now crowned by the umbral silhouette of antlers. He still wasn't used to that and hoped he never would be. Then the shadow of a *second* pair of antlers fell across the pavement, coming up from behind him. He whirled around, expecting trouble, but found only a geriatric Voyzr, shabbily dressed, looking at him hopefully.

"Excuse me, young man, do you know what time the pharmacy closes?"

Was this a trick, or was the old stag as harmless as he appeared? Chances were not every Voyzr on the planet was involved in Trath's conspiracy and out to get him. He needed to keep that in mind.

"Sorry, I'm not from around here."

Or was he?

The man thanked Chekov for his time and wandered off. *False alarm*, Chekov thought, his pulse calming. By now, daylight was fading fast and the weather taking a turn toward the blustery. A gust of wind blew a crumpled foil wrapper past Chekov's feet. Dark jade clouds rolled in, threatening rain. Thunder rumbled nearby. Were spring storms a thing in this region of Tykona? He feared he was about find out.

Finding shelter moved up his to-do list.

Not an easy task, he discovered. With night falling, shops and eateries were already closing up for the day, sealing their entrances and storefront windows behind metal shutters and/or protective energy fields. Chekov hoped he wouldn't have to hole up under an overhanging terrace or skybridge; the last thing he needed was to be picked up for vagrancy, if that was even an issue in this part of town.

Another booming thunderclap, closer than the last, brought the first spattering of rain. Shivering, he quickened his pace, anxious to put a roof over his head before the drizzle turned into a downpour. His weary limbs longed for a break as well; he had been running on little sleep all day and hadn't eaten anything since a perfunctory meal at the police station hours ago. Even Ryjo's fit, young frame was running low on reserves. *I cannot defy the laws of biology*, Chekov thought, *with apologies to Mister Scott.*

Just as he was on the brink of giving up and maybe trying to find his way back onto a transport, loud voices and music drew him around the corner to what appeared to be a lively night spot. Young humanoids, representing myriad species, streamed in and out of the multistory edifice; others, defying the weather, clustered on the pavement outside, beneath an incandescent force-field awning that pulsated chromatically in the dusk. Glowing holographic signage was projected above the wide-open front entrance:

INSOMNIA
Open Until Dawn

Works for me, Chekov thought. Judging from the percussive music spilling out from Insomnia, along with the club's name, he doubted he would be getting much sleep if he sheltered there for the night, but the temperature was dropping and the rain getting heavier, so he sprinted inside. *Beggars can't be choosers, as they say in Moscow* . . .

Insomnia was dryer than outdoors but much more disorienting. Sensory overload seemed to be the primary draw of the establishment, which struck Chekov as an unholy hybrid of an Elasian nightclub and a carnival fun house. Along with the throbbing music vibrating his bones, garishly colored lights strobed across the walls, floors, ceilings, and most every other surface, including the seats and tables. Jets of scented air, carrying everything from cloying floral fragrances to harsh chemical odors, buffeted his nostrils from all directions. A shimmering, refractive haze, producing a prismatic effect, suffused the atmosphere, obscuring his view of the entire layout. Even the gravity seemed to fluctuate randomly, leaving him constantly off-balance. Packed bodies—mammalian, avian, reptilian, amphibian, piscine, and chimerical—generated enough heat to make him almost long for the dank, damp weather outside. Steering clear of the dance floor, Chekov weaved through jostling knots of clubgoers, many dressed to party, in search of a (relatively) quiet and inconspicuous place to rest and get his bearings. He needed sanctuary, not stimulation.

"Ryjo!"

A heavy hand clamped down on his shoulder from behind. Chekov reacted instinctively, jabbing his elbow into the speaker's gut, then spinning around to place his doubled-over accoster in a headlock. To his surprise, he discovered that the man he was grappling with was not Voyzr, but simian in nature, complete with a sloping brow, cropped pink hair, and a prognathous jaw. A khaki one-piece coverall was liberally adorned with animated patches displaying bouncing alien glyphs. His lanky physique was more chimp-like than gorilla.

"What the flume?" the simian barked. "Get your rutting hands off me!"

Ryjo? Chekov registered belatedly. *He thinks I'm Ryjo?*

He loosened his grip without fully letting go. Had he jumped the gun here, after being on guard against Trath's agents all day?

"You heard him! What wrong with you?" Outraged voices accompanied rough hands dragging him away from the simian. A trio of other clubgoers held on to Chekov, one of them twisting his arm behind his back. A saggy-faced Arcturian clone, flaps of skin hanging over his face like curtains, snarled at him, his breath smelling like licorice gasoline. "You have some nerve showing your face around here again, then pulling a stunt like that?"

"You tell him!" said a Troyian, twisting Chekov's arm. His roots easily identifiable by his mint-green skin, he growled in Chekov's ear with a jarringly Nausicaan accent. "What did Brost ever do to you?"

"Why are you back anyway?" the third youth demanded. Sunken eyes and thick, leathery skin suggested that he was a Megarite, far from his people's usual stomping grounds. "Thought you were above getting rowdy with the likes of us these days?"

They taunted him over each other:

"Not looking so upstanding now, are you?"

"Serves you right for ditching us for your new Exile buddies!"

"You lost what's left of your rutting brain?"

Oops, Chekov thought. They definitely thought he was Ryjo, which meant he had indeed lashed out prematurely, only to end up outnumbered and overpowered. From what he could tell, his new acquaintances were one-time associates of Ryjo, unconnected to Trath's conspiracy, who seemed to have grudges of their own against their former comrade.

So, still bad news, but of a different caliber?

"My sincere apologies, friends." He smiled weakly at the simian, whose name was apparently Brost. "You startled me, that's all."

Starfleet combat training suggested several ways to take on multiple opponents hand-to-hand, but perhaps he could talk his way out of this misunderstanding instead. He had enough enemies on Tykona already.

"That's it?" Brost clutched his offended abdomen. Anger contorted his apish countenance. "You went all supernova on me just because I 'startled' you?"

He seemed in no mood to forgive and forget. Chekov couldn't really blame him.

"What can I say? It's been a long day. I was on edge."

With good reason.

"Is that so?" Brost swaggered toward Chekov, long arms swinging at his side. His lips peeled back to expose his sharp canines. "Well, you sure as sludge startled me!"

A hairy-knuckled fist slammed into Chekov's stomach. Or was it stomachs? Voyzr had an elaborate four-chambered stomach he was still getting used to. In any event, the punch left him gasping, and hoping that honor had now been satisfied. *Probably wishful thinking,* he thought. Brost and his pals looked like they were still spoiling for a fight.

"Ha!" the Arcturian guffawed. "Give him another one, Brost!"

"That's enough, all of you!"

A husky feminine voice intruded on the confrontation, sending a jolt through Chekov. He knew that voice, he realized, just before a scowling Voyzr woman emerged from the sparkling haze. Latinum-blonde wool was tied up in a topknot above large, literally doe eyes and a svelte snout. Eschewing traditional Voyzr attire, she sported a long green duster over a dark red halter top, trousers, studded fingerless gloves, and steel-toed boots. A twig dangled from her lips like a toothpick or cigarette. Chekov placed her at once.

Dise.

A shiver ran down his new spine. He would have "recognized" her, he guessed, even if Chief Cesss hadn't shown him her mug shot back at the police station. She'd clearly impressed herself on Ryjo's brain in a big way.

"What do you care?" Brost, his arm drawn back to deliver another punch, held his fire for a moment. "He's got this coming. You know that better than anyone."

"Damn straight!" The Troyian gave Chekov's arm another twist. "He still owes me for some low-grade stim he sold me before going straight. That sludge was no good. I want my credits back, or I'll take it out of his hide!"

More grievances issued from Brost and the others; Ryjo had obviously burned more than his fair share of bridges in these parts. *Just my luck,* Chekov thought. *Of all bodies to get stuck in . . .*

"Whatever," Dise said, unimpressed. "I claim first dibs on this sorry excuse for a buck." She cracked her knuckles, a wolfish grin belying her cervine features. "Anybody got a problem with that?"

A looming Orion bouncer, all verdant muscles and tattoos, shoved his way toward them. He grunted, visibly displeased at the sight of Ryjo. "Hoped I'd seen the last of you."

"No worries." Dise strode forward and extracted Chekov from the Troyian, who released him without further argument. She took hold of Chekov's arm. "We're going."

Brost and the others backed off as well; it was hard to tell whom they were more intimidated by, the bouncer or Dise. The latter stepped aside to let them pass. "Don't let me stop you," he said brusquely. "And don't hurry back."

Chekov also raised no objection. He had no idea whether leaving with Dise was a smart move, but he had undeniably outstayed his welcome at Insomnia. He could only play this by ear and pray that he wasn't jumping from a fist fight to a firing squad. What *did* Dise want with Ryjo?

Nothing good, he feared.

Thirteen

After the hot, sweaty maelstrom of Insomnia, the cool night air outside came as a relief. The sudden storm seemed to have passed, leaving wet pavement slick and gleaming beneath the streetlights. Chekov stepped carefully to avoid puddles and flooded potholes. Dise tightened her grip as she led him away from the club, down winding, nocturnal alleys. The evening crowd thinned the farther they got from their starting point. He mapped their course as best he could, memorizing turns and landmarks to keep from getting lost any more than he already was. His eyes scanned the shadows.

"If you're thinking about trying to ditch me, think again," she said sourly. "You don't want to do that."

"Never crossed my mind," he lied, although it wasn't as if he had any sort of haven to flee to. He might as well let this play out, while keeping his guard up. "Er, where are we going exactly?"

"My place." She shot him a warning look. "Don't get any ideas, not after the way you've been acting."

That she was talking about more than just the recent altercation at Insomnia was plainly obvious. Chekov chose his words carefully to avoid digging Ryjo a deeper hole, at his expense. Trying to explain who he *really* was would only complicate matters; like everyone else, Dise would just think he was lying or crazy.

"Thanks for the timely assist back there, by the way."

She snorted. "Somebody had to save you strutting males from yourselves." She rolled her eyes. "What were you even thinking, showing up at Insomnia again? You made it pretty clear before that you were putting all that behind you." Her expression darkened, along with her tone. "Among other things."

The bitterness in her voice did not escape him. Chekov recalled the story he had spun for Cesss back at the station, about how relations between Ryjo and Dise had soured after he cleaned up his act following his father's death. Had that scenario been more accurate than he supposed? He didn't need a tricorder to pick up the aggrieved-ex energy radiating from Dise.

Or that Ryjo's brain and body were not over her yet.

"I was . . . at loose ends," he said. "Didn't have anywhere else to go."

"And that exhibition you put on in the commercial district this morning? You had nothing better to do then, too?"

Chekov blushed beneath his fur. "You know about that?"

"A shameless buck bares all in the middle of that snooty part of town? Hard to miss. You were a media sensation for maybe an hour or two."

He groped for an explanation. "I wasn't thinking. I was clowning around and, well, it just seemed funny at the time."

"Whatever." She shrugged. "Nothing I haven't seen before."

Oh, Chekov thought, processing that. Ryjo's history with Dise was definitely coming into focus, albeit somewhat uncomfortably. He attempted to change the subject. "How much longer?"

"Like you don't know the way." She rolled her eyes again. "It hasn't been *that* long, you know."

She slowed to a stop before a long, ugly building that occupied an entire city block. Chekov had seen industrial storage containers that had more style and personality. A flickering illuminated sign identified the structure as: URBAN DORMITORY 37/FQ4.

"Coming back to you now?" she said tartly.

Releasing his arm, she peeled off a glove to let a sensor scan her palm, gaining them entrance to the building. Chekov followed her into a spartan lobby with a distinctly institutional aesthetic. Graffiti, lasered into the monochrome walls, provided the only decoration. A tiny multilegged lifeform, of indefinite phylum, scurried out of view as they entered.

Not exactly the Winter Palace.

He recalled that much of Tykona's refugee-fed labor force resided in cheap housing on the fringes of major population centers, close enough to work in more affluent districts they couldn't personally afford to live in. What had Cesss said about Ryjo working odd jobs in the service and tourist industries when he wasn't getting in trouble with the law? Chekov was getting a better sense of the life Ryjo had left behind when they swapped bodies.

"The lift's broken again," she said. "We need to take the stairs."

"Lead the way," he said without thinking, eliciting a puzzled look from Dise. "Ladies first, I mean."

"Okaaay," she said dubiously, drawing out the last syllable. "After me."

A narrow stairwell led to an underground corridor a couple of floors below the lobby. Rows of sealed doorways faced each other across the hall. Chekov held back, a few paces behind Dise, so as not to reveal that he didn't know which door was hers. Before he could find out, however, an elderly cyclops emerged from one unit. Her single eye widened at the sight of them.

"What's this?" She frowned at Chekov. "You're back with *him* again?"

"No!" Dise answered at warp speed. "Not a chance."

"Is that so? Then why—"

"Don't you have somewhere to go?"

Dise brushed past her neighbor, who huffed indignantly, to reach a scuffed door farther down the hall, where another sensor granted them admittance. Chekov followed her into her quarters, which, at first glance, was much less of a sensory assault than Insomnia. Automatic lights sputtered erratically before coming on to reveal a messy, bare-bones apartment that reminded him of his first dorm room back at the Academy. Discarded clothing littered the floor, while dirty plates and utensils waited to be sonically scrubbed. An unmade bunk, heaped with rumpled sheets and blankets, took up a quarter of the main living area; he looked in vain for a couch or recliner he might be able to crash on. In lieu of a window, a mounted viewframe displayed, in rotation, a gallery of lurid images: pillaging Orion pirates, slavering alien beasts, exploding cities and planets, and uncensored Deltan love festivals, all brazenly unsubtle and sensationalistic. A mobile composed of shed antlers hung from the ceiling, reminding Chekov of the shiv he'd been threatened with hours ago. Klingon death ballads began wailing upon their entrance. A grisly replica of a Gorn's skull, razored teeth and all, occupied a place of honor on a shelf.

At least he assumed it was a replica.

The door slid shut behind them. Dise bolted it shut for added security. That she felt this necessary did not make him feel any safer. Muffled voices and commotion from adjacent units seeped through thin walls, competing with the Klingon caterwauling. Chekov wondered if Ryjo had shared her edgy taste in music.

"I'd say make yourself at home, but that ship has sailed, thanks to you." She shrugged out of her long coat, exposing velvety russet arms, and draped it over a chair. "So, what happened? Things not work out with your new Exile compatriots?"

"Something like that."

He registered that Trath and his antlered Cossacks were indeed Exiles from Voyzr, driven from their homeworld in the aftermath of the civil war, which surely meant they were out to disrupt the anniversary celebration in some fashion, with Ryjo already in place as security chief aboard the *Enterprise*. Chekov hated to think what the imposter's ultimate objective might be.

Dise snorted. "Don't say I didn't warn you."

"I should have listened. My mistake."

If nothing else, it was evident Dise was not in league with Trath, despite being Voyzr herself. Perhaps because she was too young to have any deep attachment to her people's homeworld? That was something at least; he felt less wary in her company. It was always possible, of course, that she was simply putting on an act to lull him into a false state of security until reinforcements could arrive to subdue him, but he didn't think so. Her prickly attitude toward Ryjo, and the Exiles he'd gotten mixed up with, felt very genuine.

"Took you long enough to figure that out." She sat down on the edge of the bunk, still nibbling on her twig. "I know your dad dying messed you up, that you felt guilty about disappointing him, but . . . joining up with those fanatics? We used to laugh at them, remember, and their stupid obsession with the glorious old days back on Voyzr, then you go all in on that 'patriotic' sludge? It was like you turned into a whole different person!"

Funny you should say that.

He cleared some debris off a chair to find a place to sit. Resting his legs at last, he wondered what she was after, bringing him back to her place. A chance to have it out with him—that was, Ryjo—once and for all?

"They're not going to come looking for me here, are they?" He glanced at the sealed and bolted door, wondering if it was enough to protect them from the Exiles if they came calling. "I don't want to drag you deeper into my mess."

"So what else is new?" She spit what was left of the twig onto the floor, then got up and plucked a bottle from the same shelf holding the ersatz (?) Gorn skull. Uncapping it, she took a swig, wiped her snout with the back of her hand, then offered it to him. "You look like you need this more than I do."

He accepted the bottle. "I appreciate the hospitality."

"Don't bother. Your credits paid for that bottle after all." She invaded his space, and not in a friendly way. Her eyes flashed with indignation. "And that's another thing, what's with transferring all your savings to my account, with no warning or explanation? What the flume possessed you to do that?"

He sat up straight. "I did what?"

"You heard me," she accused him, visibly upset about it. "What was I supposed to think when all those credits suddenly landed in my palm ... after you chose the Exile's lunatic crusade over me? Were you *trying* to screw with my head, or just out to buy yourself a clean conscience where I was concerned?"

Or leaving Dise his life savings because he knows he isn't going to need them anymore.

This was not good, Chekov realized. Putting two and two together added up to a disturbing conclusion: Ryjo was not expecting to come back from his mission.

"Well?" She glared at him, snout to snout. "Say something, why don't you?"

"It's difficult to explain," he said honestly. Worst-case scenarios raced through his mind. *Is Ryjo on a suicide mission—in my body?*

"Give it a try. You owe me that much, credits or no credits." She grabbed him by the shoulders and shook him. "What's wrong with you, and why are you acting so rutting weird? I look at you and I see the Ryjo I used to run with, but something's off. Nothing you're doing or saying feels right. It's like you're a stranger to me!"

More than you know.

He had to hand it to her: She saw what nobody else had yet, that he wasn't remotely Ryjo, even if she didn't fully understand what or why—yet. A desperate, almost extinguished hope showed signs of life again. He had all but given up on anyone on Tykona comprehending what had actually happened to him, but maybe, just maybe...

"You're not going to believe me," he ventured.

"Try me."

Fourteen

"Bridge," Ryjo instructed the turbolift.

He used the short ascent to compose himself for the challenge before him. Second thoughts threatened his resolve, but no, he had already decided on the best course of action, given the dire news from Tykona. This was the right response.

I just need to pull it off.

The turbolift door whooshed open, and he strode onto the bridge with as much confidence as he could muster. Kirk acknowledged his arrival, looking over from the captain's chair.

"Mister Chekov. I thought this was your day off?"

So it was, per the current crew rotation schedule. Ensign Vicki Novak was presently manning the nav station next to Sulu. Ryjo noted with relief that Spock was not present, the science station occupied by a junior lieutenant, Benuel Miller. The last thing Ryjo needed at the moment was the Vulcan's cold-blooded logic dissecting what he was about to report.

"Aye, Captain, but something has come up that I thought you should be notified about promptly."

Uhura swiveled toward him. "Concerning that subspace message from Tykona earlier, directed to you personally?"

"Affirmative." He approached the command well. "I just received word from the central law-enforcement agency on Tykona that some miscreant on the planet has been impersonating me."

In fact, the coded transmission, from an ally highly placed in the planetary civil service, had alerted Ryjo that the real Chekov had escaped from the villa and was currently at large, evading all efforts to recapture him.

Seriously?

He had needed a moment to recover after receiving that shocking transmission in the privacy of Chekov's quarters. How could Trath and the others have been so careless, after all the planning and effort that had gone into the operation, after all he'd been asked to sacrifice? Pungent Voyzr curses had spilled from his lips, even though he'd carefully weaned himself off them in preparation for his mission. Chekov was supposed to be locked up tight, not running around free, putting the entire operation in jeopardy!

Once he'd finally calmed down, which had not been easy, Ryjo had debated long and hard about how best to handle this alarming complication. He was tempted to do nothing, trusting in his fellow Exiles to deal with the situation back on Tykona, but the more he thought about it, it seemed better to get out ahead of the problem, just in case Chekov surfaced at the worst possible moment.

"Impersonating you?" Kirk echoed. "That's damn peculiar. Why you, specifically?"

"Your guess is as good as mine, Captain."

After mulling it over, he'd concluded that it was safer to play dumb than come up with some elaborate "explanation" that might not ring true. Chances were the real Chekov would be at a loss to readily account for such an unlikely scenario.

"The *Enterprise*'s visit to Tykona *did* receive global media coverage," Uhura observed. "The imposter may have seen Chekov's name and rank in the news reports."

Thank you, Commander, he thought, grateful for her unsuspecting assistance. *I can use all the help I can get.*

"Possibly," Kirk conceded, "but still, why Chekov and not, say, Doctor McCoy, who was the actual star of our mission to Tykona?" He offered Ryjo an apologetic smile. "No offense, Commander."

"None taken," Ryjo said. "Perhaps it's because the doctor was *too* prominently featured in the press coverage of his mission of mercy, making him harder to impersonate. I, on the other hand, am positively obscure as far as the average Tykon is concerned. Nobody knows what I actually look or sound like."

"Solid logic," Kirk said, nodding. "Who is this imposter? What do we know about him?"

"A petty criminal, apparently, unlikely to cause significant harm." Ryjo neglected to mention that the "imposter" happened to be Voyzr. "From what I gather, he's more juvenile delinquent than criminal mastermind. He's no Orion ganglord, nor even a Harry Mudd."

Ryjo knew of Mudd, an incorrigible human reprobate, from his extensive study of Chekov's Starfleet exploits. He congratulated himself for coming up with that aptly biographical reference.

"And I take it this imposter remains at large?" Kirk asked.

"Affirmative, although the Tykon authorities are confident he will be apprehended shortly."

I hope, Ryjo thought.

"So, you don't deem this a major cause for concern?"

"Not at all, sir. It's irritating, and more than a little embarrassing, personally, but scarcely a security issue, let alone a crisis. Still, I wanted to keep you informed."

"Acknowledged." Kirk seemed to take the news in stride. "I suppose this is hardly the first time some scoundrel pretended to be Starfleet for prestige, perks, or profit."

"If only," Sulu said from the helm. "Remember that con artist on Colchis V who posed as a Starfleet recruiter to run some sort of Academy admission scam? Whatever became of him anyway?"

"Still serving time in a rehab facility, I imagine," Kirk said. "Starfleet frowns on stolen honor, especially when it comes to opportunists falsely representing us to remote colonies and worlds outside the Federation." Kirk turned his chair toward the communications console. "Uhura, pass this information on to Starfleet Command. Let them know what's up."

"Aye, sir. Right on it."

Ryjo started to relax a little. It appeared he had gotten away with it: painting the fugitive Chekov as a known imposter without attracting suspicion toward himself. He made a mental note to change all of Chekov's security codes as well. With luck, these precautions would prove unnecessary, but Chekov had already proved himself more resourceful than anticipated by escaping captivity and eluding Trath's operatives so far. Ryjo didn't intend to underestimate him.

"I apologize for the inconvenience, Captain."

"Not your fault, Chekov. Keep me posted on any new developments."

"Count on it, sir."

Exiting the bridge, he sagged against the wall of the turbolift, releasing some of the tension he'd been masking while trying to preemptively discredit Chekov in case he reappeared. He couldn't relax entirely, however, knowing that Chekov was still on the loose—in Ryjo's true body no less.

Where was he now, and what was he up to?

Fifteen

"Once again," Chekov said, keeping his voice low, "you don't have to come with me. You've done enough already."

"Save your breath," Dise whispered back. "I'm coming whether you like it or not. We each have our own agendas after all. You want to protect your ship and your mission. I just want to stop Ryjo from doing something terrible." Her voice cracked slightly. "I need to keep him from getting into any deeper trouble than he's already in . . . for old times' sake if nothing else."

Protesting a bit much? She clearly cared more about Ryjo than she wanted to admit. *Perhaps even to herself.*

Convincing her of the truth, that he and Ryjo had traded bodies, had proven unexpectedly easy given how well she knew the real Ryjo and that she had started out realizing that something was very much off about him. As outlandish as the notion of a "life-entity transference" was, it confirmed what she had already sensed, deep down inside. In no time at all, she'd accepted that he was Chekov, not Ryjo.

Now they were standing in a long, painfully slow line at a spaceport terminal a transport ride away from her run-down neighborhood in Jhopash, waiting to be beamed aboard the *Quintessential*, a commercial passenger cruiser heading in roughly the same direction as the *Enterprise*. A wide central concourse, packed with inbound and outgoing travelers, connected several wedge-shaped boarding areas. Winding, switchback lines led to transporter gates.

"But—" he started to protest, still reluctant to drag her deeper into this potential hazardous affair. Trath and his fellow Exiles were surely looking for him and would likely stop at nothing to prevent him from exposing Ryjo before the imposter could complete his mission of malice, whatever it entailed. Chekov hated placing Dise in their targeting sensors as well, but was that because of his natural Starfleet aversion to putting a civilian in jeopardy—or because Ryjo's protective instincts toward Dise were seeping into his own consciousness?

Possibly a bit of both.

"No buts." She held up her open palm, waving it in his face. "Don't forget, I'm holding the purse strings on this intervention, thanks to Ryjo, so you're not getting far without me."

True enough, he conceded. Ryjo's savings, lately bolstered by his inheritance from his father, had paid for their passage on the cruiser, not to mention the false IDs and disguises Dise had acquired for them via her somewhat shady connections in the city. Unfortunately, those funds were not sufficient to charter an express flight to Voyzr. The best they could manage was to set off after the *Enterprise*, with an inconvenient layover at an independent space station along the way. This was far from optimum, considering that the *Enterprise* already had a daunting head start on them and was doubtless warping toward Voyzr at this very moment.

First things first, he thought. *Get away from Tykona—and the Exiles hunting me.*

Beyond that, his plan was very much a work in progress. The odds of them intercepting the *Enterprise* or making it to Voyzr before her were vanishingly slim. His best shot? Come within standard communications range of the *Enterprise* and somehow manage to send a priority message via subspace, despite lacking any sort of proper credentials or command status. Perhaps he could somehow con or sneak his way into a communications center, aboard either the cruiser or the space station?

When in doubt, improvise—just like Captain Kirk does.

Chekov liked to think he'd learned something after serving beneath Kirk and Spock all these years. Kirk would find a way to prevail no matter what, so Chekov expected nothing less from himself. As Spock was known to say, there were always possibilities.

"*Economy boarding, keep left,*" a public-address system blared, not for the first time. "*Premium boarding to the right. For a scenic shuttle voyage to the vessel, take Zodiac Corridor to Launchpad Indigo-Eight.*"

Stuck in the discount line, they crept forward toward the waiting transporter platform, which was guarded by uniformed terminal employees scanning people's palms or other appendages to confirm their reservations and that they were in the right line. He and Dise had already checked their minimal luggage elsewhere at the terminal, with the expectation that it would be beamed about the cruiser via cargo transporters, but the snail-like pace of the line left him feeling frustrated and far too exposed. His wary eyes swept the sprawling terminal, on the lookout for any Exiles who might be conducting sweeps of the spaceport in search of him.

Chekov kept his head down, regretting that antlers rendered hats and hoods unpractical. Rudimentary disguises provided him and Dise with only a degree of anonymity. Unable to hide that they were Voyzr, what with his antlers and their snouts, they'd settled for simply trying to look like a different, slightly older, more respectable Voyzr couple. For him, this meant a woolly green wig over Ryjo's shorn, furry pate, along with a change of clothes, cosmetically applied streaks of gray to his snout, and the addition of a couple of realistic prosthetic tines to his antlers to alter their configuration, which Dise had assured him varied from buck to buck in ways very distinguishable to Voyzr eyes.

He took her word for it.

For her, she had let down her topknot and traded her latinum-blonde dye for a more natural-looking forest-green tint. She had also exchanged her flashy club outfit for a more conservative, knee-length travel dress and sensible shoes. In contrast to Chekov, she had gone easier on the gray coloring, rationalizing that nobody was looking for her, so why look *too* old if she didn't have to?

He had not argued the point.

But were their new looks sufficient camouflage? The disguises had struck him as serviceable when he'd inspected himself in a mirror back at Dise's place, but now he was having misgivings. It wasn't as though there were that many other Voyzr passing through the terminal. He'd seen only a handful so far, none of whom he'd recognized from the villa, thank goodness. Nervous, he reached up to make sure his wig was still secure.

"How do I look?" he asked. "Truly."

"Like a lucky old stag with a younger doe, that old story." She smirked at his augmented antlers. "Nice rack, too."

This did little to reassure him. "All in all, I would prefer to look like my actual self. I feel like game at the beginning of hunting season, no offense."

"Relax. Nobody's going to give us a second look."

Unless they're deliberately searching for me.

"We'll see," he said dubiously, recalling an old Russian saying that often guided him as a security officer. *Hope for the best, expect the worst.*

The line inched forward, bringing them incrementally closer to the boarding platform. He tried to force himself to relax, if only to avoid looking as though he had something to hide, until he spotted Broken-Antler and another exile prowling the main concourse.

Naturally. Heavens forbid we should get off-planet too easily . . .

Had they spotted him yet? It didn't appear so. They were still sullenly scanning the faces in the crowd, looking rather frustrated and weary. Moving quickly, Chekov slipped around Dise to put her between him and the Exiles. He embraced her, pulling her closer, and leaned in as though to nuzzle her neck.

"Whoa." She started to pull away. "Let's not get too caught up in the role."

"Shush," he whispered in her ear. "Don't look now, but we have company. Two of Trath's agents, searching the terminal, about seventy meters away."

She got the message, cuddling against him. "They ID you?"

"I don't believe so. I spotted them before they clocked me."

"Lucky for us."

But for how long? On the plus side, the Exiles were presumably looking for a solitary escapee, not a couple, unless they had already tracked "Ryjo" back to Dise. Had someone at Insomnia—that hefty Orion bouncer, perhaps—reported them leaving the fun house together? Or had they followed the credit trail from Ryjo's account to Dise's to their booking on the cruiser, albeit under fraudulent identities?

He had no way of knowing.

Chekov contemplated the line before them, which had slowed to a stop. Peering past the *many* travelers still ahead, he discovered that there appeared to be an issue with a large, obstreperous family of Tellarites who were (no surprise) arguing with the gatekeepers over something or another, holding up the line. He squirmed inwardly; every passing minute increased the odds of the approaching Exiles taking a closer look at him—and seeing through his disguise.

"Economy boarding, keep left," the PA system announced again. *"Premium boarding to the right. For a scenic shuttle voyage to the vessel, take Zodiac Corridor to Launchpad Indigo-Eight."*

Chekov saw an escape route.

"We have to upgrade. Spring for the premium boarding."

Dise balked. "That's going to photon torpedo our budget. Your dad—Ryjo's dad, I mean—didn't leave him *that* much."

He glanced ahead, where the Tellarites were still wrangling with the gate attendants. From what he could see, a supervisor had joined the increasingly heated discussion. The economy line was going nowhere fast.

"No choice. We're too exposed here. We have to get on the ship, on the double."

Taking her by the arm, he escorted her over to the much shorter and faster premium line, all while trying to act as inconspicuously as possible. Within minutes, and with the Tellarites still stubbornly bringing the other line to a near standstill, they faced a felinoid gatekeeper armed with a data slate and a handheld scanner.

"Appellations?" he asked officiously.

"Corcy bur Olfrud," Dise said, stepping forward. She tipped her head toward Chekov. "And my distinguished spouse, Sevoon mur Norder."

The attendant consulted his slate. His whiskers twitched.

"You're in the wrong line. This is for premium boarding only."

"We know," Chekov said. "We'd like to upgrade to premium boarding." He gestured toward the steadily growing economy line, which was moving only slightly faster than the congealed gelatin flows of Tanis X. "For obvious reasons."

"Are you certain, sir? There is a significant surcharge, which, to be clear, does *not* alter your accommodations aboard the vessel. Unless you also wish to upgrade to a luxury cabin?"

"Just the expedited boarding, please."

Chekov discreetly checked on the two Exiles, who were getting steadily closer to the boarding area for the *Quintessential*, although at a methodical, unhurried pace that suggested they were still looking for him, at least for the moment. He turned to Dise, anxious to hurry things along.

"If you don't mind, dearest?"

"My pleasure, sweetie." She extended her palm to the attendant. "Anything to get us on our way and off your poor, tired feet."

Chekov held his breath as the felinoid scanned her. The back-alley techno witch who'd hacked into their palm chips, overwriting the original data with false IDs (and matching credit accounts), had assured them that her work would hold up to all but the most exacting, high-level scans, but how could they be sure? This was a black market they were talking about, not the Starfleet Corps of Engineers. Chekov would've preferred to do the programming himself, but he'd been out of his element and lacking both time, tools, and resources. Better then to rely on a local talent who, in theory, was more familiar with Tykon tech and systems and actually knew what she was doing?

He hoped.

An electronic tone confirmed the transaction, along with Dise's assumed identity. The felinoid turned toward Chekov.

"If I can just verify your identity as well, sir?"

"By all means." He watched the Exiles wind their way through the terminal, getting far too close for comfort. *And make it quick, please.*

Another endless instant passed before a second tone finally allowed them access to a smaller, more exclusive transporter platform, where he positioned himself behind Dise at the rear of the platform. Peeking through an array of impatient passengers standing on the pads in front of him, he gulped as Broken-Antler turned his baleful gaze in their direction. Had the aggrieved Voyzr spotted him at last?

"Boarding will commence in ten seconds. Please remain still."

Chekov froze in place. Was that a gleam of recognition in the other buck's eyes? It was difficult to tell from the back of the transporter platform. Chekov was torn between looking more closely at his foe and turning his own face toward the illuminated transporter pad beneath his feet. Was it already too late to hide Ryjo's familiar face from his allies?

"Five seconds to boarding."

"Don't say I never take you anywhere," Dise snarked.

"Now boarding the Quintessential. *Enjoy your trip."*

The staticky tingle of a transporter beam broke his current corporeal form down to atoms.

But it failed to dissolve his worries.

Sixteen

"This is ridiculous," Kirk said. "I've taken on Klingons, Romulans, the Gorn, even 'God' not so long ago, and I trash my ankle playing racquetball?"

"Serves you right for playing cutthroat against two much younger crew members." McCoy applied a therapeutic brace to Kirk's injured right ankle in an examination room in sickbay, after previously treating the injury with a handheld physiostimulator. Kirk grunted as the doctor applied pressure to the tender area. "You're not as young as you used to be, Jim, whether you act like it or not."

"Thanks for the reminder, Doctor, but I simply landed the wrong way jumping after a tricky ball, that's all. Could happen to anyone at any age." The sudden sharp pain as he'd touched down hard on the court, badly rolling his ankle, had instantly served as a crucial damage report. "I can still climb El Capitan for Pete's sake."

"As I recall, you *fell* from El Capitan."

"Only because Spock distracted me."

"Regardless, those torn ligaments aren't going to heal overnight." McCoy stepped back from the examination table Kirk was perched on. "So take it easy for a while. Doctor's orders."

Kirk frowned. "How easy? I have responsibilities."

"Which you can carry out perfectly well from your chair or a desk. Just try to avoid putting too much stress on it, so don't push your luck in the gym . . . and no Gorn-wrestling without my say-so."

"Duly noted." Kirk gingerly pulled his boot back on, then

hopped off the table more energetically than advisable, biting back a gasp of pain as he placed his weight on both feet. The ankle in question felt better than it had before McCoy's expert doctoring, but it still smarted like the devil. "Anything you can do to speed the process along, Bones?"

"I can't just wave a magic wand and put everything right if that's what you're asking, at least not without risking unnecessary complications. In cases like this, it's often better to let the body heal itself naturally."

Not what Kirk wanted to hear, but he trusted McCoy's judgment on medical matters and knew better than to argue with him once the doctor had made his mind up. It wasn't as though he had any physically demanding activities coming up soon; he just needed to show the flag on Voyzr for the big peace celebration.

"All right, Bones. You've made your point. Now if you'll excuse me—"

An intercom whistled for his attention. *"Bridge to Captain Kirk,"* Uhura's voice announced.

He limped over to the wall unit, favoring his right foot.

"Kirk here."

"We've received an urgent distress signal from a nearby star system."

Kirk's own temporary infirmity suddenly became the least of his concerns. "Details?"

"None at present. Only a general distress signal, possibly automated."

"Acknowledged. I'll be right there." He contemplated the short hike to the nearest turbolift and braced himself in anticipation. "As soon as possible."

Ryjo suppressed a grin as Kirk hobbled onto the bridge, followed closely by Doctor McCoy, clucking after him like the proverbial mother hen. Word of the captain's unfortunate sports injury had already spread like a plasma cascade throughout the ship.

Lieutenant Jennifer Gavin, one of the two crew members Kirk had been playing against, had looked positively green when Ryjo had passed her earlier. For himself, Ryjo regretted he hadn't been on hand to personally witness the great Captain Kirk's embarrassing mishap.

Not that he allowed even a hint of satisfaction to show on his borrowed countenance as Spock surrendered the captain's chair to Kirk, who lowered himself into his customary seat somewhat more carefully than usual.

"Status?" Kirk asked. "Any updates on the nature of the emergency?"

"Negative, sir." Uhura adjusted her specialized earpiece. "Just your basic SOS, repeating on a loop. I have confirmed, however, that the signal does indeed emanate from somewhere in the Gilgio system."

On Spock's orders, the *Enterprise* had already slowed to impulse to avoid leaving the signal and its place of origin behind. They would need to reengage the warp drive to reach the Gilgio system in a timely manner. Even then, Ryjo estimated, it would take them roughly four days to reach the distress beacon, taking the *Enterprise* seriously off-course from Voyzr.

"Any vessels reported missing in that region?"

"Negative, Captain," she said. "Nor has any known vessel filed a flight plan through that vicinity."

"Acknowledged," Kirk said. "What do we know of this system, Spock?"

"Uninhabited, inhospitable, and relatively insignificant," the Vulcan reported from the science station. "Characterized by a notable lack of Class-M worlds, almost certainly because of the presence of a sizable gas giant dominating the system's habitation zone, precluding the development of more habitable worlds at a suitable distance from the system's sun. What other planets exist in the system are few and barren. In addition, the system lacks any strategic value or any unique resources, leaving it largely unexplored and unexploited to date. Most of our information on the region was obtained by long-range sensors and a few unmanned probes of less than recent vintage."

Kirk nodded. "Desolate and off the beaten track, in other words. Not somewhere you'd want to find yourself in dire straits."

"A cogent summation," Spock said, "which raises the question of why anyone would be visiting the Giglio system in the first place."

"Here's hoping we arrive in time to ask them," Kirk said, leaving unspoken the very real possibility that the automated distress signal had outlived those who had activated it. "Mister Chekov, set a course for the Giglio system."

Offal, Ryjo swore silently. His true mission did not include an unexpected detour to a lifeless system to rescue unknown parties who might already be beyond help.

"What about our mission to Voyzr, sir?" He schooled his features to remain professionally neutral. "We have little time to spare if we wish to arrive at the appointed hour."

"An unfortunate development," Kirk agreed, "but we have no choice. Who knows how many lives may be in jeopardy? That takes precedence over any purely ceremonial appearance, regardless of its diplomatic importance."

"Damn right," McCoy added.

Ryjo nodded, unable to argue the point. "Affirmative, Captain."

He could not fault Kirk's priorities, curse him, but found them personally inconvenient in the extreme. He hadn't assumed Chekov's place aboard the *Enterprise* to take part in an ill-timed search-and-rescue mission.

"Uhura," Kirk ordered, "keep trying to establish contact with whoever is at the other end of that signal and let them know we're on our way, just in case they can receive but not respond to our transmissions."

"Aye, Captain." She worked the communications control panel with practiced confidence and efficiency. "Shall I also notify Voyzr that we may be late to the embassy opening?"

"Not just yet. Inform Starfleet of the change in circumstances, but let's hold off on making our apologies to the regnant and her people. Perhaps we can still make it to Voyzr in time, depending on what we find waiting for us in the Gilgio system."

Please let it be so, Ryjo thought. In this at least, he and Kirk were on the same page.

"Course set for Gilgio system, at best possible speed."

Seventeen

"There she goes . . . again," Ryjo said. "All the way up into space."

A tremendous plume of volcanic ash and steam, visible against the blackness of space, blasted up from the moon's thin, smoky atmosphere as the shuttlecraft approached the obscure satellite, following the trail of the distress signal, which the *Enterprise* had traced to a particular moon orbiting that immense gas giant in the Giglio system. Wexx, as the moon was listed in Starfleet's database, was looking less and less inviting by the moment.

"I see it," Sulu replied from the helm of *Copernicus II*, its predecessor having been lost on Sha Ka Ree a couple years ago. "Flying into that fireworks show is going to be . . . interesting."

"To put it mildly."

Seated next to Sulu in the copilot's seat, Ryjo was glad to have Sulu at the helm. The man might be an enemy of his people and a potential threat to Ryjo's ongoing impersonation of Chekov, but Sulu's reputation as a pilot preceded him. If Ryjo *had* to take part in a risky Starfleet search-and-rescue mission, he couldn't be in safer hands than with Sulu flying the shuttlecraft.

Better him than me, Ryjo thought, *for all our sakes*.

A clearer picture of their ultimate destination had emerged once the *Enterprise* arrived at the Giglio system. Working together, Spock and Uhura had narrowed the location of the distress beacon to Wexx, which, much to Ryjo's private frustration, turned out to be singularly difficult to search in a time-effective manner, precluding any quick and easy resolution to the crisis. The moon's challenges included low gravity, an unbreathable atmosphere consisting mostly of sulfur dioxide, extreme temperatures, and violent geological activity, which Spock attributed to the moon's close proximity to the gas giant and its eccentric orbit thereof. At present, Wexx appeared to be going through some major volcanic throes, complicating the *Enterprise* crew's ability to determine the precise location of the beacon or even beam safely down to the surface. Dense clouds of smoke, ash, and more exotic materials shrouded the moon, interfering with the ship's sensors, while the space-high plumes erupting from beneath the global cloud cover made maintaining a standard orbit more hazardous than usual, forcing the ship to tread warily, shields raised. Hence the decision to send in a shuttlecraft instead, to pinpoint the source of the signal, determine the nature of the emergency, and, if necessary, care for and evacuate any survivors.

None of which got Ryjo any closer to Voyzr—and the regnant.

"I don't envy any poor souls stranded on that hellhole," Doctor McCoy observed from the passenger cabin behind the cockpit, where rows of seats lined the walls. A triangular hatchway allowed him a clear look at *Copernicus*'s wide cockpit window if he leaned out as far as his seat belts allowed. "Of all places to be in desperate need of assistance."

"That's what we're here for," Nurse Tovar said, seated beside McCoy. "I just hope we're not too late."

I suppose, Ryjo thought, *maybe*.

In actuality, a big part of him wanted to discover that they *were* too late, and that whoever sent the distress signal was long past saving, so that the *Enterprise* could get back en route to Voyzr. As it was, this rescue operation was becoming ever more complicated and time-consuming, and demanding much more of him personally than he liked or anticipated.

The team aboard *Copernicus* consisted solely of him, Sulu, McCoy, and Tovar, their numbers kept small to accommodate any injured or endangered individuals who might need to be flown to the *Enterprise* immediately. Kirk had wanted to lead the mission, naturally, but McCoy had argued strenuously that Kirk's injured ankle made traipsing around an unstable moon problematic. Not wanting his compromised mobility to hamper the operation, Kirk had grudgingly conceded the point and, with Spock best employed monitoring the moon's volatile geology from orbit, the captain had startled Ryjo by placing Chekov in charge of the mission.

Not what he had signed on for!

He'd been in no position to protest the assignment, of course. He could even see the logic behind the team selections: Chekov, all the better to track the signal to its source *and* deal with whatever security issues might arise, due to his status as security chief, along with his substantial background as an auxiliary science officer; Sulu, the ship's foremost pilot; and both a doctor and nurse to provide immediate assistance to any casualties. There'd been some brief discussion of adding an additional security officer to the party, but it was ultimately determined that Chekov and Sulu were probably sufficient to provide any needed security, especially since both McCoy and Tovar were also trained to deal with hostile circumstances. McCoy's service record, which Ryjo had studied extensively, documented that the doctor had survived more than his fair share of tough scrapes over the course of his career. Tovar's history was sketchier in this regard, as she had mostly worked in hospitals, both planetside and orbital, before heading out into deep space aboard the *Enterprise*, but her Starfleet training records suggested that she knew her way around a phaser as well as a hypospray.

Yes, it all made perfect sense, aside from the fact that he wasn't actually Chekov.

"Brace yourselves." Sulu lowered a heat shield over the front window, flying on instrumentation alone. "Entering the atmosphere now."

Copernicus plunged into Wexx's dense, smoky canopy, the shuttlecraft's own modest shields dialed up against any sudden plumes, shock waves, or flying debris. Atmospheric turbulence rocked the shuttle, justifying the safety straps binding the search party to their respective seats. For Ryjo, who had seldom ventured beyond the surface of Tykona, aside from a few stints working at an orbital casino or resort, the experience was far more unsettling than any practice session in a simulator. It was all he could do not to hold on to his seat with white knuckles, but as the real Chekov had doubtless endured many a bumpy flight before, he tried his best not to let his nerves show.

Just another day in Starfleet...

"What's the story with the signal?" Sulu raised the heat shield as they completed their rapid descent into the atmosphere and leveled out high above Wexx's surface. "Heading?"

Ryjo forced himself to concentrate on the illuminated display panel before him. He was hardly the science whiz Chekov was reputed to be, but he could operate a basic sensor array and tracking monitor well enough to zero in on an emergency beacon that was intended to be detected from deep space. As expected, the closer they got to the signal's source, the easier it became to distinguish its exact location.

"Heading ninety-seven mark one hundred."

Because Wexx rotated in sync with its orbit around the gas giant, known only as Giglio III, one side of the moon was forever facing the much larger world, whose reflected radiance shone through the smoke and ash blanketing the upper atmosphere. He squinted at the sensor bandwidth display on the control panel, which was fluctuating slightly.

"Can you go lower?" he asked. "Safely, I mean."

"That's a judgment call." Sulu divided his attention between the cockpit window and the instrumentation. "The lower our altitude, the greater the risk of a sudden eruption blowing high enough to impact us as we fly over it, but I guess going a little lower isn't going to skew the odds too much."

"*Too* much?" McCoy echoed. "Can't say I like gambling with life and limb. Don't forget, we can't help anybody if we get blasted out of the sky ourselves."

"There's an image I didn't need in my head," Tovar said. "Would it help if I crossed my fingers?"

Ryjo hoped McCoy's bedside manner was more reassuring than his unwelcome contributions as a passenger. He wasn't keen on getting himself killed in Starfleet's service either but figured that Chekov would not let himself be swayed by the doctor's habitual grousing. He needed to be decisive, stand by his command decisions, and take calculated risks in the line of duty, like a proper Starfleet officer.

"Just a bit lower," he instructed Sulu. "To get a better fix on the signal."

If nothing else, the sooner they located the beacon and dealt with this maddeningly ill-timed rescue, the sooner he could get back to his *real* mission.

"Works for me," Sulu said. "Here goes."

Copernicus dipped lower, then leveled out again at an altitude of roughly ten kilometers. They sped west, following the signal, soon passing over a large equatorial sea, which looked to have been formed by an icy comet strike ages past, before proceeding over solid land again. Ryjo thanked his ancestors that the beacon was not apparently deep underwater, emanating from some sunken vessel lost beneath the waves; that would have added a whole new level of complexity to an already difficult mission.

Topographical scans revealed vast plains broken up by towering peaks and plateaus, some as high as eighteen thousand meters. Deep ravines and hardened lava flows embellished the lifeless terrain, testifying to the moon's restless vulcanism. A sky-high plume erupted in the distance, hopefully too far away to pose any immediate threat. Swirling ash, ranging in hue from bright yellow to dull orange, obscured their view of their surface, but the signal was coming in stronger and clearer than ever. Ryjo adjusted the controls to filter out any remaining interference while silently thanking whatever Starfleet engineer had designed the apparatus to be so user-friendly.

"Getting warmer," he reported, deftly employing a human colloquialism. "We're practically on top of it . . . there!"

Sulu glanced over at the coordinates on the tracking monitor. "Got it. Heading in for a landing."

Sensors indicated the signal was emanating from what appeared to be a large, metallic structure—quite possibly a spacecraft—resting on a rocky plain at the base of a smoking volcano. Neither the rugged terrain nor the looming volcano made Ryjo eager to attempt a landing. Why couldn't they have found a nice, safe spaceport instead?

"We going to be able to touch down there?" he asked Sulu, half hoping they'd have to settle for simply surveying the situation from the air, or would that only prolong their mission? "Looks pretty rough and uneven."

"You're kidding, right?" Sulu looked askance at him. "You *have* met me?"

"Sorry," Ryjo said. "What I was I thinking?"

"Beats me." He smiled confidently. "Not to worry. I've landed ships and shuttles in worse places than this, as you well know. Remember that glacier on Kendall IV? Or that hungry bog on Bellefontaine?"

Ryjo faked a grin. "I withdraw the question."

The mottled, ocher surface of the plain came into view. Wind-blown ash limited visibility, so he couldn't make out a ship or other structure just yet, but sensors verified artificial alloys and an energy signature nearby . . . possibly half-buried beneath the surface? Contemplating the barren, inhospitable landscape below, Ryjo couldn't help wondering the same thing Spock had pondered earlier: Just what would bring anybody to this volcanic wasteland anyway?

An effort to communicate with the unseen structure elicited no answers. "Still no response to our hails," he said. "Just the same repeating signal."

"Any life signs?" McCoy asked.

"Checking." Ryjo recalibrated the sensors, kicking himself for not having already thought of that. Had anyone noticed his lapse, or had it gone unremarked in the urgency of the moment?

A trio of flashing green blips provided a further distraction, while also eliminating any last hope that there was no one left to rescue.

"Three life signs!" he announced, only partially feigning his excitement. Caught up in the task, he couldn't help feeling a rush of adrenaline, even as he concealed his disappointment that there was no chance of returning to the *Enterprise* empty-handed now. Life signs meant they were now committed to providing whatever emergency assistance was required.

"Thank heavens," McCoy blurted. "We're not too late after all."

"Nice work, Commander Chekov," Tovar said. "Good call back there."

"Thank you, Nurse."

He welcomed her vote of confidence, which eased his mind somewhat regarding her inclusion in the search party. Had he flinched inside when McCoy suggested bringing Tovar—of all people—along on the mission? Absolutely. But, as with Kirk putting him in charge, he could hardly object to including a qualified nurse in a rescue operation, even if the prospect of sharing close quarters with Tovar had worried him, considering their fraught interactions to date.

Thankfully, however, she had been nothing but cool and collected toward him so far, betraying no lingering distaste or animosity. It seemed she had no intention of letting any personal grudges or bruised feelings get in the way of them working together on this mission.

Let's hear it for Starfleet professionalism.

He dutifully notified the *Enterprise* of their status as Sulu brought *Copernicus* in for a landing. Vapor jetted from the thrusters, cushioning the impact as the shuttlecraft came to a rest on the irregular surface with only a bit of a wobble.

"Nice landing," Ryjo said, hiding his relief. "As usual."

Sulu winked at him. "O ye of little faith."

"Me?" Ryjo placed a hand over his heart. "Perish the thought."

He took a moment to contemplate the forbidding landscape visible beyond the forward window. Thick layers of fallen ash coated a rocky expanse strewn with boulders, dunes, ridges, and depressions. Blowing ash, along with the overcast sky, continued to limit visibility, although the base of the mountain, looming ominously in the near distance, could still be discerned through the smoggy, swirling, mustard-colored haze. Approximately twenty kilometers away, the churning volcano was still too close for Ryjo's comfort. He preferred his mountains nonsmoking.

"Not exactly a vacation spot." Tovar unbuckled her seat belt and came forward to take a closer look at Wexx through the cockpit window. "Makes Vulcan's Forge look like a resort on Wrigley's Pleasure Planet."

Ryjo had to agree. He suddenly felt far from home and very much out of his element. He was just a street kid from Jhopash, trying to make up for his wastrel ways. What was he doing leading a rescue mission in the shadow of an alien volcano?

"Well, let's not waste time gawking." McCoy retrieved his medkit from beneath his seat. "I don't want one of those life signs to go cold before we get to them."

"Point taken." He rose from the copilot's seat, acting as though he knew what he was doing. "Doctor, Nurse, you're with me. Sulu, watch over *Copernicus* while we investigate . . . and be ready to depart in a hurry if necessary."

"Acknowledged," Sulu said. "I'll keep the motor running, figuratively that is."

Wexx's hostile conditions necessitated donning environmental suits before exiting the shuttlecraft, which was going to slow them down even further. The suits were kept in storage compartments behind the seats in the passenger cabin. As *Copernicus* was not equipped with an airlock, the search party needed to be fully suited up, and the hatchway between the cockpit and the passenger area sealed off to protect Sulu, before any of the exit hatches could be opened. The shuttlecraft's interior would be repressurized upon their return.

Assuming all went well.

The lack of an airlock annoyed Ryjo. What had possessed Starfleet to sacrifice one just to free up more room for crew and cargo? He could only assume that some bigwig behind a desk somewhere had judged that shuttlecrafts were mostly for conveying passengers to and from Class-M worlds, and that transporters could handle any other circumstances.

Maybe not the right call, considering.

Putting on the cumbersome, multipart suit proved trickier than it looked, made harder by the fact that he had never practiced this in a simulator, only scanned the training manuals, because he'd never expected to have to do so on the way to Voyzr. At the time, back on Tykona, familiarizing himself with the bridge controls and operations had seemed a much better use of his time. He fumbled with the helmet, struggling to get it properly affixed to the neckpiece of the suit, which was not nearly as easy as the manual had made it sound. Would anybody find it odd if he reviewed the instructions posted inside the storage compartment?

"Need a hand with that?" Tovar had slipped into her own padded white suit much more gracefully, although she had yet to don her helmet. Heavy-duty gravity boots thudded against the deck as she clomped toward him, looking amused by his fumbling, although not in a vindictive way. More like the way Dise used to find his occasional screw-ups endearing . . . before the Exiles' cause came between them.

"If you don't mind." He sweated beneath both the EV suit and his uniform, worried as ever that his actual inexperience might draw suspicion. He offered her a feeble smile. "A bit rusty at this, I'm afraid. Guess I need a refresher course."

"It helps to put your gloves on *after* you put on your helmet."

She used her bare hands to help him guide the helmet into position and ensure that the seals were airtight. Filtered air began filling his lungs. A tinted visor impinged on his field of vision. He fought back a momentary attack of claustrophobia.

Just another day in Starfleet.

"There." She stepped back to admire her work, then put on her own helmet and gloves, in that order.

Ryjo tested the helmet's built-in comm system, using its heads-up controls to open up a private channel to her helmet. "Thanks for your assistance, Nurse Tovar . . . or Simone, if you prefer."

"Tovar is fine when we're on duty." Her visor largely concealed her face, but there was a touch of humor in her voice. "Bet you're glad I came along now."

"I never thought otherwise."

"Liar," she teased him.

A loud rumble penetrated the walls of shuttlecraft, and the deck abruptly rocked beneath them, causing them to stumble. He grabbed onto the edge of an open compartment and reached out to steady her. A few paces away, McCoy tottered and dropped his tricorder but managed to keep his balance as the rumbling abated and the deck settled uneasily back into place. Ryjo held on to the compartment and Tovar just in case *Copernicus* started shaking again. His heart racing, he magnetized his boots to keep from falling if this was only a brief respite.

"What in blazes?" McCoy exclaimed. "Sulu?"

"Not my doing," the pilot called out from the cockpit, which was not yet sealed off from the rest of the shuttlecraft. He consulted a display panel on the dashboard. "Just a mild seismic tremor, it looks like."

"Mild!" McCoy awkwardly rescued his tricorder from the deck; fortunately, they were built to withstand worse than slippery fingers. He shook his head in exasperation. "I knew there was good reason to leave the captain back on the ship. It'll be a miracle if we don't all end up on crutches . . . if we make it back at all."

Wary of aftershocks, Ryjo was tempted to abort the mission but knew that Chekov wouldn't turn back at this point, not with those enigmatic life signs at risk. Even McCoy, for all his grumbling, appeared no less determined to answer the distress signal. Tovar gently disengaged her arm from his grip.

"Thanks for the helping hand, Commander."

"Anytime, Nurse."

He took a deep breath of recycled air, still rattled by the tremor. On Tykona, you didn't have to worry about the ground acting up at any moment. Suppose another tremor struck while they were outside the ship? He didn't want to get swallowed up by a gaping chasm opening beneath him before he even reached Voyzr, let alone completed his mission. Dying here, as Chekov, would ruin everything and render his whole life pointless.

"What are we waiting for?" McCoy put on his own helmet. "Another damn moonquake?"

Not if I can help it, Ryjo thought. *The sooner we leave Wexx, the better.*

They ran a systems check on their suits, consuming more time, then sealed off the hatchway to the cockpit. A gust of air accompanied the search party as they exited *Copernicus* via the starboard hatch, which closed automatically behind them. They set off across the scabrous landscape, their heavy boots compensating for the low gravity. ID markers on their helmets, just above the visors, helped them tell each other apart. Peering through his own visor, Ryjo tracked the signal via a tricorder, while both McCoy and Tovar toted medkits. They moved carefully and deliberately to avoid stirring up the fallen ash any more than necessary. Harsh winds buffeted them, whistling shrilly through the audio receptors on their helmets and pelting them with grit. The cold light of the gas giant barely penetrated the heavy clouds far overhead.

"This way." He pointed northeast. "Keep close. We don't want to lose each other in the haze."

McCoy snorted. "Trust me, sightseeing is the last thing on my mind."

"You can say that again." Tovar stepped gingerly around a jutting slab of ash-dusted rock. The uneven terrain slowed them, forcing them to proceed with caution. She directed another private transmission to Ryjo: "This is not the walk in the park you promised me."

"Perhaps," he replied, unable to resist, "but don't say I never take you anywhere."

"Ha-ha."

A demanding hike finally brought them within sight of their destination: a tall, cylindrical spacecraft tilted to one side like a leaning tower. Twin nacelles flanked a tapered hull that resembled an old-fashioned rocket ship of the sort employed by many species in their first primitive attempts at space travel. Sleek, aerodynamic contours, now somewhat dented and pitted, and equally weathered fins indicated that the craft was designed for planetary landings and departures, the latter now made impossible by the fact that the bottom third of the ship was buried beneath a hardened mass of ash, rubble, and lava fragments; Ryjo surmised that a searing volcanic flow, racing down onto the plain at breakneck speed, had disabled the ship's thrusters long enough that the flow had cooled and set around them, locking the ship in place. Indeed, from the look of it, there may have been successive avalanches and lava flows after the initial surge. It couldn't blast off now without tearing itself apart, assuming that the thrusters were even operational and not thoroughly damaged or destroyed by the initial flow. Heavy layers of ash coated the trapped ship, confirming that it hadn't flown since some catastrophic eruption.

Which was when?

Ryjo looked past the ship at the mountain dwarfing them all. Thick, sulfurous fumes rose from the smoking crater at its crest. Peering through the haze, he could trace a patch of destruction back up the shattered face of the volcano, which was scarred by rockslides and lava flows. The recent tremor still fresh in his mind, he swallowed hard. Was it just his imagination or could he practically hear the volcano rumbling impatiently? How soon before it went off again?

"Well, I'll be," McCoy said, taking in the sight. He scanned the ship with a tricorder of his own. "Still reading three life signs." He turned toward Ryjo. "Any luck reaching them, now that we're right at their front door?"

Ryjo shook his head. "Not responding to hails."

Because why would anything on this mission go easily? Fate seemed to be conspiring against him.

"So now what?" Tovar asked.

Ryjo craned his head as far back as the EV suit permitted. The leaning ship was crowned with a cone; he assumed that was where the vessel's cockpit or bridge was. Increasing the magnification of his visor, he thought he glimpsed the outline of viewports—and maybe even a hatchway—beneath the concealing ash.

"We do this the hard way. Up we go, on the outside of the hull."

A sigh came over McCoy's mic. "I was afraid you were going to say that."

They clambered up the slope of the congealed volcanic debris until they reached an exposed section of hull stretching all the way to the top of the ship. Magnetizing their boots, they started up the side of the tilted spacecraft, leaving the buried portion behind. The slanted angle, possibly caused by the flows and avalanches slamming into the ship's base with great force, made their ascent somewhat less vertiginous than it might have been had the ship been entirely upright. Close up, the hull revealed more scorch marks, nicks, dents, and even one gaping tear about a quarter of the way up, its ragged edges unrepaired. Perhaps that entire level had been sealed off after the breach?

"This ship's taken a beating," McCoy observed, a few paces behind Ryjo. The older man was breathing heavily, the rasping noise audible over the comm line. "Let's hope the crew are in better condition."

The nacelles looked in bad shape as well, although the haze and layers of ash made it difficult to gauge the extent of the damage. No matter; chances were, this ship was never going to traverse the stars again. Good thing *Copernicus* could accommodate three more passengers.

Even with the low gravity easing the climb, Ryjo was also breathing hard, and missing his actual, younger body by the time they neared the top. The dusty outline of an ash-caked viewport attracted him. He started toward it, then froze as the helmet's audio receptors picked up a metallic clanging from *inside* the ship.

Someone signaling for his attention?

"I hear something! I think they know we're here!"

Probably heard our gravity boots thumping against the hull.

He rushed toward the noise, which was coming from right below the powdered viewport. Looking closer, he could just make out the seam of a hatchway under all the ash. His pulse sped up as he bent over and started wiping away the accumulated ash and grit with the palm of his glove, revealing the faint glow of an interior light filtering through the last layer of ash, which he swept away to expose:

A furry, bewhiskered face staring back at him!

Eighteen

". . . the pyroclastic flow came rushing down the mountain at a horrific speed. Imagine a glowing, red-hot avalanche of rock, ash, lava, gas, and steam, more than a thousand degrees Celsius. There was no time to fire up our engines, let alone take off, before it slammed into us. The sky went dark, blacker than night. Then came more rockslides and lava flows. The eruption went on for hours. It was terrifying. I thought we were going to die, but instead we were trapped, and still going to die, until you showed up!"

The habitat level of the *Whilom*, as the semi-entombed spacecraft was named, was cramped, aslant, and reeked of bodies and fur that hadn't been washed since the ship was disabled weeks ago. Sputtering lights testified that the vessel's batteries were running low. Ryjo's magnetized boots allowed him to keep his balance on the tilted floor, but the angle was still unsettling; he kept expecting to tumble forward or back, even with the artificial gravity turned off to conserve power. The pungent odor made him regret taking off his helmet after the search party was admitted to the ship, through an actual airlock no less.

Take that, Starfleet.

Boarding the ship, they'd discovered that the anonymous life signs belonged to the three-person crew of the *Whilom*, who had been confined to the topmost levels of the ship since the eruption, living on emergency rations and a single, straining food synthesizer that was also on its last legs. All three were Yarfites, a species of canine humanoids Ryjo was only vaguely familiar with. They were short in stature, the tallest of them standing only waist-high to Ryjo and the others, which he gathered was typical of their breed. Fitting them all into *Copernicus* was going to be no problem at all.

"But didn't you have any warning that an eruption was imminent?" Tovar asked.

She and McCoy had also removed their helmets in order to better communicate with the Yarfites, who had not required any urgent medical attention, suffering only varying degrees of malnutrition, dehydration, exhaustion, anxiety, and stress; these had been addressed via some appropriate hypospray injections, pending fuller checkups back on the *Enterprise*. Thankfully, there'd been no fatalities, which even Ryjo had been glad to hear. As frustrating as this whole rutting excursion was, he didn't begrudge the Yarfites a happy ending to their ordeal.

"On this moon?" Fressa, the ship's captain, scoffed. She was stocky and solidly built, with a flat muzzle, heavy jowls, and a pronounced underbite. Brindle fur needed grooming. Like her crew, she wore a rumpled, soiled coverall that hadn't been changed or laundered in too long. "If we took off every time there was a rattle or burp, we'd might as well never land at all."

"But I told you!" Bwoj insisted. Scruffy and excitable, he had a longer, pointier muzzle and had barely stopped yapping since Ryjo had first spied him through the viewport outside. Unable to sit still, he paced up and down the tilted deck. "You should have listened to me! I knew we were in danger!"

"You *always* think that." Fressa huffed on a vaporizer and expelled scented azure fumes through her nostrils. The fragrance did little to combat the stuffy atmosphere. "Is it my fault that for once you weren't fretting over nothing?"

"More to the point," said Dipelly, the first mate, "predicting the *when* of volcanic eruptions is not an exact science, especially on a world as seismically active as this one." Tall and rangy by Yarfite standards, with silky auburn fur, she appeared to be the crew's resident peacemaker and a welcome voice of reason, or at least that was

Ryjo's first impression. She leaned against a wall of storage lockers. "Were there tremors and venting prior to the mountain blowing up in a big way? Of course. This is Wexx after all, but was the blast going to occur in hours, days, weeks, months? There was no way to know for certain." She sighed philosophically. "In hindsight, we obviously called it too close."

You think? Ryjo thought. "If you don't mind me asking, what brought you here in the first place, and tempted you to stay too long?"

"That's what I'd like to know," McCoy said, as he packed up his medkit. He and Tovar were seated at a steeply inclined table that had been prudently bolted to the floor.

Fressa frowned. "That's our business."

"Not good enough," Ryjo said, annoyed by her attitude after all they'd gone through to rescue her and her crew. "Seems to me you've made it our business, and a hazardous one at that."

Not to mention keeping him from his true mission.

"Don't think we're not grateful!" Bwoj hurried to say. "It was only a matter of time before we starved or asphyxiated or worse. We should have never pushed our luck as far as we did, not with that volcano rumbling so close by. No treasure is worth dying for—"

"Shut your yap!" Fressa barked. "You want the whole quadrant to find out what we're up to?"

"Treasure?" Ryjo asked. "Is that what this is about, some sort of treasure hunt?"

"Wouldn't you like to know?" Fressa crossed her arms atop her chest, her protruding lower jaw lifting defiantly. "Forget it. We don't need any competition, from you or anybody else."

No wonder there had been no reports of a ship going missing in this region, Ryjo realized. The treasure hunters' paranoia and secrecy had come back to bite them when they ran afoul of the volcano. That they'd activated the distress beacon at all was a measure of just how desperate they'd become.

"Are you serious?" McCoy said, taking offense. "Starfleet is not in the business of profiteering, let alone claim-jumping. We're here to rescue you, responding to *your* distress signal. Would you prefer we turn around and leave you to your business, just to preserve your precious secrets?"

Fressa had the good sense to back down somewhat. "No, no, nothing like that. You have to understand, though. We've put a great deal of time, effort, and expense into this expedition. I don't want anybody else swooping in and claiming our prize when we're so close to finding it at last."

"What prize?" Tovar asked. "We're not out to steal from you, but yes, I would also like to know what's so valuable that we're risking our own hides to get you out of this fix."

Fressa dug in, glaring at Bwoj, who was visibly struggling to stay silent. "Not another word."

"But—"

"You heard me."

Dipelly stepped away from the lockers. "Give it up, Skipper. The expedition is over, at least for now. *Whilom* is lost. We couldn't recover the *Gale* if we wanted to, and I'm confident that we can count on these fine officers' discretion. The way I see it, we owe them some explanation after they saved us from our own recklessness."

"Yes!" Bwoj threw up his paws. "That's what I'm saying!"

"What is this, a mutiny?" Fressa huffed on the vaporizer. "Fine, but don't blame me if every scoundrel and salvage crew in the sector comes calling, looking to cash in on our hard work."

"Our lips are sealed," Ryjo said.

Fressa remained unconvinced. "And the official reports?"

Not my problem, Ryjo thought. "That's for our captain to decide, but I can't imagine he'd have any interest in disclosing your . . . trade secrets . . . to the galaxy at a large."

"That's assurance enough for me." Dipelly sat down at the table. "Have you ever heard of the *Stellar Gale*?"

Tovar perked up. "The long-lost treasure ship?"

Both Ryjo and McCoy looked at her in surprise. "You know about this?" the doctor asked.

"A little. Space mysteries have aways fascinated me, ever since I was a kid. Probably one of the reasons I joined Starfleet eventually, that and a midlife crisis of sorts. The *Stellar Gale* was a Therbian cargo ship, allegedly laden with ancient relics from an extinct alien civilization, that supposedly went missing centuries ago, in or around this sector, come to think of it. Treasure hunters, archaeologists, and amateur historians have been searching for it ever since . . . to no avail."

"Correct," Dipelly said, "but we have reason to believe that the *Gale* may have crash-landed on Wexx way back when. We've been quietly scouring the moon for months now, keeping a low profile to avoid attracting any competition, until our luck ran out, obviously."

Ryjo was intrigued, despite his own pressing concerns. "What evidence do you have that this lost ship is here?"

"More like a theory than hard evidence." Bwoj glanced nervously at Fressa before continuing. "But a comprehensive survey of the historical record turned up a hitherto-overlooked astronomical survey indicating that a vessel matching the *Gale*'s description may have taken a shortcut through the Jelasko Vortex, around the right period, which suggests that previous *Gale* hunters have been looking in the wrong direction all this time. So, if you run a new simulation, taking into account the prevailing solar winds, ion storms, orbital paths, and space-time ripples, along with that era's known trade routes, border disputes, and war zones, not to mention—"

"You get the idea," Fressa interrupted. "Bwoj may not know when to shut up, but he's done his homework, and I'm convinced we're on the right track." Her eyes lighted up. "You know, it's not too late to find the *Gale*. With the *Enterprise*'s help and resources—"

"Don't even think about it," McCoy said. "That's not going to happen."

"But it's not just about profit," Dipelly argued. "Think of the historical value of such a find. If it turns out, as we were coming to suspect, that the *Gale* is somewhere at the bottom of the equatorial sea—"

A tremor rattled the deck beneath them. McCoy's medkit bounced atop the table as everyone took hold of the nearest fixed rail, computer terminal, bunk, or tabletop. Any loose objects had already been secured by the Yarfites, no surprise. The quake lasted less than a minute but felt much longer. An aftershock from the previous quake—or a precursor to something even bigger?

Ryjo didn't want to find out.

"That's it. No more discussion. We're heading back to our shuttlecraft." He looked at the Yarfites. "Please tell me you have working pressure suits."

"Yes," Fressa said, "but—"

"Save it until we're all safely back on the *Enterprise*."

"All right," she said, the tremor having shaken some of the stubbornness out of her. "Just give us time to salvage all our charts and data."

"Way ahead of you." Dipelly produced a microtape from a pocket of her coverall. "It's not as though I haven't had time on my hands since we were stranded here."

Ryjo appreciated her foresight since it meant one less thing to haggle about. Acutely aware that another quake—or worse—could strike at any moment, he hurried things along as the Yarfites suited up and the search party redonned their helmets. The process still took longer than he liked, but they soon left the *Whilom* behind and started back toward *Copernicus*. Ryjo led the way at a rapid clip, while Tovar followed at the rear to ensure nobody strayed or got left behind.

"On our way back," he updated Sulu, whom they'd kept informed of their progress throughout. "Prepare for immediate departure."

"Make it snappy," Sulu replied. *"I'm picking up some pretty alarming seismic readings. We're talking swarms of mini-quakes beneath the surface, and rapidly building pressure inside the mountain."*

"Preaching to the converted." Ryjo glanced back at the volcano.

Venting steam had given way to thick, roiling clouds of ash, which began falling like snow. Lightning, caused by static electricity, flashed inside the clouds. Rockslides could be heard in the distance. You didn't need to be a xenogeologist to guess that the clock was ticking. He opened a line to the entire party, including the Yarfites. "Step on it, people. Time is safety."

"All right, all right," McCoy grumbled. "We're coming."

"Not fast enough," Ryjo said. "Pick up the pace, all of you. Let's get the hell off this moon while we still can."

"Aye, aye, sir." Tovar switched over to their private line. "Nicely handled back on there on the ship, by the way. You showed those fractious relic hunters who was boss, without even pulling a phaser."

"Just doing my duty."

"Well, consider me impressed."

Uh-oh. Ryjo hoped things wouldn't get complicated again if and when they returned to the *Enterprise*. His cover was probably more secure when she wanted nothing to do with him socially.

None of which mattered if they were all wiped out by an erupting volcano. The ashfall was coming down more heavily now, darkening the sky and making it harder to see even with his helmet's searchlight turned up to full. Wading through powdery accumulations of ash made a punishing hike ever more arduous. Hustling the party along as fast as he could, without acting too frantic for a seasoned Starfleet officer, he sighed in relief as, through the murky haze, he spied the *Copernicus* ahead, still waiting for them.

Thank you, Sulu.

He had to give the pilot credit. A lesser person would have already taken off by now, saving themselves rather than sticking around next to a rumbling volcano, but that wasn't the Starfleet way, it seemed. Ryjo wasn't sure he'd do the same in Sulu's place.

Something to think about later, perhaps.

"Almost there!" he encouraged the others. "Just a bit farther—"

The ground bucked beneath him, throwing him off his feet.

He crashed to the surface, amidst a blinding cloud of ash and the clamorous gnashing of subterranean plates. The quake tossed him about as though he was a Rigelian jumping pod, making it impossible to scramble to his feet. It was like trying to rise from a bouncing trampoline. Fear and rage jolted him as well. The sheer unfairness of it all, of Wexx ambushing them just as they were on the verge of escaping, was so perfectly cruel that he really should have seen it coming.

Just like the universe to screw him over one last time!

Then the shaking subsided. A gloved hand reached down through the thick yellow haze and helped him to his feet.

"You okay?" McCoy asked.

"I think so." A hasty inspection revealed that his body and, more crucially, his EV suit had not sustained any critical damage, just some minor scuffs and scratches, possibly due to the heavy ash cushioning his fall. "The others?"

"Just shaken up it looks like. Is it just me or are these damn quakes coming faster and harder?"

"Not just you." Ryjo brushed off his suit. "Everyone in the shuttle, now!"

He didn't need to repeat himself. Throwing caution to the whistling winds, the party sprinted toward *Copernicus*, its aft hatchway already opening to receive them. They dashed up the boarding ramp into the depressurized passenger area; the cockpit remained sealed off to protect Sulu from Wexx's toxic atmosphere.

"*Everyone aboard?*" Sulu asked via the comms.

Ryjo did a quick head count, just to be safe. "All accounted for." The ramp retracted as the hatchway closed. He caught a last glimpse of the smoking volcano before the hatch shut completely. Forget depressurizing the passenger cabin, he decided. They could do that later, after they were safely clear. "Get us out of here!"

"*My thoughts exactly. Buckle in! We're taking off!*"

And none too soon; he barely had time to strap himself into a seat, next to Tovar as it happened, before *Copernicus*'s thrusters ignited and the shuttlecraft lifted off. The sudden acceleration tested the shuttle's inertial dampeners, jolting Ryjo, who had to resist an urge to grab onto Tovar's hand for reassurance. *Copernicus*'s nose turned skyward, away from the moon's agitated surface.

Had they made it? Were they clear of Wexx at last?

A thunderous blast drowned out everything, including his own thoughts and a gasp. A shock wave slammed into *Copernicus*, sending it spinning out of control. Heavy objects smashed against the shuttle's shields, a barrage of flying debris battering the hull despite the deflectors. Images of granite boulders and lava bombs, as large or larger than photon torpedoes, striking the shuttle flashed through Ryjo's panicked brain with every titanic bang and impact. They hadn't outrun the volcano in time.

It had blown again—with a vengeance.

Screams and shouts filled his helmet, even as his ears rang from the cataclysmic explosion. He seized Tovar's gloved hand, who squeezed his right back. *Copernicus* spun on its axis, making him nauseous, then began to level out again. Had Sulu regained control of the shuttle? Ryjo experienced a fleeting moment of hope before *Copernicus* tilted downward and plunged back toward the surface, captured by gravity.

"*We're going down!*" Sulu announced at high volume. "*Brace yourselves! I'm trying for a water landing!*"

The equatorial sea, Ryjo realized. The one they'd flown over before, that might have claimed the *Stellar Gale* centuries ago. Was *Copernicus* about to meet the same fate—if the shuttlecraft could even make it to the sea before it crashed?

"*Hang on!*" Sulu said. "*Here we go!*"

The shuttle dived headfirst toward—what?

Nineteen

"Captain!" Uhura called out. "We've lost contact with *Copernicus*."

Alarmed, Kirk sprang from his chair. A sharp, stabbing pain forcefully reminded him of his injured ankle, and he sat back down again, no less distressed by the news.

"And the landing party?"

Uhura worked her control panel. "I'm trying to reach their individual communicators, but . . . no response so far."

"Damn it," Kirk said. Last they'd heard, McCoy and the others had successfully located a trio of marooned Yarfites and were escorting them to the shuttlecraft with all deliberate speed. In theory, they should have been on their way back to the *Enterprise* by now. "I knew I should have gone with them."

"In which case," Spock observed from the science station, "we would now be concerned for your safety as well."

"Flawless logic, Mister Spock, but cold comfort at the moment." Kirk pivoted the chair toward his first officer. "What about our sensors? Can you get a fix on the shuttle?"

"Not a present," Spock said gravely. "Wexx's turbulent atmosphere, blanketing the moon with dense, energetic clouds of particulate matter, continues to pose a challenge for our sensors." He peered into the science viewer, expertly manipulating the dials at its side. "However, I am detecting a geological event of substantial magnitude dangerously near the site of the rescue operation."

The volcano, Kirk grasped. Both Spock and Sulu had predicted that an eruption was likely imminent. Had *Copernicus* managed to take off in time?

"Life signs?"

"Undetected," Spock said, "which is inconclusive due to the sensor issues already noted, now exacerbated by an excess of atmospheric contamination and activity in the affected area."

"Keep looking, Spock. Scan the entire moon if you have to, inside and out." Kirk shifted uneasily in his chair, frustrated and anxious. "I need to know what's become of our people . . . and those stranded civilians."

"Acknowledged," Spock said. "Diverting more power to primary and secondary sensor arrays."

Kirk knew he could count on Spock to find out as much as he possibly could with the technology available to them. "And keep your ears open, Uhura, on all frequencies."

"Absolutely, sir." Worry showed on her face as she applied herself to the task with her customary focus and expertise. "It's only been a few minutes. Perhaps they'll reestablish contact once they're clear of the atmosphere?"

"From your lips, Commander . . ."

McCoy, Sulu, Chekov, Tovar, and three endangered strangers to boot. Kirk held on to hope, not about to mourn any of them just yet. Spock was right. This could just be a sensor issue. *Copernicus* could check in at any moment.

As minutes dragged on, however, with no word from the missing crew members, Kirk was sorely tempted to dispatch another shuttlecraft to search for *Copernicus*, but would that merely endanger more of his people? He fought the impulse to ask Uhura for another update. She would doubtless inform him the instant she had anything new to report.

Likewise, Spock and the others.

Wanting desperately to do *something*, Kirk stared grimly at the shrouded, unstable moon on the viewscreen. Immense, umbrella-shaped plumes of ash and smoke and debris kept shooting up from

Wexx's churning yellow atmosphere, blossoming above the moon like the atomic mushroom clouds of yesteryear. The erratic, unpredictable plumes had yet to impact the *Enterprise*, bursting only before, behind, or below their orbit around Wexx, but the shields were dialed up in case the ship found itself in the wrong place at the wrong moment. Was that what had happened to *Copernicus* and its passengers? He couldn't rule out that ghastly possibility. Wexx was a geological minefield that may have already claimed the lives of seven people, including some of his nearest and dearest.

No, Kirk thought. *I refuse to accept that, not without proof.*

"Captain," Spock addressed him.

His somber tone alerted Kirk that the news was not good. He knew Spock well enough to register that despite the Vulcan's stoic demeanor; subtle variations in Spock's manner, which might be lost on those less acquainted with him, came across clearly to Kirk.

"What is it?" He braced himself for the worst. Had Spock detected wreckage or, worse yet, proof of death? "Have you found *Copernicus*?"

"Negative, but the most recent comprehensive scans of Wexx, as best we can manage, point to an extremely dire conclusion: The eruption at the rescue site was just the beginning. Similar seismic events are occurring all across the moon, with escalating frequency and severity, connected to a vast underground magma system."

"Which means?"

"By all indications, pressures within Wexx are rapidly building toward a super-eruption of global proportions, capable of devastating continents and reshaping the entire surface of the moon."

Gasps and exclamations greeted Spock's announcement. "Oh, no," Uhura whispered loud enough for Kirk to hear. Similar sentiments could be heard across the bridge.

Kirk didn't blame his crew for reacting in dismay. "That bad?"

"Were Wexx not already lifeless, the impending super-eruption would accurately be categorized as an extinction-level event."

Kirk took a moment to process what Spock was saying. "So even if the landing party is still alive on Wexx, they don't stand a chance once that super-eruption occurs?"

"Captain," Spock said gravely, "I cannot guarantee our *own* survival."

Twenty

Am I too late?

Heart pounding, head throbbing, feeling sick to your stomach, you hurry up the stairs at the back of your father's barbershop to the all-too-humble lodgings above the shop. Trath mur Damva and a few other Exiles are waiting at the top of the stairs, muttering darkly amongst themselves. Trath subjects you to a withering look, making no secret of his disdain.

"About time you got here."

Ordinarily you wouldn't care a microbe what Trath and his fellow relics think, but this morning is different. This time it stings.

Because you know you deserve their scorn.

"I'm sorry. I only just got the news." You've spent the night in a detention cell, after getting into a brawl at Insomnia while high on stim and cheap Nausicaan happy juice. Bloodshot eyes, rumpled club gear, a busted nose, and a brutal hangover attest to yet another wasted night spent partying and getting into trouble. "Please tell me I'm not too late."

"Only just." Trath steps aside to let you pass. "He's been asking for you."

You wince, imagining your father calling out in vain for his wayward son. You push past the scowling old stags and, bracing yourself, slip into your father's bedroom, just off the landing. The modest chamber smells like a medbay, chemical disinfectants overlaying the stink of sweat, waste, and sick. The ratty curtains are drawn, the shutters closed, to grant Kletz mur Zimble some privacy and dignity in his final hours, shielded from the uncaring bustle and racket of the city streets. He's propped up in his bed, looking older and frailer than ever. You can hear his labored breathing from across the room.

"Ryjo, my boy," he wheezes. "You're here . . ."

"Yes, Dad." He rushes to his father's side. "I came as fast as I could, I promise."

A traditional Voyzr healer, clad in a ceremonial grass robe, is already in attendance. She looks at you and shakes her head dolefully.

"What happened?" you ask.

You knew your father wasn't well, hadn't been so for some time, but how had he declined so quickly, practically overnight?

"He took a sudden turn for the worse," the healer says, not unkindly. "It happens."

You refuse to accept that. "We need to get him to a hospital."

"No," your father protests as forcefully as he can manage, coughing and hacking all the while. "It's my time. I just wanted to see you once more, despite everything."

Every breath sounds like it could be his last. You take his hand, afraid to squeeze it too hard for fear of breaking it. It feels hot, feverish, and skeletal: dry, papery skin stretched tight over fragile bones. He seems to be wasting away before your eyes.

"I'm here, Dad. I'm here for as long as you need me."

You and your father have clashed frequently over the last few years, over politics, your lifestyle, your choices, your friends, his friends, pretty much everything, really, but none of that seems to matter now, not at the end.

"Ah, but look at you, what you've become." Rheumy eyes scrutinize you, taking in your disheveled, disreputable appearance. Tears leak from eyes, streaming past his silvered snout. "Instead of what you should be."

Shame and guilt hit you harder than any hangover. The smell of spilled happy juice clings to your soiled clothing like the stench of failure. You know what your father sees when he looks at you: a huge, rutting disappointment.

"I'm sorry, Dad. I didn't mean to let you down." You choke up, hot tears stinging your own eyes. "Forgive me."

"No, no!" He grows agitated, struggling to get the words out. "Forgive *me*, my son. I failed you. We all failed you, years ago. Cost you your homeworld, your rightful place and destiny..."

Coughs rack his feeble frame as you realize, to your horror, your father blames *himself* for your many shortcomings. That he's carried this guilt for who knows how long, all the way to his deathbed.

Somehow this is a hundred times worse than any final rebuke...

"Chekov?"

A hand gently rocked his shoulder, waking him. Dise peered into the upper bunk where he'd been dreaming. She stood beside the bed, dimly visible in the soft blue glow of a nightlight.

"Are you all right?" she asked. "What's the matter?"

He blinked in confusion, coming back to reality from... Ryjo's father's deathbed? The emotional scene, laden with crushing guilt and shame and anguish, clung to him even as he lifted his head, orienting himself. He switched on an overhead reading light, illuminating his bunk and exposing Dise's worried face, close enough that he could feel her breath, scented by the spiced twigs she was always chewing on. He wasn't sure why she'd woken him, but he was glad to leave that painful bedside vigil behind.

Their budget cabin aboard the *Quintessential* made Dise's compact apartment in Jhopash seem roomy. A foldout bed above the lower bunk had spared them the awkwardness of squeezing into the same sleeping space, with Chekov chivalrously taking the top bunk, which had just enough head room to accommodate his antlers... barely. Standing on the outer edge of her bunk, gripping the molded metal edge of his, she regarded him with concern. An oversized, cheaply fabricated shirt, bearing the logo of a Tykon theme park, served as sleeping attire. Doe eyes reflected the glow of the reading light.

"What is it?" he asked groggily. "Is something wrong?"

"You tell me. You were tossing and turning and groaning in your sleep. And muttering in Voyzr no less."

"Ah, sorry about that." He rolled over to face her. "Just a bad dream . . . and not even my own dream at that."

She gave him a puzzled look. "What do you mean by that?"

He hesitated, uncertain whether she wanted or needed to hear this, but decided they'd already come too far together to hold out on her now.

"I think I was dreaming about something from Ryjo's past. His last encounter with his father." Chekov's throat tightened. "A sick, elderly Voyzr dying in a room above a barbershop."

Dise inhaled sharply.

"You mean when his dad begged Ryjo, tears running down his face, to forgive him for losing Voyzr back in the day." Bitterness sharpened her voice. "Yeah, that really messed Ryjo up. It's when everything started going wrong, for him and us. I tried to help him through it, but it was no use. He was determined to make his dead dad proud of him, even though the poor old guy was well past caring. He let his dad's Exile buddies get into his head and spin him all around, convince him that he owed it to his dad's memory to take up their cause." She rolled her eyes. "And here we are, rushing across space to stop him from committing some sort of rutting insanity in his father's name."

Whatever it might be, Chekov thought. Unfortunately, Dise was not in the loop when it came to what exactly the Exiles were plotting. She could only confirm that they were endlessly bitter over losing Voyzr—and obsessed with getting revenge on the global regime that had "stolen" their homeworld from them. Perhaps by sabotaging the embassy opening, which the regnant herself was expected to attend? Maybe staging an attack on the regnant, Captain Kirk, or the peace celebration itself?

"We all failed you, years ago. Cost you your homeworld, your rightful place and destiny . . ."

Chekov felt a pang of sympathy for Ryjo after experiencing that wrenching scene through the other man's eyes. He wasn't ready to forgive Ryjo for stealing his body and his identity, not in the slightest, but he understood Ryjo better now and what was driving the grieving buck to carry out such an extremist agenda. Certainly, Ryjo wouldn't be the first troubled, rootless young person to be radicalized by a tragic loss and a future that seemed to offer few prospects.

Like Irina, he thought, *and Doctor Sevrin's other followers.*

"But I don't understand," Dise said. "How can you be dreaming about Ryjo's past? I thought his mind was in your body and vice versa?"

"It's not that simple. I'm no expert on 'life-entity transferences,' but my understanding is that there's a degree of, I don't know, psychic entanglement involved. We're connected somehow, subconsciously, telepathically, maybe even metaphysically, with some part of Ryjo's psyche still imprinted on his brain and neural pathways. Back when Doctor Lester switched bodies with Captain Kirk"—an incident he had told Dise about when he'd first tried to convince her that he wasn't really Ryjo—"their minds began to shift back and forth as the transference started to reverse itself. That hasn't happened to me yet, I haven't suddenly found myself back in my own body for a moment, but I do sometimes get flashes of Ryjo in my head. Memories, images, feelings."

"About me?" she asked.

"Occasionally," he admitted. "For what it's worth, you made a big impression on Ryjo. His feelings for you run deep."

In his brain, in his body.

"Oh, I see."

An awkward pause ensued. Chekov found himself acutely aware that he was alone in the night, and sharing confidences, with the lovely doe—Ryjo's former lover no less. How much of his growing attraction to her came from Ryjo and how much of it was perfectly natural on his part? Certainly, Dise was smart and sexy and vibrant enough to pique any man's interest, especially under the circumstances. What was Ryjo thinking, choosing the Exiles over this woman?

But what about Simone Tovar?

He felt a twinge of guilt for thinking this way about Dise instead, although it wasn't as though there was actually anything serious between him and Tovar just yet; that romantic connection was mostly hypothetical at this point, so he was hardly betraying Simone by also being attracted to Dise, for extenuating reasons. As a celebrated Russian lyricist once said, when you're not with the one you want, want the one you're with.

And all the more so when you're not even you, lying in bed wearing nothing but a pair of synthetic trunks and another man's pelt?

"My apologies for waking you," he said finally.

"Not to worry. I wasn't getting much sleep anyway."

He couldn't miss the melancholy in her voice. "Want to talk about it?"

"Maybe," she said. "It's stupid, though. I mean, Ryjo and I aren't even together anymore. His doing, not mine. And now he's up to his antlers in all this Exile craziness, mixed up with Trath and his fanatics, who are serious bad news. I ought to be glad to be rid of him. Wash my hands and walk away."

"But?"

Her eyes grew moist. "I worry about him, you know. We go way back, have been through a lot together, good and bad." She wiped her eyes with her hand. "And I just rutting miss him."

Chekov tried to comfort her. "He misses you too, very much."

"You can feel that, really?"

"Yes."

Painfully so, at this very moment.

"I'm sorry he's not here to tell you that himself." He attempted to lighten the tone. "Not that I object to enjoying your company in his place, mind you. Thank goodness his subconscious led me to you; I don't know what I would have done without your brilliant assistance. Ryjo did me a big favor by being unable to forget you."

"That's something I guess." She smiled wanly. "As faux Ryjos go, you're not so bad yourself, Pavel Chekov. For a mentally displaced human, that is."

"High praise indeed."

"You bet it is." A thoughtful look came over her face and she nodded to herself, as though making a decision. "In fact . . ."

Grasping the handholds to one side of the bunks, she climbed into bed with him. "Scoot over."

"Er, what are we doing here?"

"Like I said, I can't sleep." She snuggled up next to him. "And I miss those arms around me . . . among other things."

He knew just what she meant, in a way. He couldn't help feeling the heat and promise of her lying next to him, warm and inviting. He was only human, or Voyzr, or some combination thereof. But should they be doing this?

"I'm not him," he reminded her.

"I know." She nuzzled his neck, provoking feelings both new and strangely familiar. Velvety limbs entangled him. "Just let me pretend . . ."

Twenty-One

Oasis Station was an independent deep-space station, jointly operated and subsidized by a consortium of regional systems and commercial interests, that served as a hub for interstellar travel throughout the sector. Chekov and Dise watched from Oasis's observation deck as a private yacht approached the station's docking ring a few levels below. The yacht was a streamlined, copper-colored ellipsoid maybe twice as a large as a standard Starfleet shuttlecraft.

But not remotely Starfleet, alas.

"No good?" Dise asked.

"I doubt it."

A mounted display panel listed all the vessels docked, expected, or departing Oasis at present. According to the display, the yacht, named *Xoline*, was registered out of Wuvoga III, a notorious haven for smugglers, pirates, fugitives, and dissolute expatriates fleeing scandal and/or prosecution. Hardly the sort who might be inclined to help him alert Starfleet or the *Enterprise* to an imminent threat.

"So much for that idea." She leaned against him, reflecting their newfound intimacy, and nibbled on a bar of moss-flavored taffy she'd picked up aboard the cruiser. "Worth a shot, I suppose."

The *Quintessential* was temporarily docked at Oasis to take on or unload passengers transferring from one ship to another; the cruiser was also taking advantage of the station's facilities to restock, refuel, and perform any necessary maintenance. Meanwhile, passengers like Chekov and Dise, who were continuing on to Voyzr, could disembark and sample Oasis's varied amenities during the layover.

He'd hoped a Starfleet vessel, or at least a Starfleet-adjacent ship, might be docked at Oasis, so he could try to send a priority subspace communique to Starfleet, or perhaps even catch a ride to chase after the *Enterprise*. Unfortunately, they were well beyond the Federation's jurisdiction, and Starfleet had no real presence in this neck of the galactic woods. The odds of finding a Starfleet ship at Oasis had always been a long shot.

"Time to try another tack," he said. "Wish me luck."

She squeezed his hand. "Go get 'em, stag."

The station's security office was one level up from the observation deck. He felt a flicker of apprehension as they approached it, recalling his frustrating encounters with the police on Tykona, but he was determined to get the message across this time, even if that meant fudging the truth a bit. Dise, who had her own reasons to be leery of law enforcement, stayed outside, playing lookout just in case the Exiles' reach extended to Oasis.

"Can I help you?" a gray-skinned humanoid asked from behind a counter. A scarlet sash distinguished Oasis's security forces from the station's other personnel, who also sported crisp tan uniforms. A name badge identified him as Sergeant Zagulla.

"I hope so. I need to report a criminal conspiracy posing an immediate threat to an upcoming diplomatic function on Voyzr."

"You don't say." The sergeant raised an eyebrow. "Well, that's something I don't hear every day. What kind of conspiracy?"

"I don't know all the details," Chekov said honestly, "but I have good reason to believe that radical Voyzr terrorists have placed an undercover agent on the *Starship Enterprise* as part of a plot to disrupt the opening of a Federation embassy on Voyzr."

"I see." The sergeant looked Chekov over, his expression professionally neutral. His gaze lighted briefly on Chekov's antlers while he tapped away at a control panel behind the counter. "And you know this how?"

Careful, Chekov thought. *Nothing about life-entity transferences this time. You're just a concerned citizen tipping off the authorities to a dangerous extremist plot.*

"I have friends and associates who run in the same circles as some of the conspirators. One of them let slip what was up, thinking I shared their political sympathies." He strove to look conflicted. "Which I do, more or less, but I draw the line at terrorism. I don't want to inform on anyone, but I can't in good conscience keep this information to myself. I needed to report it to someone, quietly if possible."

The sergeant maintained his poker face. "This isn't a Federation starbase, or a Voyzr one for that matter. What exactly do you expect us to do with this information?"

"Contact Starfleet, or the *Enterprise*, or the relevant authorities on Voyzr. Just pass the warning along so they can take action as needed. That's all I'm asking."

"Hmm." The sergeant peered at a terminal below the counter, situated so the display was not visible to Chekov. "Speaking of Starfleet, I see that they sent out an alert last week, about someone impersonating a Starfleet officer."

"Really?" Chekov's heart leapt. Had Ryjo already been exposed? He should have known that Captain Kirk and the others would see through the deception. "That's just what I'm saying. There's an imposter aboard the *Enterprise*, posing as Commander Pavel Chekov."

The sergeant shook his head. "Uh-uh, that's not what the alert says. Just that there was some shady young troublemaker running around Tykona, claiming to be this Chekov person." He eyed Chekov suspiciously, his expression sliding from neutral to hostile. "What is your name, sir? And where exactly do you hail from?"

"Is that necessary? I would prefer to remain anonymous."

"Your name, please," the sergeant said, more sternly.

"Er, Sevoon mur Norder. From Voyzr, obviously."

The sergeant squinted at him, as though trying to penetrate his disguise. Chekov feared Ryjo's mug shot was gracing the sergeant's computer terminal as they spoke, and that Zagulla would soon discover that "Sevoon" had just arrived from Tykona, if the sergeant hadn't called up that information already.

"Are you certain of that, sir?"

Chekov didn't like how this was going. With that Starfleet alert poisoning the waters, he wasn't sure how he was going to convince Zagulla—or anyone else—that he was the real Pavel Chekov without invoking the body-swap, which was a proven nonstarter.

"Yes, of course. How could I not know my own name?" *Don't answer that,* he thought. "May I ask if you intend to pass my report on to the proper authorities, as you see fit?"

"Tell you what, why don't we take this into the back," the sergeant said, not answering Chekov's question. Two more guards emerged from the rear of the security office, no doubt summoned electronically. "Where we can ask you a few more questions about what precisely you think you're up to here."

Chekov did not see anything positive coming from that interview.

"Never mind." He backed up toward the exit. "I've done my part. You can take it from here."

"Hold on!" The sergeant beckoned to the other guards, who started toward Chekov. "We're not done here."

Chekov begged to differ. He darted out of the office into the busy corridor outside, where Dise leaned against a wall, still chewing on the taffy. Visitors and station personnel streamed past them in both directions. Antigrav lifters conveyed luggage, cargo, and supplies across Oasis. Hover-scooters assisted those who preferred riding to walking, due to age, infirmity, a proclivity for lower-gravity environments, or simply a desire to rest their legs.

"What is it?" Dise sprang from the wall, instantly picking up on his hasty exit. "Didn't go well?"

"Move!"

He grabbed her by the hand and they dashed down the teeming corridor, even as the red-sashed guards burst from the office, looking about for him. Heavy foot and lifter traffic provided a welcome degree of concealment as they wove through the crowd, exploiting whatever cover was available. They hurried as quickly as they could without obviously fleeing, while apologizing for cutting in front and between people.

"Sorry. Excuse us. Coming through."

With luck, people would assume they were just rushing to make a scheduled departure, or so Chekov hoped. Were the red-sashes actually pursuing them? He had no idea and was in no hurry to find out. It occurred to him that the one good thing about being far outside the Federation's borders was that Oasis's security forces might not be too motivated to apprehend him on the UFP's behalf. A delinquent Voyzr passing himself off as some random Starfleet crew member was not their problem; at most, he was only guilty of wasting their time with a bogus story, which, Chekov feared, was almost certainly not going to be communicated to the *Enterprise*.

Mission unaccomplished.

Packed ramps and escalators brought them down to the docking ring, where they sought refuge in a public meditation lounge offering a serene escape from the hubbub of the station. Low lighting, tinted partitions, and white noise generators created a peaceful sanctuary for weary travelers, fortuitously cut off from the circular corridor outside. Chekov and Dise nestled into a secluded nook at the rear of the lounge, as far out of sight as possible.

"Let me guess," she said in a low voice. "They didn't give you a medal for doing your civic duty?"

"Far from it." He glanced around to make certain no one was eavesdropping before filling her in on his less than productive visit to the security office. "I have to give the Exiles credit; they've done a good job of discrediting me in advance. We can write off anybody outside the *Enterprise* taking me seriously."

"And on the *Enterprise*?"

"I like to think I can make my case, given a chance. Like I did with you."

She nodded. "Because they know the real you that well."

"Exactly." He shrugged. "And, if that doesn't work, a Vulcan mind-meld can always settle matters."

"Can't say I like the idea of somebody poking around in my brain." She shuddered at the thought. "But I suppose that's old hat for you."

He thought of Khan, Gorgan, the Zetarians, the Beta XII-A entity, and his present situation. "You have no idea."

"So now what?" she asked.

"Let's get back to the cruiser. I'm not sure how hard they're looking for me, but the sooner we're back in our cabin the better."

And then hope against hope that the *Quintessential* made it to Voyzr in time . . .

Warily, they exited the lounge and made their way back toward the boarding area for the cruiser, ducking out of sight whenever they glimpsed a red sash. Chekov noted with some relief that no alarms or alerts were sounding, which led him to hope that Oasis did not consider him a major security issue. It was entirely possible, in fact, that they might prefer to let him slip away on the next ship leaving the station, making him no longer their problem. Ryjo was just a petty criminal after all, not the sector's most wanted.

Shops, eateries, arcades, and other attractions lined the inner circumference of the ring, across from the entry and departure gates. Dise cast a longing eye at some of the shops and snack bars as they hurried past them.

"Too bad we can't afford a change of clothing, or a stiff drink, but our credits are running low as is."

He was all too aware of that. Springing for express boarding back on Tykona had put a substantial dent in their budget. That had been a necessity, though, not a splurge. "Let's hope you don't have to put up bail to get me out of a detention cell."

They soon arrived at the correct gate, which led to a long radial arm jutting out from the docking ring in order to accommodate vessels too large to dock directly onto the ring as that luxury yacht had earlier. Uniformed attendants, representing both the station and the cruise line, occupied a desk at the entrance to the gate, keeping track of who was coming and going from the

Quintessential. Chekov wasn't concerned about the gatekeepers; their hacked ID chips had already passed muster a few times already.

It was something else that stopped him in his tracks.

"Uh-oh." He ducked behind a souvenir stand, tugging Dise along with him. "We have another problem."

"Namely?"

"Some unwelcome acquaintances from Tykona, lurking around the gate, watching for me."

Broken-Antler and four other Voyzr, to be precise, loitering just outside the entrance, looking over everyone coming on or off the *Quintessential.* Sullen expressions made it clear they were here on business, not pleasure. Chekov had seen more affable Klingons.

Not exactly the welcome wagon . . .

"Offal." Dise poked her head around the side of the souvenir kiosk. "Oh yeah, I recognize a couple of those bucks from Trath's herd. Bunch of Exile losers." She scowled at them. "They don't look too friendly, do they?"

"The one with the bandaged antler has a definite grudge against me." He shrugged. "I may have been a little rough with him at the villa."

"Picco?" She smirked. "No wonder I like you." She yanked her head back, her grin vanishing as though vaporized. "Rutting hell! I think he clocked me!"

Sure enough, a rapid glance confirmed that Picco and three other Exiles were heading their way, leaving two of their confederates behind to stand watch over the gate. Baleful expressions left no doubt that, unlike at the spaceport outside Jhopash, Chekov and Dise had not avoided being spotted this time around.

And the chase is back on, he thought. *Here we go again.*

Twenty-Two

Abandoning the kiosk, Chekov and Dise took off back down the circular corridor, hoping to lose their pursuers in the crowd. He wondered what the Exiles hoped to accomplish. Drug him into submission, then stow him in a ship's cabin or cargo hold until Ryjo completed his mission?

"Sorry!" Dise glanced back over her shoulder. "Didn't mean for him to see me!"

"Not your fault." They couldn't count on always spotting their hunters without being spotted themselves. "They'd be onto us the moment we tried to reboard the cruiser."

But what about Dise? Would the Exiles want to keep her captive too—or would they consider her expendable?

"It's me they're after," he said. "You should veer off and make yourself scarce."

"Not a chance. Besides, they know I'm with you now, if they didn't before. That makes me a loose end they can't afford to leave dangling."

He wished he could dispute that.

A line of impatient travelers, waiting at another gate, blocked their path. Glancing back, he saw the three Exiles gaining on them, fast-walking through flowing currents of humanoid life-forms. Picco smiled coldly as he made eye contact with Chekov. His left hand was tucked into the outer pocket of a rumpled jacket, clutching . . . what? A hypospray? An agonizer? A bony shiv?

Nothing good, Chekov was sure.

"Out of the way! Sorry!"

He and Dise shoved their way through the line, eliciting plenty of vocal protests. It closed behind them, briefly hiding them from the Exiles. He hoped they would have a harder time getting past the incensed queuers, but knew the line wouldn't delay Picco and company long.

A hover-scooter was parked outside a salad bar. He ran over and jumped onto it, dragging Dise behind him.

"Hop on!"

"Don't mind if I do!" She plopped into his lap. "Not the snazziest getaway vehicle, but—"

He hit the ignition button before she could finish the sentence. The scooter lifted off from the floor and started off down the corridor.

"Hey!" a geriatric Caitian cried out from a table. "I was using that!"

Consider it commandeered, Chekov thought. He pushed the scooter to its limited velocity, leaning on a warning buzzer to clear their path. Visitors and Oasis employees scurried out of their way as he took a tight curve around the ring, momentarily leaving the footbound Exiles behind.

"Smooth move," Dise said. "You definitely know how to show a doe a good time."

But for how long? Their headlong spin in the scooter was bound to attract station security in no time, and even if it didn't, the ring would soon bring them right back to where they started, outside the gate to the *Quintessential*, where more Exiles were waiting for them. And then what? They couldn't keep zooming around the docking ring forever.

We need to find someplace to hole up and catch our breath.

An unattended check-in desk, at a currently vacant gate, snagged his attention. He hit the brake and pointed at the empty boarding area.

"Over there, behind the desk."

"Got it."

"But first, give me that taffy."

Surrendering the gooey treat, she hopped off the scooter and scrambled toward the potential hiding spot, where she furtively ducked beneath a rope and dived behind the desk. That no crowds were waiting at the vacant gate was a bonus. He took a moment to rig the scooter to keep going by using the sticky taffy to hold the forward-drive button down, then jumped free of the moving vehicle, which sped on without him. Chekov watched it go, then hurriedly joined Dise behind the counter. Crouching to keep his head down, he held a finger to his lips. She pantomimed zipping hers.

And just in time. Within minutes, urgent footsteps pounded past them. Chekov didn't dare sneak a peek, but recognized Picco's voice among others.

"Keep looking! They can't have gone far, I can still hear the scooter!"

"Says the gullible yearling who let him escape in the first place! We wouldn't be chasing him halfway across the sector if you hadn't let him get the better of you before!"

"Bury it, will you? Just find him . . ."

Their voices receded along with the footsteps, disappearing down the corridor, but Chekov still waited several moments before whispering:

"I think they're gone, for the time being."

"But how did they find us?" Dise asked. "All the way out here?"

He was wondering that, too. "Who knows? Maybe Picco *did* spot me back at the spaceport, right before we boarded the cruiser, or perhaps they traced the credit trail from Ryjo's account to yours to our flight reservations." He recalled worrying about that earlier at the spaceport back on Tykona; maybe it had just taken the Exiles a while to follow the money all the way to Oasis. "I'm more worried about how they managed to intercept us despite our head start."

"I have an idea about that," Dise said. "Rumor has it the Exiles have deep pockets, filled by donations from 'patriotic' Voyzr both on Tykona and off-planet, including some die-hard loyalists back home on Voyzr." A furrow creased her velvety brow. "Come to think of it, Ryjo even hinted once that the Exiles were receiving aid, covertly, from galactic powers opposed to the Federation."

"Like the Klingons," Chekov guessed. That made sense; what with Voyzr's strategic location, the Klingons would definitely gain from souring relations between Voyzr and the UFP. "It would hardly be the first time they meddled behind the scenes where your homeworld is concerned."

Like egging on the civil war two decades ago.

"So they say," she said. "Point being, Trath and his allies have friends in high places and the resources to get agents from Tykona to here in a jiffy."

"*And* get their hands on top-secret body-swapping technology," he observed. If they could pull that off, arranging an express trip to Oasis was well within their abilities. "For all we know, they hitched a ride on a cloaked bird-of-prey."

"We could use one of those ourselves right now," she said.

"Don't I know it. We can't go back to the cruiser; it's not safe now even if we could slip past the watchdogs at the gate, but we can't stay on Oasis either."

"Which means?"

"We need to find another way off the station." He stood up cautiously and looked around. Assorted travelers were passing by the inactive boarding area, but no Voyzr that he could see. He helped Dise to her feet. "Let's get moving before our friends circle back this way."

"Any destination in mind?"

"Yes, actually." A new plan was coalescing in his mind. "Remember that glitzy yacht we saw docking earlier? You probably don't need a full crew to operate a private vessel that size . . ."

She beamed at him. "I like how you think, Pavel. We'll make a renegade of you yet."

"What can I say? You're a bad influence."

"Don't sell me short. I'm the *best* bad influence."

Eyes open, heads down, they tracked down the gate where *Xoline* was docked, as helpfully indicated on mounted display panels. Unlike the *Quintessential*, the yacht was small enough to attach directly onto the docking ring instead of to a longer extension. They arrived just in time to see a mixed party of humans, Mazarites, Catullans, and miscellaneous other sentients disembark from the yacht, looking enviably giddy and carefree.

"Come along, friends and gentlebeings," said an elegant lady whose aristocratic air and fashion sense pegged her as an expatriate Ardanan, most likely a sky-living upper-cruster who had decamped to Wuvoga III to escape Ardana's ongoing egalitarian reforms. Her arms were draped over the shoulders of two comely companions while the rest of her conspicuously merry entourage followed in her wake. "What quaint diversions shall we avail ourselves of first? The spa? A holographic rec room? Fine dining? Exotic libations?"

"Any or all!" enthused a trim Edosian youth. "I'm up for anything after being cooped up in that boat for days now."

"Now, now, my tri-armed lovely, don't forget: That's *my* yacht you're talking about..."

Perfect timing, Chekov thought as the party headed off to explore Oasis's myriad attractions, leaving *Xoline* behind. *Now we just need to find a way aboard.*

"Heads up." Dise pulled him aside, into a thicket of visitors milling about an overtaxed information booth. "We've got trouble coming, both ways."

He saw at once what she meant. A contingent of red-sashes were coming their way from the right, while Picco and the other Exiles had doubled back in search of them, advancing toward them from the left.

With the gate leading to *Xoline* in between.

"How are we going to get on that boat now?" Dise whispered in his ear. "Any bright ideas?"

"Just one, but you're not going to like it."

She pulled back, eyeing him narrowly. "Why not?"

"We need a distraction. Or rather, *I* need a distraction."

"What—?" Doe eyes widened as she grasped his meaning. She shook her head vehemently. "Forget it. You're not ditching me now."

"It's the only play left to us. In your own words, *somebody* has to stop Ryjo before it's too late, for his sake as well as for everyone else's, and that only happens if I can get on that yacht without anyone seeing." He placed his hands on her shoulders. "Which is where you come in."

She glared at him, looking betrayed, but unable to refute his reasoning. He suddenly envied Mister Spock's emotional detachment; he assumed Spock wouldn't feel so guilty and gutted for reaching the only logical conclusion.

"Don't let anything happen to him, you backstabber."

"No promises, but I'll do my best."

"You'd better."

Looking away from him, she turned her fierce gaze on the twin obstacles converging on them. Her expression hardened.

"Fine." She shook her head. "The things I do for you stupid bucks."

She strode out into the open, straight toward the Exiles.

"RYJO!" Her voice rang out over the general hubbub as she stopped in front of Picco. "How many times do I have to tell you to leave me alone! And that goes for the rest of your tick-infested herd as well!"

Picco froze, taken aback by her unexpected outburst. Heads turned in their direction as she got right up in his snout, all but spitting in his face. The red-sashes quickened their pace, marching briskly toward the disturbance.

"What the rut, Dise?" Picco sneered at her, seeking to regain the upper hand. His accomplices closed in on Dise, surrounding her. He lowered his antlers menacingly. "Where is he? Tell us now and maybe we'll go easy on you."

"I've already told you!" She raised her voice even higher, if that was possible. "I wouldn't couple with you if you were the last stag in the quadrant. Why can't you get that through your sorry excuse for a rack!"

The security guards arrived on the scene, led by a hefty officer whose canary-yellow skin and bushy orange hair and eyebrows reminded Chekov of a certain unwanted admirer on Triskelion years ago. A Nemar, as he'd since learned.

"Excuse me, is there a problem here?"

"You bet there is!" Dise shoved Picco away from her, creating an opening for the guards. "Maybe you can stop these mangy losers from stalking me all the way from Voyzr, just because Ryjo here can't take no for an answer!"

"Ryjo?" the officer said. "The Starfleet impersonator?"

"Wait? What?" Picco was thrown for a loop again. "That's not me!"

"Save the moose droppings, Ryjo! You're not fooling anybody!" Dise radiated disdain. "He's bad news, Officer, believe me!"

"Is this true, sir?"

Picco shook his head. "Don't listen to her. This is just a . . . misunderstanding . . . among friends."

He and the other Exiles squirmed uncomfortably in the spotlight. A growing ring of curious spectators observed the dramatic confrontation with interest. A muscle-bound Orion male, whose emerald body mass rivaled the bouncer at Insomnia, guffawed out loud.

"What are you looking at, green-genes?" Dise taunted him. "You think this is funny? Feast your eyes on this!"

Six fingers flung an obscene gesture at the Orion, who, predictably, didn't take it well.

"You gamy fawn! Who do you think you are?"

Fists clenched, he lumbered at Dise, giving the security guards another fractious element to contend with. Making matters worse, the Orion had friends, who waded into the fray on his behalf. All at once, Dise's heated denunciation of Picco threatened to erupt into a full-fledged brawl to rival Chekov's youthful free-for-all against the Klingons on another space station many light-years away.

Minus the tribbles.

That's my cue, he thought. By now, nobody was looking at him as he snuck away from the scene, counting on the red sashes to keep Dise safe from both the Exiles and the provoked Orion. At worst, she might end up in a detention cell for a few days, which might be the safest place for her, especially compared to what he might be heading into when and if he caught up with Ryjo.

I'll be back for you, he promised her, *after.*

Turned out he wasn't the only person distancing themselves from the escalating fracas in the corridor. A nervous-looking Bolian, wearing a tan uniform minus sash, ducked into a doorway labeled "Oasis Personnel Only." Seeking sanctuary from the ugly scene?

Chekov saw an opportunity.

Ignoring the posted warning, he furtively followed the Bolian into what proved to be a stark off-white service tunnel, thankfully underpopulated at the moment. His footsteps echoed in the narrow passageway, alerting the Bolian, who turned to see who was behind him. A hairless blue face frowned at Chekov.

"This area is off-limits to visitors. You don't belong here."

"More than you know." Chekov flashed a disarming smile. "Still, perhaps you can help me . . ."

A karate chop dropped the Bolian to the tiled floor, less gracefully than a Vulcan nerve pinch, perhaps, but just as effectively. Chekov quickly divested the unlucky Oasis employee of his uniform and changed into it. Not a perfect fit, but it would have to do. A quick inspection of a nearby utility closet yielded a transparent bottle of cleaning solution, along with an assortment of freshly laundered towels and wipe cloths.

Very handy, he thought. *I can use these.*

He stowed the unconscious, undressed Bolian in the closet, then stepped back out into the corridor, where he was gratified to see the manufactured commotion was still underway, keeping everyone fully occupied.

Thanks, Dise. This is above and beyond.

With a pristine white cloth draped over the bottle, he quietly approached the docking port leading into *Xoline*. An intercom unit was mounted to one side of the port, serving as a doorbell of sorts. Had all aboard departed the yacht, or had someone been left behind to mind the store while *Xoline*'s owner and her entourage amused themselves? A paid crew member or domestic perhaps?

He tried the intercom to find out.

"Hello? Hailing *Xoline*?"

The refined, green features of a Troyian gentleman appeared on a miniature viewscreen. "Who is calling?"

"Station Hospitality, with a complimentary bottle of fine Benecian champagne for our prestige visitors."

He held up the draped container of cleanser.

"I see. Very well."

A hatchway slid open, allowing Chekov to step directly from the docking ring into *Xoline*. He was greeted by the rather austere-looking Troyian, who gave off a definite "family retainer" vibe. He swept an appraising gaze over Chekov.

"Her Ladyship is not presently aboard, but I shall convey your employer's compliments on her return."

"By all means." Chekov lobbed the bottle at the other man. "Catch!"

Caught off guard, the Troyian instinctively lunged to catch it, offering Chekov another opportunity to deliver a well-aimed karate chop. Both bottle and greeter hit the deck, the former rolling harmlessly across the tiles. Wincing, Chekov massaged the uncalloused edge of Ryjo's hand, which was apparently not accustomed to being employed as a weapon, twice.

Ouch.

Gaining access to *Xoline* was worth the discomfort, though. He swiftly closed the hatch behind him, then deposited the Troyian in one of the yacht's emergency escape pods, to be dealt with later. From there, he hurried to the flight deck. As he'd hoped, the helm controls were happily basic, intended for amateur spacefarers with too many credits to burn. He strapped himself into the pilot's seat and fired up the engines while disengaging *Xoline*'s docking clamps.

His preflight routine did not escape Oasis's notice.

"*Attention,* Xoline," a voice announced over the yacht's comm system, which was still plugged into the station. "*This is Oasis Traffic Control. You are not cleared for departure.*"

He briefly considered ignoring them, but decided against it. He didn't want to get snagged by a tractor beam or whatever other mechanisms Oasis might have in place to prevent unauthorized exits. He hit Reply on the comm controls.

"My sincere apologies, Oasis, but we need to depart at once. We are experiencing a critical radiation leak from our warp engine. I cannot guarantee that we will not blow up your valuable docking ring if we remain any longer."

There was a pause on the other end of the line before:

"*Our sensors detect no excess radiation aboard your vessel, nor any evidence of a potential warp-core breach.*"

"Not yet, perhaps, but I'm certain I can arrange one if you do not allow me to depart posthaste."

If there was one thing he'd learned from Captain Kirk, it was when in doubt, bluff.

"Do you read me, Oasis?"

"*Who is this? Identify yourself!*"

"No time for that, I'm afraid. We're leaving now. I don't advise you try to stop me." A further glance at the control panel informed him that *Xoline* was armed with a rudimentary phaser array. Not enough to take on the *Enterprise* or a Romulan warbird, but sufficient to discourage any would-be pirates looking for easy prey. "Charging phasers now."

"*Wait! Don't do anything rash!*"

He could practically smell the perspiration streaming off whoever had the bad luck to be running traffic control this shift. He felt bad about ruining their day, but . . . priorities. There were larger matters at stake.

"Just let me go and I'll be out of your hair for good."

Another pause, not quite as long as before.

"Acknowledged, Xoline. *You are cleared for departure. Please don't come back."*

"I appreciate your cooperation. *Xoline* out."

Chekov sighed in relief, dialing down the phasers. Ideally, he'd be able to return the yacht to its rightful owner in due time, but that could wait. Undocking from Oasis, he paused only long enough to eject the escape pod holding the Troyian, confident that the station would recover him in no time. Then he warped away from Oasis, leaving Dise behind.

He wondered if she would ever forgive him.

Twenty-Three

"*Copernicus* to *Enterprise*, do you read us? Repeat: *Copernicus* to *Enterprise*..."

Sulu tried a few more times before admitting defeat. "No use. We're too far deep, under more than a thousand meters of scalding water seething with metallic sulfides. I can't get through."

Of course, Ryjo thought. *Why should anything ever go our way?*

To Sulu's credit, *Copernicus* had survived its death-defying plunge into Wexx's equatorial sea, only to end up stranded on an unstable seabed far beneath the waves. Between the crash landing and the barrage of flying rock and lava bombs before that, the shuttlecraft's thrusters and the starboard nacelle were thoroughly trashed. It seemed nothing short of a miracle that the hull was still intact, despite a few ominous bulges in the interior bulkheads and the tortured creaks and groans from the duranium walls enclosing Ryjo and the others. A protective heat shield covered the cockpit window, blinding them to the alien depths outside. Tinted red emergency lights provided the only illumination, while the temperature inside the ship was steadily rising, despite whatever was left of the shuttle's deflectors. External sensors indicated that, even this deep, the water outside was nearly one hundred degrees Celsius, thanks to the gravitational pressures heating up the moon's core, as well as several underwater hot springs. The latter, Ryjo gathered, would account for the thick brew of exotic metal sulfides surrounding *Copernicus*.

"That's just dandy," McCoy grumbled. He and Tovar were busy tending to whatever injuries, minor and otherwise, the landing party and their Yarfite charges had sustained from the rough landing, including bruised ribs, bumps, contusions, sprains, and even, in Fressa's case, a broken arm. A hand scanner whirred as McCoy used it to check Bwoj's vitals. "We come answering a distress signal and end up being unable to send one ourselves."

"At least we're still alive." Tovar applied a brace to the neckpiece of Dipelly's pressure suit, to address a preliminary diagnosis of whiplash. "I thought we were goners when we went into that spin." She wiped a sheen of perspiration from her brow. "Remind me why I decided to go explore space again?"

"Temporary insanity?" Ryjo was definitely having second thoughts about infiltrating Starfleet. The way things were looking, he was never going to make it to Voyzr to complete his mission. He was going to die a failure.

Sure, life-support was still functional for the time being, and they had even managed to repressurize the shuttle's interior so they could remove their helmets, but despite the heat, they'd kept their environmental suits on and their helmets close at hand in case *Copernicus*'s structural integrity failed and they had to abandon the vessel in a hurry. Sulu had donned an environmental suit as well, after reopening the hatchway between the cockpit and the passenger compartment.

"So there's no chance of lifting off on our own?" Tovar asked. "After some typically ingenious repairs?"

Sulu emerged from the cockpit, shaking his head. "That nacelle's taken too much damage. Not even Scotty could make this bird fly again under these circumstances. *Copernicus* is not going anywhere."

"And life-support?" McCoy asked.

"Holding for the moment, but not indefinitely," Sulu said. "I'm diverting most of whatever power we have left to life-support, keeping the shields at a bare minimum, pulled back to reinforce the hull's structural integrity, but that's just buying time. Maybe five hours at most."

"Until what? The life-support fails, before or after the hull caves in?" Bwoj paced up and down the length of the compartment. He threw up his arms in dismay. "Either way, we'll be lost at the bottom of this cursed sea forever . . . just like the *Stellar Gale*!"

Fressa's right arm was in a sling, courtesy of McCoy, but she stroked her chin with her free hand. "Speaking of which, now that we're beneath the surface anyway, I don't suppose we can use your state-of-the-art Starfleet sensors to see if the *Gale* is resting anywhere nearby?"

"Seriously?" Bwoj gaped at his skipper, aghast. "Do you even hear yourself? Forget the treasure! We're all going to die here because you were too stubborn to lift off in time. I warned you, but did you listen? No, and now we're—"

"That's enough, Bwoj," Dipelly said, intervening a moment before Ryjo could. She grimaced as she turned her sore neck toward her agitated crewmate. "What's done is done. We all knew this moon was perilous, but we dared it anyway, based on your brilliant research and theories. Treasure-hunting is a risky business; danger comes with the quest."

"Hear, hear!" Fressa said. "So, about those sensors . . . ?"

"Not an option," Ryjo said, having already tried to put *Copernicus*'s sensors to more practical use, such as charting where exactly they had come to rest and what the surrounding deep-sea terrain was like. "The same contamination that's blocking our comm signals is fouling our sensors just as badly."

"Oh." Fressa's jowly face sank as it finally dawned on her that the glorious crusade for which she'd sacrificed so much had been scuttled for good.

Ryjo knew how she felt. *The regnant can sleep easy tonight.*

"So now what, Commander Chekov?" Dipelly asked. "What's our next move, if any?"

All eyes turned toward Ryjo, who silently cursed the cruel fate that had put him in this position. It wasn't supposed to be this way; this wasn't his crew, his people, or his mission. How had he become responsible for all of their lives? And why should he even care what became of Tovar and Sulu and the others? They were Starfleet, the enemy, not Voyzr.

Even if it didn't feel that way at the moment.

"I am open to suggestions," he said. "Anyone?"

"Maybe we should abandon ship?" Tovar said. "Swim to the surface in our EV suits and try to contact the *Enterprise* from there?"

"Swim?" Bwoj's voice jumped an octave. "I can't swim!" He looked to his compatriots. "Tell them I can't swim!"

"We could hold on to you," Dipelly volunteered. "Carry you to the surface."

"But even if we can make it all the way up, despite people's injuries," McCoy said, "there's no guarantee we'd be able to contact the ship, what with that volcano spewing heaven knows what into the atmosphere. And then what, we end up adrift in the middle of the sea, kilometers from shore?" McCoy reloaded a hypospray. "Not that dry land is much better, considering we can't even breathe the air. At the risk of being a wet blanket, what would we really gain by attempting such a desperate stunt?"

Sulu shrugged. "Could make it easier for the *Enterprise* to locate us. Holding out long enough to be rescued might be our best bet."

"Assuming the *Enterprise* hasn't already moved on by now," Ryjo added. "I hate to say it, but they have no idea we survived that eruption, let alone the crash. Chances are, they've given us up for dead and are back on course for Voyzr."

Without me, he thought bitterly.

"You're joking, right?" Sulu shot him a startled look. "Captain Kirk and the others would never give up on us so quickly. If there's even a *chance* we're still alive, the captain will move heaven and earth to save us. You know that as well as any of us!"

"Amen!" McCoy scowled at Chekov. "Maybe I ought to give that thick Russian skull of yours a closer look... to rule out a concussion!"

"Sorry!" Ryjo kicked himself for underestimating the other men's loyalty to their captain. He hadn't thought he was disparaging Kirk by suggesting that the *Enterprise* might reasonably consider them lost, but he'd obviously crossed a line in a very un-Chekov-like manner. "I don't know what I was thinking. Just a bit rattled, I suppose."

"That's one way to put it," McCoy grumped. "Have a little faith in Jim Kirk. He'll come through for us if he can. Why, even Spock—"

An undersea tremor shook *Copernicus*, tilting it sharply to port and causing all aboard to grab for the nearest handhold. Bwoj stumbled, smacking into the closed aft hatch. An open medkit fell from the seat it was resting on, spilling its contents onto the deck. Ryjo's helmet, which he'd stowed beneath a seat in the passenger compartment, rolled away from him. Bulkheads moaned in distress as he staggered after it, terrified that the hull would buckle at any moment. Something thudded heavily outside the shuttlecraft, the noise and impact only partially muffled by sea and steel. It felt like *Copernicus* was under assault, from above and below.

Is this it? Are we done for?

As before, the quake lasted only moments but felt like forever. *Copernicus* settled back down on the seabed, now listing to one side. Ryjo remembered to breathe again. He was still shaking, even if the seabed wasn't.

"Everyone okay?" McCoy called. "Sound off if you're hurt!"

A hasty roll call determined that, fortuitously enough, no one had incurred any significant new injuries, but Ryjo took little comfort from this given that the overall danger persisted. Recovering his runaway helmet, he worried about when the next tremor would hit and how hard. It was all too easy to imagine *Copernicus* flipping over altogether or rolling down a hill, maybe into a bottomless, deep-sea ravine. And what had caused that ponderous thud outside? Falling ejecta from the volcano? An underwater landslide? A massive rock formation collapsing far too close to them?

"We need to get a look at what's out there," he concluded, "before we make any decisions about to do next. For all we know, we're right on the brink of a cliff or about to tumble into a steaming volcanic vent." He took in the anxious faces listening to him and decided Chekov would want to offer a sliver of hope for morale's sake. "Or maybe we're resting safely on a wide-open plain, clear of any immediate hazards aside from the obvious. In any event, we can't afford to stay blind to what's outside. We need to survey the landscape."

"Can't argue with that," McCoy agreed. "How do you propose we do that?" He glanced at the starboard hatch. "Send a scout out for a swim?"

Bwoj flinched at the word "swim." Dipelly clapped a hand around his muzzle.

"Maybe later." Ryjo indicated the front window, which was currently covered by the opaque heat shield. He looked to Sulu. "What do you think? Can we risk raising those shutters, just to look around?"

"We can try. The transparent aluminum looks intact from this side, having been protected by both the heat shield and our deflectors when we crashed into the sea. In theory, it should be able to handle the extreme pressure, with just a little assist from our shields, such as they are . . ."

His voice trailed off worryingly.

"But?" Ryjo prompted.

"Hang on to your helmets, everybody, in case we spring a leak."

Ryjo swallowed hard. Was he making the right call? Would the real Chekov make a different one? Phantom antlers itched furiously. It was all he could do not to reach up and scratch the nonexistent prongs.

Playing it safe, he and Sulu went so far as to don their helmets before reentering the cockpit. McCoy, Tovar, and the Yarfites watched from just outside the open hatchway behind the cockpit, which could be sealed off at a moment's notice. Ryjo contemplated the dense steel heat shields blocking their view of what lay beyond. Who knew what they'd see once the shields were lifted?

"Ready?" Sulu's finger hovered above the control panel.

Ryjo nodded. "Do it."

Sulu pressed the button and the heat shield retracted. Ryjo braced himself in case the exposed window could not hold up to the pressure of the depths, causing the sea to invade *Copernicus* with untold force; back on Tykona, he'd heard tales about leaks on submersible vessels producing high-pressure torrents strong enough to kill or maim. For once, however, providence was with them and the window remained intact (for now). He switched on the forward landing lights to reveal:

A rocky underwater landscape not unlike the rugged volcanic plain they'd just departed, complete with low ridges, shallow declivities, and boulders both weathered and worryingly not, all coated in a yellowish slurry that looked like a mixture of accumulated sand, clay, and ash. Peering into the murky liquid, Ryjo did not spot any obvious hazards. No undersea precipices or chasms threatened, although some bubbling hot springs could be glimpsed several meters away.

"Okay, that's better than I expected, relatively speaking." A monitor on the control panel reported that the near-boiling temperature outside the shuttlecraft had remained more or less stable. "Not exactly a prime locale for snorkeling, but—"

Something large and glowing swam past the window.

"What in Sam Hill?" McCoy blurted over a chorus of startled gasps, interjections, and, in Bwoj's case, a high-pitched yelp. "I thought this moon was supposed to be lifeless!"

"Apparently not." Ryjo scoured the scene outside, trying to catch another glimpse of *whatever*, but the nameless life-form had vanished as swiftly as it had appeared. "Guess we're too deep for any previous scans to have detected their life signs from above."

"Or maybe a tremor released it from a subterranean cave system?" Dipelly speculated. She shrugged. "Just a theory."

"Either way, Starfleet's going to need to update their database," Sulu said. "Maybe send a new automated probe designed for deep-sea exploration."

"Assuming we make it back to the *Enterprise* to inform anyone."

Tovar hugged herself. "I don't know about you, but I'm having second thoughts about the whole swimming-to-surface option."

"You and me both," Sulu said. "I suppose it's too much to hope that we're talking about a couple of friendly humpback whales."

George and Gracie, Ryjo thought, catching the reference to one of the crew's more recent voyages. "We should be so lucky."

"Terrific," McCoy said. "So we can't abandon ship, but we can't stay here much longer either. Talk about a real-life *Kobayashi Maru* situation."

Ryjo got that reference too.

Unfortunately.

"Excuse me." Bwoj tentatively raised his paw. "I may have an idea."

Twenty-Four

"*Enterprise*! Hailing *Enterprise*! Please respond!"

Warping away from Oasis, Chekov tried to contact the ship on a civilian frequency, employing *Xoline*'s merely adequate comm system. Prior attempts to utilize Starfleet's priority channels had proved ineffective; Ryjo had apparently changed all of Chekov's classified access codes, shutting him out of the network.

Just what I would have done, he thought, *in his place.*

Without recourse to Starfleet's extensive network of subspace beacons, there was no telling when or if his hail would reach the *Enterprise* at this range, or what sort of time lag might hinder their response. Presumably, the *Enterprise* was almost to Voyzr by now, if not there already. Chekov pushed the stolen yacht beyond its recommended velocity in a desperate attempt to make up the distance between him and the ship he truly belonged on. Trying to convince Captain Kirk and the others that he was the real Chekov just over the comms was going to be challenging enough without long-distance time delays.

Still, he had to try.

"Hailing *Enterprise*—"

An urgent buzz interrupted him, drawing his attention to the comm display panel before him. A systems alert flashed in Federation Standard:

Transmission Failure

"What the devil?" Seated at the helm of *Xoline*, he fiddled with the comm controls, only to find himself blocked on all frequencies.

A chill ran down his spine as he identified the problem immediately. His signals were being jammed—but by whom? He was traversing deep space outside any inhabited system. By all indications, there was no other vessel in the vicinity.

Unless...?

A Klingon bird-of-prey—a smaller *B'rel*-class scout ship, to be precise—uncloaked on his sensors, flying parallel to *Xoline*. Chekov's pulse raced at the sight of the other ship's ominous silhouette, instantly recalling what Dise had told him about the Klingons possibly lending covert support to the Exiles. Was this the same cloaked ship that might have delivered Picco and his cohorts to Oasis in pursuit of him? That seemed more than likely.

But how had they found him here in deep space? The flashing message on the comm panel hinted at the answer.

My comm signals! he realized. By trying to hail the *Enterprise*, he had been broadcasting his location to anyone tracking him.

And painting a target on Xoline.

Reacting quickly, he raised the yacht's rudimentary shields; they were far below Starfleet-level defenses, but they were all he had. Proximity alerts wailed as sensors warned of a torpedo-shaped object zooming straight for *Xoline*. Chekov attempted an evasive maneuver, banking hard to port, but the torpedo was too close and too fast. He flinched in anticipation, unsure if, even shielded, the yacht could survive a photon torpedo strike.

Good thing I left Dise behind...

The torpedo slammed into *Xoline*, exploding on contact with her shields. The impact knocked the yacht out of warp and sent it spinning off course but, to Chekov's relief and surprise, did not bring total annihilation. Finding himself unexpectedly alive, he saw that the blast had reduced *Xoline*'s shield intensity by only fifty percent, far less than he'd expect from a military-grade Klingon torpedo. A rapid scan of the diagnostic displays showed damage across the boards, but not enough to leave the yacht dead in the water. He could only assume that the Klingons had deliberately reduced the torpedo's explosive yield—to avoid destroying *Xoline* completely?

"*Attention, fugitive vessel!*" a guttural voice barked over the comms; clearly, the Klingons were not jamming their own transmissions. Static indicated that *Xoline*'s own comm system had not come through the torpedo attack unscathed. "*You cannot escape or defeat us in battle. Surrender at once.*"

Surrender? After only one pulled punch? It was unlike Klingons to avoid a battle, even one as obviously lopsided as this. More proof that the Exiles, along with their Klingons allies, needed him kept alive—for Ryjo's sake?

This did little to reassure Chekov. Even if the Klingons were not immediately intent on reducing him to space dust, he was in no hurry to enjoy their infamous "hospitality" anytime soon, especially when he had more important places to be.

"Excuse me," he attempted to hail the Klingon ship, uncertain if they could even hear him despite the jamming field and the torpedo-inflicted injury to *Xoline*. Preliminary readings suggested crippling damage to the yacht's long-range transceiver antenna. "It appears there's been some sort of misunderstanding—"

"*Silence!*" Electronic hisses and crackles punctuated the Klingons' bellicose response. "*Lower your shields and prepare to be boarded!*"

A viridian tractor beam latched onto *Xoline*, squeezing her tattered shields. Chekov resisted an urge to fire back at the bird-of-prey with the yacht's meager phasers; he was hopelessly outgunned and he knew it. He wasn't going to be able shoot his way out of this, but perhaps there was another option, one the Klingons wouldn't see coming?

"Acknowledged. Just give me a moment to shut down the deflectors. I'm afraid the controls are somewhat less than responsive, after the torpedo and all. I need to do this carefully, just to be safe . . ."

"*No tricks, Starfleet! Yes, we know who you are!*"

"I'm sure I don't know what you mean. Starfleet, me?"

Keep him talking, Chekov thought, stalling for time as he

systematically began stripping down the shields protecting *Xoline*, dissolving the complex lattice of energized gravitons comprising the field so that, from the Klingons' vantage point, it would certainly seem as though he was dismantling the shields layer by layer, albeit in a rather laborious fashion. One by one, the constituent elements of the deflector field were peeled away, so all that remained was a localized zone of ionized gamma rays leavened with a very specific concentration of free neutrons, not unlike the byproducts of archaic nuclear-fission reactors . . .

"What is taking so long? Lower your shields or suffer the consequences!"

"Just a moment. I'm almost finished . . . There!"

He turned a dial, but instead of eliminating the gamma field as well, he expanded it so that it blossomed outward toward the bird-of-prey and was almost instantly sucked up by the Klingon vessel's tractor beam, which pulled it straight into the bird-of-prey—before the beam blinked out entirely.

Yes! Chekov thought. *Always wondered if that trick would work.*

Just a few years ago, while temporarily stranded in the late twentieth century, he'd had occasion to infiltrate the reactor room of a primitive nuclear-powered aircraft carrier, where he had unfortunately been taken into custody by some notably unfriendly American military personnel. Attempting to escape, he discovered that the radiation from the carrier's archaic nuclear-fission reactor had rendered his communicator and hand phaser inoperative for reasons he had been in no position to examine at the time. Later, however, after that tumultuous excursion to the past reached a successful conclusion, saving all life on Earth, and he had returned to his own, substantially more advanced era, he had delved deeper into precisely how those specific emissions had disabled his gear, while also taking advantage of the opportunity to study the specs of the Klingon ship they had captured around the same time. A *B'rel*-class bird-of-prey, as it happened.

Searching for potential vulnerabilities that might be exploited later, it had occurred to him that perhaps one could re-create, on a somewhat larger scale, the same effect that had knocked out his equipment on that aircraft carrier three hundred years ago, disabling its weapons and sensors, if only temporarily. Certainly, what he had learned from the late *HMS Bounty* suggested this trick might work at least once, before the Klingons developed an effective countermeasure.

Once was enough for Chekov. Holding his breath, he reactivated *Xoline*'s warp engine and took off at top speed. No torpedoes, phasers, or tractor beams pursued him as he resumed course for Voyzr and the *Enterprise*.

He glanced warily at the comm panel, remembering how the Klingons had located him before.

No more open hails until I'm right in Voyzr's backyard, he realized. *It's silent running until then.*

Twenty-Five

"You sure you want to do this?" Tovar asked. "What with that creature out there?"

She held on to his helmet as Ryjo ran a safety check on his environmental suit to ensure that it was still operational after the crash, quakes, and spills, while exchanging his magnetic gravity boots for levitation boots. Groaning bulkheads added urgency to the procedure, as if anyone trapped aboard the sunken shuttlecraft could possibly forget the fix they were in. His gaze drifted toward the forward window, watching out for *whatever* had swum past it before. That they now knew that the sea outside was not entirely lifeless did give him pause.

"Doesn't seem like I have much choice, not if we want to get through to the *Enterprise*." He turned toward the rear of *Copernicus*, where Sulu, Bwoj, and Dipelly were hard at work assembling a makeshift communications buoy out of a standard-issue signal enhancer, a remote-controlled surveillance drone, and an emergency flotation device. Acrid fumes contaminated the pressurized atmosphere as Dipelly employed a beam welder to solder two components together. Ryjo's nose wrinkled. "How are we doing there?"

"Just a few more minutes." Sulu hunched over the buoy, using a trident scanner to cross-connect the control circuitry. "Don't want to cut corners where this gadget is concerned, especially without Scotty on hand to pull off a miracle in record time."

"I couldn't agree more," Ryjo said. "Take the time to do it right. Just not *too* much time."

Sulu nodded. "Acknowledged . . . and then some."

Everything—their lives, Ryjo's undercover mission—depended on Bwoj's plan: to deliver a floatable signal enhancer to the surface of the sea in hopes of finally making contact with the *Enterprise* despite the depth and contamination of all the water above *Copernicus*, assuming Captain Kirk was indeed still searching for them, of which Sulu and the others remained utterly confident. Ryjo had his doubts, but he kept them to himself to preserve his cover. Given their lack of viable alternatives, he could only hope, for all their sakes, that Kirk's people knew their captain better than he did. Otherwise, they were almost surely doomed to drown beneath alien waves.

The catch? Since there was no guarantee that the improvised buoy would work perfectly the first time out, without needing any last-minute adjustments or fine-tuning, *somebody* had to accompany the buoy to the surface to make certain the remote connection to *Copernicus* worked, that the hailing frequencies to the *Enterprise* didn't need to be tweaked, that the buoy stayed afloat, and, not incidentally, to defend it from any lurking aquatic life-forms.

"Ready when you are," Ryjo said. "More or less."

"Not in that big a hurry to brave the depths?" Tovar said. "Can't say I blame you. Don't think we don't appreciate you taking this plunge for us. You're a brave man, Pavel Chekov."

If only. Once again, though, he hadn't had much of a choice. As mission leader, he'd briefly flirted with delegating Sulu, but that seemed out of character for Chekov. For better or for worse, he still felt obliged to avoid attracting suspicion—just in case he somehow survived to make it back to the *Enterprise*.

"Just doing my duty," he said, as Chekov might. "Unless you're volunteering?"

He was kidding, naturally. This was no job for a nurse or a doctor, nor something that could be trusted to one or more of the rescued civilians.

"You wish," she joked back. "Guess I can't really complain about being in this situation. I wanted to break out of my comfort zone and check out the far frontier . . . and here we are." She chuckled wryly. "Be careful what you wish for."

He glanced at the buoy-assembly team, who looked like they still had a ways to go. Meanwhile, McCoy was tending to Fressa's broken arm by administering a fresh dose of painkillers and healing agents. Time enough then, Ryjo concluded, for he and Tovar to engage in a bit more conversation, if only to keep his mind off his impending ascent through the perilous waters outside.

"You said something about a midlife crisis before?"

"Pretty much." She inspected his helmet for any hairline cracks or loose fittings. "Don't get me wrong. Medicine and nursing will always be my true vocation, but a few years back, with my fortieth birthday looming on the horizon, I felt like I needed a change of scenery at least, after working in planetside hospitals and clinics for most of my career. As it happens, I once worked with Doctor McCoy, back when he was taking a sabbatical from Starfleet after your original five-year mission, so I reached out to him, told him I was interested in broadening my horizons, and, long story short, he pulled strings to get me assigned to your brand-new *Enterprise*." She took in their daunting surroundings, with the dim emergency lighting, creaking bulkheads, and flagging life-support. "Mind you, getting stranded underwater on a dangerously volcanic moon was not exactly what I had in mind . . ."

"Not really on my to-do list either," he replied, "but as we say in Russia, life is what happens when you're making other plans."

Including assassination plots, it seemed.

"Truer words, et cetera." She handed him the helmet, then stepped closer to brush his hair away from his brow, as though inspecting him for any previously undetected bumps or bruises. "Suit looks fine, but how are you holding up? No concussions after all?"

"Not that I know of." He found her touch and proximity and outgoing personality more stimulating than he should. Guilt pricked him as he recalled not just his mission but Dise also. "What's your diagnosis, Nurse?"

She unhooked a medical tricorder from her suit. "Let me see about that." She scanned him from head to toe, then consulted the display panel. "Hmm. Slightly elevated blood pressure, heartbeat, adrenal levels." She smirked at him. "Should I be flattered, or are you just stressed about your big swim to the surface?"

He wasn't sure how to answer that. *Forgive me, Dise.*

"I decline to answer on the grounds that it might—"

"Look sharp!" McCoy shouted. "It's back!"

All heads turned toward the cockpit window to see a pulsing, blue-white glow come surging out of the murk toward *Copernicus*. At first, all that could be discerned was a large, amorphous shape vaguely defined by bright, strobing flashes, but then the shuttlecraft's landing lights exposed an immense, jellyfish-like creature reminiscent of the monstrous slime nettles of the Hylera Basin. Its translucent, bell-shaped head was at least a meter high and across. Undulating tentacles streamed behind it like luminous party streamers.

"I'll be damned!" McCoy gaped at the beast.

Hopefully not, Ryjo thought. Was the sea creature dangerous? He didn't spy any obvious fangs or claws or spikes. *Perhaps it's harmless and merely curious about us . . .*

A sparkling tentacle lashed out at *Copernicus*. Lightning blazed beneath the sea in the form of a blinding, white-hot flash that forced Ryjo to avert his eyes. Energy crackled loudly as an electrifying jolt clashed with the shuttlecraft's already flimsy shields, which barely overlaid the contours of the hull. The landing lights flared, then went black, so that all that could be seen was the glowing jelly retreating back into the swirling mustard slurry before vanishing from sight completely.

Okay, not so harmless then.

He scrambled into the cockpit, despite his heavy boots and padded EV suit, and tried to reactivate the landing lights. Blue spots danced before his eyes as they recovered from the flash.

"No use," he announced after a few frustrating moments. "I can't get the searchlights back on. The circuits are fried."

"That may have been the intent," McCoy said.

"How do you mean, Doctor?" Tovar asked.

"You saw that thing, all lit up like a pulsar chandelier. If it's territorial, it might have seen *Copernicus* as competition, so it targeted our brightest lights first."

"But what did it hit us with?" Fressa asked between puffs on her vaporizer, which she stubbornly persisted in employing.

Ryjo studied the relevant readings on the dashboard. "Nearly as I can tell, that tentacle delivered a powerful bioelectric surge, on the order of several gigajoules."

"Lovely," McCoy said. "A huge electric jellyfish, armed with lightning bolts. Just what we *didn't* need."

Cowering behind the other Yarfites, Bwoj peered apprehensively at the forward window. "Why hasn't it attacked again, to finish us off?"

"Maybe it needs time to recharge?" Sulu speculated. "Or only wanted to take out our lights like Doctor McCoy suggested?"

"Could be." Ryjo was suddenly grateful for the subdued red emergency lighting inside *Copernicus*. He lowered the heat shield anyway, to hide their interior lights. "We should probably reduce our visibility to be safe."

"Hang on!" Fressa protested. "How are we going to see that thing coming with the window covered?"

"Is that likely to make a difference in the outcome?" Ryjo exited the cockpit. "With our forward lights out, we'll barely have any advance notice anyway. If we can possibly avoid provoking that . . . lightning jelly . . . by going dark, we ought to give it a try."

"And if it's simply recharging before taking another run at us?" Fressa asked. "Or if there are more of those creatures swimming around out there?"

"No way of knowing that," Ryjo admitted, "although if we're right about it being territorial and not liking competition, perhaps it's the only specimen in its territory."

"Perhaps, maybe, if . . ." Fressa expelled a jowlful of azure vapor. "None of that is very reassuring, Commander Chekov."

Tell me about it, Ryjo thought. "All the more reason to get hold of the *Enterprise* sooner rather than later." He stomped down the passenger cabin toward the buoy on which their futures depended. "Where do we stand with our composite lifesaver?"

"Ready to go." Sulu put down the trident scanner. "It's as good as it's going to get under the circumstances, although I confess I was briefly distracted by our gooey, galvanic friend out there."

"You don't say."

Ryjo took a moment to refamiliarize himself with the signal enhancer's controls, another bit of Starfleet tech he'd never actually handled before, not even in simulations. Fortunately, they looked straightforward enough, and manipulable even when wearing gloves.

He hoped.

"Wait a second," McCoy said. "Let's rethink this. Does Chekov *really* need to babysit that buoy, now that we know how dangerous that creature is?"

"And if the remote link to *Copernicus* doesn't connect at first?" Ryjo appreciated the doctor's concern for "Chekov," but he had already thought this through. "Or if the beast tries to zap the buoy with its tentacles?"

McCoy faltered. "That would cook our goose but good, I guess, but I still don't like the idea of you taking a swim with a sea monster."

"Don't worry." He slapped the phaser affixed to his hip. "I'm set to kill."

"Kill?" Sulu raised an eyebrow. "You mean stun, don't you? We're the invaders here. For all we know, that life-form is sentient, or even just an endangered species. We can't just go in phasers blazing. Starfleet protocol—"

"Phasers on stun, of course." Ryjo switched the setting on the weapon before attaching it back to his suit. "Sorry. Got a little carried away there. I just didn't want to take chances with your lives all depending on me."

"No shame in that," McCoy said. "The pressure of the deep is nothing compared to the pressure of being responsible for the lives of others. Trust me, I know that too well." He placed a hand on Ryjo's shoulder. "Stun first, but if that doesn't do the trick . . . do what you must to stay alive. We'll back you up."

"You said it, Doctor." Sulu gave Chekov a pat on the back. "All for one and one for all, as they say. Just don't think I'm going to let you win our next bowling match because you get to play hero this time."

"Not even one extra frame?"

Joking aside, all this heartfelt support and camaraderie unsettled Ryjo. He was not Chekov, and these people were not really his friends and crewmates.

Even if they *were* all in this together right now.

"Watch your back out there." Tovar came forward, squeezing past McCoy and Sulu. For a moment, he thought (hoped?) she might give him a kiss for luck, but she simply squeezed his hands before assisting him with his helmet again. "You can do this. I have faith in you."

"Thank you, Nurse."

"Call me Simone."

Twenty-Six

Copernicus's lack of airlocks again posed a problem. Since they could hardly cram six humanoids into the cockpit, even with the Yarfites' diminutive statures, everyone aboard had to helmet up before they gradually lowered the aft force field and, just as cautiously, opened the rear hatchway. Pushing against the incoming water, Ryjo exited *Copernicus* with the buoy clipped to his suit by a short cable. Sulu and the others would flush the shuttlecraft after they closed the hatch, then suit up again upon Ryjo's return. *If* he returned.

This had better be worth it, he thought.

Using emergency climbing gear stored aboard *Copernicus*, he anchored one end of a long tether to what appeared, for the moment, to be a solid chunk of seabed. Was it secure enough to hold fast through another seismic event? He wanted to think so, but . . .

One more reason to get a move on.

To speed his ascent, he activated the thruster rockets on his levitation boots, which propelled him toward the surface, dragging the buoy with him, the tether playing out behind it. A heads-up display inside his helmet allowed him to monitor his rise so he could angle his legs as needed to keep speeding in the right direction. A good thing, too; it would be all too easy to get lost and disoriented in these murky currents. If there was any sunlight filtering down from above, Ryjo couldn't see it, possibly because the sky was still bedimmed by volcanic ash and smoke? Phaser in hand, he watched anxiously for the telltale glow of the lurking lightning jelly. A slower, less dramatic climb might be less likely to attract the creature's notice, but Ryjo chose to err toward speed rather than stealth. Time was running out for *Copernicus*, and despite his crew's faith in Kirk, who knew how long the *Enterprise* would stick around searching for them? The shuttlecraft's bulkheads and life-support were on borrowed time.

Plus, he simply didn't want to spend any more time in this scalding, jelly-infested soup than he had to.

His helmet's searchlight swept the swirling murk. He'd debated switching the light off entirely to avoid attracting unwelcome company, but swimming blind carried its own risks as well, such as colliding with some undersea reef or outcropping, besides being, honestly, just too scary to contemplate. He needed to see *something* of where he was going, if only for his own peace of mind. What if another huge stony fragment or lava bomb came plunging out of nowhere?

"Chekov to *Copernicus*. Can you read me?"

Nothing but static responded, just as they'd feared. The adulterated sea was interfering even with their personal communicators. The best he could hope for was that he could establish a comlink with *Copernicus* once the buoy was up and running. Until then, he was on his own.

Which, in a very real sense, he had been ever since he'd first beamed aboard the *Enterprise* posing as Chekov. All this time, he'd been surrounded by strangers who didn't and couldn't know the real him, leaving him very much alone, with no one else to rely on.

But not like this.

I could use another voice to keep me company. Maybe Tovar's?

Blue-white flashes strobed the sea, speeding toward him. Ryjo fired the phaser, a crimson beam sizzling through the umber liquid, causing it to bubble and steam. His first shot missed the oncoming creature, reminding him that he wasn't actually a trained Starfleet marksman and that none of his simulations had involved *underwater* target practice. Frantically, he fired again, this time grazing the jelly's bulbous, bell-shaped head. A coruscating red glow flared against the monster's electric-blue pulses as it darted away, boiling yellow froth obscuring its retreat. Ryjo looked about anxiously, reeling the buoy in closer, uncertain of how effective the phaser had been.

Had the beam stunned the beast? Repelled it? Or merely made it angry?

Peering out through his helmet's visor, he cursed how it limited his field of vision. Ascending through three-dimensional space, there was no way of knowing which direction the jelly might attack from next. He upped the power to the booster rockets in his boots. According to the heads-up display, he still had roughly two hundred meters to go before he reached the surface.

Not that this guaranteed safety from the lightning jelly.

A luminous pulse, out of the corner of his eye, alerted him just in time as, quite un-stunned, the creature came rushing at him from an angle. A blazing tentacle whipped toward him with alarming speed. Unable to swing the phaser around fast enough, he kicked up his legs to blast the swinging tentacle away with the boosters in his boots. The desperate maneuver sent him pinwheeling out of control. He held the buoy tightly against him with one arm, protecting it with his body, while his other hand kept a tight grip on the phaser. Dropping his only real weapon would be a death sentence for sure.

Tumbling head over heels, he used a voice command to switch off the thrusters, then tried to arrest his spin by kicking his legs and flailing with his free arm, while dreading the jelly's next attack—which was not long in coming.

A pulse strobed above him. He fired wildly, missing his target, and an electrified tentacle lashed against the back of Ryjo's suit, delivering a vicious jolt that caused him to spasm in shock. He convulsed within his suit. His heart missed a beat.

And then his suit went dead.

His searchlight blinked out. The heads-up display vanished. And worst of all, the constant hum and buzz of the suit's life-support functions fell silent, including the rebreathing apparatus.

Ryjo gasped, then clamped his jaws shut to hold his breath. Dazed and trembling, his nerves tingling from the shock, he still had the presence of mind to be properly terrified by the realization that his insulated suit, which seemed to have spared him from the worst of the jelly's lightning bolt, had been shorted out by the jolt, which left only one question to be answered: What would kill him first, suffocation or the creature?

The jelly appeared in no hurry to finish him off. Ryjo watched, his cheeks bulging with used air, as the beast lazily circled him, as though waiting to see if the intruder's light had been extinguished for good.

Right, Ryjo thought. *It left* Copernicus *alone after it knocked out our exterior lights. Guess I'm safe as long as my suit stays dark.*

So, suffocation then . . .

With the suit's cooling system down, the burning heat of the sea began to penetrate the insulated layers protecting Ryjo. This was the least of his concerns, however, since he would run out of oxygen well before he boiled to death.

Lucky me.

Then, to his surprise, flickers of color appeared before his eyes. He fought to keep from gasping as the heads-up display within his helmet began to come back to life. Photonic images, visible only to Ryjo, declared:

System Rebooting

Hope flooded him. Maybe he still had a chance after all, if the suit didn't take *too* long to restart—and some Starfleet engineer had been bright enough to prioritize the air supply in the reboot sequence.

It was going to be close. He was already feeling light-headed, a different variety of darkness infringing on the periphery of his vision. Starving lungs ached for relief. He clenched his teeth, trying to preserve his last precious breath as, one by one, assorted heads-up icons and displays manifested before his ever-foggier eyes. He couldn't hold on much longer . . .

Restart Complete

The suit started humming again. Fresh air flowed from the rebreather. Ryjo sucked it down hungrily, just as the helmet's searchlight came back on, shining in the dark—and attracting the lightning jelly once more.

Rut Starfleet protocols, Ryjo thought. His head clearing, he switched the phaser to maximum and fired dead-on at the approaching creature. A crimson glow suffused the jelly, overpowering its own innate luminosity, before it dissolved into atoms, leaving Ryjo alone in the deep at last. He panted loudly.

Would Chekov have resorted to lethal force quite so quickly? Ryjo didn't know or care. Preserving his cover wasn't going to do the Exile cause any good if he got himself killed before completing his mission. Now he just had to hope that McCoy was right about the jelly defending its territory, and that no new creature moved in to claim the dead jelly's turf before Ryjo could deliver the buoy to the surface.

Only a couple hundred meters to go.

With some effort, he got himself pointed in the right direction again and reactivated his levitation boots. One last push got him to surface without further incident, and he found himself bobbing in the waves beneath an ashy, overcast sky of mixed ocher and umber. Flakes of ash continued to fall like snow upon the sea, coating its surface with a gritty film that was immediately replaced almost as soon as its accumulated mass began to sink beneath the waves. The sludgy expanse stretched all around him as far as he could see, with no solid land in sight. *Copernicus* had clearly crashed many kilometers beyond the shore.

Just as well. Ryjo had no desire to return to the quaking volcanic plain they had barely escaped from before. Focusing on the task at hand, he activated the buoy's flotation system, which was comprised of an inflatable ring augmented by waterproof antigrav units that could be calibrated to adjust for the weight of the object or individual being supported. Making sure that calibration was correct so that the buoy didn't sink back into the depths was among the reasons Ryjo had needed to accompany the buoy to the surface. The antigravs also helped stabilize the buoy, compensating for the waves and the pull of the tether anchored to its base. He gave the tether just enough slack to allow it to bob above the waves without being submerged.

That and protecting it from the lightning jelly.

Had the creature's attack damaged the device? Ryjo anxiously inspected it by the light from his helmet but detected no obvious scorch marks or charring. He could only assume that his suit had protected the buoy from the jolt when the tentacle lashed him from behind. They'd lucked out that the strike hadn't hit the buoy directly, when it was nestled against his chest. As it was, all vital systems appeared operational.

But would that be enough to reach the *Enterprise*?

He wasted no time finding out. Gloved hands successfully activated the signal enhancer, which was already preset to the *Enterprise*'s emergency frequencies. A few more tweaks and he synched his helmet's comm system to the buoy; in theory, the enhancer would boost the signal enough to reach the *Enterprise* now that it was no longer coming from the bottom of the sea.

"Chekov to *Enterprise*. Can you read me?"

He held his breath, fearing that his perilous ascent had been in vain. Had the volcano thrown too much exotic matter into the atmosphere? Had Captain Kirk indeed given them up for dead and continued on to Voyzr? Did fate have one more dirty trick to play on them?

"Repeat, Chekov to—"

"*Enterprise* here, Chekov!" Uhura's voice came over the line. It was faint and scratchy, broken up by pops and crackles, but it came through nonetheless. "Stand by while I clean up the signal on our end."

It worked! Ryjo exulted. *That crazy Yarfite's plan saved us all.*

Provided, that is, he told the whole truth about *Copernicus* and the other people still trapped in the sunken shuttlecraft a thousand-plus meters below. He had yet to attempt establishing a comlink to *Copernicus*, so he *could* try informing the *Enterprise* that he was the sole survivor of the crash, which might increase his own chances of being rescued in a timely manner, thereby getting him closer to completing his mission—at the cost of the others' lives.

Tovar. Sulu. McCoy. Dipelly. Bwoj. Fressa.

He knew what Trath and other Exiles would want him to do, but could he really go through with it? Simone's voice echoed in his mind:

"You can do this. I have faith in you."

"Enterprise to Chekov." Uhura's voice, now much clearer, hailed him again. "What is your status?"

Twenty-Seven

"Time is of the essence, Captain." Spock looked up from the scanner at his science station. "The super-eruption I warned of earlier appears to be imminent."

"Can you be more precise, Spock?"

"Not with total accuracy, Captain." He sounded pained by the admission. "Seismology is not an exact science, and certainly not when it involves the complex variables of a largely unexplored moon. Sensors indicate, however, that the extreme tectonic pressures beneath Wexx's crust are rapidly approaching critical. We are likely talking hours at most. Possibly less."

"Understood." Kirk contemplated the cloudy, ocher sphere on the viewscreen, where they now knew *Copernicus* and its passengers were stranded and in desperate need of rescue, and not just from the coming cataclysm. According to Chekov and Sulu, the shuttlecraft's life-support systems were on their last legs, posing yet another mortal threat to the landing party. "Are you suggesting that we've run out of time to rescue our people?"

"Negative, Captain. The safety of the many does not always outweigh the lives of a few, as my own unlikely resurrection attests. I merely apprise you of the risks entailed . . . and the need for haste."

"Duly noted." Kirk nodded. "Keep me posted."

"I will endeavor to do so."

Kirk gravely faced the daunting task ahead, as did everyone else on the bridge. Their earlier jubilation at discovering that the search party was still alive had given way to somber recognition of just how dire the crisis still was. Rescuing their imperiled crewmates, not to mention the three Yarfites, was going to be both difficult and dangerous. They had a plan, but there was no guarantee they could pull it off successfully. Split-second timing would be required, too many things could go wrong, and the clock was ticking . . .

Let's get on with it, Kirk thought. "Take us down, Lieutenant Miller. Yellow alert. Shields up . . . for the present."

"Aye, sir."

Benuel Miller, subbing for Sulu at the helm, took the *Enterprise* out of orbit, descending into Wexx's roiling atmosphere. To his right, Ensign Vicki Novak occupied the nav station. Despite their relative youths, having never served on the old *Enterprise*, both were fully qualified, well-trained officers who had more than earned their postings upon the bridge; still, Kirk couldn't help wishing that Sulu and Chekov were at the conn for these tricky maneuvers—instead of being among those in need of rescue.

Sulfurous yellow and black clouds, densely laden with ash, filled the viewscreen. Compared to the relatively serene emptiness of space, the turbulent cloud cover seemed positively chaotic. Kirk could practically hear hot gas and steam whipping past the hull, pelting the deflectors with volcanic ejecta. Wexx's atmosphere was nearly as unstable as its surface.

"Exiting upper atmosphere," Miller reported, sticking to the plan. "Altitude one thousand meters and falling. Approaching crash site."

Thanks to the comlink Chekov had established between *Copernicus* and the *Enterprise*, Spock had finally been able to pinpoint the shuttlecraft's location beneath a vast equatorial sea suffused with heavy concentrations of metal sulfides. But even with the buoy enhancing the signal, *Copernicus* was still too deep beneath the waves to confidently transport its passengers to safety. According to Scotty, there was much more to be done before he could even try to lock onto Sulu and the others. Descending into Wexx's atmosphere was just the first step.

"Acknowledged," Kirk said. "Keep a close eye out for any volcanic plumes or lava bombs."

"Aye, sir." Novak monitored the tactical displays at her station. "On it."

Just the same, Kirk didn't intend to lower their shields until *Copernicus* could do the same, and then only for as long it took to beam everyone back to the *Enterprise*. He hadn't forgotten watching all those explosive plumes blast up into space. He could only imagine what it must be like for Chekov right now, adrift at sea on an unstable moon that was violently coming apart at the seams.

Hang on, Pavel. We're coming for you.

Ryjo clung to the buoy for dear life, as well as for the lives of everyone still trapped aboard *Copernicus*. Ultimately, he hadn't been able to bring himself to betray Tovar and Sulu and the others depending on him. He rationalized that the risk of being caught in that lie was too great, that "Chekov" would never be trusted again if the *Enterprise* somehow managed to detect the crashed shuttlecraft and the life signs aboard it, but he knew he was fooling himself. The truth was, he couldn't have lived with himself if he'd left them to drown, even if half of them were Starfleet and the other half foolhardy treasure hunters who'd brought this on themselves. They'd all been through too much together for Ryjo to abandon them now.

I can still complete my mission, he told himself. *I can still kill the regnant ... afterward.*

At the moment, though, the waves were getting progressively higher and choppier, churned up by undersea tremors and the occasional large chunk of rocky debris crashing down from the sky. If not for the cable binding him to the buoy, he would have already been swept away from it by now. Meanwhile, the relentless ashfall was growing heavier by the minute, so that he constantly had to wipe the abrasive yellow sludge off his visor and the buoy, as well as keep adjusting the antigrav controls to prevent the buoy from sinking beneath the sodden weight of the ash. The *Enterprise* had offered to try to beam him up first, now that the signal enhancer could help them get a decent lock on him, but Ryjo had opted to stay with the buoy until everyone aboard *Copernicus* could be rescued, if possible. He'd already gone too far to desert his post now; if he was resolved to save Tovar and the others, for whatever reason, he was going to do whatever it took.

All in, he thought. *No half measures.*

He wiped more gunk off his visor with the back of his glove before checking in with Sulu, mostly just to hear another voice.

"Chekov to *Copernicus*. Can you still read me?"

"Loud and more or less clear, thanks to you."

Sulu sat at the cockpit controls, Tovar beside him, while McCoy and the Yarfites hovered in the hatchway behind them, everyone still in their EV suits and holding on to their helmets. The shuttlecraft's comm system had more capacity and range than their handheld personal communicators and helmet comms, so they relied on it to keep in touch with Chekov and the *Enterprise* now that the buoy was in place and operational. He relished the sound of his friend's voice coming over the line. Chekov had gone ominously silent after exiting *Copernicus* earlier; the wait to hear if he'd successfully made it up from the deep had been hard on everyone's nerves. More than once, Sulu had been tempted to go looking for him.

"How are you managing?" he asked.

"Haven't been electrocuted by a hostile jelly for a while, so there's that," Chekov responded. *"I could ask you the same."*

"Don't," Sulu said. "We can compare notes once we're back where we belong, in much more comfortable accommodations."

In fact, conditions aboard *Copernicus* were steadily deteriorating, despite their best efforts to conserve power and maintain life-support. They had largely succeeded in flushing the interior of the shuttlecraft after Chekov's departure, although puddles of murky liquid made the deck slippery, and muddy yellow sediment had clung to every surface, requiring strenuous efforts to wipe the seats and bulkheads clean. A harsh, sulfurous odor suffused the already stale and sweaty air within both cockpit and cabin. Sulu had attempted to confiscate Fressa's vaporizer, but she had argued, not entirely unconvincingly, that the scented fumes helped relieve the general miasma; in the end, Sulu had not contested the point, concluding that the vaporizer's value in keeping the testy Yarfite pacified outweighed whatever marginal impact it had on their overall situation and chances. It wasn't as though a few stray puffs were going to tip the scales one way or another.

Undersea moonquakes continued to shake *Copernicus*, the jarring tremors increasing in both strength and frequency, placing additional strain on the already beleaguered hull. A worrisome bulge on the aft hatchway looked slightly larger every time Sulu looked at it, while apportioning power between the shields and life-support had become a delicate balancing act that was at best only buying them a little more time. The emergency lights in the passenger cabin were dimming as he prioritized keeping the cockpit controls and display panels lit. Artificial gravity had been switched off entirely, so only Wexx's much weaker gravity kept their feet planted on the deck and provided a sense of up and down. The reduced gravity made Sulu feel slightly "bouncy" and off-balance.

"*At this point, a packed cargo bay would feel comfy by comparison,*" Chekov replied. "*Or even a Jefferies tube.*"

"Pretty sure we can do better than that. I'm thinking drinks by the swimming pool."

Tovar leaned in toward the comm receiver. Perspiration shone upon her face as the temperature inside the shuttle steadily rose. "Works for me. I'll take a large Finagle's Folly or two."

"*Nyet on the pool. I've had enough waves and splashing around to last me all the way to Voyzr.*"

"Can't imagine why," Sulu quipped. "Seriously, though, we all owe you, big time. I see a commendation in your future."

"*It was the least I could do, considering.*"

"Nothing least about it," Tovar said. "We're talking above and beyond in my book."

Sulu couldn't agree more. Chekov may not have been himself lately, for reasons Sulu couldn't quite fathom, but he had definitely come through when it counted, just as he always had before.

That was the Pavel Chekov he'd known for decades now. The one he was proud to call his friend.

"Incoming!" Novak called out from the nav station, her eyes fixed on the tactical display. "Plume coming on fast!"

A sky-high column of superheated rock, ash, and gas slammed into the *Enterprise* at thousands of kilometers per hour. The volcanic cloud briefly obscured the viewscreen before being dispelled by the deflectors. The impact jarred the bridge even through the shields as the ship powered through the spreading, umbrella-shaped plume. A data slate vibrated off an auxiliary duty station behind Kirk, clattering onto the deck. Microtapes rattled in the tape holder on the right armrest of Kirk's chair. Uhura's earpiece was shaken loose, but she caught it before it hit the deck.

"Status?" Kirk demanded.

"Shields holding." Novak held on tightly to the nav panel. "Only fractional loss of strength."

"Putting the plume in our rearview sensors," Miller said. "Continuing descent toward equatorial sea."

"All departments checking in." Uhura refastened her earpiece. "No major damage or injuries reported."

"Acknowledged."

Kirk was relieved to hear that the *Enterprise* had come through the plume unscathed, mostly. Still, he didn't want to subject the ship to many more such blasts, before or while they lowered their shields to beam the landing party to safety. And then there was the brewing super-eruption to consider; from what Spock had said, they didn't want to be anywhere near Wexx's surface when that occurred.

Was he making the right call here? He couldn't help questioning his decision to proceed with the rescue mission, even while judiciously hiding any doubts from the crew. Was it fair to risk the lives of four-hundred-plus men, women, and beings to try to save seven lives that would otherwise be lost? Even Spock couldn't foretell exactly when the super-eruption was going to hit. For all they knew, the *Enterprise* was only moments away from destruction.

Then again, the *Enterprise* was no pleasure cruiser, loaded with innocent civilians counting on a safe voyage. Every member of Kirk's crew had accepted the risks when they joined Starfleet and accepted a post aboard this ship. They knew they would be facing danger and that their survival was not guaranteed, just as they needed to know that their captain would not abandon them if there was any chance of saving them.

We're not out here to play it safe.

"How much longer, Helmsman?"

"Leveling out at six hundred meters above the surface," Miller reported. "Circling above crash site. Thrusters on full."

Only six hundred meters, Kirk mused. *Way too close to a moon that is erupting all across its face . . . and building toward an apocalyptic explosion.*

"All right," he said. "Here's where things get complicated." He turned toward Miller, who had already engaged the telescoping targeting scanner at the helm. "Fire up the tractor beam."

Twenty-Eight

Ryjo had to admire the audacity of Kirk's plan: to bring the *Enterprise* low enough to lock onto *Copernicus* with a tractor beam and drag it to the surface, despite the sizable challenge of employing a tractor beam through large quantities of liquid instead of the vacuum of space. At that point both the starship and the shuttlecraft would simultaneously drop their shields long enough for Mister Scott to attempt to beam everyone off Wexx at last, with the buoy making it possible to lock onto the communicators in their helmets, both Starfleet and Yarfite. Preferably before another volcano or moonquake did *Copernicus* in for good.

All because Kirk had not given up on them, just as Sulu and McCoy predicted.

He's loyal to his own people, I'll give him that.

Even if he's no friend to mine.

He listened in as Uhura's voice came over the link: "Enterprise to Copernicus. *We are in position above you.*"

Ryjo tilted back his head and wiped his visor with his glove, irrationally hoping to spy the *Enterprise* high in the sky, but of course all he saw was smoke, clouds, and a blizzard of ash falling down on him, fouling his visor again. He had to take Uhura's word for it that the *Enterprise* was here to save them.

If they could.

"Proceeding according to plan," she said. *"Brace for tractor beam."*

But could the shuttlecraft's already compromised hull withstand the force of the tractor beam and the stress of the ascent? That was the question that worried Ryjo and seemingly Kirk as well. Ideally,

Copernicus would drop its shields now to allow the tractor beam to get a better grip on the sunken vessel, but instead *Copernicus* had been instructed to keep its fraying shields in place, reinforcing the hull, until it was securely above the waves. Even so, Ryjo wasn't fully convinced that the shuttlecraft would hold together that long. The bulkheads had been threatening to buckle even before he'd exited *Copernicus*, and that had been nearly two hours ago. Phantom antlers that couldn't actually fit inside his helmet ached to be scratched or rubbed against a post.

He prayed this hadn't all been in vain.

"Ready when you are, Enterprise," Sulu responded. "*We're in your tender— Whoa, you feel that?*"

A thunderous rumble, coming over the link, drowned him out.

Another tremor?

Now?

"Sulu!" Ryjo shouted. "What is it? "What's happen—?"

Before he could finish, a surging wave washed over him with seismic force, dislodging his grip on the buoy and sweeping him away from it. Waves buffeted him, carrying him under and tossing him about. He groped for the cable connecting him to the buoy, then felt it tug sharply on him, yanking him back.

Don't snap! Please don't snap!

As ever, the quake-driven surge lasted only a few endless moments before subsiding. Panting inside his helmet, he kicked his way to the surface, where the crashing waves were once again only fierce, not overpowering. Grabbing onto the cable with both hands, he pulled himself back toward the buoy, while trying frantically to contact *Copernicus* to make sure Sulu and the rest were still okay. Was the tether still secured to the seabed? If it had been shaken loose by this latest quake, he and the buoy could be swept away from the shuttlecraft, making it harder for the *Enterprise* to lock onto *Copernicus*.

"Sulu, *Copernicus*, can you hear me? Please respond!"

No one answered.

"*Enterprise*? Chekov to *Enterprise*?" Still no responses. "No, no, no . . ."

Had they all lost contact with each other? On the bright side, that implied the problem wasn't simply that *Copernicus* had gone dead, with all the ghastly possibilities that raised, since the *Enterprise* was silent too, and they wouldn't have been knocked offline by an underwater quake, which suggested that maybe something had happened to . . .

The buoy!

Hand over gloved hand, he dragged himself through the pounding waves and heavy, clinging sludge until he reached the equally mud-encrusted device—and discovered that, despite the tether, it had been flipped over by the seismic surge.

"Ordure!"

Clearly, the buoy wasn't working upside-down, with the primary antenna dish submerged and out of alignment. Ryjo blamed himself for allowing the tether a little *too* much slack. This wasn't good; the whole plan depended on all parties being able to communicate and coordinate with each other, and Scott needed the signal enhancer to lock onto the landing party and the Yarfites despite all the ash and interference in the atmosphere. Furthermore, just to make matters worse, the buoy was already starting to sink beneath the weight of the ashfall again, and Ryjo couldn't get at the antigrav controls to compensate for the extra mass. If worst came to worst, he would have to unclip himself from the buoy to avoid being dragged down with it.

Unless I fix this.

He seized the flotation ring, which was mercifully still intact. Heaving with all the strength left in Chekov's maddeningly middle-aged, merely human body, he tried to flip the buoy back over, but he couldn't get any leverage with his feet dangling underwater instead of braced against something solid. Kicking and splashing like a panicked waterfowl wasn't doing any good, while his heavy boots felt like rutting anchors . . .

My boots! My levitation *boots!*

They were his only chance, if the booster rockets still had enough juice for one more liftoff.

"Voice command! Ignite boosters!"

The boots fired, thrusting him upward with force enough that he was able to flip the buoy back into the correct orientation. He instantly switched off the boosters to avoid shooting up into the sky, dragging the buoy behind him. As it was, both the cable binding him to the buoy and the tether anchoring the buoy to the seabed were tested severely before he splashed down into the waves, briefly sinking below the surface, before swimming back up to the buoy. He scrambled to dial up the antigrav units, then rebooted the comlinks.

"*Copernicus, Enterprise*! Can either of you hear me now?"

Uhura replied at once: "*We read you, Chekov. We lost you for a few minutes, but we have you back.* Copernicus?"

"Ready and waiting," Sulu answered. "*Bring us home.*"

"Helmets on, everyone!" Sulu called out. "And strap yourselves in. This could be a bumpy ride!"

"Oh, joy," McCoy said. "Just when I was getting comfortable."

Bulkheads keened in distress. Sulu swallowed hard and gave *Copernicus*'s dashboard an encouraging pat.

Hang on just a little longer.

The shuttlecraft shook, much as it had during each new quake, but this time Sulu felt *Copernicus* rise from the seabed, captured by the tractor beam. The pilot in him would have preferred to lift off under their own power, with him in control of their ascent, but they were all just passengers now. The *Enterprise* was calling the shots.

"Hang tight," he said over his helmet comm, as much to himself as to the others. "We're in good hands."

As long as they don't squeeze us too hard.

Clinging to the buoy like a space-suited barnacle, Ryjo watched wide-eyed as a shimmering blue curtain of light shone down from above, turning the mustard-colored clouds purplish as it passed through them on its way to spotlighting the frenzied yellow waves no more than fifty meters away from him. He had to admire the precision of whoever was aiming the tractor beam, targeting *Copernicus* while carefully skirting both Ryjo and the buoy. A concentrated stream of gravitons penetrated the tossing surface of the waters in search of the stranded shuttlecraft more than a thousand meters below.

I never realized before just how beautiful a tractor beam can be.

Another stony chunk of volcanic debris splashed down in the distance, increasing his anxiety. He kept telling himself that the odds of an ejected volcano fragment crashing into the sea exactly where he was floating were comparable to winning the jackpot at a crooked casino in Jhopash, but it would be just like fate to flatten him when he was on the verge of rescue. Somehow knowing that escape was almost at hand only made the possibility all the more nerve-racking.

Maybe he *should* have let the *Enterprise* beam him up first?

Then, right where the tractor beam was focused, a churning fountain of purplish froth heralded the sight he had been waiting for. *Copernicus* rose from the depths, breaking through the waves. In the rippling blue glow of the tractor beam, the much-abused shuttlecraft looked as though it had been through the wars, its once-gleaming hull scorched and battered and coated with gunk. The trashed starboard nacelle was nothing but scrap metal and pulverized coils, conduits, and circuitry. Not even the shuttle's name was visible beneath all the damage.

But it wasn't stuck at the bottom of the sea anymore!

"We did it!" Sulu announced, monitoring their ascent via the altimeter on the control panel. What was left of the external sensors confirmed that *Copernicus* was now surrounded by air, not liquid. Toxic air, to be sure, but air nonetheless. "We're out of the drink!"

And just in time.

Cheers and laughter greeted the news. Tovar high-fived him from the copilot's seat. Fressa blew celebratory smoke circles toward the ceiling, while Dipelly applauded.

"Hallelujah," McCoy said. "Never thought I'd find myself pining for a good old-fashioned transporter beam."

"Don't forget!" Bwoj bounced up and down in his seat. "The buoy was my idea! If I hadn't thought—"

The bulging aft hatchway caved in, admitting a rush of swirling ashes and gas, and setting off a cascading structural collapse. Screaming bulkheads gave way, twisting and shearing away from each other. The ceiling lurched downward, causing Sulu to duck his head instinctively. All at once he felt like a sacrificial probe being crushed by the gravitational forces of a singularity it had been sent to explore. The deck buckled beneath his feet. White-hot sparks sprayed from the control panel.

"*Copernicus!*" Scotty's unmistakable burr issued from the speaker. *"Lower your shields at once!"*

Ryjo watched in horror as *Copernicus* crumpled before his eyes, its wounded hull succumbing to the force of a tractor beam powerful enough to raise it from the deep. Moments later, the sublime blue radiance vanished, leaving behind a mangled mass of compacted wreckage that foundered briefly before sinking out of sight . . . for all time?

Ryjo's throat tightened. Had Tovar and the others been beamed away in time, or were they also headed back to the bottom of this hellish sea? If they had even survived the shuttlecraft's collapse.

"*Enterprise!*" he hollered. "Please tell me you've got them!"

A tingling sensation washed over him as a transporter beam cut off his pleas by breaking him down into atoms.

"Captain!" Spock said urgently. "Wexx's internal pressures have peaked. The super-eruption is almost upon us."

"Damn it." Kirk pounded a fist into his palm. Had they run out of time after all, and with their shields down no less? He stabbed the intercom button on his armrest. "Scotty! Do you have them?"

The engineer replied from the transporter room, where he was personally operating the control console. *"Everyone from* Copernicus *is safe, Captain. Locking onto Chekov as we speak."*

Kirk exchanged a worried look with Spock, whose furrowed brow and grave demeanor fully conveyed the extremity of the moment. The danger was not lost on the rest of the bridge crew as well; Kirk could virtually feel the tension in the air. Uhura had a hand to her earpiece, listening intently. Miller wiped perspiration from his brow while muttering darkly in Pennsylvania Dutch. Novak's hand hovered over the shield controls. Everyone in earshot knew just how close they were calling it.

"Scotty?" Kirk asked.

"Chekov aboard, Captain. A bit muddy, but—"

That was all Kirk needed to hear.

"Raise shields!" he ordered. "Get us out of here. Full impulse!"

"Aye, aye, sir!" Miller and Novak said, almost in unison.

The ship took off at a steep angle that tested the ship's inertial dampers, climbing out of the atmosphere through sulfurous yellow skies that quickly thinned. Pressed into the back of his chair by the sudden acceleration, Kirk peered anxiously at the viewscreen, seeking the welcome vacuum of space. If they could just leave the self-destructing moon behind before—

"Wexx is erupting," Spock said loudly. "All hands, brace for impact."

A titanic roar, exceeding the detonation of Earth's legendary Krakatoa in volume, accompanied a shock wave that struck the *Enterprise* with a force many orders of magnitude beyond the volcanic plume that rattled the ship earlier. The bridge tilted upward to an almost ninety-degree angle before righting itself. Lights flickered and warning klaxons sounded. A standing yeoman, who had not had time to secure herself, slammed into the protective rail around the command pit and tumbled over it, even as the moon-shaking blast hurled the *Enterprise* out and away from Wexx.

Or whatever was left of it.

Twenty-Nine

"The sheer quantity of ash, smoke, and other particulates produced by the super-eruption pose an even more formidable challenge to our long-range sensors," Spock reported, "but by my estimates, approximately 3,450 cubic kilometers of materials were ejected during the event, and the climactic blast was on the order of more than one million megatons."

Kirk listened to Spock's summary in the *Enterprise*'s main briefing room, where they were meeting with the rescued Yarfites. Also in attendance was Ensign Welles, filling in for Yeoman Munro, who was currently resting in sickbay after her nasty tumble on the bridge during their narrow escape from Wexx. Doctor McCoy, happily back where he belonged, had assured Kirk that she would make a full recovery. Meanwhile, Kirk's own ankle was starting to feel better as well.

"So you're saying there's little chance the *Stellar Gale* might have survived?"

Fressa, her injured arm in a fresh, more lightweight sling, looked stricken by this assessment. Along with her two companions, she had been provided with clean coveralls tailored to fit Yarfite proportions. Kirk had also tactfully arranged to have levitating seats on hand so the short-statured rescuees could sit comfortably at the conference table without any loss of dignity, just as he had the last time the *Enterprise* had hosted a delegation of Ithenites.

"That would be extremely unlikely," Spock said. "If the wreck in question had indeed rested somewhere on Wexx, perhaps at the bottom of the sea, it is almost surely lost now. A pity; it would have been a find of significant historical interest."

"That's it then." Fressa's jowly face fell. She fumbled plaintively with her vaporizer, which Kirk had strictly forbidden her from using anywhere except in the privacy of her guest quarters. "We've lost our ship and the treasure."

"But we still have our lives," Dipelly reminded her. She had shed her neck brace after receiving a follow-up examination aboard the ship. "Once again, Captain, we're very grateful for that and deeply regret the loss of your shuttlecraft."

Fressa eyed Kirk worriedly. "Er, we're not going to be billed for that, are we?"

"Not to worry," Kirk said. "We don't charge for saving lives."

Starfleet Command wasn't going to be pleased at having to replace *Copernicus* again, only a couple of years after the Sybok affair, and Kirk didn't like being short-handed in terms of shuttlecrafts, but this was simply the cost of business as far as he was concerned. They had a duty to respond to distress signals and render whatever necessary aid they could, even if that meant sacrificing some valuable hardware once in a while.

"That's very good of you," Fressa said, visibly relieved. "Please don't think me ungrateful, Captain. We wouldn't be here if not for you and your valiant crew."

"We're happy to have been of assistance," Kirk said. "I'm just sorry we couldn't salvage your ship as well."

Chances were, the *Whilom* was nothing but a smoking crater now, or else buried beneath tons of molten lava. Not that, according to the landing party, it was ever going to fly again anyway.

"But what's to become of us now," Bwoj fretted, wringing his paws. "Where are we to go?"

Good question, Kirk thought, which was one of the reasons he'd convened this meeting. "As it happens, we're due at Voyzr shortly. Our schedule is tight"—too much so, after their extended detour to Wexx—"so there's no time for any additional stops or side trips along the way, which means you're our guests until we reach Voyzr, at which point you can disembark there, or we can drop you off at the nearest starbase after we've concluded our business on Voyzr. If you're in need of further shelter or transportation, there are staff and facilities at most starbases that can help you get back on your feet again and safely back to Yarfa."

"Thank you, Captain," Fressa said, "but that won't be necessary. We're not entirely destitute. I still have favors I can call in, contacts throughout the sector, and untapped resources put aside for emergencies. Just get us to Voyzr and we'll be back in business in no time." She turned to Dipelly. "Isn't that so?"

"Absolutely, Skipper. In fact, I've been thinking. Remember that junked Izarian freighter a certain former business associate was hawking in Asteroid City not too long ago? As I recall, that could probably be made spaceworthy again without spending too many credits, or maybe we could cut a deal to get any vital parts or repairs in exchange for just a modest slice of the proceeds of our next expedition, whatever that might be."

"About that," Kirk said, both amused and curious, "what do you have in mind now that the *Stellar Gale* is presumably lost for good? If you don't mind me asking."

"Well . . ." Bwoj glanced around, his gaze lighting briefly on Ensign Welles *and* a potted fern in the corner before lowering his voice. "You ever heard of the Lost Scepter of Null-Zero?" Canine eyes gleamed with excitement as he hurried on without waiting for a reply. "Story goes that, roughly five centuries ago, a notorious master thief heisted a priceless relic from the hidden burial vault of a proto-Nausicaan priest-king. The thief, known only as 'the Primrose Phantasm,' was reportedly captured and executed by a royal death squad or a rival cult of interplanetary freebooters, depending on which account you choose to believe, but the Scepter was never recovered. Legends persist that she hid it in somewhere in the Yannah Belt, but

I've long wondered if perhaps that was deliberate misdirection, and she actually stowed it in the last place anyone would ever expect."

Spock raised an eyebrow. "I take it your recent mishaps have not discouraged your zeal for such quixotic ventures. Nor persuaded you to take up less hazardous pursuits?"

"You underestimate the thrill of the quest." Fressa chortled, her chops quivering. "Treasure-hunting is in our blood, Mister Spock. It's what keeps our hearts pumping."

"Even when it nearly stopped those hearts permanently?"

"No risk, no reward, I always say."

"And that goes for all of you?" Kirk asked. "No offense, Mister Bwoj, but my understanding is that you appeared rather disenchanted with treasure-hunting while trapped on Wexx."

"That was before you saved us," Bwoj replied. "True, I may have expressed some misgivings before, but I was under severe emotional duress. Now that the crisis is past, I can think more clearly, and I'm convinced that the Scepter is out there, just waiting to be found on—"

He caught himself before saying too much.

"Fascinating," Spock said, bemused.

"Well, we wish you luck in all your future endeavors," Kirk said, "and I couldn't be more pleased that all concerned have been recovered from Wexx without serious loss of life or limb. A most satisfactory outcome."

"Very much so." Dipelly glanced around the briefing room. "Speaking of which, Captain, where are Commander Chekov and the others? I was hoping to thank them again now that we've all had a chance to recover from our ordeal."

"I'm sure you'll have your chance on the way to Voyzr," Kirk said. "At the moment, however, I believe they're enjoying some well-deserved rest and recreation."

"To the *Copernicus*. May she rest in peace."

Glasses clinked as Ryjo, Tovar, and Sulu toasted the deceased shuttlecraft that had briefly sheltered them from the volcanic furies of Wexx. They shared a table on the fringes of the *Enterprise*'s impressive botanical garden, which boasted an abundance of lush, multicolored flora from all across the quadrant. Panoramic viewports offered a view of distant stars, while an artificial breeze wafted gentle fragrances along the many leafy paths winding through the garden. A freshwater stream fully stocked with a wide variety of tropical fish gurgled softly in the background. A convenient snack bar provided both drinks and refreshments. A pleasant change, Ryjo had to admit, from the hellish moonscape they had just escaped. Starfleet certainly took good care of its people.

"A shame the good doctor couldn't join us." He sipped on a White Russian for the sake of his cover. Disturbingly, he was starting to develop a taste for them. "I gather he's busy tending to all the crew members who got knocked about by the shock wave?"

Ryjo himself had been thrown from the transporter pad almost immediately upon being beamed back to the *Enterprise*. For a few moments there, he thought he'd been rescued just in time to go down with another ship.

"So he says." Tovar put down the Finagle's Folly she'd promised herself before. The dark green beverage was said to pack quite a punch. "But if you ask me, he's just delighted to be back home in sickbay. Not that he'd ever admit it."

"At least he cut you loose to unwind a little." Sulu treated himself to a Risan mai tai, garnished with fresh fruit. "Despite all the bumps and bruises filling sickbay."

"Nothing he can't handle with an assist from the beta and gamma shift nurses," Tovar said. "And after what we went through on that rescue mission, he can hardly begrudge me some much-needed down time. He's a doctor, not an ogre."

"We can all use a break," Sulu said. "I don't know about you two, but I feel a lot more human now that I've had a warm meal, a sonic shower, and a good night's sleep."

"I know what you mean," Ryjo said, although "feeling human" was still not a phrase that sat comfortably with him, even if it did technically apply at present. *But not for too much longer.*

Their fellow crew members—*no*, he corrected himself, Sulu's and Tovar's fellow crew members—were also milling about in the garden this afternoon. Many of them swung by to congratulate the trio on their death-defying escape and express relief at their continued well-being. The warmth and sincerity of their sentiments were hard to resist. Ryjo caught himself basking in the camaraderie, envying Chekov the tight bonds between Kirk's people.

Too bad he had to betray them . . .

"Sure you don't want a sip?" Tovar offered him a taste of her Folly. "You don't know what you're missing."

"Well, if you insist."

Careful, he thought. He had to keep his wits about him, especially in front of Sulu and where Tovar was concerned. Now that they'd escaped from Wexx, he needed to focus on his mission once more. Then again, he didn't want to appear suspiciously antisocial. Staying in character required a certain degree of congeniality.

The drink had a definite kick to it, leavened by a sweet, spicy flavor he couldn't quite place. He could all too easily see it loosening his tongue, dangerously so, if he overindulged.

"Very nice." He pulled back, withdrawing his lips from the edge of the glass she was holding out to him. "As I understand it, Finagle was actually born in a Russian colony on Grushenka V . . ."

"Is that so?" Sulu chuckled. "Next you'll be insisting that Finagle is actually short for Fingalski."

"*Da*. That goes without saying."

The overhead lights began to dim, simulating twilight according to the ship's internal clock. Artificial moonlight began to filter down from above. Tovar polished off her drink and rose to her feet. She smiled down at Ryjo and held out her hand.

"You know, it occurs to me that somebody still owes me a moonlit walk in the garden." She glanced at Sulu. "If you don't mind us leaving you to your own devices, Hikaru."

"Don't let me stop you." He winked at Chekov as he leaned back in his chair, nursing his drink. "I'm fine where I am. Enjoy."

Just my luck, Ryjo thought. *Sulu knows how to take a hint.*

Now what was he supposed to do?

Not that he wasn't tempted to enjoy a romantic stroll—or more—with Simone Tovar. She was quite appealing for a human, and he was undeniably drawn to her, all the more so after their shared brush with death on Wexx. What's more, his own future was growing shorter the closer they got to Voyzr and the fatal culmination of his mission. This might very well be his last chance to enjoy a woman's tender embrace. Why shouldn't he seize the opportunity before it was too late?

On the other hand, all his earlier reasons for keeping Tovar at arm's length still applied. The closer he got to her, the greater the risk that she might see through his cover, endangering his mission. This undercover routine was tricky enough without trying to finesse a love affair on top of everything else. Plus, honestly, it didn't feel right to romance Tovar under false pretenses. Assassinating an enemy leader for the sake of the cause was one thing; toying with Simone's affections, setting her up for even greater heartbreak down the road, was something else altogether. He was an undercover operative, not a monster.

He couldn't do that to her.

"Can I get a rain check on that?" He declined to take her hand, knowing full well just how badly this would go over. "I'm still feeling rather beat and that last drink has gone to my head. I think I'll turn in early if that's all right by you."

Her stunned expression stabbed him in the heart. Her face hardened as hurt ignited into anger.

"Unbelievable! Just when I thought that we were finally . . . Tell you what, *Commander*, I've had quite enough of your mixed signals. Thanks for saving our lives and all, but don't come looking for me the next time you decide to run hot instead of cold. I'm through."

She turned and walked away.

"Are you kidding?" Sulu stared at him, aghast. "I mean, you know I have your back no matter what, but what the hell is wrong with you?"

Ryjo sighed.

"Trust me. It's better this way."

Thirty

You shudder as the eel wriggles its way up your cheek, leaving a slimy trail on your skin. It's inside your helmet with nowhere to go except into your brain. You want to rip the helmet off and yank the pincered creature away from your face, but Khan's people won't let you. You can only suffer, your heart pounding in fear, as the eel burrows into your ear . . .

A chime brought Ryjo back to the present and himself. Starting, he woke to find himself at his desk in Chekov's quarters, where he must have dozed off while reviewing the latest updates on the security arrangements for the embassy opening. No surprise there; he hadn't been sleeping well lately.

Can't imagine why, he thought. *Given what lies ahead for me.*

Trying to shake the ghastly dream/memory from his mind, he reached out and responded to the chime. "Chekov here."

Uhura's face appeared on the screen of his desktop computer monitor.

"Sorry to disturb you, Chekov, but we're approaching Voyzr."

"Thank you, Uhura. I will be ready."

Signing off, he took a moment to gird himself for what was to come and recover from that all-too-vivid flashback to Chekov's harrowing ordeal on Ceti Alpha V. That Chekov's memories were already starting to filter into his own dreams was not a good sign. Doctor Morval had assured him that he would have time to complete his mission before the transference reversed itself, but perhaps she had miscalculated; this was an experimental technique after all. They might be calling it closer than anticipated.

Good thing we're finally arriving at Voyzr, just in time.

Against all odds, his mission was finally near completion, provoking a complicated mix of emotions. He felt excited, resigned, anxious, and relieved all at once. On the one hand, he was about to strike a great blow in his father's memory, despite the universe's best efforts to derail him. On the other hand, he was about to die a murderer . . .

No, he corrected himself. *An assassin. A martyr for my people.*

Either way, it would all be over soon.

A quick sonic shower helped to wash away some, if not all, lingering unease from that horrific nightmare. He changed into Chekov's dress uniform, then unlocked a private storage compartment and extracted what appeared to be an ordinary, standard-issue Starfleet hypospray, which had gone completely unnoticed when he'd brought it aboard the *Enterprise* upon his "return" from Tykona. The camouflaged weapon, expressly designed to avoid attracting undue attention, had been waiting patiently to fulfill its ultimate purpose—and seal his fate forever.

We're almost there.

A turbolift brought to him to the transporter room, where Kirk and Sulu were already waiting, with Scott standing by to beam them down to the gala opening of the embassy. After departing Wexx, the *Enterprise* had pressed its engines to reach Voyzr at practically the last minute. Like Ryjo, Kirk and Sulu were also decked out in their dress uniforms, befitting their status as guests of honor on account of their "historic" actions on Voyzr twenty years ago. As neither Spock nor McCoy was present when Kirk supposedly brought "peace" to the planet, they were remaining aboard the ship, with Spock commanding the bridge in the captain's absence and McCoy presiding over sickbay.

Thankfully, Tovar was not slated for this diplomatic call since she hadn't even been a member of the crew when the original

Enterprise first visited Voyzr before. Days had passed since he had deliberately rejected her in the garden and, for better or for worse, they'd had little contact since. On the rare occasions they encountered each other in the corridors, she walked briskly past him without a word, while somehow still conveying a frosty attitude.

Just as well, he thought. *Maybe this will make it easier for her after "Chekov" comes to a bad end, turning assassin.*

Sulu looked up as he entered. He had tried to talk to Ryjo a few times about that scene with Tovar, but Ryjo had managed to fend off his well-intentioned inquiries without being too brusque about it, at least long enough to arrive at this moment, which, luckily, was neither the time nor the place for such a discussion.

"Looking sharp," Sulu said. "Who knew you cleaned up so well?"

"Likewise." Ryjo's amiable grin belied his nerves. "Reporting for duty, Captain."

"Very good, Mister Chekov." Kirk turned to Scott. "Please inform the embassy that we are ready to beam down."

"Aye, sir."

"I assume all proper security protocols are being observed." Ryjo shrugged apologetically at Scott. "Just doing my job."

Security was airtight around the event. Entry to Voyzr space was being closely monitored and restricted, while the embassy itself was heavily guarded by shields and Voyzr security forces, with multiple levels of encryption, passcodes, and clearances required at every juncture. In deference to Voyzr's sovereignty and the regnant's attendance, the landing party was leaving their own phasers behind.

Hence, the doctored hypospray.

"No offense taken," Scott replied. "Every precaution that can be taken has been taken. We're just waiting on you to transmit the final passcode before they lower the shields around the embassy."

"Happy to oblige."

Ryjo strode over to control console. In his capacity as security chief, he had been heavily involved in setting up these procedures and kept apprised of the latest codes. After confirming that they were indeed on the prescribed secure channel, he keyed in the final code and sent it down to the planet.

"*Thank you*, Enterprise," a voice replied from the comm unit on the control console. "*You are cleared to beam down. We look forward to greeting you.*"

The three men took their places on the transporter pad. Sulu grinned at Ryjo. "Beats taking a shuttlecraft into a volcano zone. If nothing else, this excursion should be a lot more pleasant than our last one."

I wouldn't count on it, Ryjo thought.

The hypospray weighed heavily in the pocket of his maroon jacket.

"Hailing *Enterprise*! This is an emergency! Please respond!"

Chekov risked trying to contact the ship again as he approached the Voyzr system, reluctantly slowing to sublight velocity. After his close call with that bird-of-prey, he'd refrained from transmitting any signals that might draw the Klingons down on him again. Moreover, *Xoline*'s crippled long-range transceiver array had proved beyond repair, limiting his ability to communicate across great distances in a timely manner. Was he now close enough to the *Enterprise* to get through to them at last—or did he still need to get even closer to them?

The silence greeting his hails strongly suggested the latter.

He had pushed the hijacked yacht past its limits to get to Voyzr as fast as possible, but time was running out. By his calculations, the ceremony at the embassy should be getting underway anytime now; whatever Ryjo had planned was about to go down—with disastrous consequences for the regnant, Voyzr, the Federation, and even Ryjo himself. He needed to warn Captain Kirk and the others before it was too late.

"*Warning: inertial dampers overheating,*" a computerized voice announced as yet another alert icon started flashing on the cockpit control panel. "*Immediate maintenance advised—*"

Chekov muted the warning, as he had all the previous ones. He already knew that the headlong flight from Oasis Station was taking a toll on *Xoline*. The control panel was lit up like the Scarlet Nebula, with one system after another edging into the red zone. He suspected he was killing *Xoline*, driving it too hard like a lathered steed ridden until it drops, and he felt a twinge of guilt with regard to the yacht's actual owner, but he couldn't worry about that now. All that mattered was stopping Ryjo while there was a still a chance. *Xoline* just had to make it to the final stretch.

"Hailing *Enterprise*! Repeat: Hailing *Enterprise* . . ."

Someone else responded instead:

"*Attention, unidentified vessel. This is Voyzr border security. You are approaching restricted space. Identify yourself and your purpose.*"

A proximity sensor detected an object moving to intercept *Xoline*. Increasing the magnification and scan resolution revealed that the object was an automated space buoy, about half the size of the yacht, marking and patrolling the perimeter of Voyzr space. One of several drone buoys, Chekov recalled from his study of Voyzr's planetary defenses, with the drones just the first layer of planetary security. The order itself was being relayed by the buoy from a monitoring station elsewhere.

"*Repeat: State your identity and purpose.*"

There was no good answer to that query. What was he supposed to tell them, that he was a fugitive Voyzr piloting a stolen vessel? That was not going to get him close enough to the planet in time to do any good, and especially not while the embassy opening was underway. At best, he'd be turned away, if not detained indefinitely.

Still, he had to say something.

"Er, this is the *S.S. Grigori*, requiring an emergency stopover at Voyzr. Request permission to achieve orbit around planet."

A false name and registry number wasn't going to hold up to close examination, but might make it a little harder to identify *Xoline* as a hijacked spacecraft, while the yacht's sorry condition and myriad systems overloads could lend credence to his "emergency" cover story if and when *Xoline* was subjected to any security scans. He just needed to get close enough to Voyzr to contact the *Enterprise*, which was presumably already in orbit around the planet.

"*Negative,* Grigori. *Our orbital space is currently a no-fly zone. Remain where you are until assistance can be dispatched.*"

"No time for that, I'm afraid. My situation is urgent. Please allow me to proceed with all due speed."

Sensors indicated two more drones converging on his location.

"*Negative,* Grigori. *Sit tight and await inspection.*"

Chekov muttered under his breath. He had been afraid of this, being well acquainted with the heightened security measures surrounding the anniversary celebration, some of which he had personally proposed before having his body stolen. The irony was neither lost on him nor appreciated.

Xoline did not slow down.

"*Attention,* Grigori . . . *or whoever you are. Turn back immediately.*"

"Sorry. This is not possible."

He muted the transmission, seeing no further point in dissembling. On the viewscreen before him, the first of the automated buoys came into view, blocking his path. No surprise, the drone was shaped like an intimidating rack of antlers, at least three times the size of those of a terrestrial moose, all polished steel plating and incandescent lights and sensors. *Xoline* banked to starboard to evade it, but, as anticipated, the drone corrected its own course to match him, as it would surely do again and again, with yet more drones rushing to join the blockade.

He didn't have time for this.

Xoline's defensive phasers targeted the buoy. Cobalt beams sliced through the vacuum and the drone as well, bisecting it. Sparks flared in the dark of space before quickly extinguishing. The yacht veered to avoid the floating wreckage, then resumed its original course in open defiance of Voyzr's express instructions. Chekov set his jaw in determination.

All right, he thought. *We are crashing this party—with extreme prejudice.*

Firing on the buoy was only going to make his approach all the more alarming and suspicious, of course, and with good reason. He wouldn't let a rogue, trigger-happy vessel anywhere near Voyzr or the *Enterprise* either, if he was in charge, and certainly not during a major diplomatic event. Any hope of talking his way past Voyzr's defenses had just gone out the waste disposal unit.

And more drones were on the way.

Sensors indicated two buoys on his tail and a third on track to intercept him any moment now. Chekov made a beeline for Voyzr anyway; there was no time to find a sneakier, more circuitous route to the planet. He recharged the phaser batteries, so he was armed and ready when the next drone darted into view, dead ahead. Without waiting for another warning, he opened fire at once, only to see the beams break against the buoy's now-raised shields, producing brilliant blue flashes of Cherenkov radiation, named after the great Russian physicist Pavel Cherenkov no less. This proud bit of scientific history brought little comfort to Chekov, who realized that the drones were not going to be taken unawares by another sneak attack. Having learned from their predecessor's demise, the other buoys had taken appropriate countermeasures—and would likely respond in kind.

The tips of the metallic antlers lit up.

"Red alert!" he blurted out of habit, hastily dialing up his own shields, just as the drone opened fire with a barrage of phaser beams targeting his engines and propulsion units. Chekov admired its restraint while simultaneously being shaken by the impact of the beams colliding against *Xoline*'s shields. More blinding blue flashes, now right outside the yacht, paid tribute to Russian science and nomenclature, while battering the pleasure craft's somewhat less than Starfleet-quality deflectors. Within moments, *Xoline*'s already compromised shield strength had been diminished by another seventeen percent. Gauges and status displays on the control panel flashed even brighter, or else gave up the ghost entirely, pointedly reminding him that, already overtaxed, the yacht was in no condition to sustain heavy fire.

"*Gavno!*" he swore.

Reluctantly, he took evasive action, zigzagging through space in all three directions, even though every abrupt change of direction delayed his progress toward the *Enterprise*. The drone stuck with him, its phasers still glancing off *Xoline*'s shields. Chekov cast a pained look at the empty copilot seat beside him; he could really use Sulu at the helm right now, instead of having to single-handedly evade the drones *and* attend to the system failures and malfunctions being reported all over the board. Precious energy needed to be diverted from propulsion to the deflectors, further slowing their flight. Automatic fire-suppression systems activated in both a luxury stateroom and the galley; he had to trust that *Xoline* could put out the blazes on her own, even in her exhausted state. Was that smoke he smelled wafting into the cockpit? Or simply burning circuitry in the control panel?

Changing course, the second buoy charged straight at him. Chekov had no intention of playing chicken with a lifeless mechanism that had no actual flesh and blood in the game, so he dived below the oncoming drone, barely avoiding a head-on collision and taking another blast to blast to the yacht's topside. He banked sharply to port, then veered back toward Voyzr. He may be no Sulu, he reminded himself, but he had logged more than his fair share of hours piloting everything from workbees to shuttlecrafts to two different *Enterprise*s, while also spelling Sulu on a captured Klingon bird-of-prey as well. He wasn't about to be outflown by a pack of glorified boundary markers.

Granted, I could really use a cloaking device right now, he thought, briefly pining for the late *HMS Bounty*.

But perhaps he could still pull another ace from his sleeve?

Executing a loop, he turned the yacht's stern toward the lead drone, then ejected all of *Xoline*'s remaining escape pods at once. Three emergency lifeboats, each capable of sustaining up to four standard humanoids, filled the empty space between the yacht and the drone like so much chaff, drawing the drone's fire and briefly shielding *Xoline* long enough for Chekov to remotely trigger the self-destruct mechanisms he'd jury-rigged in the pods on the way here, while the yacht was flying on automatic pilot across deep space. Just in case he ran into more Klingons or other hostile parties.

The pods exploded, spewing smoke, shrapnel, and blazing plasma in all directions. As hoped, the expanding clouds of gas and wreckage confused the drone's sensors and provided cover for *Xoline* to dart past the drone and get out ahead of it, zipping past the outer moons and planets of the system toward Voyzr itself—and the *Enterprise*.

Not that he'd escaped the buoys for good. He was under no illusion that his improvised "smoke screen" would lose them completely. Aft sensors quickly verified this grim assessment; as the clouds dispersed, the three drones regrouped and accelerated after him, gaining rapidly.

How long could he stay out in front of them?

"Attention, hostile vessel!" A stern voice overrode his mute command, either by force from their end or perhaps simply because some algorithm in the yacht's computerized brain decided Chekov *really* needed to hear this. *"An armed patrol ship is headed your way and will not permit you to advance any farther toward Voyzr. Do you understand me?"*

Only too well, as it happened. Chekov was fully aware that such patrol ships constituted a second ring of defense for Voyzr, on top of the hostile drones now closing in on him. A quick glance at a flickering display panel confirmed the ship speeding toward him; within minutes he would be caught between the drones behind and the manned patrol ship ahead, with the latter between him and the *Enterprise*. A classic pincer move.

"Power down your weapons and surrender. Be aware that we will not hesitate to use lethal force."

Chekov could not say the same. Blasting a drone was one thing, but he couldn't risk firing on a piloted vessel for fear of harming innocent Voyzr security personnel who were just doing their job. That would be unconscionable, as well as a diplomatic catastrophe in its own right.

A drone blast from the rear jolted *Xoline*, chipping away at her shields, which were down to twenty-nine percent, and herding the yacht toward the oncoming patrol ship. Sparks erupted from the control panel, causing him to recoil in alarm, but tiny burns stung his hands and face regardless as he hastily rerouted key systems to auxiliary circuits, then hopped over to the copilot's seat instead. The artificial gravity wobbled, resulting in a momentary wave of nausea. Blood rushed from head to his feet and back again.

Alone in the cockpit, Chekov was again glad he'd left Dise safely behind on Oasis. He was going to get to the *Enterprise* or die trying, and he'd just as soon not get anyone else killed in the process.

Thirty-One

"Captain Spock," Uhura said, "we have a situation."

"Elaborate, Commander."

Occupying the captain's seat on the bridge, Spock had anticipated no urgent developments while the *Enterprise* orbited Voyzr, awaiting the landing party's return from the ceremonies at the embassy. Prior to Uhura's announcement, he had made use of the time by observing the efficiency and performance of every crew member stationed on the bridge, while simultaneously studying the latest Starfleet briefings on the covert power struggles within the Klingon High Council, particularly with regard to the rise of a certain Councilor Gorkon, who appeared to have the chancellorship in his sights, *and* contemplating certain subtle refinements to the ship's multiphasic sensor array. Had he been human, he might have been annoyed by the unexpected interruption.

Had he been human.

"A small vessel, of uncertain origin, is making an unauthorized approach to Voyzr, ignoring demands from the planetary defense forces to turn back," Uhura reported. "I've been monitoring their communications, and the mystery ship has already opened fire on an automated border buoy and a patrol ship has been dispatched to intercept it."

"I see." Spock dismissed all irrelevant matters from his mind. A rogue ship charging toward Voyzr at this particular juncture was indeed cause for concern. He turned toward the science station, where Ensign Morag Fraser, a recent Academy graduate with a strong backing in science, was currently posted. "Do we have this vessel on our scanners?"

She nodded. "Coming into range now, sir."

"Onscreen," Spock said.

An image appeared on the main viewer, displacing an orbital view of Voyzr. Blurry at first, the image sharpened to reveal a sleek, copper-hued yacht that, to his Vulcan eye, appeared more ostentatious than strictly necessary. At first impression, the civilian craft did not present a particularly menacing aspect, but appearances were often deceiving. The cetacean probe that had recently posed a mortal threat to Earth had not bristled with weapons and armor either.

"Can we identify this vessel?" he asked.

"Working on that, sir."

Fraser was already consulting the *Enterprise*'s computer banks, no doubt running the yacht's profile through the ship's library of databases. From what Spock could see, she was going about it in a suitably efficient manner; nevertheless, he was tempted to reclaim his usual post, suspecting that he might well be able to isolate any relevant data more quickly. Logically, however, his first duty was to oversee the entire situation in the captain's stead. Delegation was a fundamental component of effective leadership.

"Commander Uhura, hail the Voyzr defense authorities and ask if they require assistance."

"Aye, sir."

"Captain Spock," Fraser said, swiftly enough. "The vessel in question matches the description of the *Xoline*, a private yacht recently stolen from Oasis Station."

Spock raised an eyebrow. "Stolen by whom, Ensign?"

"Give me a moment, sir. Accessing the report filed by the station."

He once again yearned to be at the science station himself. "Without delay, Ensign."

The incursion in progress was becoming increasingly worrisome. To what illicit purpose was the stolen spacecraft invading

Voyzr's space? Spock was reluctant to hypothesize without sufficient data, but the timing of this event, occurring in sync with the major diplomatic event transpiring on the planet, was highly suspicious. He doubted it was a coincidence.

"Captain Spock." Uhura looked over at him. "Voyzr says they have the matter in hand. We are instructed to let them deal with it."

"Acknowledged." A hint of a frown betrayed his dissatisfaction and growing unease. While he appreciated the importance of allowing the local authorities jurisdiction over their own space, he was also conscious of his own duty to defend both the *Enterprise* and the embassy opening. "Please inform them that we remain available to render whatever assistance they may require."

"Aye, Captain."

In need of further data to properly evaluate the situation, he turned back to Fraser.

"Ensign?"

"I have it, sir," she said, looking both proud and a little flustered. "Details are sketchy, but the *Xoline* is believed to have been stolen by one Ryjo mur Zimble, and get this, he's an expatriate Voyzr with a criminal record, whose last known address was on Tykona!"

"Tykona?" Uhura echoed. "Didn't Chekov say something about someone impersonating him on Tykona?"

"He did indeed." Spock steepled his fingers beneath his chin as he considered this new complication. He regretted that Chekov himself was not presently on hand to be consulted, but rather accompanying the captain on Voyzr. "The plot, as they say, thickens."

"There has to be a connection," Uhura said, "but why would the imposter be racing toward Voyzr? Chekov said he was just a petty criminal."

"True," Spock said. "It is peculiar, however, that he failed to mention that the imposter was Voyzr . . . if indeed he was aware of that." He studied the yacht on the viewscreen, which appeared to be heading directly toward them. "Inform the Voyzr of our discoveries regarding the identity of both the ship and its pilot."

"And then, Mister Spock?"

"Hail the unknown vessel."

"*Hailing* Grigori. *This is the* U.S.S. Enterprise, *currently in orbit around Voyzr. What are your intentions?*"

Uhura's voice, even broken up and distorted by static, was music to Chekov's ears. He should have known his altercations with Voyzr's defense forces would not escape the *Enterprise*'s attention, and their comms were more than sufficient to instantly reach him as he neared the planet, approaching transporter range. Perhaps he was still in time to stop Ryjo after all? He didn't need to completely convince Uhura that he was Chekov; he just needed to alert Captain Kirk to the *possibility* of an imposter having taken his place.

"Uhura! It's me, Chekov! There's no time to explain, but the 'Chekov' who returned to ship is an imposter, working for dangerous Voyzr extremists—"

"*Repeat:* Enterprise *hailing* Grigori. *Can you read me?*"

"What?" Chekov jabbed the transmit button with his finger. "Yes, I can read you! Can you read me?"

"*Attention,* Enterprise," a Voyzr voice broke in. "*This is not your concern. Please refrain from involving yourself in this matter.*"

"No!" Chekov protested, apparently to deaf ears. "This is very much their concern!" He pounded the control panel in frustration, even as he recalled sparks erupting from that same panel as *Xoline* was being blasted by the drones. Smoke continued to permeate the air aboard the ship. Had even the short-range transmitters been taken out as well, just when he needed them most? That would be too cruel. "Chekov to *Enterprise*! Can you read me?"

"*Apologies, Voyzr,*" Uhura said diplomatically, "*but we have reason to believe this incursion may relate to a recent incident involving one of our officers. We are merely seeking confirmation of this fact.*"

"It is absolutely related!" Chekov blurted. He was encouraged to hear that Uhura and the others suspected something was amiss, *and* he was tormented by his apparently inability to explain it all to them. "Voyzr, please inform *Enterprise* that their suspicions are correct! There is a saboteur in their midst!"

"Acknowledged, Enterprise. *Nevertheless, you are directed not to interfere. Any inquiries can be submitted through the proper channels* after *we have dealt with the intruder. Refrain from any further attempts at communication with the incoming vessel. Voyzr out.*"

Chekov's heart sank. It seemed the Voyzr defense force could no longer read him either. After that last battle with the drones, on top of the photon torpedo strike earlier, any transmissions were one-way only. He could receive but not send.

Which left him only one last desperate option.

"*Voyzr to intruder. Halt at once. This is your final warning.*"

The patrol ship came into view, both on the sensors and on the yacht's viewscreen. Its streamlined, crescent-shaped contours were familiar to him from his briefings on Voyzr's planetary defenses. He didn't need any further scans to guess that the Voyzr ship had its disruptor cannons locked on *Xoline.* Not quite visible, but almost within transporter range, was the *Enterprise.* The patrol ship, he knew, was not equipped with transporters.

This was going to be close.

Appearing to comply, he powered down the impulse engines, letting the yacht coast forward on momentum alone, while simultaneously lowering his shields.

Then he killed the life-support as well.

"Captain Spock!" Ensign Fraser called out from the science station. "*Xoline* has powered down, and its life-support is failing fast."

Spock instantly entered this data into his computations. "Time frame?"

"Very urgent, sir. The ship is venting air at a precipitous rate, and there are indications of fire and smoke spreading rapidly through the ship. A possible radiation leak as well."

"All at once?" Uhura reacted in surprise. "This seems very sudden."

"Indeed," Spock agreed. A cascading catastrophic failure, or was there more here than met than eye? Nothing about this crisis lent itself to ready explanation. "Life signs?"

"Just one, sir," Fraser responded. "Registering as Voyzr, as expected."

The alleged imposter, Spock presumed. "Shields?"

"Down, sir." She turned away from the console, visibly anxious. He overlooked her emotional display given that she was both young and human. "He doesn't have long."

"Understood."

He arrived quickly at a decision. He had already calculated that hailing *Xoline*, in the interests of achieving a clearer picture of the situation, outweighed a marginal violation of the Voyzr's instructions to leave the matter entirely to them. Now, with a Voyzr life at stake, the equation had become even simpler.

"Helm, bring us within transporter range." He hit the intercom button on chair's armrest. "Mister Scott, prepare for an emergency beam-out." He nodded at Fraser. "We are sending you the precise coordinates now."

"Aye, Captain," the engineer replied. *"We're on it, don't you worry."*

"That was not in doubt."

"And the Voyzr?" Uhura asked.

"They are in no position to save the intruder. We are," Spock stated as the *Enterprise* left orbit. "Inform them, with apologies, that we are intervening solely to prevent an imminent loss of life."

A thought occurred to him: Was it possible that the imposter had deliberately engineered the emergency to provoke just this response on the part of the *Enterprise*? There would be a certain logic to that, if one was willing to gamble their very life on it.

A fascinating theory, if nothing else.

Thirty-Two

"Welcome back to Voyzr, gentlemen. Glad you could make it in time."

The new Federation embassy had its own state-of-the-art transporter room, where Ryjo, Kirk, and Sulu were greeted by a mixed delegation of Voyzr and Federation personnel. Ryjo understood that although the embassy would technically be Federation property once it officially opened today, Voyzr was still taking the lead on security matters, particularly with regard to the regnant's visit. He could work with that.

"Thank you again for having us," Kirk said as the landing party stepped down from the transporter platform in their crisp dress uniforms. "Sorry to call it so down to the wire, but we ran into some unavoidable delays on the way."

"So we understand," said the youngish Efrosian woman who'd addressed them before. Prominent cranial ridges could be mistaken for a Klingon's if not for her bright blue eyes and voluminous mane of snow-white hair. A conservative suit befitted her role as a member of the embassy's staff. "The ambassador regrets that he's unable to welcome you in person, but he's presently occupied with a number of last-minute matters concerning today's events."

The ambassador was a Vulcan, Ryjo recalled. He and his staff had already relocated to Voyzr months ago to oversee the construction of the embassy and lay the groundwork, diplomatic and otherwise, for today's formal opening and dedication.

"I quite understand," Kirk said. "This is a historic occasion, long in the making. I'm sure Ambassador Torek wants to make certain everything goes off without a hitch." He smiled graciously at all present, deploying his famous charm. "We're honored to take part in the proceedings, which mark an important step forward for both Voyzr and the Federation, deepening our already established bonds of peace and friendship and ushering in a new era of even greater mutual support and cooperation."

"Well said," she replied. "In any event, the ambassador anticipates meeting you at the reception following the ceremony, if not before. In the meantime, I'm the ambassador's aide, Hy'Loq, and I'll be looking after you during your stay with us."

"Our babysitter, in other words." Sulu smiled at her. "I promise, we'll be well-behaved."

"I expect nothing less." She gestured toward the uniformed Voyzr officer standing beside her. "And this is Major Nonnd, who is in charge of security for this occasion."

"You may rely on me and my guards." His stern tone and stiff, military bearing made it clear that he took his responsibilities very seriously. He plucked a communicator from the waistband of his kilt and issued a curt command. "Starfleet guests received. Restore all shields."

Ryjo recognized their hosts' names from prior briefings and subspace correspondence. "It's a pleasure to finally meet you both in person."

A genial pose belied his taut nerves and roiling emotions. If all went well, he had only a few more hours to live. Chances were, he would be immediately killed by Voyzr guards after assassinating the regnant, but if not, he would have to find another way to dispose of himself before the life-entity transference could reverse itself. Since the whole point of his mission was to implicate Starfleet in Zavetta's death, thereby driving a wedge between the Federation and her corrupt regime, he couldn't risk Chekov revealing the truth, as improbable as it was, once he regained the body Ryjo was wearing now. Originally, the plan had been for Trath to instantly execute Chekov (in Ryjo's body) upon confirmation of the regnant's well-deserved demise, but Chekov's escape from the villa had complicated that. Last Ryjo had heard, via coded communications, the real Chekov remained at large despite the Exiles' best efforts to recapture him.

Where is he now? Ryjo fretted. *And what is he up to?*

With Chekov still in the wind, it was up to Ryjo to make sure neither of them survived the next few hours. He glanced furtively at the disruptor pistol clipped to Nonnd's belt, as well as at the weapons carried by the various guards on hand. Nonnd obviously wasn't taking any chances when it came to protecting Kirk and the other dignitaries attending the embassy opening.

When the time comes, it shouldn't be too hard to provoke him into killing me . . .

Soon.

Imaginary antlers itched like crazy, chafing on Ryjo's nerves, as further pleasantries and felicitations were exchanged and he was forced to play along to preserve his cover just a little bit longer. He found himself torn between dreading his rapidly impending extinction and wanting to get it over with already. Moments ticked by both too quickly and not quickly enough.

"Anyway," Hy'Loq said, "let me escort you to a private lounge where you can relax and review today's schedule. As you know, we have a full slate of events planned, including the speeches and dedication ceremony itself, global and interstellar media opportunities, a formal reception, and—"

Nonnd cleared his throat. "Ahem."

"Oh yes," Hy'Loq said, a trifle abashed. "As you're honored guests, I can naturally wave you past most of the security checkpoints and procedures, but if each of you wouldn't mind submitting to a brief security scan?"

"By all means," Kirk said for all of them. "I'd expect nothing less under the circumstances."

Nonnd produced a handheld device that resembled a standard

tricorder. One by one, the three men allowed themselves to be scanned. Per prior agreement, they had all beamed down unarmed, bringing only their communicators and a few personal items, which they presented for inspection. Sulu had only some breath mints and a pocket-sized data slate loaded with local history and guidebooks, Kirk disclosed the lightweight ankle brace under his right boot, while Ryjo handed over the hypospray in his pocket as though he had nothing to hide.

"A hypospray?" Kirk asked.

"Prescribed by Doctor McCoy," Ryjo lied. "A minor analgesic and anti-inflammatory, on account of my bruised ribs and some lingering aftereffects of being shocked by that electric jellyfish on Wexx." He turned to Nonnd and Hy'Loq. "I'm afraid I'm just slightly a bit worse for wear after our 'detour' on the way here."

"Don't let my friend's modesty fool you," Sulu added, backing him up. "He and I wouldn't be here today if he hadn't put himself on the line for us, taking some hard knocks in the process."

Ryjo couldn't help being amused by Sulu's unwitting assistance in explaining the hypospray away. If nothing else, their near-fatal mission to Wexx had spared Ryjo from having to invent some other minor ailment or injury, as originally planned. His ordeal on the volcano moon made having a hypospray on his person perfectly plausible.

Or so he hoped.

Kirk eyed Ryjo with concern. "You up to this, Chekov?"

"I'm fine, sir. Nothing to worry about. It's just that, as Ms. Hy'Loq said, we have a busy day ahead and I didn't want any inconvenient aches and pains to keep me from being at my best."

Kirk nodded, seeming to take him at his word. "Well, I suppose none of us are quite as young and spry as we used to be. Can't expect to bounce back as quickly as we did back in our heyday."

"I don't know about that, sir." Ryjo shrugged. "I like to think I'm still quite the spring chicken, as they say in Vladivostok."

Sulu grinned. "No comment."

"Nothing chicken about you, Chekov, young or old." Kirk turned to Nonnd, subtly favoring his bad ankle. "Everything in order, Major?"

"So it seems."

Nonnd returned the hypospray to Ryjo, who tucked it back into his pocket, within easy reach. *Thank you, lightning jelly.*

"Thank you for your cooperation, gentlemen." Nonnd nodded at Ryjo. "Take pride in those aches and pains, Commander. Injuries received in the line of duty are a badge of honor."

"Thank you, Major. If it's all the same to you, though, I'd prefer these badges to be a little less uncomfortable."

"I imagine so," Hy'Loq said. "So, now that we've concluded that necessary bit of business, shall we make our way to the lounge? Drinks and refreshments are waiting."

"Lead the way," Sulu said buoyantly.

Ryjo wondered what was on the menu. *My last meal?*

A chronometer on the wall reminded him that his time was running out. He swallowed hard and started to reach for his phantom antlers before catching himself. He'd had months to prepare himself for the inevitable conclusion of his suicide mission and had thought he'd made his peace with the prospect of dying for his father's cause, but now that his final breath was drawing near . . .

"You sure you're all right, Pavel?" Kirk asked him quietly as they followed Hy'Loq out of the transporter room into the corridor beyond. His keen eyes had apparently not missed Ryjo's unguarded moment, although he seemed more sympathetic than suspicious. "Something bothering you?"

Ryjo damned Kirk for being so perceptive—and himself for letting his last-minute jitters show.

"Not really. Just anxious that everything goes off smoothly after all we've gone through to get to this point." He mustered a wry smile. "You know how it is with security chiefs. We never stop worrying. Comes with the position, I suppose."

Kirk smiled back at him. "I'll let you in on a secret, Commander. It's the same with starship captains."

"You carry it well, sir."

Still smiling, Ryjo bolstered his personal deflectors against Kirk's undeniable charisma and supportive command style. He fully understood now why Kirk's crew were so loyal to him; he was a good captain to serve under, as demonstrated by his fearless efforts to rescue the stranded landing party from Wexx's volcanic fury. It was hard not to admire and respect him, despite his unforgivable interference in Voyzr's affairs.

"The trick is not to let it get to you," Kirk advised, "while also always expecting the unexpected."

Sorry to disappoint you, Captain, Ryjo thought, with a genuine twinge of regret. *This time you are not going to see it coming.*

Thirty-Three

"My apologies for the delay," Hy'Loq said. "I'm afraid the regnant is unavoidably detained. I'm assured she and her party will be beaming in shortly."

"No problem," Kirk replied. "We're at your disposal."

"Thank you for understanding. At least this gives me an opportunity to familiarize you with the setting and staging, in lieu of a full-fledged rehearsal."

The ceremonies were to be held in a spacious open-air courtyard within the embassy, beneath a fortuitously clear blue sky. Although it had been evening aboard the ship when the landing party had departed for the planet, it was a sunny afternoon in this hemisphere of Voyzr. Ryjo wondered if actual Starfleeters ever got used to this sort of transporter lag when beaming from one time zone to another. An invisible force field shielded the courtyard from shifts in the weather as well as more substantial threats.

Aside from a certain undercover assassin, that was.

A levitating stage occupied one end of the courtyard, facing row after row of empty seats awaiting throngs of invited guests, spectators, and the press, all of whom had been carefully screened by security, Ryjo knew. Armed guards were already discreetly positioned on interior balconies overlooking the site, as well as along the perimeter of both stage and courtyard and at every entrance. In addition, the stage itself would be shielded from the audience once the ceremony began. Ryjo repressed a smirk. Little did Major Nonnd know that, despite all these elaborate precautions, the true threat was already on stage with him, getting a grand tour along with Kirk and Sulu.

I made it, he thought. *I'm here, right where I'm supposed to be.*

The stage itself was accessed by a doorway at the back connected to a staging area inside the northern wing of the embassy. Two diagonal rows of seats, angled outward toward the front of the stage, flanked a central aisle which led to a podium bearing the arrogant, antlered seal of the postwar global coalition. Technicians were busy conducting sound and holo checks in anticipation of the event, which would be covered live by both Voyzr and Federation media. Sentient life-forms across two quadrants would be watching—and were about to be shocked to their cores when a decorated Starfleet officer killed the regnant before the eyes of the galaxy.

Anytime now.

"You'll be seated here as the ceremony begins." Hy'Loq indicated three chairs on the lefthand side of the stage. "After some brief opening remarks by local dignitaries, the ambassador will take the stage to address the audience, then introduce the regnant, who will enter via the door at the back. Following her address, she will ask you each to come forward, one at a time, and accept a distinguished-conduct medallion for your heroic actions twenty years ago. In the interest of saving Captain Kirk for last, you will be called in reverse seniority, starting with you, Commander Chekov. No offense."

"None taken," Ryjo said. "I much prefer it this way. The captain is a tough act to follow."

Not that the regnant would live long enough to reward Kirk for his meddling decades ago. Ryjo was indeed grateful that he wouldn't have to wait impatiently for his opportunity to come face-to-face with the regnant.

It will all be over soon.

His stomach churned uneasily. Despite the generous spread available in the visitors lounge, including Bolian tonic water,

Andorian tuber roots, *plomeek* soup, and chocolate ice cream, he had been too on edge to do more than sample a few of the more exotic delicacies, mostly to be polite and avoid attracting attention. Knowing that you were about to kill and be killed was not good for one's appetite, it seemed. So much for enjoying one's last meal.

"Excuse me," Nonnd said, taking a call on his communicator. Ryjo listened in as the security head replied to a subordinate. "Clear them away from the entrances and secure areas, but *gently*. This is a peace celebration after all; we don't want any violence or undue force marring the occasion."

Frowning, he lowered his communicator.

"Is there a problem, Major?" Kirk asked. "I couldn't help overhearing."

"Nothing too serious. There are some demonstrators out front protesting the opening of the embassy, getting in the way of the VIPs arriving for the celebration." Nonnd shrugged apologetically. "I regret to say not every Voyzr welcomes the Federation's involvement in our affairs, even after all these years."

That's putting mildly, Ryjo thought. He was gratified to hear of the protests but knew that peaceful demonstrations were not enough to shake the Federation's growing hold on his homeworld, let alone prevent Voyzr from joining the UFP somewhere down the road, cementing forever the vile regime that had driven the Indees into exile. More decisive action was required if ever Voyzr was to be reclaimed by those who fought and died and suffered back in the war.

No second thoughts, no regrets. He stiffened his resolve, despite his nervous stomach. *I've come too far to turn back now.*

"Dissent is a sign of healthy society," Kirk observed. "In my travels, I've occasionally run across cultures where everyone agreed on everything and there were no conflicting views. There was almost aways a fly in the ointment: mind-warping spores, all-powerful artificial intelligences, cultural stagnation, coercive brainwashing technologies, you name it. Peaceful protests and vigorous, even heated debate are good things in my book. Sentients aren't meant to live in *total* harmony with each other. That's unnatural and, speaking from experience, more than a little dystopian."

"I suppose," Nonnd conceded, "but it can be a rutting nuisance sometimes, pardon my language."

"That it can be," Kirk said, chuckling. "I take it that, in your estimation, these protests are not likely to derail today's festivities?"

Nonnd shook his head. "Not on my watch."

"Glad to hear it," Sulu said. "I'd hate to think I got dressed up for nothing."

Likewise, Ryjo thought. It would be bitterly ironic if anti-Federation protests aborted his long-awaited chance to frame Starfleet for the regnant's murder. "I know we can count on you, Major, to prevent any disturbances from disrupting this historic occasion."

"Speaking of which," Hy'Loq said, putting down her own communicator, "I just got word that the regnant is ready to beam in and will be with us shortly."

"Shortly" proved to be a tad optimistic, but it wasn't long before the regnant, formerly Field Marshall Zavetta, joined them on the stage, accompanied by a small army of advisors, aides, and bodyguards. A rack of ceremonial, gold-plated antlers proclaimed her authority, regardless of her gender, while her traditional woven-grass gown was impeccably tailored. Once-chartreuse curls had dulled somewhat with time, but her shrewd doe eyes remained as sharp as ever. Although she now presided over a so-called "coalition" government, Ryjo could never forget that she had once commanded the enemy Republic forces during the war. His mother, and many other kinfolk, had died fighting her troops. That she now claimed to represent all of Voyzr was an insult to their memories.

Even still, it was . . . unsettling . . . to finally meet the woman you were about to murder.

Assassinate, he corrected himself. *Not murder.*

"Captain, Commanders," she greeted them, clasping each of their hands in turn. "So good to see you all again, and under much happier circumstances than when first we met."

"And looking forward to even better days ahead," Kirk replied. "We've all come a long way since that rather unconventional summit meeting two decades ago. You and your people are to be commended for the peace and progress you've achieved since bringing an end to your civil war."

"Thanks to you and your valiant crew," she said.

"We're proud to have played some small part in nudging you in the right direction."

"Via a bit of unorthodox transporter diplomacy," Sulu quipped, "and a surprise visit to an underground reactor room."

Zavetta laughed. "Which turned out well for all concerned."

Not for everyone, Ryjo thought, biting his tongue. All this smug, self-congratulatory chitchat regarding the epic betrayal that had led to his father dying in shame and exile on Tykona turned Ryjo's already queasy stomach. He struggled to maintain a cordial façade while fingering the hypospray in his pocket. It occurred to him that, if he wanted to, he could kill the regnant here and now.

The seemingly innocuous hypospray was actually rigged to disperse, via an aerosol spray, a toxic mist that would kill any humanoid who inhaled it, causing the regnant to expire both quickly and dramatically.

It would be so easy. The regnant was right in front of him, gloating over the ignoble end to the war. All he needed to do was swiftly fish the camouflaged weapon from his pocket, spray the toxin in her face, and his mission would be complete. Her eyes would bulge in their sockets, her throat would close, her brain would hemorrhage, and she'd be dead before anyone could stop him, right before the eyes of everyone present.

But *not* in front of an entire audience of spectators, both in person and watching from all across the planet and the galaxy beyond. *That,* he reminded himself, was the history-making spectacle he and his comrades had worked so hard to engineer. He had to be patient and wait just a while longer, no matter how tempting it was to get it all over with once and for all—before he could lose his nerve.

"Places, everyone!" Hy'Loq called out. "We're almost ready to begin."

Thirty-Four

Thick black smoke filled *Xoline*'s cockpit, choking him. Flames crackled and roared throughout the dying yacht, consuming whatever oxygen remained after Chekov vented most of the breathable air in a last-ditch attempt to force the *Enterprise* to intervene. He felt the scorching heat of the fire at his back as it burned toward the cockpit, tempting him to try to reactivate the fire-suppression system even though that might defeat the point of putting his life in immediate jeopardy. Lacking transporters, the Voyzr patrol ship could not save him; only the *Enterprise* could if they recognized his peril in time, despite his maddening inability to directly communicate his distress.

Seemed like a good idea at the time, he thought. *Or at least not an entirely terrible one.*

He coughed raggedly, the fumes aggravating his already starving lungs. His head dipped toward the helm, his antlers scraping the controls, as he started to lose consciousness, gasping for breath between racking coughs. Darkness, airless and overpowering, encroached on him within and without. Had his last desperate gamble simply gotten him killed instead, agonizingly short of his goal?

Hurry, Enterprise, *I'm blacking out . . .*

Flames engulfed the cockpit.

He bolted awake, coughing violently. His Voyzr lungs felt as rough and raw as the surface of Ceti Alpha V after most of its atmosphere was torn away. Groggy and disoriented, his head aching, he looked about in confusion, discovering the antiseptic white walls of . . .

Sickbay!

"Easy there." Doctor McCoy placed a firm but gentle hand against Chekov's chest, pressing him back down onto a biobed. The unmistakable background hum of the *Enterprise* soothed Chekov after the crackling inferno aboard the burning yacht. McCoy leaned forward, examining Chekov's eyes, which were red and stinging. "You had a close call, whoever you are. We barely beamed you out in time, but not fast enough to spare you a nasty case of smoke inhalation and some minor burns. How are you feeling?"

"Like I just—" he started to say, only to be cut off by a jagged coughing fit that felt as though he was trying to forcefully expel both lungs. Tears stung his eyes. His head throbbed.

McCoy glanced away from Chekov. "Nurse, some water, please."

"Way ahead of you, Doctor." Simone Tovar stepped forward to offer Chekov a small plastic cup. "Take your time. Sip it slowly."

Jubilation shone through the fogginess clinging to his brain. His crazy stunt had worked after all; he was back on the *Enterprise* at last, among familiar faces. He lifted the cup to his lips. The cool water brought a degree of relief to his parched, scratchy throat.

"Thanks," he croaked. Ryjo's voice, which he'd gotten scarily used to, was now barely recognizable. "Simone."

She blinked in surprise. "Have we met?"

"Never mind that," McCoy said, scowling. "Now that you've got your voice back, mostly, maybe you can explain what in tarnation you were up to out there, daring your fellow Voyzr to blow you to atoms?"

Forcing you to come to my rescue, Chekov thought, *in the nick of time.*

In time . . . oh no!

Alarm swept away his momentary relief and euphoria at finding himself alive and well back on the *Enterprise*, as he recalled the clear and present danger that had sent him racing across the sector to reach the ship before . . .

"Wait! How long was I out? The captain . . . the embassy opening . . . has it started yet? Am I too late?"

"Too late for what?" McCoy gave him a puzzled look. "What's this all about?"

Chekov seized on the fact that neither McCoy nor Tovar appeared to be shaken by some recent disaster or tragedy as far as he could tell. Perhaps Ryjo hadn't done the Exiles' dirty work yet?

"Just tell me, please!" he said anxiously. "Where is Captain Kirk?"

"He beamed down to the planet a short while ago. Why do you ask?"

"And... Chekov?"

"He and Mister Sulu accompanied the captain, not that this ought to be any of your business. Why are you so all-fired worked up about this anyway? Is there something you want to tell us?"

Chekov hesitated. He knew what McCoy and Tovar saw when they looked at him: an outlaw Voyzr of suspect motives, a stranger to them both. Peering past the doctor and nurse, he spotted an armed security officer looking on warily, ready to take action if he got out of line. He was probably lucky, Chekov realized, that he hadn't woken up in restraints after the way he'd come careening into the system, *Xoline*'s phasers blasting.

"No time," he said, shaking his head.

Given a chance, he was sure he could convince either McCoy or Tovar of his true identity, or at least open their minds to the possibility, but there wasn't a moment to lose. As far as he knew, Ryjo was about to strike at any second, with surely catastrophic results. The Exiles would not have gone to such extremes just to embarrass Starfleet. Something far more dire was about to go down, if it wasn't already too late.

"I need to speak with Spock! Right away!"

Thirty-Five

"Vulcan, too, had its civil wars in the days of our distant ancestors, turning kin against kin and bringing our world to the brink of destruction, but, like you, we found a way to a lasting peace that united our once-divided people . . ."

The Romulans may beg to differ, Ryjo thought, sitting restlessly through Ambassador Torek's predictably dry, dispassionate, and self-righteous oration. Seated on the stage between Kirk and Sulu, before a packed crowd of spectators and the media, Ryjo struggled not to squirm as he waited anxiously for the ambassador to wrap up his remarks and get around to introducing the regnant, who remained backstage, frustratingly out of reach. Sweating beneath his increasingly uncomfortable dress uniform, Ryjo kept an approving smile pasted on Chekov's face as, time and again, he was forced to applaud his enemies and the "glorious" accomplishments of the regime that had driven his people into exile.

It was torture.

The ceremony, which had started late, was dragging on interminably as far as Ryjo was concerned. He'd already endured a seemingly endless parade of politicians, civic leaders, celebrities, a poet, a preacher, and other speakers before Ambassador Torek had even taken the stage to begin his speech, which was enough to try any non-Vulcan's patience, even if they weren't on edge, primed to carry out a political assassination.

Can we please just get on with it?

He ought to be grateful for the delays, he supposed. He should be in no hurry to get himself killed killing another. He should savor these last few minutes of existence, but how could he when his final act was going to be his very first murder?

Unlike some of the Exiles, he'd never killed anyone before.

Think of the cause, he thought. *My mother's sacrifice, my father's shame. The bright and shining future I could have had if not for the very "peace" now being celebrated right in front of me.*

He tried to work himself up, to stoke his patriotic fury, but found this difficult while smiling from his seat between two men who trusted him and who had stood behind him when all seemed lost. At least, he consoled himself, he'd helped saved several lives before taking one. That had to count for something, didn't it . . . in the grand scheme of things?

I'm Voyzr, not Starfleet. I have a duty to my—

A sudden wave of dizziness hit him. Reality seemed to spin around him, blurring from sight. Something shifted inside him, like a full-body shudder that suddenly wakens you from a dream. Then the dizzy spell passed, his vision cleared, and he found himself . . .

In sickbay?

Sterile walls surrounded him, replacing the embassy courtyard. He was sitting up in a biobed in the sickbay aboard the *Enterprise*, which he'd previously visited to be treated for his injuries on Wexx. Tovar leaned toward him, a worried look on her face. Nearby, McCoy was arguing with somebody via the intercom:

"I don't know why, Spock! He just insists that he has to see you on the double. Says it's a matter of life and death."

"What is it?" Tovar asked Ryjo. "What's wrong?"

He gasped out loud, realizing what had happened. The transference had reversed itself. He was back in his own body!

Which meant that Chekov . . .

"Doctor!" Tovar called to McCoy. "I need you here. The patient—"

The world blurred again, unmooring him. One moment he was in sickbay, frantically wondering what to say or do, then he was back onstage at the embassy in a human body again. He started, almost tumbling from his chair.

Kirk caught his arm, steadying him.

"What's the matter, Pavel?" he whispered. His worried look mirrored the one Tovar had given Ryjo only moments ago. "Are you all right?"

"It's nothing, Captain." Ryjo hastily tried to cover his lapse. He tugged at his collar. "Just a little warmer here than I expected, or maybe Doctor McCoy's prescription went to my head for an instant." He faked a reassuring smile. "I'll be fine, sir."

Inside, however, he was melting down, trying to make sense of what had just transpired. Doctor Morval had warned him that such momentary reversals might occur as the transference began to wear off, but they'd expected that he'd be able to complete his mission before that became an issue. *Not so*, it seemed. His anxiety mounted as the full implications sank in. How long did he have before he and Chekov switched bodies again, possibly for good?

And how had the real Chekov ended up back on the *Enterprise* at this crucial moment, albeit still in the wrong body? And if Ryjo had just abruptly found himself in sickbay, Chekov must have briefly reclaimed his true body here on Voyzr, although apparently not long enough to alert Kirk and Sulu before finding himself back in sickbay.

He must have been just as startled and disoriented as I was.

But what was Chekov up to on the *Enterprise* this very moment? Something about demanding to talk to Spock?

I'm running out of time, in more ways than one.

"And thus, in conclusion," the ambassador said from the podium, "it is only logical that I now introduce the esteemed regnant of Voyzr, the honorable Zavetta bur Nafine . . ."

Finally!

Ryjo fished the doctored hypospray from his pocket.

Thirty-Six

"You asked to see me?" Spock said.

The *Enterprise* was back in orbit around Voyzr, so Spock had few qualms about leaving the bridge in the capable hands of Mister Scott as he responded to the urgent summons from sickbay. With the crisis regarding the rogue yacht resolved, aside from the unruffling of administrative feathers over the *Enterprise*'s unsanctioned intervention, Spock was indeed curious to hear from the outlaw Voyzr at the heart of the recent emergency. There were questions that required answers, including why the rescued pilot was demanding to speak with him personally.

"Captain Spock!" The stranger sat up in the biobed, which was flanked by both McCoy and Nurse Tovar. A young Voyzr male, he appeared unduly excited by Spock's arrival. "Thank goodness!"

"Ryjo mur Zimble, I presume?"

"No, Spock! It's me, Chekov!"

McCoy's jaw dropped. "Come again? Last time I checked, our Chekov didn't have antlers."

Tovar looked equally startled by the patient's unexpected declaration.

Spock raised an eyebrow.

"I know what it looks like!" the Voyzr said, as though anticipating their disbelief. "But remember Janice Lester? How she switched bodies with the captain? The same thing happened to me! Ryjo stole my body back on Tykona . . . and has been posing as me this whole time!"

Janice Lester?

Spock recalled that incident well, along with the more recent reports of a Voyzr criminal impersonating Chekov.

"Hang on," Tovar said. "Are you saying that wasn't the real Chekov down on Wexx?"

"Wexx?" He gave her a puzzled look. "What and where is Wexx?"

McCoy scowled. "Chekov would know that."

"Not if I wasn't in my own body at the time!" the Voyzr argued, not illogically. On the surface, he appeared desperate to convince them of his improbable claim. But was he telling the truth, feigning, or simply delusional?

"You know," McCoy said, "Chekov *was* acting a bit strangely down on Wexx."

"Yes! Because it wasn't me!" The patient spoke rapidly, addressing each of them in turn. "Doctor, back on Mudd's planet years ago, there were five hundred identical female androids all named Alice. Nurse Tovar—*Simone*—I asked you out on a date the last time I visited sickbay, to get vaccinated before my shore leave."

McCoy glanced at Tovar, who nodded in confirmation.

"Mister Spock," the Voyzr continued, "you defended the real Captain Kirk, trapped in Lester's body, when she took over the ship and placed him on trial. You believed him when nobody else did. I need you to mind-meld with me to prove that I'm telling the truth!"

Were he fully human, Spock would be taken aback by such an audacious request. Being Vulcan, he said merely:

"A mind-meld is not something to be undertaken lightly, let alone on the basis of an extravagant claim unsupported by any definitive evidence."

Logically, he could not automatically dismiss the man's story. The Lester incident incontrovertibly demonstrated that such transferences were possible, if extremely rare. On the other hand, the assortment of personal anecdotes he'd cited to support his claim were all information he could have obtained by other means, although Spock was admittedly at a loss to explain how an alleged petty criminal from Tykona could be privy to classified Starfleet files concerning Janice Lester's short-lived takeover of the original *Enterprise*—and why Ryjo would attempt such an outrageous deception at all?

"The mind-meld would be the evidence!" the patient insisted, growing increasingly agitated. "Look, we could go back and forth for hours, with me trying to come up with memories and details that only the real me would know, but there's no time for that. What if I am telling the truth and an imposter *is* at the embassy right now, attending the celebration with Captain Kirk and Sulu? Can you risk taking that chance?"

"Dear Lord," McCoy murmured, understandably troubled by the possibility. "Spock, you don't think . . ."

"I do not know, Doctor, which is precisely the problem."

It occurred to him that this could be a ruse to distract him as part of a larger plot against the *Enterprise*. A mind-meld rendered both parties psychically exposed and vulnerable at the best of times, so he was reluctant to engage in one while in command of the ship. It was one thing to leave Mister Scott in charge of the bridge while he was occupied elsewhere aboard; it was another thing for him to surrender full possession of his faculties while in command, and all the more so when circumstances remained cloudy.

Now was not a good time for his mind to be compromised.

Nevertheless, the patient's logic was sound. If Chekov's body *had* been appropriated by an imposter pursuing a covert agenda, it was vital that they learn this immediately.

"Very well." He came around to the side of the bed, within reach of the patient, whoever he truly was. "Doctor, Nurse, please stand by to intervene should anything untoward occur." He peered into the patient's large, cervine eyes. "Prepare yourself. The fusion of minds can be a deeply affecting experience."

The Voyzr gulped. "Hopefully, you won't have to go *too* deep just to prove I'm really me."

Spock shared that hope. "We shall see."

He placed his hands against the patient's temples, resting his fingertips lightly on the Voyzr's velvety fur.

"My mind to your mind, my thoughts to your thoughts..."

As always, he experienced a not entirely irrational moment of trepidation as he lowered his own mental barriers and reached out telepathically to another's psyche. He pushed past this instinctive reaction, for necessity's sake, and joined with this stranger who claimed to be Chekov.

"My mind to your mind..."

Your mind to my mind, the stranger echoes as their thoughts become one. At once, Spock is struck by a surge of emotion that threatens to swamp his own equilibrium: *Urgency! Anxiety! Desperation!*

Memories flood him/they, carrying them backward from this moment. They are in sickbay, trying to warn themselves before it is too late. They are briefly down on Voyzr, attending the opening alongside Kirk and Sulu. They are waking in sickbay, still alive after all. They're at the helm of *Xoline*, coughing and choking and fading to black...

Coughing, Spock broke the meld before he passed out. His lungs aching, he took a deep breath as though he'd literally just escaped from a burning, smoke-filled spacecraft. His eyes stung, his throat felt raw, even as a single, overpowering imperative resounded in his brain:

Time is running out! The imposter has to be stopped!

"Well?" McCoy looked back and forth between the two men. "What's the verdict?"

"He speaks the truth, Doctor. Chekov speaks the truth."

Tovar gasped. Her hand went to her chest.

The patient—Commander Pavel Chekov, serial number 656-5827B—was pale and panting, overcome by the meld. Relief shone in his alien eyes. He sagged back onto the bed, his vital message delivered at last. A deep sigh escaped him.

"I did it," he whispered. "We did it."

Spock shared his fatigue. Ideally, he would prefer to take a few moments to compose himself, but Chekov's relentless sense of urgency was now his. On shaky legs, he staggered across the ward to the nearest intercom wall unit. He stabbed the button not quite hard enough to damage it.

"Spock to Uhura! Patch me through to the captain at once!"

Thirty-Seven

". . . and so it was that I first met our honored guests under extraordinary circumstances. At the time, the war seemed endless, our people hopelessly divided and at odds, but Captain James T. Kirk and the selfless crew of the *Starship Enterprise* risked their own lives and freedom to help us find a better way and finally bridge the divisions that cost us so dearly . . ."

Kirk noted that the regnant had only obliquely alluded to the Klingons' role in perpetuating the war. He supposed that admitting that both factions had been manipulated and played for fools didn't fit the celebratory tone she was going for.

Can't say I blame her, he thought.

Zavetta had already been speaking for several minutes before she segued into introducing Kirk and his officers. He straightened his jacket, readying himself to get up and cross the stage to accept his medallion after Sulu and Chekov had their individual moments in the spotlight. He glanced discreetly at Chekov to see how the ailing officer was faring. From what Kirk could tell, Chekov was putting up a brave front but was clearly ill at ease. Sweat trickled down his temple, belying the forced smile on his face. He fidgeted with something in his pocket—the hypospray, Kirk assumed—as though tempted to give himself another dose of the painkiller. He sat stiffly in his chair, one foot tapping restlessly against the stage floor, and occasionally reaching for his scalp before retracting his hand. Kirk guessed Chekov couldn't wait for the ceremony to be over.

Just a bit longer, Kirk silently assured the other man. It was too late for Chekov to excuse himself now; the regnant would be calling him up to the podium shortly, in recognition of his heroic deeds twenty years ago, but Kirk resolved to confer privately with him after the proceedings. Chekov had done his part toughing it out through this whole diplomatic dog-and-pony show, but he probably didn't need to attend the subsequent reception, holo ops, and so on if he was truly unwell.

Or perhaps I should just have McCoy beam down to give him a quick checkup?

Kirk's communicator beeped. He frowned and quickly silenced the chime. The *Enterprise* should know better than to hail him during the ceremony, unless, he realized, this was a genuine emergency.

"Kirk here." He kept his voice low to avoid interrupting the regnant's speech. "What is it?"

"Captain!" Spock said forcefully, his tone immediately conveying the seriousness of the communication. *"You need to hear this. That is* not *Chekov with you. His body has been stolen . . . just as Janice Lester stole yours."*

"What?"

Decades-old memories, never to be forgotten, came rushing back: of being trapped in Janice's body while she took command of the *Enterprise* in his. But as far as he knew, Starfleet had that ancient Camusian machinery locked up tight?

"There is no doubt, Captain," Spock said. *"I have verified it conclusively."*

Shocked by the news, Kirk turned to stare at Chekov, who looked back at him nervously, sweating and swallowing hard—like an imposter who fears that the jig is up? Kirk tried to wrap his head around what Spock had just told him. What he saw was a man he'd known and trusted for more than twenty years now, but if Spock said he was an imposter . . .

"Captain?" Spock said. *"Do you read me?"*

". . . and so it is my great pleasure and privilege," the regnant said, "to ask Commander Pavel Chekov of the *U.S.S. Enterprise* to come forward to accept this honorary medallion along with our undying gratitude . . ."

Chekov—or whoever—rose to his feet and started toward her, walking briskly but solemnly, as though not to arouse suspicion. Kirk caught the silvery glint of the hypospray clutched in his right hand.

The hypospray!

"Stop!" Kirk sprang from his seat and dashed between "Chekov" and the regnant, blocking the other man. "Get her out of here!" he shouted to Zavetta and her guards. "Now!"

"Kirk?" she said, puzzled. "What is this?"

Startled gasps and exclamations arose from both the audience and the assorted VIPs on the stage. Off to one side, Hy'Loq and Major Nonnd also looked stunned and alarmed. Sulu gaped in surprise, understandably baffled. He jumped to his feet.

"Captain?"

There was no time to explain or refer him to Spock. Hell, Kirk barely understood what was happening himself, but he knew he didn't want that hypospray anywhere near the regnant.

That's no mild analgesic. I know that much.

"You need to trust me!" Kirk yelled at Zavetta, Nonnd, and anyone else who needed to hear it. "The regnant's not safe!"

Getting the message, Voyzr security forces surrounded Zavetta and hustled her off the stage, along with Ambassador Torek, who had been seated on the opposite side of the stage following his oration. Armed guards swung their weapons toward "Chekov," who stood frozen in the spotlight, looking distraught and uncertain, his scheme apparently falling apart before his eyes. Kirk abruptly realized that not only Zavetta's life was in danger. Chekov—or rather his body—was only seconds away from being eliminated by a Voyzr sharpshooter.

And where would that leave the real Chekov?

"Hold your fire!" Kirk called out to the guards. "This isn't what it seems!"

Offal! Ryjo thought. *Kirk's ruined everything!*

He watched in dismay as the regnant was rushed to safety, beyond his reach, leaving him stranded onstage with a murder weapon but no target. Frightened spectators ducked for cover or else bolted for the exits. Kirk faced him from only a few meters way, clearly aware of the truth. *But how?* Ryjo wondered before the obvious answer hit him:

Chekov.

He had warned Kirk in time.

Ryjo couldn't believe it. After all he'd gone through, after all he'd endured and sacrificed to get here, after giving up everything—Dise, their life on Tykona, even his own youth and body, his entire mission had come crashing down at the last moment. It had all been for nothing!

"Stay back!" He brandished the lethal hypospray. "Don't come nearer, any of you!"

What was he supposed to do now? Glancing around, Ryjo found himself exposed and surrounded, with nowhere to go and no place to hide. Not even Chekov's borrowed body acted as camouflage anymore. His phantom antlers might as well have been visible to one and all.

"Chekov!" Sulu rushed to his side, unaware that his friend was actually high above them in the *Enterprise* at that very moment. "What's going on? What are you doing?"

Panicked, not knowing what else to do, Ryjo stepped behind Sulu and grabbed him by the waist with one arm while holding the hypospray up to Sulu's face with his other hand.

"Nobody move! Or he's a dead man!"

"Don't shoot!" Kirk ordered the guards, unsure who was in more danger: Sulu, Chekov, or both. Unfortunately, the Voyzr security forces were not under his command, so he could only hope that the regnant's fulsome praise only moments ago granted him some small measure of trust and credibility on the part of her people. "Major Nonnd!" he called to the grizzled security head, who'd remained onstage to attend to the crisis. "I can't explain, but we need to take 'Chekov' alive! Trust me on this, please!"

The major nodded grimly. He held up a hand to signal his forces to hold off . . . for now. Kirk knew that, even with the regnant no longer in immediate jeopardy, the taut situation remained both volatile and potentially deadly. One angry, anxious, trigger-happy sniper and "Chekov" would be dead.

If he didn't kill Sulu first.

"Keep back!" the imposter warned. "I'm not bluffing! I'll kill him if anyone comes for me!"

"Pavel?" Alarm and confusion showed in Sulu's eyes. Kirk could only imagine how utterly lost and at sea the imperiled helmsman must be. As far as Sulu knew, the man holding him hostage, threatening his life, was his best friend. "Why are you doing this?"

"I'm sorry, Sulu," the imposter said. "This isn't how it was supposed to go."

Since the regnant is still alive, Kirk guessed.

"Listen to me, whoever you really are." He held up open palms in an attempt to de-escalate the confrontation. "I don't know exactly what you were up to or why, but it's over now. There's no reason for anyone to get hurt, you included. Put down that device and let Sulu go."

For a moment, Kirk wondered why Spock and a full security team hadn't beamed down to assist him yet, then he recalled that the embassy was shielded against transporter beams. *Possibly just as well*, he reflected; there were already too many armed and edgy people in the mix without risking a fraught, high-tension face-off between Starfleet and Voyzr security personnel.

"You're wrong! It's not over! It can't be!" The imposter shook his head. "Listen to me, everyone! I am Commander Pavel Chekov!"

he shouted for all to hear. "Representing the United Federation of Planets!"

"No, you're not," Kirk said, despite what his eyes and ears were telling him. Was this what it had been like for Spock and McCoy and the others when Janice went berserk in his body? Kirk still found it hard to except that the agitated, dangerous man before him was not really Chekov. "You can drop the act. I know all about the transference."

"I . . . I don't know what you're talking about!" he shouted even louder and more frantically. "I am Chekov! Death to the regnant and her pathetic regime! The Federation will conquer your pitiful world!"

"Don't listen to him!" Kirk feared that "Chekov" would provoke a sniper into taking him out, while sparking a major interstellar incident to boot. "This man is an imposter, trying to sabotage the peace celebration!"

Or so Kirk deduced. Hopefully, Spock could provide a fuller account of the imposter's identity and motives when this crisis was over, one way or another. Right now, Kirk needed to keep this standoff from ending in bloodshed—for everyone's sake.

"Imposter?" Sulu said. "What—?"

"Keep quiet!" The false Chekov pressed the business end of the hypospray against Sulu's mouth. "This isn't over! I can still . . ."

His voice—Chekov's voice—trailed off. An anxious, unsteady expression betrayed his inability to come up with a viable course of action.

"You can still what?" Kirk challenged him, growing steadily angrier at this would-be assassin who had usurped Chekov's body, just as Janice Lester had once stolen his and infiltrated the *Enterprise*. He struggled to keep his rage in check as he sought to talk the imposter down. "Kill Sulu? Me? Get yourself killed by one of these guards? What purpose will that serve?"

"What purpose will that serve?"

Ryjo wasn't sure. Not about anything.

Could he really bring himself to kill Sulu or even Kirk, after Wexx and all they'd gone through together on the way to Voyzr? The regnant? She was a political figure, an abstraction whom he'd hardly known as a person, but Sulu had been nothing but a staunch friend to the man he'd thought Ryjo was. They'd nearly died together on Wexx, and they'd had each other's backs the whole time, starting with Sulu keeping *Copernicus* waiting until the rescue party returned, even though the volcano was about to erupt at any moment. Kill Sulu? Maybe, just maybe, if his mission depended on it, but now that there was no hope of assassinating Zavetta?

He couldn't do it.

"Rut it." He let go of Sulu and shoved him toward Kirk, then turned the hypospray toward his own face. At least he could still carry out one part of his mission: eliminating himself to keep Chekov from exposing the conspiracy after the transference reversed itself.

But, wait, hadn't Chekov already done that, aboard the *Enterprise*? How else could Kirk have caught on? Was it already too late to stop Chekov from exposing the others? Or was there still a chance to protect his fellow Exiles by killing himself?

He exhaled to empty his lungs.

"Don't do it!" Sulu yelled. "I have no idea what's going on, or who the captain believes you are, but I know you don't want to do this, no matter how strangely you've been acting lately. You fought too hard to survive, to save us all on Wexx, to throw that all away now!"

"Listen to him," Kirk said. "It doesn't have to end like this. Not for you, not for Chekov. Don't kill a body, a life, that doesn't belong to you."

Ryjo faltered. "I don't . . . What else is there to do?"

"Let Chekov get his life back. He deserves that, even if you don't want it anymore."

Ryjo's finger lingered on the trigger of the hypospray.

Do it, he thought. *My life is over. I'm a failure. There's nothing left for me.*

So why couldn't he bring himself to press down on the trigger? Trembling, tears streaming down his borrowed face, he willed himself to go through with it, only to find his whole body—Chekov's body—rebelling against him. Was it his own natural instinct for self-preservation staying his hand, or Chekov's own flesh fighting to stay alive? Or the imprint of Chekov's unconscious mind surfacing to save itself?

Ryjo honestly couldn't tell anymore.

Do it! Do it now!

The courtyard started spinning again, flinging him away from this place, this body . . .

"No! Not yet!"

Thirty-Eight

Sickbay went away. One minute, Chekov was in a biobed, recovering from the mind-meld while worrying about whether Spock had managed to warn Captain Kirk in time; then, after a sudden wrenching sense of dislocation, he found himself back onstage on Voyzr, aiming a hypospray at his face.

Bozhe moi!

He hurled the device away from him, not entirely sure why. Dizzy and off-balance, he tried to adjust to his new surroundings. Kirk and Sulu stood nearby, eyeing him warily, near an abandoned podium. There seemed to be a lot of shouting and confusion and racing footsteps in the background.

What's happening? Chekov thought. *What did I miss?*

"Get that hypo," Kirk directed Sulu. "Cautiously." He approached Chekov slowly, seemingly ready to take him down if necessary. "You made the right call. Now surrender peacefully before somebody takes a shot at you."

Surrender?

His head clearing, Chekov belatedly noticed an armory's worth of disruptor rifles and pistols aimed at him by a great number of very unhappy-looking Voyzr in uniforms. Ryjo had clearly put a target on Chekov's body.

"Oh boy."

Thinking fast, he raised his hands above his head and got down on his knees. Middle-aged joints impressed on him that he was not in Ryjo's much younger body anymore.

Thank goodness.

"It's all right," he said. "Nobody do anything rash."

He braced himself for another transference, expecting to be yanked back to Ryjo's body at any moment, but then a moment passed, and another, and he remained where he was, physically and mentally. Had the transference finally reversed itself for good, or was that too much to hope for?

"That's the first smart thing you've said." Kirk strode over to him, accompanied by Sulu. He glared at Chekov with obvious anger. "How dare you impersonate a member of my crew, hijacking his body?"

Oh, Chekov realized. *He thinks I'm still Ryjo.*

"It's me, Captain!" he said, even as Voyzr guards stormed the stage, converging on him. "Ryjo is gone. I'm myself again, cross my heart!"

Kirk balked, anger giving way to uncertainty. "Chekov?"

Antlered guards swarmed around them. They seized Chekov and dragged him roughly to his feet. "Come with us, human!" a surly buck ordered. Copper antler rings identified him as a corporal. "You've caused enough trouble for today!"

"Hold on!" Kirk shoved his way past the guards. "I need to talk to him."

"Back off, Starfleet!" the corporal said. "We'll take it from here."

Kirk stood his ground. "I just saved your regnant's life. Give me one minute with my officer . . . or did you miss Zavetta's whole speech about how much your planet owes me and my crew? Forget the damn medal. Just give me this minute!"

"I don't take orders from you, human!" the corporal said. "Now back off, or do I have to—"

"That's enough, Corporal." An older Voyzr, whom Chekov recognized as Major Nonnd of the regnant's personal security detail, marched into the discussion. He scowled at the captain. "All right, Kirk. You have your minute, but no longer. This—whatever this is—is in our hands now."

"Thank you, Major." Kirk brushed past the corporal to peer into Chekov's eyes. "Pavel? Is that really you?"

"In the flesh, sir. My own flesh, if you know what I mean."

"More than I'd like," Kirk said. "The transference? It's reversed itself, like it did with me and Lester?"

"I believe so, Captain." Chekov shrugged as much as he could with guards holding tightly on to his arms. "But I seem to be the victim of an unfortunate case of mistaken identity."

Nonnd snorted impatiently. "Time's up." He nodded at the guards. "Take him away . . . and don't even think about trying to stop us, Kirk, not if the Federation wants to keep its rutting embassy."

"Respectfully, Major, you don't understand what just happened. Allow me to explain!"

"You'll have your chance, believe me. I don't know why you seemed convinced your officer posed a threat to the regnant, or why he's apparently lost his mind in front of the entire galaxy, but rest assured that I *am* going to want an explanation . . . after we take Commander Chekov into custody."

The guards started to haul Chekov away, none too gently. He looked back over his shoulder at Kirk and Sulu. The latter started after Chekov, no doubt to intercede on Chekov's behalf, but Kirk placed a hand on Sulu's shoulder, restraining him. He shook his head.

"We'll straighten this out, Chekov," Kirk called out. "Count on it."

Chekov nodded, sympathizing with Kirk's position. He knew too well the difficulties of having to convince authorities that body-swapping was a thing, and given that Ryjo had apparently just tried to harm the regnant in full view of numerous witnesses . . . well, he could hardly blame the Voyzr for wanting him locked up for the time being.

But how far had Ryjo gotten before he was stopped?

"The regnant?" he asked, needing to know. "She is safe? Unharmed?

"No thanks to you, human!"

Relief flooded Chekov, despite his own predicament. He hadn't been too late after all, and Ryjo was presumably still alive as well, securely stowed away in sickbay. So he'd kept his promise to Dise as well.

"I am very glad to hear it."

"I'll bet."

He allowed himself a wry smile.

"You'd be surprised."

"No! Not yet!"

In sickbay once more, Ryjo tried to trigger the hypospray, but his hand was empty. The lethal instrument was still down on Voyzr, in Chekov's grasp.

He had waited too long—and missed his chance.

Just like he'd failed to kill the regnant backstage when he'd had the opportunity.

And the most shameful part?

The overwhelming sense of *relief*.

He wasn't dead—or a killer.

"Chekov? Ryjo? Who the devil are you right now?"

McCoy eyed him dubiously while a clearly stricken Tovar looked on, appearing more shaken than he had ever seen her. She hugged herself as though freezing. The looming security officer came forward, one hand on the phaser at his waist, just in case the Voyzr in the bed posed a problem.

That won't be necessary, Ryjo thought. His mission was past saving. There was no point in lashing out or trying to make a run for it. *Where could I go anyway?*

"Not Chekov," he confessed.

Tovar gasped. "So it's true? You were Chekov all along?"

"Since Tykona." Her crestfallen expression added to the guilt weighing him down. "I'm so sorry. I never meant to hurt you or toy with your feelings. I was just . . . trying to maintain my cover."

"And this?" She indicated his true Voyzr form, reclining in the biobed beneath a shiny silver blanket. "This is the real you? This 'Ryjo' person?"

He nodded. "Pleased to meet you finally. As myself, I mean."

"So it was just an act?" Her voice was bitter, her eyes wet. "All of it?"

He shook his head, feeling the comforting weight of his antlers again. At least they didn't itch anymore.

"Not all of it." His own throat tightened. "You're a remarkable woman, Simone. I wish I could have gotten to know you for real."

Her face hardened.

"That's Nurse Tovar to you."

Thirty-Nine

"What's happening?" Trath demanded. "Someone find out what's happening!"

The villa was in an uproar following reports that the assassination attempt had failed and "Chekov" had been taken into custody. While it was clear that the regnant was still alive, it was less evident what had gone wrong, where Ryjo was now, what if anything the real Chekov had to do with the fiasco, and what this meant for the Exiles now and in the immediate future. Voyzr rushed about in disarray, talking over each other, as they struggled to come to grips with the collapse of their ingenious plan.

"What if Ryjo talks?" Vonnu fretted. No longer occupying the body of Grigori Ratikin, the distressed buck anxiously rubbed his antlers against a doorframe on one side of the living area. "What if he's *already* talked? We need to clear out while we can. Destroy all the evidence and cover our tracks!"

"It has to be Chekov!" a doe named Mymbi insisted. "He alerted Kirk somehow." Her gaze was glued to a computer console, absorbing whatever dire news or rumors she could find. Six fingers drummed nervously on a tabletop. "I knew we should have aborted the operation after he escaped! I knew it!"

"After all our work and planning?" Vonnu shot back, no doubt recalling the life-entity transference he'd endured for the sake of the cause. "We'd gone too far to turn back by then."

"But it was only a matter of time before Chekov informed Starfleet!" she insisted. "Especially after he caught that cruiser off the planet!"

"Easy to say now! But how were we to know—"

"Silence!" Trath trumpeted. "I need answers, not bickering. Get hold of our contacts on Voyzr, the Klingons, anyone! We need facts, details, hard information, not useless speculation!"

"But, sir!" Vonnu said. "We're not safe here. For all we know, the entire operation has been compromised!"

Good, Jacqueline Morval thought. Watching from the sidelines, forgotten amidst all the general consternation and finger-pointing, she took a certain bleak pleasure in seeing the Exiles unravel along with their scheme. Alas, she couldn't linger to savor the schadenfreude. This was the moment she'd been waiting for, regardless of the outcome of Ryjo's mission.

I need to move quickly.

Unnoticed in the tumult, she slipped out of the room and strode briskly to the private room where Ratikin, back in his own body once more, was still being held at her insistence. Trath had wanted to eliminate the Russian after that transfer had reversed itself, putting Vonnu back into his own body, but Morval had argued that she needed to monitor Ratikin post-transference, just in case there were any unexpected side-effects to a human-Voyzr body-swap that might have an impact on Ryjo, Vonnu, or future applications of the Camusian transfer technology. This was mostly nonsense, conjured out of a blizzard of impressive-sounding technobabble, but it had kept Ratikin alive until now.

Saving him once and for all was going to be trickier.

A biometric scan granted her admission to the locked chamber, where she found Ratikin under restraint in a biobed, watched over by a single guard, who was accustomed to her coming by to check on her patient. The twitchy buck appeared just as anxious and confused as the Voyzr she'd left in the living area. He lurched from his chair as she entered, desperate for an update.

"Is it true what they're saying? That Ryjo failed? That he was captured before he could kill the regnant?"

"So it seems." She fished a hypospray from a pocket of her lab coat. "Trath says we need to bug out immediately. He wants me to drug the prisoner for easier transport."

"What?" Ratikin strained at the straps binding him to the bed. The large, bearded Russian was looking understandably wan and debilitated after weeks in captivity, most of it in another being's body. "Where are you taking me now?"

Patience, she thought. *You'll find out soon enough.*

She ignored Ratikin as she focused on the guard instead. The turmoil spreading through the villa worked to her advantage. Nobody was thinking straight or paying much attention to her.

"Okay." The guard headed toward a nearby intercom unit. "Let me just confirm this with Trath."

"No need."

The hypospray in her hand was a prototype of the one provided to Ryjo for his mission of murder, albeit loaded with a considerably less deadly payload. Holding her own breath, she sprayed the distracted buck with a potent but nonlethal anesthetic gas. A soft hiss was followed by a heavy thud as he dropped limply onto the floor. She stepped over him.

"*Yebena mat!*" Ratikin gaped at her from the bed. "What are you doing?"

"Saving your life, if possible."

She had been planning this for some time, fearing that both she and Ratikin would be judged expendable once Ryjo killed the regnant. That the assassin's mission had instead ended in failure did not change things; if anything, her life expectancy, and Ratikin's, had probably diminished even more now that the Exiles were going to be frantic to cover their tracks.

"What about Chekov?" he asked. "Is he in danger too?"

"No idea." She'd never had occasion or opportunity to inform Ratikin that his friend was in the wind. She claimed the fallen guard's disruptor pistol, then hurried over to the bed and undid Ratikin's restraints. "He got away from us a while ago, although there's reason to believe that he may have made it back to Starfleet by now."

"Pavel escaped?" The man's face lit up at the news. "I should have known he'd find a way to give you the slip, after all his daring adventures aboard the *Enterprise*. How did he manage it?"

"No time for that." She helped him out of the bed, then retrieved a robe from a storage closet. "Rest assured that wherever Chekov is, he's light-years away from here."

He nodded. "So where now?"

"Just come with me." She aimed the disruptor at him. "And act like you're still my prisoner."

Exiting the room, leaving the gassed guard on the floor, she marched him at gunpoint to a fortified vault in the basement of the villa. Originally intended as a "panic room" for a wealthy expatriate tax-sheltering on Tykona, it had been repurposed by the Exiles to protect Morval's insidious pride and joy:

The Transference Wall.

The vault was the most secure site on the property, its dense armored shielding built to withstand all but the most high-powered home invasion. Fortunately, she still had full access to the chamber . . . for the time being.

She submitted to a computerized scan, then keyed in a priority access code. A reinforced duranium door slid open and she prodded Ratikin through it. The door slid shut behind them as they found a single guard on duty inside, watching over her creation.

The Wall occupied the far end of the vault. Not the original artifact discovered on Camus II, which remained tightly secured and restricted by the Federation, but a re-creation reverse-engineered from the original, based on Morval's classified knowledge and files. Horizontal rows of embossed alien glyphs filled two large vertical panels. When the device was activated, constellations of miniature white stars filled the deep negative spaces between and within the glyphs, accenting them, but when dormant, as now, only shadows filled the gaps. Morval couldn't imagine Trath would ever leave the Wall behind, no matter how hastily the Exiles cleared out of the villa. It was too valuable a resource to sacrifice unless absolutely necessary. If nothing else, he'd want to keep her alive long enough to oversee its disassembly, transport, and reconstruction elsewhere.

Not that this would keep Ratikin alive another day.

"*Nyet!*" The Russian panicked at the sight of the Wall, which had stolen his body from him all too recently. "Not again!"

"Quiet!" She wished she could reassure him, but his fearful reaction helped sell the act she was putting on for the guard. "You can cooperate, or I can stun you into submission. Your choice."

The guard glowered at Ratikin. "What's he doing here?"

"Trath wants to put Vonnu back into Ratikin's body, just in case the authorities come calling. He and Vonnu are on their way now."

Ratikin's face fell. "But . . . you mean this was all just a trick? I don't understand . . ."

Shut up, Morval thought, *before you blow my entire plan.*

"What's he talking about?" the guard asked.

"Not your problem." She swung the disruptor toward him and pulled the trigger. A brilliant turquoise beam rendered the guard's concerns moot. He crumpled to the floor.

"Oh," Ratikin said. "I get it now."

"I would hope so." She relieved the guard of his sidearm and communicator, then turned to face the Wall. "Step out of the way."

Switching the setting on the disruptor, she hesitated for only an instant before opening fire with the disruptor. Carved glyphs glowed brightly before melting into unintelligibility. Sparks and smoke erupted from the arcane circuits and crystals built into the Wall behind the glyphs. An ear-piercing alarm went off in response overhead, terminating any further attempts at stealth. Trath would be onto her soon, if he wasn't already.

"Whoa." Ratikin backed away from the devastated Wall. He grinned, happy to see the dreaded mechanism wrecked. "Not that I'm complaining, but what did you do that for?"

"Leverage."

Destroying the Wall rendered her less expendable. Trath and

the Klingons *might* be able to build a new one without her expertise, based on the data they had already extracted from her, but it wouldn't be easy—and the prospect of that challenge might be enough to give them pause before disposing of her too quickly.

Assuming that mattered to Trath at this point.

"But why the change of heart?" Ratikin asked.

How to explain it? Self-preservation, in part, but that wasn't all of it. Repentance, perhaps, along with an aching need to atone for her crimes, or maybe she wasn't so compromised that she could just stand by and let an innocent pawn like Ratikin lose his life simply to eliminate a loose end. She couldn't save herself without at least trying to save him as well.

Perhaps there was still hope for what was left of her conscience? Frankly, she had been surprised by just how *relieved* she'd been to hear that the assassination plot had failed. Neither the regnant's nor Chekov's blood was on her hands after all, so she'd be damned if she let Ratikin be killed anyway.

"It's the least I can do," she said. "Believe me."

She didn't wait for Trath to discover the full extent of her rebellion. After muting the alarm, she engaged a manual lock, securing the vault from the inside, then availed herself of the guard's communicator.

"Paging Trath."

He responded almost immediately, his outraged face appearing on the communicator's miniature display screen. Rubbery black nostrils flared indignantly.

"What do you think you're doing, Doctor?"

"Ensuring my survival . . . and Ratikin's. I've taken custody of my patient and destroyed the Wall."

"You did what?!" Trath glared at her from the screen. If looks could kill, she'd be smoldering ashes. *"Have you lost your mind, Doctor?"*

"More like I'm clinging to the last strands of my humanity. You want a new Wall, I need assurances that neither Ratikin nor I will be disposed of."

And then? To be honest, she hadn't yet figured out a long-term solution to the Ratikin problem. Perhaps he could be comfortably stowed away, with a new identity, on some obscure world under the Klingons' jurisdiction, or maybe just persuaded, by a judicious combination of bribes and threats, to keep his mouth shut? She wasn't sure precisely what the future held for him, just that he wouldn't have a future if she didn't act now.

"I'm in no mood to bargain," Trath said, "and you are in no position to make demands."

"Are you sure about that? I'm locked up tight in the vault. Can you get to me before the authorities come knocking on your door—or do you want to leave me for them to find?"

"That would not go well for you, Doctor. Have you forgotten that you are a traitor many times over and party to an assassination plot?"

Hardly. But maybe she had been trapped on this hellish runaway bullet train for too long. It was time to jump off, regardless of the consequences.

"Probably still safer than in your hands . . . unless you can guarantee our safety."

Part of her was sorely tempted to just sit tight in the vault until the authorities came looking for Ratikin, then take her chances in terms of prosecution. Perhaps she could cut a deal in exchange for testifying against Trath and his fellow Exiles? On the other hand, what if nobody came calling, at least not before Trath's people succeeded in breaking into the vault? The Exiles had friends in high places after all. Suppose they managed to squash any investigation here on Tykona? It wasn't as though Starfleet or Voyzr had jurisdiction in these parts, and Trath's allies in the Tykon government had every reason to want to hush this matter up. She and Ratikin might well be on their own, and they couldn't hole up in the vault forever. Plus, if she was brutally honest, she would just as soon avoid exposure and incarceration if she could.

"*You overestimate your value, Doctor, which is diminishing every* moment this ill-advised insurrection persists. Wall or no Wall, you are not exactly convincing me that your survival is in my best interests."

"Maybe, but what about the Klingons? How are they going to feel about you costing them a valuable asset, not to mention my specialized knowledge regarding life-entity transfers?" She smiled as she twisted the knife. "As is, I can't imagine they're very happy about your botched assassination plot. Do you really want to risk upsetting them even more?"

Trath's eyes widened in alarm, his arrogant manner evaporating faster than a puddle on Vulcan's Forge. Seeming at a loss for words, he needed a few moments to find his voice again, in a notably more conciliatory tone.

"This is absurd, Doctor. We should not be haggling at a time like this. I understand that we are all under strain after the failure—"

A burst of static cut off his words. The display screen went blank as the communicator abruptly went dead. The overhead lights crackled and flashed before going out entirely, throwing the vault into total darkness.

"What is it?" Ratikin's voice cried out. "What did you do?"

"This isn't me," she said, unable to see a thing. *Then what—or who?*

The lights came back on again, and a booming voice emerged from the villa's public-address system:

"Attention, all residents! This is Tykon Civil Security! You are surrounded by ground and air forces. Your transporter frequencies are jammed. Orbital phasers are locked on your location. Lay down whatever arms you possess and surrender to lawful detention.

"You have thirty seconds to transmit your assent."

Morval's shoulders sagged as she lowered the communicator. This was it then. She could stop strategizing and scheming; for better or for worse, the runaway train had reached the end of the line.

"Good news, Mister Ratikin. It seems you'll be going home soon, and in your own body no less."

"And you?" he asked.

"I'm getting no more than I deserve."
Now only two final questions remained.
Would Trath surrender peacefully?
Unlikely, she judged.
And could the vault block a concentrated stun blast from above?
Moments later, a sudden jarring shock answered both questions.

Forty

"Thank you, Uhura. Kirk out."

Chekov looked on worriedly as Kirk put down his communicator after receiving a priority transmission from the *Enterprise*. They were gathered in the regnant's office on Voyzr as Kirk attempted to negotiate a prisoner exchange with Zavetta and her people. Also present were Sulu and Ambassador Torek. Chekov stood apart from Kirk and Sulu, flanked by two looming security guards. Fluorescent blue prison togs had replaced his dress uniform, although Kirk had prevailed upon the regnant to have any manacles or alternative restraints removed for the duration of the meeting. Chekov appreciated the courtesy, but he wouldn't be entirely at ease until he was back in uniform once more.

Still, at least he was himself again.

"Good news," Kirk reported. "Starfleet reports that Tykon forces have successfully raided the villa and rounded up the conspirators, just as they promised."

"As well they should," Major Nonnd huffed. "After harboring that den of vipers!"

As Chekov understood it, the authorities on Tykona had been placed in a very embarrassing situation by the Exiles' activities. Foreign nationals being abducted and body-swapped on their planet did not make Tykona look good and/or encourage tourism. Never mind a Starfleet officer and a foreign head of state being targeted by a conspiracy hatched on Tykon soil. Under pressure from both the Federation and Voyzr, they'd agree to apprehend the malefactors in exchange for all parties playing down Tykona's role in the incident.

"And Grigori?" Chekov asked.

"Alive and well," Kirk said. "He's being looked after now but is said to be in good shape despite his ordeal."

"Thank heavens!" Chekov sighed in relief. Grigori's fate had been weighing on him ever since he'd been forced to leave him behind at the villa. It felt good to finally shed that burden at last, no matter what happened to him personally. "You have no idea how glad I am to hear that!"

"I think I have an inkling," Kirk said, smiling. He turned back to Zavetta, who was sitting behind her desk, presiding over the meeting. "So, back to business. Do we have a deal? Ryjo for Chekov?"

Ryjo, back in his own body as well, was still in custody aboard the *Enterprise*, making him a useful bargaining chip—if they could convince the regnant that Chekov's identity had truly been stolen.

"So you're quite certain," Zavetta said, "that your prisoner is the man who tried to kill me, not Commander Chekov?"

"This has been confirmed by Mister Spock," Kirk reminded her. "In addition, we have Ryjo's sworn confession."

"Such as it is," Nonnd grumbled.

According to Kirk, Ryjo had so far declined to implicate his co-conspirators by name, no doubt out of some residual loyalty to his fellow Exiles, but he'd come clean about the life-entity transference and his temporary hijacking of Chekov's body, all the way up to his attempt on the regnant's life.

To clear Chekov's name now that his mission had failed?

The regnant sighed wearily. "It's still a lot to swallow, no offense. If it were anyone else offering a defense this outlandish, I'd be extremely skeptical, but coming from you, Kirk . . . well, you did help bring peace to Voyzr decades ago *and* you just saved my life, and those are no small things. If you say this 'Ryjo' is the guilty party, not Chekov, then I suppose we must take you at your word. Certainly, we do not wish to prosecute the wrong person, despite the evidence of our own senses."

"It *is* the logical choice, Regnant," Torek said. "As a Vulcan, I can attest to the reliability of Captain Spock's mind-meld evidence, as well as to the fact that psyches—what we call *katras*—transcend our physical forms and can, under special circumstances, be transferred from one body to another for indefinite periods of time."

Chekov nodded. Along with his own recent experience, he recalled Spock's *katra* being temporarily relocated to McCoy's brain before applied Vulcan telepathy sorted that all out. A chill ran down his spine; one wanted to think that one's mind and body were inseparable, but apparently that was far from the case.

"That's all very well and good," Nonnd protested, "but we all saw 'Chekov' go mad onstage, menacing the regnant, taking Mister Sulu hostage, threatening to kill himself before being taken custody. How are we supposed to explain letting him go free?"

"We stick to the official story," Kirk said. "That the would-be assassin was an imposter made to look like Chekov. And that the real Chekov was being held captive elsewhere but escaped in time to alert me at the last moment." He shrugged. "We just keep the 'outlandish' body-swapping business to ourselves."

"Which narrative has the virtue of being essentially true," Torek observed, "omitting only a few troublesome specifics."

"Precisely," Kirk said. "As a celebrated human author once wrote, a little inaccuracy sometimes saves a ton of explanation."

Torek raised an eyebrow. "A scientist might not agree with that sentiment, but, as a diplomat, I find it quite cogent."

"Very well," Zavetta said. "You have your deal, Kirk. Chekov goes free in exchange for Ryjo."

Relief flooded Chekov. He had never doubted that Captain Kirk would come through for him in the end—well, mostly never—but having that expectation fulfilled came as welcome news nonetheless, letting his frazzled nerves relax at last. After being kidnapped and chased all across the sector, he hadn't wanted to spend another hour locked up on Voyzr. He'd spent enough time imprisoned or hiding these last few weeks. He couldn't wait to sleep in his own bed again—and resume his proper post on the *Enterprise*.

"Thank you, Madame Regnant," Kirk said, looking somewhat relieved as well. "We appreciate you taking into consideration the highly unusual circumstances in this case. With your permission, may we proceed with the exchange?"

"By all means." She nodded at Nonnd. "Lower defensive shields."

Chekov gathered the official residence was still on a high-security footing after the close call at the embassy. No surprise there.

"Yes, Regnant." He issued a terse order via a communicator, then awaited confirmation before giving Kirk the go-ahead. "You are clear to proceed."

Kirk made use of his own communicator. "Kirk to *Enterprise*. You may deliver the package to these coordinates."

"Aye, Captain," Scotty replied. *"He's ready to be dropped off, and good riddance."*

The high-pitched whine of a transporter beam heralded three sparkling columns of light that coalesced into the solid forms of Ryjo and two watchful Starfleet security officers. Chekov gazed at the downcast Voyzr, who was clad in a plain red coverall. Their eyes met across the spacious office, and Chekov repressed a shudder; after peering out from within Ryjo's body for weeks, it was unsettling to look at it from the outside.

He wondered if Ryjo felt the same.

Nonnd stepped forward to receive the prisoner. "Ryjo mur Zimble?"

"None other." Ryjo's gaze dropped to the carpeted floor. Sounding defeated, he did not seem inclined to offer any resistance. He scratched an antler. "I'm stuck being me again."

"And you confess to having attempted to assassinate the regnant at the peace celebration?"

"That was me, in Chekov's body." He glanced over at Zavetta. "Nothing personal. Just politics."

"You'll forgive me if I take attempts on my life personally," she said coolly. "Major, get this treacherous buck out of my sight."

"You heard the regnant." Nonnd gestured to his officers, who claimed Ryjo from his Starfleet chaperones, leaving Chekov unguarded. "Take him away. Chekov's cell is waiting for him."

"Wait!" Ryjo pleaded, more animated than before. Plaintive eyes entreated Zavetta and Nonnd. "I'll go quietly, I swear, but with your permission, may I say a few words to Captain Kirk and his officers first? I owe them that much."

Zavetta looked at the captain. "Kirk?"

"Fine." He regarded Ryjo stonily. "Let's hear what he has to say."

Ryjo took a deep breath. This was likely to be his last and only chance to speak to these men before he was sent away forever. He had to make it count, if only for his own peace of mind.

"First off, I want to apologize for lying and deceiving all of you when I was posing as Chekov. For what it's worth, I misjudged you and the crew of the *Enterprise*. Regardless of your interference on Voyzr decades ago, you were far more than the arrogant meddlers I'd always been told you were. Despite myself, I couldn't help coming to respect, even admire, your courage and integrity. Betraying you was harder than I ever expected it to be."

He turned toward Sulu. "Sulu—Hikaru, you were a good friend to the person I was pretending to be, not just on Wexx but aboard the *Enterprise* as well. Honestly, I envy the real Chekov having a friend like you in his life. I hope he appreciates it as much as I did."

"More," Chekov said, frowning. "Make no mistake of that."

"Look," Sulu said solemnly, "you lied to my face, impersonating my best friend, and took me hostage at the embassy. Don't expect me to forget that, but . . . I can't discount the fact that you saved my life on Wexx. I'll give you that much, even if you only did it because that's what Chekov would do."

Fair enough, Ryjo thought before turning to the man whose face he'd been wearing all the way from Tykona to Voyzr. It was strange looking at it now, like a reflection from another life.

"Commander Chekov, I don't really know you, despite all my research. We only briefly met on Tykona, but, playing you, I came to understand why your friends and crewmates held you in such esteem. If I distinguished myself at all during my stint aboard the *Enterprise*, it's because I was trying hard to live up to the standard you set."

"For your own ulterior reasons," Chekov pointed out, not incorrectly. "Let's be clear here. You stole my body and tried to frame me for murder. That's not something I can readily forgive, but I *understand* you now, more than I might like. And as for friends . . . you should know that Dise never stopped caring about you. She saw something of value in you, beyond your crimes, and still does. If I were you, and I was, I would not take that lightly."

"Dise? You met Dise?"

"I would not be here without her," Chekov said. "She kept you from becoming a murderer."

Dise was responsible for Chekov stopping him? Ryjo was rendered speechless by this revelation. He couldn't begin to know how to feel about it. That was going to take some time to process. Maybe even an entire life sentence.

"Is that all?" Kirk asked crisply. "Have you had your say?"

Ryjo glanced around. The regnant and her guards also looked impatient to have him carted off to whatever cell awaited him. He suddenly had a hundred questions to ask Chekov about Dise, but it was clear his time was almost up. He was lucky to have been allowed this much grace at all.

"Just this: It was an honor to serve under you, Captain, if only for one voyage."

Nonnd's guards escorted Ryjo out of the office.

"What's going to happen to him?" Chekov asked.

"Voyzr has no death penalty," the regnant said, "if that's what you're asking, but he did come within moments of killing me, sabotaging Voyzr's relations with the Federation in the process. He's facing a long prison term."

Chekov nodded. "I see."

"I have to ask, Commander, why the concern for one who stole your very life from you . . . and almost had you damned as an assassin in the eyes of the galaxy?"

"Don't get me wrong. I don't excuse what he did or tried to do, but there's a wise, old Russian saying about how you can't really know somebody until you've walked a mile in their shoes." No longer under guard, Chekov crossed the room to join Kirk and Sulu before the regnant's desk. "As it happens, I just traveled light-years wearing much more than Ryjo's boots. Again, I can't condone his actions, but I can comprehend what drove him to make some very bad choices. It's hard to trade lives with someone without developing some sympathy for them and regretting the mistakes they've made."

Kirk nodded knowingly. "If only . . ."

"So who is this Dise person?" Nonnd asked. "Somebody we need to investigate?"

"To the contrary," Chekov said. "You owe her a medal."

"Speaking of which," the regnant said, "we have one last bit of unfinished business."

Rising from behind her desk, she removed an ornate wooden box from a drawer, which she opened to reveal three exquisitely carved wooden medallions nestled on a cushion.

"Allow me to finally present you gentlemen with these well-deserved honors, for past *and* present services to Voyzr."

Forty-One

"How the hell did the Voyzr Exiles get their hands on that top-secret Camusian technology?" Kirk wanted to know. "I thought Lester's infernal discovery was supposed to be tightly under wraps?"

Fleet Admiral Lance Cartwright occupied the viewscreen in Kirk's office. A furrowed brow and somber countenance conveyed his concern over recent developments. A deep, resonant voice issued from the screen.

"Believe me, Jim, we're just as troubled about this security breach as you are. Maybe more so."

"With all due respect, sir, I doubt that. Not unless you've personally had your body and identity stolen by that device."

Cartwright did not take offense at Kirk's retort.

"I don't blame you for being upset, after what happened to you and *Chekov*. We're doing everything we can to get to the bottom of this incursion. Current intel points to a compromised Federation scientist named Jacqueline Morval, who is presently in custody on Tykona and reportedly willing to talk in exchange for immunity and/or a reduced sentence. We're in the process of trying to get direct access to her, but as you know, Tykona has no formal extradition treaty with the Federation, so that's taking longer than we'd like. Hopefully, we can question her sooner rather than later."

"And in the meantime?" Kirk pressed. "How do we know that transference know-how is secure?"

"We can't, not yet. Our investigation is still in its early days. Rest assured, though, that we're cracking down hard on security regarding anything to do with ancient Camusian science and relics. We're *running new, in-depth background checks on all of Morval's colleagues and associates, while also reviewing the security clearances of everyone with access to that research, which is going to be much more restricted going forward. And Tykon Civil Security confirms that the device used on Chekov and Ratikin has been destroyed."*

Kirk wished he found all that more reassuring.

"All reasonable precautions, Admiral, and obviously overdue. I just hope the genie isn't already out of the bottle."

A blank screen replaced Jim Kirk's image on Cartwright's computer screen. He sank back into his chair, feeling the weight of the four-leafed insignia on his right shoulder even more heavily than usual. Multiple, redundant security measures protected the privacy of his office at Starfleet Headquarters but couldn't keep out the constant worries and dilemmas that came with the job.

"Well?" he asked.

Colonel Patrick West emerged from the inconspicuous corner where he'd been silently listening in on Cartwright's long-distance conversation with Kirk. As cool and collected as ever, he smoothed his dapper mustache with a finger.

"Our probe is leaving no stone unturned. If there are more leaks, we'll find them, along with any further evidence of Klingon subterfuge. Kirk's not wrong to be concerned, however. I strongly recommend that this 'turnabout' technology be placed under the sole authority and auspices of Starfleet Intelligence."

Cartwright had heard this argument before. A hawk by nature, West typically came at every issue from a strictly military perspective, always proactive with regard to defense and security. He was first and foremost a soldier, always phaser-focused on defending the Federation from any and all threats. Possibly to a fault.

Then again, the Federation *did* have enemies, and Chekov had confirmed that the Klingons were up to their filthy elbows in this latest covert attempt to foment trouble between the Federation and its allies. Cartwright knew too well that the Empire was forever scheming to gain an edge of their rivals. Generations of unremitting hostility between the Klingons and the Federation had taught him that the Klingons would stop at nothing to achieve their barbaric aims, no matter how vicious and underhanded the means. Klingon "honor" was an oxymoron.

"I don't know," he said. "Civilian scientists might bristle at having to report to Starfleet or having the entire project taken out of their hands entirely."

West scoffed. "Scientists like Morval?"

"Touché," Cartwright conceded. "If the Klingons can get to Morval, who knows where else we might be vulnerable? Maybe we should just shutter the whole endeavor altogether. Bury the data as deep as we can and declare Camus II off-limits, period."

"I wouldn't go that far," West said. "If nothing else, this close call demonstrates the enormous potential of turnabout tech when it comes to undercover operations. The Exiles taught us a valuable lesson. Now imagine that technology being applied properly . . . in the right hands, of course."

"Ours, for instance?"

West shrugged.

"Better us than those bloodthirsty Klingon bastards."

Forty-Two

"So that's the real you?" Dise asked from the viewscreen.

Chekov realized that she had never laid eyes on his actual face before. "I'm afraid so."

"Weird. Not going to lie. That's going to take some getting used to."

They were speaking via a priority subspace channel from Oasis Station, where she had been released from custody thanks to Kirk's long-distance intervention. That Starfleet had compensated *Xoline*'s owner for the destruction of the yacht had also gone a long way toward persuading Oasis to drop any charges regarding Dise's role in abetting Chekov's theft of the spacecraft.

"Thanks for pulling strings to get me off, though," she said, "and for keeping Ryjo alive, despite everything."

"Well, I can't take full credit for either of those." He sat at the workstation in his quarters, facing a desktop computer monitor. "Captain Kirk did most of the heavy lifting after I managed to get back to the *Enterprise*, thanks in no small part to you."

"But the important thing is Ryjo survived . . . and we kept him from killing anyone."

"With 'we' being the operative word," Chekov stressed. "So what's next for you? Back to Tykona? If you lack funds to secure passage back home, I'm sure Starfleet can arrange something, given your pivotal role in averting an assassination *and* a diplomatic catastrophe."

"You bet they owe me a lift, especially after you blew most of my credits on that rutting cruise." A twig dangled from her lower lip. "But not to Tykona. I want a free ride to Voyzr . . . and the opportunity to visit Ryjo in whatever hole they've got him stowed away in. On a regular basis."

Ryjo's confession had spared everyone the messy spectacle of a public trial. He had been sentenced to a protracted prison term almost immediately. He had not contested the charges or the sentence.

"I can put in a good word for you with the regnant and her people," he promised, "but are you sure want to relocate to Voyzr for that long? Ryjo is not going to be a free man anytime soon, if ever."

She shrugged. "What can I say? Somebody has to help him get through this rough stretch, even if he did bring it on himself. He's going to need a friendly face, and who else is there but me?"

"You are a loyal friend." Chekov felt a mild pang of jealousy. "He doesn't deserve you."

"Look who's talking," she teased. "Besides, it's about time I checked out our fabled homeworld. I've never been obsessed with it the way the Exiles are, but I'll cop to some curiosity about my roots. If nothing else, it might be nice to live on a planet where the average Voyzr isn't some grumpy Indee loser still nursing a grudge over a war that was lost before I was born. Who knows? Perhaps I'll fit in better on Voyzr than I ever did on Tykona. Maybe even get a real job. Make something of myself."

"I wouldn't be at all surprised."

An awkward silence ensued as Chekov pondered how to bring up the intimacies they'd shared aboard the *Quintessential*, and what exactly that might or might not mean for them now that their shared adventure was over. Meeting Dise, and getting close to her, had been the only bright light during that whole harrowing stint in Ryjo's body, but was there any sort of future for them, especially with her heading off to Voyzr to support Ryjo during his confinement? And did he truly want to pursue that? Painful experience had taught him just how challenging cross-quadrant relationships could be.

"Anyway," he began, "about what happened on the cruiser. Between us, I mean . . ."

"Oh, that." She squirmed, avoiding his eyes. "Look, Chekov, it was great and all, and absolutely what I needed just then. No regrets, no complaints, I swear, but—" He recognized the telltale tone of a woman trying to let a guy down easily. "Honestly, I'm not into older males . . . or humans."

At least he wasn't allergic to vodka anymore.

He took a bracing sip of a White Russian, his taste buds once more savoring its familiar kick and flavor, as he sat on the sundeck overlooking the *Enterprise*'s Olympic-sized swimming pool. Artificial sunlight glinted off the rippling water, where any number of off-duty crew members were enjoying themselves. The sundeck was sufficiently distant from the pool that neither he nor Simone Tovar had to worry about getting splashed on.

"Thanks for agreeing to meet with me," he said, "despite everything."

"Not your fault some imposter took your place." She attempted a casual shrug, less than convincingly. This encounter was obviously awkward for her.

"Just the same, I figured it couldn't hurt to clear some air."

Sulu had filled him on Tovar and Ryjo's rocky interactions while the Voyzr was posing as him. Chekov was both resentful and jealous that Ryjo had spent more time with her than he had, even forming some sort of connection. He hoped that, on top of everything else, Ryjo hadn't messed up his own chances with Tovar.

Carefree squeals and laughter rose from the pool. "Nice location, by the way," he said. "Can I ask why you suggested this place in particular?"

"No associations with the imposter, to be honest. He wanted nothing to do with the pool after our subsea misadventure on Wexx."

Chekov nodded. "I heard about that."

"It's so strange." She looked across the table at him, a pensive expression on her face. "Realizing that, after all of that, I barely know the real Chekov. No offense."

"Understandable." He felt a sudden urge to punch Ryjo. "For what it's worth, it's really me this time. The guy you vaccinated in sickbay before all this body-swapping craziness."

"That seems like forever ago."

"Tell me about it, but . . . perhaps we can start over? Pick up where the real me left off?"

"I don't know. It's going to be hard to get past my history with the false 'Chekov.' You look and sound just like him . . . even though I realize, intellectually, that was more like him looking and sounding like you."

His heart sank. "Was the fake me that awful to you?"

"I wish! That would make the big reveal that he was lying to me the whole time a lot easier to take. Problem is, there were times—" She hesitated. "You don't mind me talking about him, do you?"

"Go ahead. Sounds like you need to get it out of your system."

"Okay, just wanted to check." She took a swig of pure Altair water. "There were times, especially down on Wexx, when he seemed like a stand-up guy, heroic even. Chances are, I wouldn't be here if he hadn't stepped up after *Copernicus* crashed, and there were moments when I truly felt something real happening between us . . . before he suddenly turned around and gave me the cold shoulder again." She chuckled bleakly. "In hindsight, I guess all those mixed messages make sense. Small wonder I could never figure out where I stood with him. He literally wasn't who he was pretending to be."

Chekov winced inside, hearing about her confused feelings regarding Ryjo, but he moved past it. He wasn't about to let a little thing like a temporary life-entity transfer derail his own mission to get to know Simone Tovar better. He had his own life back and he intended to make the most of it.

"No secret agendas here, I promise. What you see is what you get."

She smiled. "That would be a pleasant change, I admit, and maybe seeing Ryjo in his true form does help me wrap my head around the idea that you aren't him. But starting over from scratch with the real you? I'm not sure."

"Not entirely from scratch," he reminded her. "We *did* have sickbay, and I believe I still owe you a walk in the garden."

"True," she conceded. "There is that."

"Besides, from what Sulu tells me, it sounds as though you liked my doppelgänger best when he was acting the most like me."

She laughed, much more lightly this time.

"That's one way to look at it, Commander."

"Call me Pavel."

ACKNOWLEDGMENTS

Hard to believe that this is my twentieth *Star Trek* book, not counting various novelettes and short stories. This would not have been possible without the support and contributions of such past and present *Trek* editors as John Ordover, Ed Schlesinger, Marco Palmieri, Margaret Clark, Jaime Costas, Kimberly Laws, and, most recently, Sarah Schlick. I've also benefited from the able oversight of Paramount/CBS, as embodied by John Van Citters, Paula Block, Dayton Ward, and others. Writing for *Star Trek* has always been a collaborative enterprise (pun intended), and I couldn't ask for better skippers on this decades-long voyage. And I'd be remiss if I didn't mention ace copyeditor Scott Pearson, who has kept me honest for several books now, and who heroically took over the actual editing of this particular novel during difficult circumstances, as well as my agent, Russ Galen, who has been with me since the beginning. Thanks again, Russ.

Sadly, Margaret Clark passed away during the writing of this novel, but her expert editing and insights are all over it, going back as far as the original outline. If, for example, you enjoyed the whole subplot with Simone Tovar, you can thank Margaret for that; it was her idea to give Chekov a potential love interest aboard the *Enterprise*, just to complicate the imposter's mission even more. *Identity Theft* is a better book because of her.

And the same can be said of the many books and stories we worked on together over the last several years. Margaret was always very engaged and supportive—and thoughtful and patient when need be. She was also great fun to hang out with at conventions and chat with over the phone, usually at great length. Her loss is a tragedy to all of us who knew and worked with her over the years—and to *Star Trek* in general.

Finally, as ever, Karen has been my copilot this entire trek and for every other adventure we've shared together, past, present, and future.

ABOUT THE AUTHOR

GREG COX is the *New York Times* bestselling author of numerous *Star Trek* novels and stories, including *Lost to Eternity, A Contest of Principles, The Antares Maelstrom, Legacies: Book One: Captain to Captain, Miasma, Child of Two Worlds, Foul Deeds Will Rise, No Time Like the Past, The Weight of Worlds, The Rings of Time, To Reign in Hell, The Eugenics Wars (Volumes One* and *Two), The Q Continuum, Assignment: Eternity, The Black Shore, Dragon's Honor* (with Kij Johnson), and *Devil in the Sky* (with John Gregory Betancourt). He has also written the official movie novelizations of *War for the Planet of the Apes, Godzilla, Man of Steel, The Dark Knight Rises, Ghost Rider, Daredevil, Death Defying Acts*, and the first three *Underworld* movies, as well as books and stories based on such popular series as *Alias, Buffy the Vampire Slayer, CSI: Crime Scene Investigation, Farscape, The 4400, The Green Hornet, Leverage, The Librarians, Roswell, Terminator, Warehouse 13, The X-Files, Xena: Warrior Princess,* and *Zorro*. His first original novel, *Hungry as the Grave*, is forthcoming.

He has received six Scribe Awards, including one for Life Achievement, from the International Association of Media Tie-Writers. He lives in Lancaster, Pennsylvania.

Visit him at: www.gregcox-author.com